10/13/01

To - Best wishes,
Watch for De
Davies

(Bristledifoy)

Novels by Robert Charles Davis

Plutonium Murders
The Doomsday Kiss
A Time to Die
Ghosts of the Dead

Robert Charles Davis has been a
practicing physician for fifteen years.
Most recently, he has completed four novels,
with three others in progress.

The Doomsday Kiss

By Robert Charles Davis

An Alex Seacourt Thriller

THE DOOMSDAY KISS
The Second Alex Seacourt Thriller
A Novel by Robert Charles Davis M.D.

Horizon Press
32436 Old Franklin Drive
Farmington Hills, Michigan 48334
(248) 539-2979
(248) 539-2980 (fax)
Seacourt@Concentric.net (e-mail)

Library of Congress Cataloging-in-Publication Data
Davis, Robert Charles
The Doomsday Kiss / Robert Charles Davis
An Alex Seacourt Thriller
Horizon Press, 1998 Farmington Hills, Michigan

p.   cm.
ISBN 0-890248-02-9

1. Seacourt, Alex (Fictitious character)—Fiction. I. Title.
PS3554.A85 D66   1997
813/.54—dc21   97-00000
CIP

Printed in the United States of America
HP 10 9 8 7 6 5 4 3 2 1

In The Doomsday Kiss, his second adventure, Dr. Alex Seacourt again holds the fate of the world in his hands. With the help of a young stunt pilot and a fellow doctor whose secret past has troubling implications, Alex must battle a mad woman with a vial of deadly virus, a group of rogue CIA agents and just about every cop from Nevada to California. While this book is fiction, the technology and intrigue lie just under the surface of current events. Dr. Davis will draw you into a frightening world that at times seems all too real. You'll be dodging bullets, flying stunt planes, crash landing the shuttle. And you'll never quite be sure who your friends are. Alex Seacourt, the hero from the thrilling Plutonium Murders, is a thinking man's Bond.

The Doomsday Kiss

Dedicated to my mother—whose unselfish,
tireless research made this book possible.
And to my daughter,
whose love is my daily inspiration.

Robert Charles Davis

Acknowledgments

I owe many people my deepest gratitude.
First, thanks to Alice Gustafson, Greig Davis and Jerry Weiner, for believing in me and this project. To the following for their contribution and editorial assistance: Jenna Girard and Joe O'Donnell.
To the staff at Horizon Press: Lydia Dawood, Mike Richotte, Sheryl Ross, and Angela Sucharski. Lastly, special thanks to all the readers who have supported my efforts and made suggestions—without each of whom this book—and little else—would be possible.

The Doomsday Kiss

CHAPTER I

"*Kill him!*"

Dr. Alex Seacourt had gotten himself into a pickle. He had tried to help his friend—he was the good guy—just trying to be there. That's what friends were supposed to do, weren't they? And now they were going to kill him—mow him down in the prime of his life.

And...he didn't even know why.

"*Kill him!*" the assassin yelled as the four others locked-n-loaded their automatics. "*Get him now! You two up there, you two down here!*"

Alex had nowhere to run, nowhere to hide. If he didn't think cat-fast on his feet; if he didn't come up with a nick-of-time solution, he'd be Swiss-cheese riddled with lead—dead! What was he going to do?

"*Kill him, now!*"

The Doomsday Kiss

Two Days Earlier

Oleg Shlyapnikov, assistant to the First Chief Directorate, KR Line—Counterintelligence and Security for the FSB (Federal Security Service), formerly the KGB, had arranged for Alex to attend the Consumer Electronics Show (CES) and particularly the BetaTec exhibit.

Alex had just finished three months of intensive training: one in Washington D.C. at the Pentagon; one at the Federal University of Rio de Janeiro in Rio's Guanabara Bay, with the cooperation of President Fernando Henrique Cardoso and the PMDB (Brazilian Democratic Movement Party); and one in Moscow at the FSB (KGB Headquarters) in Dzerzhinshy Square at the Yasenevo Main Building.

Alex was selected from over 11,000 physicians to participate in an international training seminar on anti-terrorist germ warfare. In part, he was chosen because of the geographic location of his practice—Salt Lake City, Utah; and also because of his educational experience —he was Board Certified in Internal Medicine and Emergency Medicine, and had worked as a practicing physician for the last twelve years.

One hundred and fifty doctors participated from the United States; 290 from other countries. The training was the ultimate result of the thawing of the cold war.

The purpose of the seminar was to teach physicians how to respond immediately to a biologic weapons attack by terrorist groups such as the Japanese Supreme Truth cult who were responsible for the nerve gas subway assault that killed eight and injured 4,700 in early 1995, radical Islamic extremists like the Hizaballah and Hamas, North Korean political extremists, and even local fanatics such as the Idaho Neo-Nazi White Supremacists.

In 1972, the United States and Soviet Union banned biologic weapons and destroyed those that were stockpiled. However, other nations such as Iran and Iraq, both of whom employed this sort of weapon, had not.

The cultivation of botulism toxin, anthrax and even Ebola virus was relatively easy. They could be brought into nearly any nation in innocuous-looking luggage. One scenario would have all of Manhattan exposed to anthrax from a boat misting tainted water from the Hudson River. Only 1/1,000,000 of a gram of anthrax was needed. The odorless, tasteless agent would kill an adult in one day, causing shock and massive bleeding from the lymphatic system. One pound of anthrax spores produced enough toxin to wipe out the majority of the population of New York City.

Biologic weapons were cheap to build and the methods had already been extensively published by the Army in the 1950s and 60s in the scientific literature. For a terrorist, on a small scale, it would be akin to making moonshine.

The Office of Emergency Preparedness, along with a number of international organizations, governments and the FSB's KR Line—Counterintelligence and Security—had begun training regional "medical strike teams" to respond in the event of such a terrorist cataclysm.

Alex's training, along with that of the other physicians, was intensive and involved mock emergencies such as the release of botulism toxin and sarafan nerve gas in major metropolitan centers. This encompassed not only the treatment of the afflicted and the use of protective gear, but also the schooling of others in response to such emergencies, and techniques of direct confrontation with the terrorists—including overpowering them both physically and psychologically.

Because of international threats, the training was divided into the three geographic regions: Washington D.C. (North and Central America), Moscow (Asia, Europe and Africa) and Rio de Janeiro (South America and Australia). The enrollment of physicians was likewise apportioned into thirds and rotated monthly from one region to the next. There were never more than 150 doctors at any one location at one time.

While in Moscow, Shlyapnikov had proctored Alex during his on-line anti-terrorist germ warfare computer training. Shlyapnikov taught Alex how to access the FSB's Borzov Antiterrorist Intelligence Network (BAIN) from the World Wide Web. In addition, he instructed Alex on computer software and hardware capabilities—which would tie-in with his community medical mission statement.

Shlyapnikov also arranged for Alex to stop at the CES in Las Vegas on his way back to Salt Lake City from a BetaTec exhibit in Moscow. BetaTec had a "demo-stage" software that was the state-of-the-art medical office database, and was necessary to complete Alex's participation in his anti-terrorist germ warfare training.

The name of the software was *LAV-10*.

Alex agreed to go.

CHAPTER 2

Las Vegas had that flash-card recognition. Mention its name and it evoked quicksilver images of luxurious hotels, high-stakes gambling, bawdy production shows and the frantic pursuit of provocative, often ribald entertainment twenty-four hours a day, 365 days a year.

Las Vegas was Sin City, Disneyland for adults, a place to immerse oneself in decadence and booze-soaked forget-me-nots. It was a hedonistic Shangri-La, the quarter to leave one's sorrows behind, a dream for instant riches—only to return home with the problems of reality therapeutically awash.

Las Vegas was also where, ten years earlier, Alex finished his residency training in Internal Medicine at the Southern Nevada Memorial Hospital, now renamed University Medical Center. Southern Nevada Memorial Hospital was a 560-bed medical center with more than 800 physicians on staff. It was affiliated with the University of Nevada School of Medicine, operated residency programs, and was a Level II Trauma Center.

Alex had spent three long years there, some of the toughest in his life. It was being on call every night and then thirty-six-hour shifts that got to him the most. Often, he felt like he was the walking dead. He'd physically and mentally pushed himself to the absolute limit and then beyond. When he finished work, he was past burn out. His mind was a fried clutter of synapses, blurred with multiple symptoms, patient diseases and diagnoses mosaicked into a collage of their frail faces.

Nevertheless, he loved Vegas.

Alex was heading west on East Desert Inn Road toward Paradise. Though he had lived in Vegas for several years prior to moving to Salt Lake City, in all the time he had spent in Sin City, he had never attended the CES.

Shlyapnikov had prepared an itinerary for Alex that not only included BetaTec, but also Motorola, General Instruments, Sony Electronics, Microsoft, and a zillion other gizmo-inundated places. All told, Alex planned to spend three days in Vegas, not only at the Las Vegas Convention Center but also at the Las Vegas Hilton, Caesar's Palace, and Cashman Field Exhibition Hall, among others.

Shlyapnikov had made arrangements for Alex to be at BetaTec at noon. He was to ask for Roscoe J. McMahon III, the CEO, and was to inquire about the *LAV-10* software. He would be given a demo copy.

Alex had never heard of *LAV-10*, due to the electronics industry changing rapidly—that coupled with the fact that *LAV-10* probably wasn't for sale to the public yet.

Alex parked his forty-eight mile odometer, burgundy rental car. He found a spot nearly a mile away. It was that crowded. He relished the walk, especially after three months of intensive and sometimes boring instruction.

He looked toward the street and could see the hotel monoliths: the MGM, the Mirage, Bally's, the Imperial Palace. The next thing he knew, he was at the entrance to the Las Vegas Convention Center. He flashed the I.D. that Shlyapnikov had given him, and slowly walked through the throng of consumers and ubiquitous exhibitors.

The BetaTec booth was sixty-by-seventy feet and displayed a 3-D ten-foot high laser hologram of a surrealistic magician with a yellow aura that projected out of his face. His hair was bright red, his face magenta, his retinas and jacket shamrock green. He wore a black and fluorescent green polka dot tie. Two-thirds of the way down the dots melted into herringbones. In his left hand he held before his face a Phantom of the Opera mask. The domino was white and rectangular. A tufted eyebrow spiked in an outward flair. The iris was the only colored portion. It was a fluorescent green. The man's three fingers holding the mask were smudged. Underneath were the words: "*BetaTec holds the future to your dreams.*"

Alex walked to the eerie booth. He approached the pitchman who too was wearing the strange leprechaun outfit. His name was Max Hobart and he had his name laser-printed on a BetaTec name tag, in fluorescent digital 3-D. His face was fat and he had a full head of jet-black curly hair. A thick mustache covered his upper lip. He was handing out BetaTec twelve-page color brochures as he introduced himself with a firm handshake and bright smile.

Alex shrugged. He prepared to meet the corporate huckster when a man in his late fifties suddenly fell to his knees in front of him. The man was retching and his skin was ashen white. He held one hand to his head, the other to his stomach.

"Can I help you? I'm a doctor." Alex knelt as some of the elbow-room-only conventioneers stopped to gawk, while others shuffled by. The man did not look up. Alex gazed into his dense black hair with angry sprinklings of gray. Alex bent lower and crouched next to him. "Can I help you?"

A woman with platinum-blond hair, rose-water complexion, dark sunglasses and cherry-red lips, placed her hand on Alex's shoulder. She wore a black miniskirt, black stockings and black pumps. Alex looked up.

"He'll be okay."

"No, really let me help him, I'm a doctor." The fallen man did not respond.

"He'll be fine," she irritably said as she stepped between Alex and her much-senior paramour. The scent of her perfume was thick. She smelled of lilacs.

"Are you sure?" Alex stood as the girl put her arm around the man and in a low voice whispered into his ear. Alex could see the man's plump manicured fingers trembling. His nailbeds had turned turpentine green.

"I'm positive," she replied.

"But..." Suddenly, another man, wearing a dark suit and Ray-Ban sunglasses, squatted down to give the man a hand.

"Please..." she said as the Ray-Banned man assisted the sick man. He wrapped the invalid's right arm over his powerful shoulder, and helped him up, lifting also at the waist. "We don't need your help." She looked worried.

They helped the man through the crowd, bumping through a thicket of people.

"Really, I can give you a hand, I think he needs medical attention," Alex said as he stood and walked with them. Alex could see the pale green color was rapidly spreading from the man's fingertips up his forearms.

"No," she said. She had hold of him under his other arm. "We're all right."

"Honestly..." The two sped through the conventioneers, walking at a brisker pace. Alex was not paying attention. He accidentally ran into a group of Asian businessmen with their Chinese-Eurasian interpreter. They had their guidebooks open and she was pointing with her pen and speaking in rapid-fire Mandarin dialect.

"*Wo men xing cheng biao shang de di yi zhan shi song xia chan pin zhan shi hui. Wo zhi xiang ti xing ni wo men jian zai la si wei jia si de xi er dun fan dian de Le Montrachet...*"

When Alex bumped into them, two of the Asian men fell backwards onto the linoleum flooring. They were elderly, and one had a baton walking staff. Alex was embarrassed. He reached down to assist the septuagenarian, while the interpreter helped the other. "I'm sorry." They said something in Chinese and bowed to him. Alex feigned a bow while he tried to find the sick man with a rapid scan of the crowd. By the time he had picked up and returned both the briefcase and the rosewood cane to the seventy-six year old, the fleeting three had disappeared.

CHAPTER 3

After most of the day had slipped away, and having discovered that he had just missed Roscoe McMahon because he had stopped to help the sick man, Alex decided that he had had just about his fill of the CES. It was too crowded for him, especially after three months of grueling training. In addition, Max Hobart and several other account representatives from BetaTec told Alex that there was no such animal as an *LAV-10* software, nor any demo software waiting for him.

Alex thought that he might have gotten the name wrong, though he was sure he had not, so he decided to fax Shlyapnikov in Moscow once he got back to Salt Lake City and hook up with the program there. Maybe he could have the software downloaded onto his office computer via the Borzov Intelligence Network and the World Wide Web.

Alex had already seen more than enough exhibits and there were still more on his itinerary, not to mention others that he was interested in. He had been there most of the day.

It had been nearly ten years since Alex had seen Dr. Joanna Knight.

They were soul mates at one time. Jo was Chief of the Pathology Department at University Medical Center. She was 52 but looked to be in her early forties, had auburn hair, and stood nearly five feet, seven inches tall. She was rugged, with her idea of fun being a nine mile hike from the head of Kyle Canyon at Cathedral Rock to the twelve-thousand foot peak of Mount Charleston. It was the switchbacks and pines, the white firs that were surrounded by vertical cliffs and the pair of unnamed waterfalls that were most dramatic in early spring. That's what made Jo's motor run.

Alex had trained under her during a one-month rotation the first year of his residency program. They had hit if off immediately.

It wasn't a sexual thing, though it could have been. It was about chemistry. They clicked. Though their points of view and politics were different: he an independent who really never gave much thought to the importance of politics, and she a polemic who chose whatever side was controversial, whether it be liberal or right-wing conservative. She just liked to make people think.

Alex admired her. She was as sharp as a tack and taught him about more than just pathology. She taught him about life, the transcendental, and to delve into the essence of his time-bound existence. They discussed subjects as diverse as Nietzsche, Sartre, Spinoza, hard rock and heavy metal. They played chess, went to movies, the ballet and car shows.

She gave Alex a gift. She made him think about other things. It made him open up his blinded eyes and look at life from a broader perspective.

In the three years that Alex trained at Southern Nevada Memorial Hospital they were the best of friends.

Then he moved. After the great times, the wonderful talks, they just drifted apart after Alex relocated to Salt Lake City to open his practice. A rift of patchwork time had since separated them with few telephone calls and fewer letters. Maybe each was waiting for the other to take the initiative.

Today he was going to surprise her and breach that gap.

When Alex arrived at the hospital he stopped at the front desk. Behind the receptionist were eight portraits of the County Commissioners. None of them wore a smile. Alex had Jo paged and waited. He read a dog-eared issue of *People*. There was an article about Madonna and her newfound Catholicism, another on the plight of the American tobacco farmer, and one detailing Senator Bob Dole's heroism during World War II.

After nearly twenty minutes there was still no response. The lobby clock read 6:03 p.m. Alex presumed that she might be busy in the pathology lab, so he decided to walk to the pathology department, which was down the hallway toward the emergency room just before the ambulatory care center.

There were few workers in the lab. Most had gone home. Those that hadn't weren't particularly talkative. After speaking with a disinterested few, he eventually found a stuffy, lab-coated tech who said he knew where to locate Dr. Knight. She was called away for an emergency autopsy.

That was strange.

The autopsy room at University Medical Center was a place that Alex never liked, nor got used to. Kitty-corner between the main hospital building and the Diagnostic Outpatient Clinic, it was down a hallway on the first floor near the trash dump, and just east of the 1800 Building.

The autopsy room was colder than any other room in the hospital, which wasn't saying much, since Alex thought hospitals had a tendency to freeze their patients to death. There was a mobile cart for transporting the body to the morgue, an autopsy table with holes to allow water and fluids to drain, a small-parts dissection table with drains, a scale to weigh each organ and a tank for delivering water to the table and collecting fluids. The light was tinged in a ghoulish fluorescent hue, but not intentionally so. Alex hated the place.

"Jo, it's me," Alex exclaimed with his arms wide open, ready for a "gosh-I-haven't-seen-you-in-ages" hug. He got the opposite. She was in the middle of an autopsy. She was masked and gowned and her nonsterile surgical gloves were pulled tight. She had already made the midline "Y" incision across the chest from shoulder to shoulder, crossing down over the breasts; then from the lower tip of the sternum, a midline incision extending the entire length of the abdomen to the pubis. She had cut through the ribs and cartilage exposing the heart and lungs. She had already taken a sample of blood from the heart after opening the pericardial sac to determine the blood type of the victim.

The heart, lungs, esophagus and trachea were removed en bloc; and each organ had been weighed, its external surface examined and then sliced into sections to evaluate the internal structure. Microscopic slides of tissue from the organs needed to be prepared.

The organs of the abdomen had been removed, weighed and examined. The room smelled like mothballs. Sweat beaded on Jo's brow. He had never seen her sweat before, except once when she thought that a cadaver she had been working on died of the plague, and that she wasn't informed of it in the first place. She was finishing her 120 word-a-minute dictation—then she said, "Oh my God...Alex." But it wasn't the reaction that he would have expected. She was frightened, scared, as if she was involved in something terrible.

"Hey, I thought that I'd stop by and say hi to an old friend. Maybe take you out to dinner. You still eat dinner nowadays, don't you?" He hadn't had anything to eat since this morning except for a greasy hot-dog with onions and relish. He was starving.

She wore a worried look. She had just finished the "C" intermastoid incision made from over the top of the skull, cutting all the way through the scalp down to the parietal bone. She had pulled the scalp over the front of the face and had cut it away, and was in the process of removing the front quadrant of the skull.

"Could you give me a hand?" she asked.

"Sure." He was hesitant.

"Be careful not to touch anything until you've gloved and gowned."

"No problem. You okay?"

"No."

"If you want me to come back..."

"No, please Alex, I need a hand. My resident hasn't shown up yet."

"Sure." Alex slid on a disposable surgical gown and a pair of nonsterile latex gloves.

"Make sure you put something on your feet, and a splash guard too."

"Do you want one?" he asked. Jo wasn't wearing her's.

"Yes, please."

Alex removed one from the top shelf of a glass-front cabinet, split open the see-through thermoplastic wrapping, and placed it over her head. He took a clean tissue from his pocket and wiped off her sweltering brow. Then he slipped down the splash guard and from the rear adjusted the plastic band with a quarter-sized twist screw. When he did, he sensed her turmoil. She hesitated momentarily with her vibrating bone saw and said, "I'm sorry. It was just last-minute. You startled me."

"You needn't apologize."

"I do," she said as she restarted the awkward electric saw and made the last cut through the frontal bone.

"There."

She slowly removed the skull and exposed the underlying meninges and cerebral spinal fluid. There was a heat-liberating reaction. The cerebral spinal fluid, normally clear, was jellatoid and translucent purple.

"What the..."

"Jesus Christ," Jo said as if she had seen this before. It was then that her resident came in.

"Sorry Dr. Knight, I was on my way home when I got your page."

"That's all right, Melissa. If you could quickly gown up." Alex glanced at Jo's young resident. "Melissa, this is Dr. Alex Seacourt. Dr. Seacourt, this is my second-year pathology resident Dr. Graham." Jo was about to press the floor pedal control and dictate into the mike that hung from the ceiling, when she abruptly had second thoughts. She looked at Alex. "How 'bout a raincheck. Sunday? Is that okay?"

"Sure."

"Look, I'm going to be here for awhile..."

"No problem Jo..."

"Alex," she said as she moved between him and his view of the brain and the bizarre cerebral spinal fluid. "I've...really got to get this done. So...let's just say Sunday at six. How 'bout it?"

"Fine. But what the heck is that?" He said, gesturing to the grossly abnormal cerebral spinal fluid "I've never seen..."

"Oh, the CSF. More than likely a DMSO overdose."

Out of instinct Alex knew that she wasn't telling him the truth. He never heard of anyone dying from DMSO, though he was sure it could happen. He once had a patient who had gallons of the stuff injected IV by some quack Las Vegas naturopath. The woman, he didn't remember her name, smelled like rotten eggs and garlic—like

DMSO, which wasn't this smell. She had spent two-and a-half weeks in the Intensive Care Unit and survived. He had never forgotten that odor.

"Okay," he said as he walked toward the door. Dr. Graham finished sliding into her disposable, paper gown. "Nice to meet you," Alex said to Dr. Graham.

"You too," she replied.

"Six, okay. Meet me here," Jo said.

"Sure." It was then, out of the corner of his eye, that Alex noticed that the cerebral spinal fluid had begun to change to a normal color and consistency. He sensed that the room had actually warmed. There was some sort of reaction occurring. *Jo...* he wanted to say something but the words would not come.

Ten years ago she was his best friend. And...she had just given him the coldest shoulder he had ever gotten. It didn't make sense. The autopsy didn't pan out. She was in too big of a hurry to get him out of there. Also, the room smelled like mothballs. That was wrong, real wrong. Did the smell come from the body? *It couldn't have been...*

People change, and certainly Jo might have, but that wasn't the Dr. Joanna Knight that Alex had known. That was someone else entirely.

CHAPTER 4

In five minutes he was going to blow Aeromexico Flight 900 to kingdom come. Allah would be proud of him, as well as the Hamas whom he served with the unwavering blind devotion of his life. Khalifa Ali Al-Megrahi would fulfill his destiny...he would serve his God and exalt just punishment on the unholy.

He could envision the passengers' screaming faces—the abject terror. He was proud of what he was about to do.

Israel had long ago declared war against the Hamas and Islamic Jihad, and eventually Palestinian leader Yasser Arafat had publicly ordered the dismantlement of all terrorist organizations. Arafat, however, was a traitor. There would be "no further negotiations with the 'wackos'." Arafat himself had condemned his legion's mission as "dangerous terrorist acts."

But Khalifa Ali Al-Megrahi, whose flower germinated from Hebron, the only Palestinian city on the West Bank still under Israeli control, had a mission.

The Israeli government had waged a $100 million war against

the Hamas. The homes of suicide bombers were destroyed. Eight hundred guards were posted at bus stops to give commuters a sense of security in light of a rash of suicide bombings in Jerusalem and Tel Aviv. A barbed-wire security fence was built along the border with the West Bank, and all known Hamas activists were arrested and their offices shut down.

Their bombs, however, had not killed or maimed enough. Fifty-seven people in one nine-day period. Then, 103 people dead and 105 wounded outside a mall in Tel Aviv during the holiday of Purim. And, despite the confusion in their ranks, and as some said a loss of control by its leaders—he, Khalifa Ali-Al-Megrahi, had a charge. He would up the ante. The stakes would become international, and if their plan was successful the Hamas would have the world by the balls.

The flight from Mexico City to Los Angeles was three and a half hours. Russian Ambassador Vladmir Perov, who neither liked flying nor the turbulence that was usual over the Baja and Sea of Cortes, was already airsick. His attaché gave him a pill to ease the nausea. He washed down the tablet with banal airplane champagne.

The flight to L.A. was longer than Perov anticipated. His feet itched, especially his cracked heels. They smelled too bad to kick off his tired shoes. He had been cursed with the problem since his youth in Leningrad. He had tried just about everything, including an anti-fungal cream that seemed to help, but stung his raw skin and gave him pinhead-sized, beet-red sores. In addition, he had diabetes and high blood pressure for which he took other pills that made him drowsy and upset his stomach.

"What time do you anticipate we'll arrive?" Perov asked the pleasant stewardess.

"Forty-five minutes," she replied accommodatingly. She was having difficulty managing her cocktail tray. She didn't want to spill any of her beverages on her important passengers, the delegates from the World Health Organization and the Russian, Indian and Korean ambassadors. They had been working on an enigmatic cure for Alzheimer's disease, one that could only be manufactured in outer space. With the United States' assistance, a consortium of nations had gone into the Alzheimer's research business, and if preliminary reports were correct, they would have the panacea ready for manufacture and FDA testing by mid-February.

"More champagne?" she asked. The stewardess noticed that Perov had just about finished his glass.

"No, thank you." His English was perfect. He placed his hand on his stomach. He could feel the churning as the pill he took began its machinations.

She then asked Perov's two attachés if they wanted drinks. The aides-de-camp declined. The stewardess returned to the kitchenette to stow her tray.

The overhead light chimed: *"Fasten Your Seat Belts."*

"Ladies and gentlemen, we've entered some moderate turbulence. Could you please return to your seats," the captain said first in Spanish then in English.

"Next time," Perov said, "Let's take a night flight. The turbulence isn't so bad in the evening. I'm getting too old for this."

"Yes, Mr. Ambassador."

Perov's stomach made a vulgar gurgling sound. He wasn't sure if it was the medicine working or the champagne bubbles causing a fracas.

Khalifa Ali Al-Megrahi was cautiously adjusting the device in one of the eight tail-section bathrooms. The C-4 plastic was packed in envelope-thin compartments and sewn into the waistband of his underwear, on the skin side of the elastic. The detonator was concealed in a Papermate Metal Roller pen which he had clipped inside his left shirt pocket along with his heavy-framed glasses and airline ticket. He looked like an engineer.

The pen was designed to escape detection by the airport metal detectors. Inside was a small alkaline battery with nonmetallic plastic contacts, capable of delivering a charge of five volts—which was more than enough to detonate the 226 grams of C-4 that he carried.

The detonator was activated by Al-Megrahi opening the pen. The tip was a decoy. It had just enough black roller ink to write and could be used just so long as the cap was not seated on the rear of the pen. The tip, however, was also the triggering device. By setting the pen's cap on the back end of the pen, the battery contact was engaged. To discharge the device, Al-Megrahi needed only to push down hard on the ink-end roller ball and the circuit was closed. The alloy clip, which held the pen in place in Al-Megrahi's pocket, had two miniature contact points at the end. One was the positive contact, the other the negative.

Al-Megrahi said his homage to Allah, then removed the metal roller pen from his shirt pocket. He opened it, then unzipped his pants and pulled them down slightly. In front, on the inside, was a faded red label with misspelled English writing. It read: "Haines." With his mallard-yellow thumbnail, Al-Megrahi scratched off the label and exposed the contact points. He then gently seated the pen into the elastic band. He aligned the clip with the contact points.

His brown corduroy pants were designed so that they were baggy enough in the waist and crotch so the insidious device could be placed underneath without a bulge.

Al-Megrahi checked his pen. He lightly fingered the black roller-tip. His plan was to return to his seat and then detonate the 226 grams of C-4 directly under Russian Ambassador Perov.

The 747-400 would be blown up and Perov would be instantly vaporized. There would be no trace of him or his treachery.

Overheard the captain announced, "Ladies and gentlemen, I apologize for the unexpected turbulence. We will be increasing our altitude from 24,000 to 30,000 feet to see if we can get above the turbulence. Please be patient."

When the next updraft jolt buffeted the plane, the Aeromexico 747 was climbing out of flight level 250 toward 350. Simultaneously, Al-Megrahi was making last minute adjustments in the restroom. He was manipulating the roller-tip through his corduroys to ensure that he would be able to blow up the plane on his first attempt.

When the bomb detonated, the 747's tail blew off.

Initially, the front two-thirds of the jet survived the blast, along with 175 petrified passengers. But, without a rudder and elevators it was only a matter of seconds before the four-engine 747-400 spiraled toward a grave just 30 miles south of San Jose del Cabo, Baja, Mexico, where the Pacific Ocean meets the Sea of Cortes.

Had the plane's first class and business sections burst into flames, death might not have been so gruesome. But as it was, the eighteen-second death spiral was more horrifying than even Al-Megrahi could have imagined.

The Doomsday Kiss

Washington, D.C.
Office of the President

President Bill Climan was sitting at his desk, reading *USA Today*. Climan liked to scan the paper because it gave him a sense of the nation, the mood and vicissitudes of his constituency. His advisers supplied him with synopses of all the major daily newspapers: *The New York Times*, *The Washington Post*, *The Chicago Tribune*, *The Miami Herald*, *The Rocky Mountain News*, *The Dallas Morning News* and *The LA Times*. But this was something he preferred to do on his own—it made him feel thorough.

President Climan stood and walked into the bathroom. He splashed water onto his weary face and looked at himself. "My, my," he said with dissatisfaction. The bags under his eyes had become more prominent since he was elected. In public, and especially for the cameras, he covered them with vanishing cream. That was his reluctant secret.

It was then that Chief of Staff Creighton Debry came in. "Mr. President, I'm sorry to interrupt you."

"Not a problem, Creighton. Have a seat," Climan said through the bathroom door without turning to face the Chief of Staff.

Creighton sat in the green room, in one of the tufted-back armless chairs. The burgundy leather was crisp and crinkled under his weight. He felt at ease in the room, with its mellowed oak paneling, warm beams and placid stenciled ceiling. There was a conversation area which was formed on one side by a 19th-Century English mantel and hearth. The carpet was antique jewel-red and golden wheat.

Climan finished rinsing his face and then returned to the green room. He set his newspaper on top of his leather-topped desk. The paper was well-scanned, and the pages were not returned to their sharp creases. "Speak to me," he urged.

"No offense, sir, but why do you read that rag?"

"I read that rag, Creighton, because *that rag* lets me, lets us, have a pulse on America...and that's why us has been elected."

"Sorry, Mr. President."

"Now, what's on your mind?"

"We have a situation."

"A situation? What do you mean?"

"Mr. President you're familiar with *LAV-10* and *Space Station*

Mir-Kennedy I?"

"Yes...why?"

"I think we've got a big problem."

"Go on."

"Mr. President, at 1:54 Eastern time, Aeromexico Flight 900 from Mexico City en route to Los Angeles was blown up."

President Climan looked at his watch. It was 2:30 p.m.

"On board, among others, were the World Health Organization contingency and Russian Ambassador Vladmir Perov, Indian Ambassador Sonjay Singh and South Korean Ambassador Park Dae Jung."

"Are you sure about Perov?"

"Yes, Mr. President."

"Was he involved with *LAV-10?*"

"We think he might have been covertly attached, Mr. President."

"Who do you think was responsible?"

"We don't know yet."

"And Ambassador Perov—was this a direct blow against him, or the World Health Organization contingency and the other ambassadors?"

"I don't know Mr. President, but I've arranged a call with President Cheka in forty-five minutes. I took the liberty of contacting Cheka's Kremlin liaison. Cheka's en route from Beijing to Moscow. I thought this would give us some time to get the ball rolling."

"Good. Get me directors Gates and Fitzpatrick in my office in fifteen minutes. Also, I need General Peterson on video conference. He's in Houston isn't he?"

"Yes, Mr. President."

"Debry."

"Yes."

"This is bad, real bad...isn't it?" Climan said as he shook his head in disgust, then pounded his fist into the leather mat on the center of his desk.

"Yes, Mr. President."

CHAPTER 5
Las Vegas, Nevada

"Alex?"

"Yes." Alex Seacourt answered the telephone on the second ring. He was still sleepy and disoriented. "Yeah, who's this?"

"Jo."

"What time is it?" Alex looked up toward where he thought the hotel electric clock was, but wasn't.

"Eight thirty. Sounds like I woke you up."

"Yeah, that's okay. Don't worry about it."

"Alex you need to come over right away."

Alex propped himself up against the backboard and then hung his legs over the end of the bed. He pushed the brown cotton blanket toward the foot of his bed. His sheet just covered his waist. He had been up most of the night gambling. That's what they all do when they come to Vegas. That's what he did.

He coughed the sour evening's air that lingered in his lungs from the casino where he had stayed until 3:30 in the morning, playing blackjack and drinking Stoli vodka. He had broken even. He was just killing time and thought about going home Sunday afternoon.

"Someone took a shot at Melissa."

"Melissa who?"

"My resident, Dr. Graham."

"Did you call the police? Why...are you calling me?"

"Alex, just come."

"Jo."

"The body's gone Alex. Please, can you be here in ten minutes. I'm scared."

"I don't understand."

"Please Alex, just come. I'll explain when you get here."

"Okay."

That was enough for him. Alex thought back to the bizarre autopsy. Within twenty minutes, he had showered, dressed and was on his way.

Despite his shower he smelled like stale cigarettes and vodka. Maybe it was his clothes from last night that he had slipped on in a hurry. He looked disheveled, and had the rapid-fire *haute couture*.

The assiduous Dr. Joanna Knight was pacing in front of the hospital's main entrance. She was a bundle of frazzled nerves. Her long, white lab coat hung past her knees, and the buttons were undone. It jib-flapped as she paced. She took skittish drags on her cancer stick, then spit out the smoke and briskly inhaled. Her bifocals hung from her neck on a granny chain. She wore black slacks and a button-up man's lumberjack plaid shirt with a pocket in front. Inside her pocket she had a white-vinyl pen holder with two pens, one pencil with its lead pointing out, and a disposable blue Bic lighter.

Alex was going to park in the rear, but when he saw her in an uncharacteristic fit, he double-parked his car underneath the six-story Ambulatory Care Building near the front entrance.

"What's up?"

"Jesus Christ, Alex," she said as she threw her Marlboro Light to the ground and fired up another one, "walk with me."

That's one thing that Alex remembered about her, she always did her best talking when she was walking. "Let's walk," she'd say. And Jo, then Dr. Knight when he was in his pathology rotation during his first year of Internal Medicine Residency, would walk with Alex. They would make three one-mile loops around the medical center.

"She was shot at."

"Dr. Graham?"

"Yeah."

"Who did it?"

"I don't know."

"Why would someone shoot at her?"

"I'm..."

"Did she call the cops?"

"Yes...Alex, the body's gone."

"What do you mean gone?"

"I mean 'gone' as in as if it never existed."

"What? What are you talking about, Jo?"

"And there were some men, some government men that I'd never seen before..."

"Slow down."

"Sorry." She took a throaty puff of her cigarette. "There were some men. Some men in expensive suits who showed up at the hospital yesterday, about noon when I was finishing my dictation on the cadaver. They told me to leave, and I said 'who the heck do you think you are!' And then, the administrator came in and told me to take the day off."

"What?"

"Yeah, the hospital administrator told me to take the day off."

"I don't get it."

"So, after arguing for a few minutes about my responsibility, etc., I was told to leave or I'm fired."

"Fired?"

"Yeah. Me, Dr. Joanna Knight, pillar of this institution."

"So what was that all about? Did you straighten it out in the morning?"

"That's the thing, the next day—the locks were changed to my autopsy room. So, I thought 'yeah this is just some nonsense that has nothing to do with me;' you know, I'd just call security and get them to let me in, so that I can finish my work and straighten up any mess that those guys left."

"Who were they?"

"I don't know."

"Well, why do you think that they...."

"Alex, security wouldn't let me in. Could you believe those bastards? They said I didn't have authorization. I said 'what the heck', so I called George's butt at home."

They had turned the corner on Shadow Lane off West Charleston and were heading north on the narrow end of the hospital's drive. In Alex's periphery he spotted a gray '96 Taurus that made the turn behind them, then pulled into a Food Mart's parking lot and stopped. They left their engine idling. Two men were in the car.

"George?"

"Yeah, George Jaffe, that pompous bureaucratic administrator that kisses everyone's rear end but mine. He's been here for about a year since you left."

"Yeah, I remember that they were going to replace Taylor or something."

"So you know what his wife tells me?"

"No, what?"

"That he's going to be out of town on business until next Friday, and that if I called—and why would I even call that jerk—to tell me that I'm on sabbatical until he comes back. His wife said that they've been trying to get ahold of me since I stormed out of the office yesterday.

"Wouldn't you get pissed off if you got kicked out of your office, YOUR OFFICE by two goons...YOUR OFFICE that you've been in for the last twelve years."

"I don't know. Maybe."

"Well the point is, I smelled something wrong with that autopsy, real wrong. And my gut just told me..."

"Where did you go?"

"Got myself a bottle of Chivas, turned off the phone and got drunk."

"Jo, doesn't sound like you."

"I know."

Her smoldering cigarette died. She stopped, threw it on the pavement, and angrily snuffed it out. She pulled a pack of Marlboro Lights out of her lab coat pocket. Alex stopped, bent down and pretended to tie his shoe. The gray Taurus that had parked at the Food Mart had eased onto Shadow Lane, then crept off onto the gravel shoulder. It looked like one of the men was watching them through a pair of binoculars.

"We're being followed."

31

"What?" Jo asked as she fired up another cigarette. "No kidding. I wouldn't expect less. And don't worry, you don't need to say don't look around, 'cause I saw those bozos already."

"Yeah..."

"So I said to myself...this is my goddamn office and no one's going to keep me out of there. What are they going to do, fire me? Where are they going to find someone to teach the first and second year residents, chair the Tissue Committee, preside over the Quality Management, Morbidity and Mortality, Critical Care, Infectious Diseases, and Ethics Committees—and be Vice-Chief of Staff; not to mention my job! I bet I give those bastards one hundred hours a week!"

"Calm down."

"So, I broke into my own office. And guess what, Alex?"

"What?"

"No records, no tapes, no cadaver, no nothing. It was picked clean."

"Son-of..."

"See, I told you. But you know, they don't have everything."

"What do you mean?"

"Alex, remember that cerebral spinal fluid, how it came out thick...gelatin like."

"Of course. I'd never seen anything like it."

"And how after maybe 30 seconds it seemed to change back to a normal consistency, and then the room heated up."

"Are you kidding?"

"Well, I made a slide."

"A slide?"

"Yeah, a slide that I forgot to label. A slide that I stuck in my top desk drawer, that I meant to label later, but got caught up in other things. So I broke into my office, just like a thief. Everything was gone that had to do with the autopsy except for my slide. So I ran some tests."

"And what did you find?"

"*Alex, we're dead.*"

CHAPTER 6

The gloom that Dr. Knight had cast outside the University Medical Center was pea-soup thick. Alex was scared, but he didn't want to admit it. *What kind of conspiracy was this where the feds abducted a cadaver, got rid of any evidence, and threw Jo out of her office?*

"Alex, what do you know about AIDS?" Jo asked as they walked past the rear of the 1800 Building. In front of them there was another nondescript vehicle, a tan Chevy Lumina. It pulled up facing them as they approached the Emergency Room entrance at the rear of the Medical Center.

"I don't get you? What do you mean, 'we're dead.'"

"Alex, tell me what you know about AIDS?"

"Jo, this doesn't make sense."

"Please, humor me."

"Are you serious?"

"Alex."

"All right. Just about what every doctor knows...AIDS or Ac-quired Immune Deficiency Syndrome was coined by the CDC in the early '80s. In the beginning, almost all deaths from AIDS occurred in homosexual, bisexual and IV drug abuser populations. In the late '80s the scientific community realized that AIDS was not just a disease that could be spread through homosexual intercourse."

"What else?"

"Come on Jo. Is this a test?"

"Go on."

"I don't know...the usual stuff: That some goofballs believe that AIDS might be a derivative monkey virus that broke loose from an occult Langford, Virginia CIA Chemical Research Lab in the very late '70s and early '80s. Others suggest that AIDS has been around for a long time, but perhaps is a mutated virus that manifested itself in the San Francisco Bay area and was spread by some French Canadian TWA steward in the heyday of the American bathhouses. Apparently, Pierre or Jacques knew he was infected and wanted to leave his pathetic world with something to remember. Nice guy."

"And?"

"Jo."

"Please."

"The Socratic method? I'll amuse you. Human Immunodeficiency Virus, or HIV is society's executioner. HIV is a virus that is usually transmitted from person to person by passage of blood or body fluids such as semen and vaginal secretions. Urine, sweat, and saliva are not considered to be infectious. Patients engaging in unsafe sexual activity and intravenous drug use with needle sharing account for most cases of HIV infections, though sexual contact or passage of blood via sexual contact have caused an increase in the heterosexual numbers of new AIDS cases.

"Once infected by HIV, there is usually an asymptomatic phase lasting five years or more, sometimes up to ten years, though a very small minority of people thus far can go a lifetime after testing positive for HIV and never develop AIDS. Immunodeficiency, the 'I' portion of HIV is a description of the disease...do you really want to hear this?"

"Go on Alex, please."

"I feel like I'm...Anyway, the 'I' part of HIV is a description of the disease process. Immunodeficiency means that your body begins to lose its ability to fight off infections, first recognizable by the progressive destruction of white blood cell lymphocytes. The particular type of lymphocytes that are destroyed are T-helper or CD4+ cells.

"As the T-helper lymphocyte number drops, the unwary host becomes susceptible to opportunistic infections, malignancies, or different types of cancers.

"An opportunistic infection is—just as it sounds—opportunistic. This type of infection takes advantage of a situation that normally is not present in the body, that is, the low number of T-helper lymphocytes that fights off infection; and we get sick. Opportunistic infections that are commonly associated with AIDS include pneumocystis pneumonia, mycobacterium infections, candidacies—or yeast infections, herpes, etc. All of these infections, and many more that I have not mentioned, are normally organisms, fungus, protozoa, viruses and bacteria, that a healthy person can fight off.

"Testing for HIV generally requires an enzyme-linked test, called an ELSIA screen, that binds with the AIDS antibody that our body's white blood cells produce in their attempt to battle off the HIV virus. The ELSIA test, if positive, is followed by a confirmatory Western Blot. In most cases this 'window period' lasts about six weeks to three months. In some patients, a positive HIV test may not occur for six months to two years, and rarely, not at all.

"Finally," Alex said as he crunched over some splayed loose gravel that was scattered across the asphalt, "HIV infection can affect every organ system in the body. The first signs of HIV disease or AIDS, when one no longer has just a positive HIV blood test, but is now getting sick—are weight loss, weakness, malaise and anorexia. Unexplained fevers are common. Lung diseases, nervous system disorders and a body-wide mycobacterium infection occurs. Bacteria and fungi infection that would never in a million years concern us, can run rampant. And..." He took an irritated breath.

"And?"

"For example," he sighed. He didn't like being treated like a resident physician giving morning rounds report to his attendings, "approximately one-quarter to one-third of AIDS patients get Kaposi's Sarcoma, which involves skin and mouth lesions, which are those unusual purple and black lesions that AIDS patients get on their face, neck, arms, legs, abdomen. Another sign of AIDS, and usually one of its first manifestations, is another skin condition called seborrhea dermatitis, or a resilient dandruff all over the patient's body. In later stages, AIDS patients tend to get shingle infections, herpes simplex, eye, heart, lung, gastrointestinal tract problems, kidney involvement, etc…Am I done teacher?"

"Very good, but not quite."

"Treatment?"

"Yes."

"Come on."

"Go on, Alex."

"None really. Maybe AZT, ZDU, DDI, Ritonavir, and other antiviral agents which slow or prevent viral replication, but have limited effect and are nothing more than a Band-Aid. There is some talk about the development of a vaccine, and also some RNA protease inhibitors that allow AIDS to be treated as a chronic disease along with traditional medications…That's it…So what's the point?"

"So…I got some information through the grapevine…"

"The grapevine?"

"Well, okay, Ed."

"Ed? Ed who?"

"Ed the janitor."

"Ed the janitor—that's a reliable source?"

"Considering what just happened out of the blue in my autopsy room, and my career—I'd say that that source was pretty reliable."

"Go on."

"Well, Ed the janitor," Jo scoffed, "didn't like what he saw going on with my autopsy room being expropriated—so Ed stuck his nose in where it didn't belong."

"So?"

"Well…he broke into one of their cars."

"*Their cars?*"

"The feds."

"The feds?"

"At least I'm pretty sure they were the feds. Anyway Ed found a note scribbled on a piece of paper with the names Frank K. Bennett, M.D. and Lansing F. Darling and the date 1993. Underneath were a couple of other lines. He wrote them down as best as he could remember."

"And…" Alex said as they turned the last corner onto Tonopah. The two men in the second car were carefully watching them. One was perpetually smoking a cigarette. His window was cracked and he flicked the ashes out of it.

"The House Permanent Select Committee on Intelligence."

"That's it? So what does that mean?"

"Well, I'm not quite sure, but I was up most of the night surfing the Internet...until I finally got what I was looking for..."

"That's interesting."

"What?"

"Nevermind. I was just thinking...the Internet. Go on."

"It's CIA, Alex, CIA. The House Permanent Select Committee on Intelligence was formed on July 14, 1977 after allegations of wrongdoing by U.S. Intelligence agencies like the CIA. The Senate established the Senate Select Committee on Intelligence (SSCI) on May 19, 1976."

"Yeah."

"So these committees, along with the Armed Services, as well as the Foreign Relations and Foreign Affairs Committees, were charged with authorizing the programs of the intelligence agencies and overseeing their activities. The 1980 Intelligence Oversight Act established the current oversight structure by making the SSCI and HPSCI the only two oversight committees for the CIA. The SSCI and HPSCI receive all CIA finished intelligence products."

"What about Frank Bennett, M.D. and Lansing Darling?"

"I was drawing all kinds of blanks on them, then I linked up with the AMA Computer Data Bank Physician Masterfile in Chicago. I figured I could at least check out this Dr. Frank Bennett character. It turns out that Frank K. Bennett doesn't exist, at least never as a licensed physician in this country. So I thought, maybe Ed got the name wrong, maybe he meant Bennett Frank, or Bennett Franklin, or something."

"What did you find?"

"There was a Bennett K. Frank, M.D."

"No shit."

"Yeah...and he worked, get this, as a special adviser to the HPSCI from 1980 until 1992."

"Did he work for a congressman?"

"No...the CIA."

"Why would the CIA have a physician as a special adviser to the Oversight Committee?"

"That's what I asked myself...why? So I did some further investigation into Dr. Frank and guess what his training was all about?"

"I give up?"

"*Virology and immunology.* He's a Ph.D. and M.D. trained from the University of Pennsylvania and University of Chicago. He received special scholarship funding from the National Security Agency. A big shot."

"This is getting spooky."

"So, I said to myself, what's the deal with Lansing Darling. I thought I should go look at the CIA."

"I suppose you found that on the 'net' also?"

"Yes, I did. It took me longer than squat, but I finally tapped into the University of Wisconsin database at Madison, of all places. They have a Citizens Watchdog Committee dedicated to the public oversight of the CIA."

"You mean some radical student group that is already probably heavily under surveillance by the CIA is your information source?"

"Yes. Well, to cut to the quick, Dr. Bennett K. Frank and Lansing F. Darling are both listed in the CIA's Book of Honor."

"What's that?"

"It's a memorial carved into the north marble wall of the foyer of the CIA Headquarters Building—for those who have *lost their lives in the service of their country.*"

"You mean *they're both dead?*"

"That's right."

"Anything else on Lansing Darling?"

"Nothing, except that his name's in the Book of Honor and his memorial star—nada."

"So you got a dead man whose death..."

"Oh yeah, there's one more thing about the autopsy."

"What's that?"

"The cadaver, aside from the bizarre cerebral spinal fluid, had a normal examination, except..."

"Except?"

"He..." she was hesitant to answer.

"He what?"

"He had a facial expression—like he'd been scared to death."

"Scared to death?"

"That's what I said."

"So, to rehash, let me get this straight...you had a stiff who might have been frightened to death, and had a translucent, gelatinous purple cerebral spinal fluid. No big deal except for the fact that your dictation, your tissue and organ specimens and notes are gone."

"That's correct...except for the slide."

"What did you do with...wait a second...what does all of this have to do with AIDS?"

"Let me ask you a hypothetical question, Alex—what kind of work do you think that Dr. Frank did for the CIA as an adviser for the Oversight Committee?"

"I don't know. But what does this have to do with AIDS?"

"So, what if I told you that I took some of that specimen on the slide and just for the hell of it ran an ELSIA test?"

"Why would you 'just-for-the-hell-of-it' run an ELSIA test?"

"I don't know. But let's just suppose I did."

"Okay, so let's just say you did. So?"

"So, the ELSIA test was positive."

"Wait a second, Jo." Alex stopped dead in his tracks. "Why would you even run an ELSIA test on the slide. I mean, there's a hundred other tests you could have run."

"True. But I can't tell you that now."

"So you have a virologist/infectious disease guy and someone else that are both on the CIA's Book of Honor, both dead, a dead someone whom we performed an autopsy on, and cerebral spinal fluid that you just happened to do an ELSIA test on. But you won't tell me why the ELSIA test was positive, even though you've got an idea why."

"That's correct."

"So you want my advice? Oh, I forgot, we have two cars that have been following us ever since we began walking around the hospital. Tell me about your resident."

"Dr. Graham?

"Yes."

"She's a second year resident in pathology, assisted me in the autopsy after you left."

"Yeah, I remember."

"She was shot at last night, in front of her apartment building at the Tropicana Royale Apartments, on Tropicana between Eastern and Maryland Parkway."

"Bad neighborhood?"

"No, good. Never had any problems there."

"So what did she do?"

"Called the cops. And then they booked her on suspicion."

"In jail?"

"Yes."

"For suspicion of what?" Alex asked, infuriated. They began walking again, but this time Alex paced briskly in frustration.

"I don't know. All I know is that I spoke with her boyfriend this morning when I called her at home. He said she was in jail for suspicion. So I called the Las Vegas Jail, and she wasn't there, then I called the Clark County Detention Center Jail and she wasn't there either."

"You mean that she disappeared?"

"Neither place had any record of her ever being booked."

"So why are you talking to me and not the police?"

"Good question."

They turned the last corner and began walking down West Charleston back toward the hospital entrance. Jo was holding out. There was something important that she wanted to tell Alex. Yet, she wouldn't divulge it. So why did she call him for his advice? "What did you do with the slide?" Alex asked suspiciously.

With hesitation she replied, "Sent it to USC, to a friend of mine in immunology."

"Who?"

"Why?"

"Come on Jo, do you want me to try to help you or not? Isn't that why you called me here?"

"Yes."

"Well."

"Livingston."

"Livingston what?"

"I can't tell you."

"Jo, cut it out! Are we going to play guessing games all day, or should I just leave?"

"Just Livingston."

"So what's Livingston's deal?" Alex said throwing his hands into the air in disgust. "Why did you send it to him?"

"He's a friend."

"Jo, I need to know. It doesn't make any sense. Why did you do an ELSIA test on the CSF?" She did not answer. "Jo, I mean, I'm not a pathologist, and God knows that I haven't done an autopsy in forever, except for helping you the other day...but an ELSIA? Come on."

"Alex. I can't tell you why and that's that."

"So what do you want me to do?"

"I don't know. Maybe I just needed to tell someone. Maybe I should go to the police."

"Maybe? Good idea." Alex kicked some of the scattered loose gravel as they returned to where they started. Jo reached into her pocket for another Marlboro Light. She quickly lit up. Her normally rock-steady hands were shaking. Alex looked behind her. The first car, the gray Taurus, had reappeared.

"Jo, maybe you should get out of town, take a few days off, get lost or something."

"Alex, I think that..." she paused for a long time. She gazed up at the stars, the few that pierced through the neon-tinged, Vegas night. "...my past has caught up with me."

"What Jo? What's going on?"

"Alex you have to leave."

"Jo, you need my help. Please."

"Alex, go."

"Jo." She abruptly pushed him away. She flicked out her cigarette and then tersely walked through the automatic sliding entrance doors. Alex was dumbfounded.

That was it. Alex had known her for years, and she was still to-the-point; sometimes needing someone to vent to. Alex listened, gave her his feedback. But this time it was different. He sensed that Jo was in grave danger. She had been locked out of her autopsy room, the body, her dictations, her notes, and tissue and organ samples had disappeared.

Jo had one slide left, one that she inadvertently forgot to mark...or did she forget to mark it on purpose. And then she ran an ELSIA test. That made no sense at all. Why run an AIDS test on her John Doe, when the patient looked as healthy as a horse. And he wore a wedding ring. Alex remembered seeing it now.

"That's it...this guy wasn't gay. No way, no how."

Jo said the dead man looked like he had been scared to death, like he had come face-to-face with the grim reaper. What was Jo not telling him, *and why hadn't she already gone to the police?*

CHAPTER 7
Space Station Mir-Kennedy I

M*ir-Kennedy I* was a compilation of the previous Space Station Mir and the space shuttle-constructed *Kennedy Space Station*. Operational on December 7, 1993 at 2:30 A.M. *Space Station Mir* was equipped with ten solar panels, the *Mir* Core module, Kvant, Kvant-2, Kristall, Spektr, docking module, Soyuz-TM and Progree-M. It had a mean altitude of 409 kilometers. Eleven U.S. and Russian missions were completed in 1994-95.

In mid-1996, the United States began the construction of Kennedy Space Station. This United States/Russian designed platform was built in two interconnecting hoops, each with a diameter of 612 feet, or five shuttle lengths. The "hula-hoops," as they were later known, interlocked—with one running along the X-axis and the other the Y-axis. At a later date, a Z-hoop would be added. The Z-hoop was scheduled for completion in August 1997.

In a complex maneuver which required three extravehicular "tugs," approximately two-thirds of the previous *Space Station Mir* were cannibalized to fit into the center of hoops X/Y. Once done, *Mir* attached to hoop-X at Kristall module, adding additional living quarters, a hydroponics lab, a hydrophilic earthen-like soil greenhouse, an observatory, and research modules.

X-hoop's function was to provide simultaneous docking at the two 180 degree opposing poles. In addition, it provided life-support systems, two biologic bays, a one-third circumference metallurgics unit, a computer complex and a biologics production lab for the manufacture of three zero-G products: Draculase, a fast-acting drug for dissolving blood clots that cause heart attacks; 4TC, an Alzheimer's drug which prevents atrophy of acetylocholine-transmitting neurons and their target nerve cells, and recently approved by the Food and Drug Administration; and an E. coli bacteria which produces spider silk which is ten times stronger than silk and other suture material.

Y-hoop had a modified circumferential Velcro running track and sports training equipment that were affixed to the hoop's perimeter, and was used to prevent bone mineral loss, muscle atrophy, and to build resistance to radiation exposure. Additional rebreathing and emergency electric power and fuel back-up systems made up the remainder of the Y-hoop.

Instead of crew members sleeping in cramped two-by-six-foot beds, they now had private sleeping modules. Though the room was bathroom-size, there was access to digital satellite TV, on-line telecommunications on the Internet, and video-phone communication.

Eventually, when the Z-hoop was added to *Mir-Kennedy I*, the space station would be placed into a one-half orbital spin along the Y-hoop axis, which would create partial gravity. This "earth-normalization" would not disrupt activity in the X- or Z-hoops, which were already designed on a thirty-two degree X-axis angle, so that once the space station went into one-half gravitational spin, the respective hoops would also adapt one-half gravity, but through the erect, vertical axis.

From the telescopic platform of *Space Station Mir-Kennedy I*, the mysteries of the universe came into sharp focus. Immense clouds of interstellar hydrogen were seen boiling away by the intense ultraviolet light of newly birthed stars. Wispy tendrils of towering gas and dust thunderheads nearly six-trillion miles high, which were the cradle of newborn stars, came into sharp, unencumbered focus.

"Have you ever seen anything so beautiful?" Biologics Engineer Maya Mukhina asked Mission Commander Scoop Jackson. Jackson ran the show at *Mir-Kennedy I*. He was the archetypical leader. After graduating valedictorian from high school, and with a congressional recommendation from U.S. Senator Nathanal "Billy" Clark, he attended the Air Force Academy. It was there that he acquired his moniker as editor of the student newspaper, *The Warrior Update*. They called him "Scoop" because he had an eye for a flashy story and was able to push the envelope just far enough to not cause a brouhaha with the establishment—just to juice up the cadets.

After graduation from the Academy, his first assignment was flying McDonnell Douglas F-15 fighters out of Eglin Air Force Base, Florida. In 1981 he transferred to C-17 Globemaster 3s at Edwards Air Force Base, California, eventually making his way to the B-1B program at Ellsworth Air Force Base in Rapid City, South Dakota.

His career had changed in the spring of 1985 when, as a lieutenant colonel, he test-piloted the prototype USA/Northrop Grumman "Spirit of St. Louis" General Electric F118-GE-100 turbofan B-2. Scoop was instrumental in working out the bugs which eventually brought to fruition the maiden flight of the B-2 on July 17, 1989.

After the B-2 success story, Jackson was promoted to general and took a position in Washington on the staff of the National Security Council. After a while, flying a desk just didn't cut it. He jumped at the chance to start astronaut training in Houston six years ago.

Maya on the other hand, was the inverse. Her mother, Katrina, was a prima ballerina assoluta who danced with the Bolshoi. She was the first to introduce more than dance to ballet with Boris Sankin's *Rhythms of the Planet Ensemble*, while at the same time performing Tchaikovshy's *Swan Lake* and *Sleeping Beauty* with the greatest of elegance and grace.

Maya's father, Demitrov, was a teacher and research scientist at the Academy of Sciences of the U.S.S.R., the Presidium at Lenin prospeckt south of Gorky Park. It was her father's work in experimental biologic engineering that interested her, and it was in his footsteps that she followed while attending Moscow M.V. Lomonosov State University. There she received her degrees in virology and genetic engineering. Maya was assigned to *Mir-Kennedy I* and was one of two biologic engineers.

"It doesn't get much more beautiful than this," Jackson remarked.

He wasn't alluding to the heavens. She held fast her gaze into the space telescope where she was studying the Cartwheel Galaxy.

The focus of her fascination was a galaxy 500 million light-years away in the constellation Sculptor. It was once a graceful spiral the size and shape of our Milky Way. A small galaxy had, however, smacked though its center, sending shockwaves outward at 200,000 miles per hour pushing dust and gas in front of it. The debris was caught up in a galactic tsunami, and was compressed and ignited into billions of new stars.

"I mean, if you think of it, there has to be a God. How else could all of this have happened?" she asked.

Jackson studied her waist and voluptuous hips. He thought of making love to her last night. Eighty-six days in space in close confinement was enough to stir emotion in any person. "You know," he said, taking his eyes off her waist and looking back into the heavens, "have you seen the Cat's-Eye Nebula?"

"No, should I?"

"Yes. We'll be in position in about," he looked down at his watch, "Zero nine hundred."

"And what's so special about the Cat's-Eye?" she asked. She looked at him with an inviting simper as she stepped down from her harnessed viewing seat and stood next to him. He was tall, five-foot ten as compared to her five-foot three. "Meow," she purred sweetly as she placed her left arm around his waist, and with her right, weaved her delicate fingers through his short, graying hair. "Meow. What's so special about the Cat's-Eye?"

He kissed her on the forehead, then they embraced in a moment of anticipatory desire. "It's...three-thousand light-years away in the constellation Draco. It looks like one of those marbles you might have played with as a kid. You know those?"

"Yes."

"It's an orange ball of gas that forms the iris of the eye, which in actuality is the outer atmosphere of a star glowing brightly in the pupil, blown off in a slow-motion explosion that many stars undergo as they die..."

"Is that so..." she gently kissed his neck.

"Yes...that's so." His composure was unpinning. "But the gas," he continued, "known as a planetary nebula for its spherical shape, has an intricate structure that suggests something unusual's going on."

"And what's that," she asked as she glided her left hand down below his waist, over his inflight coveralls.

"Huh, huh. It's...we think that the..." he was having a hard time concentrating, "star at the center of the structure may actually be two stars so close together that we can't tell them apart. Most of the gases according..." she stroked the outside of his trousers, "Maya."

"Shu..." She continued with her impish business.

"Maya," he pulled away. "Let me finish."

She immediately pressed next to him, not willing to let him go, and in a schoolgirl voice said, "Go on."

"Behave."

"Yes, master."

"Now...most of the gas, according to this theory, comes from the larger of the two stars, but the smaller star is still spewing jets of hot gas..."

"Hot gas?" She gazed at him mischievously—and deliberately in a light brush—swung her left hand against his groin.

"Hot gases that created the wispy curlicues and bright arcs that form the outer edges of the cat's eye!"

"In the death throes?"

"Why do you do this to me when I'm trying to speak to you?"

"I'm sorry. I didn't mean to make you mad," she replied coyly, but she was really on top of her game. "Did I?"

"Maya...look, I'm trying to tell you about a lot of neat stuff..."

"You mean like HH1 and HH2 named after Berbi and Haro—infant stars that burp out gaseous lumps when their gravitational fields gobble up too much surrounding material too quickly, and black holes that lurk at the core of many galaxies like those confirmed by Hooland Ford at Johns Hopkins. That stuff?"

"Funny. I was just trying to tell you about the Cat's-Eye, 'cause I thought that it was pretty neat."

"You know Scoop, the only cat's-eye that I want," she again rubbed him below the waist, over his coveralls. This time he responded by pulling her tight in a passionate embrace. He hotly pressed his lips against hers and lunged his tongue deep into her mouth. He kissed her hard for a minute.

"Now that's the kind of black hole I like," she mumbled.

He held her tight and didn't utter a word. She could feel his heart pound.

"Tell me you love me," she said. She stopped her school-girl taunts.

He was stoic, and his emotions were difficult to get in touch with, but Maya was a remarkable woman, and she believed that she could draw him out of his shell.

"I..."

"What?" she asked.

"Nothing."

"Is it hard for you to say...I love you? Do you think...that the feelings between us are...artificial because of our confinement? Something that wouldn't have happened had we not been here?"

"No, no...it's not that." He looked into her hazel eyes. "It's just...I mean...I didn't plan this."

"Is love ever planned?"

"I don't know. Falling in love with you. My life's already very complicated."

"And so is mine. What makes you think you have a monopoly on that?"

"I don't."

"Then?"

"I don't know. It's just...not simple...If things were different."

"I know what you're thinking Scoop. You're thinking that you were weak. That you shouldn't have given in to your primal desires. That we shouldn't have been with each other last night...that we shouldn't have made love."

He thought that the notion of "night" was humorous, especially up here. There was no day nor night, just Mission Control's clock. Was it 0900 or 2300? "Yes," he honestly answered.

"Those thoughts have crossed my mind—being with you Scoop. But just like bees are to flowers, some things in life go together. I didn't plan on meeting you. In fact, if you would have asked me, and I was certainly asked dozens of times when I trained for this program, and before I was ever assigned here, my answer would have always been that my career came first. That's how I saw it. But...it's part of the mystery of life. Things just happen—sometimes when two people work closely together it just happens."

"I suppose that's true."

"I'm not trying to pressure you. In fact, that's the opposite of what I want to do. All I'm saying is—I'm being honest with you—

sharing my feelings with you. It's just something that happened. Do you understand?"

"I do."

"Then...how do you feel?"

"I don't know. I agree with everything that you said. I also didn't plan on anything. I..."

"What?"

"I don't know."

"Go on."

"Well, I've been married before, once, to my high school sweetheart...for twenty years. About three years ago, I took it pretty hard...She died in a car accident."

"I'm sorry."

"It wasn't your fault...We didn't have any children. It wasn't that we didn't want to, she just couldn't. In fact, if I wasn't instrumental in the construction of Mir-Kennedy I, then I probably wouldn't have been considered for this mission. The political climate is such that a married-with-children Mission Commander is more palatable in NASA's eyes."

"You were the best man for the job."

"I suppose."

"So, I don't know if this is the right time, but I wanted to tell you what I'm feeling. That I love you. You're under no obligation whatsoever, except that I want you to be honest with me regarding your feelings when you want to talk about them."

"Honest?"

"Yes."

It was then that the "code red" alarms blared, and the flashing emergency lights screamed.

"What is it?" Jackson toggled on his voice-activated right-ear headset with earphone, clip and microphone. A cable connected his headset to a small control unit which he had clipped to his waistband, and a rocker switch allowed him to select either the onboard intercom or external communication. The intercom setting on the rocker switch was marked ICOM; the transmit position XMIT PTT. There was a volume control on top of the box and a *push to talk* mode.

"We've got an emergency in the Biologics Production Lab," Commander Vrubel railed from the Communications Center.

"Gregov! It's Gregov!" Maya shouted.

CHAPTER 8
Mwanza, Tanzania
on the Shores of Lake Victoria

"You okay?"

"No, I'm not."

"What's wrong?"

"I feel hot."

"Hot as in all over, or just your forehead?"

"Just my forehead."

"Do you want some water?"

"Yes."

The Bantu Serengeti National Park game warden's wife got out from under her flowered sheets and damask bedcover. She slid on her slippers and walked across the teak floor to the kitchen. She opened her refrigerator and removed a pitcher of ice water. She poured it into a glass while she tightened her robe. It was 10:00 P.M. and her husband, Abeid Nyerere had just gotten home. She had put their baby down several hours earlier. Outside she could hear the sounds of the game preserve: the cackling hyenas, the trumpeting elephants, and the lions roaring.

She filled the glass two-thirds full, placed a few butternut cookies onto a china plate that her grandmother Karume had given them as a wedding gift, turned off the light and returned to the bedroom. Abeid loved his cookies. They calmed down his sometimes obdurate temper.

When she returned to the bedroom Abeid was shivering. He was sweating profusely and his color had turned ashen-gray. He was lying on his side in anguish.

"My little teddy bear, are you alright?" She kissed him on the cheek and quietly set the glass on the end table next to him. Enough luminescence came through the window in the full-moon eve that she didn't need to turn on the night-light.

She walked to a chest of drawers. On top was a box of tissue in a hand-carved coverlet. She removed several sheets and returned to his bedside to tenderly dab his brow.

"Do you need some aspirin?"

"Thank you, that feels good."

"Do you want some?"

"I'll be fine. I just have the flu."

She kissed him a second time on his cheek, then set the Kleenex next to the cookies and water. He hadn't touched them.

"Have some water please."

"I will."

At one in the morning, their nine-month-old baby awoke. The game warden's wife heard Rolanda's yammers through the infant monitor that she had turned on low and was on her end table side of the bed.

"Abeid, Abeid," she rolled over. She gently nudged him but he did not respond. It was his turn to feed their child. "Abeid." She got a little irritated, then she remembered that he wasn't feeling well. She pushed her side of the covers back, got up and slipped on her bathrobe for a second time. With the lights out, she walked to the kitchen, opened the refrigerator and removed one of the six-ounce bottles she had earlier prepared.

After thirty seconds in the microwave, the bottle was skin-touch warm. She checked it, pressing it onto the fleshy inner surface of her forearm. Sometimes the center of the bottle heated less than the circumference, and she learned after experimentation, that she needed to shake the bottle after it warmed to glean a sense of temperature.

Fifteen minutes later, the baby was fed and changed and Abeid's wife was heading back to bed.

She was dog-tired and could barely keep her heavy lids from falling shut. As she snuggled next to Abeid she said, "You have the most darling little child ever." Then she rolled over and cuddled her arm around Abeid's teddy bear furry chest. He was cold. At first she didn't notice it and almost fell back to sleep. Then, "Abeid," she shook him. "Abeid." He did not respond.

She reached over him and turned on the night-light on his side of the bed. "Abeid," she said as she looked down at his face. He had a look of horror, as if he had seen a ghost and then died of a heart attack in his sleep. His eyes were wide-open and his mouth was agape. He was turpentine green. "Abeid!" she screamed.

Seoul, South Korea
Kyongsin Electronics Corporation International

The board meeting was tumultuous. At stake was the direction the multinational electronics concern was going to forge over the next five years. Kyongsin Electronics was the third largest electronics corporation in the Pacific rim and was a global force to be reckoned with.

Kim Young Mun was the iron-fisted CEO who ran Kyongsin Electronics. His reputation as a tyrant was justly deserved. Yet, he was not a demagogue without a calling—which was to give the consumer the best possible product at the lowest possible price, which at the same time made him a deep-pocket billionaire.

Mun was known to have a "hands on" approach that involved every aspect of his company's business. Aside from chairing the bi-weekly board meetings, he was often found with shirt sleeves rolled up, tie tucked in, in the trenches on the assembly lines—or in the electronic showrooms at Sello, a global electronics retailer; or at their mining operations in Thailand, Malaysia, and New Guinea.

Yearly, Mun logged over 300,000 miles in his Gulfstream G-5. He was a tireless worker.

The board was in heated debate over Kyongsin Electronics' mission statement. Chun Knojong, the president of Paekche Teck, a subsidiary Taiwanese textile manufacturer, stormed out in disgust after he kicked his chair backwards and threw his leather-bound itinerary across the marble conference table. Though Mun was an inquisitor, he encouraged hot-tempered disagreement, since he ultimately made the final decisions. Nevertheless, he believed great ideas sprung out of diversity.

At first it was Mun's executive assistant Pusang Yoo who noticed that Mun was not his normal self. Mun's proclivity was to manipulate the meeting like a puppeteer.

"Director Mun, are you all right?" Yoo asked as he stepped forward to pour him a second glass of fresh carrot juice.

Mun took a handkerchief out of his shirt pocket. It was perfectly folded and positioned square-end-up in his pin-striped suit. He waived off Yoo and dabbed his forehead. He was sweating profusely.

Park Dae, Mun's Director of Asian Operations for Kyongsin, threw a tantrum and hurled his pen across the table at Doo Chun Hwan, the Director of North American Operations, then apologized, pretending that the pen slipped out of his hand and that Park Dae wasn't a "jack-ass" like Konjong. The twenty directors were in such a rage that they barely noticed Mun get up from the board table and walk into his executive bathroom, which was directly behind his director's chair and to the right. Besides, he had excused himself before during other raucous board meetings, and had encouraged that the lively debate not stop because of his need to use the facilities, especially since the board meetings often ran over five hours.

When Mun had not returned after fifteen minutes, Yoo knocked on the bathroom door. When there was no answer after the second knock, he gently pushed open the door, "Director Mun?" There was no response.

Yoo entered the anteroom. It was darkly lit in charcoals and emerald with three overhead TV monitors. They had different views of the conference room. Next to the wall was a six-foot long ottoman. Below the monitors was a small table with magazines on it: *Korean Economic Report, Korean Business Review, Maekryung Business Week, Forbes*—all the most recent issues. Below the third monitor was a twisted-cord telephone.

In the adjacent room was a small bathroom with a sink, vanity mirror, and a small medicine chest. There was also a shower/Jacuzzi combination, bidet and toilet. Yoo could hear the water running through the closed door.

"Director Mun?" he asked with genuine concern as he reticently tapped on the door. There was no answer. He knocked again and repeated his inquiry. Still no answer.

After waiting thirty seconds he knocked loudly. Then, he cautiously pushed open the door.

Standing, frozen in rigor mortis, was CEO Kim Young Mun. His petrified hands were planted on the sink's edges for balance. He was staring into the mirror. He had torn off his tie and ripped open most of his starched shirt, popping off several of the buttons.

He had splashed water onto his face and his glinting, hairless chest. His shirt was sopping wet. Around his stomach, the unopened portion of his shirt stuck to his skin in a puddle.

Mun's eyes were frozen open, his skin was greenish white; his lower jaw ghoulishly sagging. He had an abhorrent expression on his face. *He looked like he had seen a ghost.*

CHAPTER 9

The deceptive salvage rust-bucket, the *Maria Santini* rocked re-lentlessly in the billowing swells thirty miles off the coast of the tip of transpeninsular Cabo San Lucas, just above the Cedros Trench. Beneath lay the diatomic silts and ocean clays that made salvage diffi-cult. The deep Gulf water was thermally stratified, which caused oxy-gen deficiency at intermediate depths and made intact recovery more probable.

The *Maria Santini* had arrived at the site of the wreckage within thirteen hours of the Aeromexico Flight 900's demise. Diving for re-covery and investigation of the cause of the explosion was best handled immediately since deep-water currents along with rich salt waters, tended to rapidly change the environment of the crash site.

Fortunately for the *Maria Santini* and its crew, Aeromexico Flight 900 was blown up in the tail section, according to the pilot's report, before radio contact was lost. This meant that the forward and possi-bly mid-fuselage sections of the aircraft were likely intact, or at least the wreckage would be dispersed over a more confined area.

With the help of the NSA's PSYTEP North American infrared spy satellite, and using the *Maria Santini's* sophisticated ocean searching equipment, the crew found the bulk of the wreckage at a depth of 1,210 feet, spread over a three-quarter mile area. A descent short line was dropped, consisting of a floating "ploy" lined with a large buoy at the surface and a forty pound shot-weight which sat on the seabed floor. A smaller counterbalance was secured to the top end of the shot line which allowed the line to slide freely through a loop on the buoy, thus removing all slack from the line.

Theodore, a small submarine that was the cousin to Alvin—the submersible used in the search of the Titanic—went down first. Theodore also had a small tethered robot to penetrate and photograph areas within the wreckage. Thirty minutes after Theodore's descent, the *Maria Santini* had found the remains of the first class cabin.

Simon, a remotely operated vehicle was lowered in preparation for the JIM Suit divers. The ROV was capable of penetrating into the 747's first class cabin through business class. The port side of the plane's fuselage was crushed and the opening was not large enough for Theodore, and the insertion distance was too far for its limited-mobility concatenating robot.

Simon was tethered to the surface by an umbilical line which carried electric power and communication cables. After an additional seventeen minutes, twenty seconds—Simon, or as the crew preferred to call it, "*Chipmunk No. Three, The Flying Eyeball*," worked its way into the remains of the first class compartment.

"Any sign of Ambassador Perov?"

"No, Captain."

"And the briefcase?"

"Not yet."

Vince Eddy, the ROV specialist, powered Simon through as much of the first class cabin as he could. Color pictures instantaneously beamed up to Eddy's monitor on the helm, in the crusty wheelhouse, where Captain Nathaniel Henry manned the *Maria Santini*.

"Send down the JIMs," he ordered his first mate. The JIMs had been in ready. Within two minutes of the command, they were overboard and rapidly descending

Each of the JIM Suit divers (named after Jim Jarratt, who dove the forerunner of this system to five hundred feet in Loch Ness) allowed a single diver to move and work at depths up to fifteen hundred feet. The JIMs were one atmosphere diving suits and were solid with movable joints, similar to a suit of armor. The suit had its own life support systems and utilized mechanical hands to perform manual tasks at depth. While the JIM suit allowed a single diver to move quite freely on the sea bed, it was not as effective for mid-water use. Also, at sea bottom, the JIM was clumsy. The divers were connected by a hundred-foot communications tether and each was lowered by an overhead miniboom.

"Whatdaya got?" a surly Duke Roberts asked as he followed his Chief Petty Officer's lead on the fungating volcanic floor.

"What a mess," CPO Eric Hodges said as he trudged in mechanical slow-motion. He looked like a Jules Verne moon-walking astronaut. Hodges wore the Roman numeral nine on the back of his suit next to the humpback shell that covered his hydreliox supply.

"That's the truth," Al Giddings piped as he stopped to shoot video that was transmitted up to the *Maria Santini*.

"Let's tighten up," Hodges ordered as he turned to inspect his crew before they entered the 747-400

Aeromexico Flight 900, at least the stern, had broken into three pieces once it struck the ocean floor. The business class section had splintered at the galley and cargo elevator bay, and slid approximately 120 meters north of the middle and rear sections of the 747.

The belly of the four-engine Rolls-Royce RB211-524 jet had in part disintegrated with ocean impact, then broken apart when it came to a sudden halt on the ocean's unforgiving floor.

"Be careful."

The most precarious aspects of wearing JIM suits when diving for wreckage are toppling over and not being able to right oneself, or getting stuck in a confined space; usually the result of shifting debris or structural instability.

They entered through a hole that had been torn in the plane's fuselage midway forward of business class. The remnants of the dead were strapped into their seats—at least some. This suggested to Hodges that despite the jet's tail being blown off, the Boeing 747-400 did have some maneuverability before it crashed into the ocean. This was the opposite of what was thought. If the jet had gone into a spiral and immediately plummeted, there probably wouldn't have been an intact cabin. The fact that there were recognizable bodies suggested that the pilot attempted to maneuver the 747 onto the ocean's surface.

Despite best efforts, however, the crash landing still had to be substantial, since most of the ceiling between business and first class was violently smashed upward. There was barely walking room.

The three JIM Suit divers made their way carefully through the business-class section. Giddings, the last on the tether, remained in business class while CPO Hodges and Roberts worked their way above.

The milieu in first class was gruesome. There was little more than crawl-space room between the seats and crumpled ceiling. Grisly body parts and blood had been spewed onto the ceiling, while others floated in suspended animation between the rows. Neptune-blue seawater was tinged crimson.

"What number was Perov in?"

"3-A," Hodges replied. As he carefully made his way through the bulkhead, the plane shifted. A grinding creak smacked through the brine—and the 747-400 rocked ten degrees to the port.

"You okay?" Hodges turned to give Roberts a hand. Roberts had been thrown onto his left knee, but signaled that he was all right with a thumbs up as Hodges shuffled back to help him.

"Okay down here," Giddings replied. Giddings then looked over his shoulder back at the opening through which they came. The opening had closed partially, as the plane had rolled to its left. "I don't think we have much time. One more shift and we don't have a way out."

"Barry," Captain Henry spoke from the helm where he had been monitoring their progress. "Get out of there. I'm reading seismic upheavals all over the place!" Henry scanned the seismographic strips that his ensign had just handed him from the telemetry room.

"No dice captain. Five more minutes, and we should find what we're looking for."

"Sorry Barry, you've gotta come topside, now!"

"Captain, just five more—we're right on top of the situation. Give me five and I'll have Perov."

"Five more, that's it. But if we have one more tremor, I'm pulling the plug."

"That's a go."

Another quake rocked the 747-400. Hodges braced himself between two first-class seats and Roberts was thrown backward.

"Everyone all right?" Hodges gut-checked.

"Affirmative," Roberts crisply replied.

"Affirmative," Giddings answered. "Our escape route's shifted. We need to get our rear ends out of here." Then another mild tremor rattled the plane. Giddings realized that the plane wasn't shifting with the ocean floor, but was falling into an opening fault.

"What's going on down there?" Henry asked.

"I think we're sitting on a fault line," Giddings replied, "and we better make quick work of things." He was referring to Hodges and Roberts above him, "or we're unequivocal grass." Another tremor, this one moderate, shook the unstable plane, as if in response to Giddings' declaration.

"Wait a second," Roberts said. He glanced briefly behind Hodges and to the left before falling backward. There appeared to be a lonesome hand with something shiny attached to it. It was difficult to ascertain in the deep-water gloom. Roberts quickly worked his way aft to seat 8-D, shining his helmet light in his path. He pushed one cadaver out of his way, then a second.

"Wait a..." Roberts precariously reached down. He had difficulty sliding between the seats, and at the same time distinguishing real objects from their murky shadows. He gripped a hand that was attached to a handcuff, and the handcuff in turn to an attaché case.

"I've got..." then he pulled out from under the seat the rest of the hand that was attached to the smashed briefcase. The extremity had been jaggedly severed at the shoulder. He shoved his way between the first class seats and into the serrated isle, and up a row. On the floor he saw it: *What was left of Perov. His face had that look. His eyes were wide-open in ghastly fright. His mouth was agape. His skin was white—as a bleached sheet...It was as if he had seen a ghost.*

CHAPTER 10

FSB Directorate Shlyapnikov had booked Alex at the Desert Inn. Alex wasn't one of those glitzy high-roller players—really nothing more than an average Joe who liked to go to Las Vegas once in awhile with the guys. He had, however, his fill of gambling while living in Vegas during his Internal Medicine training. In fact, nowadays he played very little. He didn't like to lose.

The Desert Inn, which was built in 1950 and had six hundred rooms, was recently refurbished. It was across the street from the Galleria and south of the Frontier Hotel. Though it wasn't a hotel with a famous erupting volcano atop an artificial mountain, and it didn't have the replica of an eighteenth-century sea village, surrounded by rock cliffs, palm trees and nautical artifacts perched atop a blue-water lagoon—it was a nice place to stay.

The DI was a "joint" that courted the *whales*—the gamblers with zigzagging psyche and superstitious quirks who'd win or lose millions at a sitting, and who might demand rooms with white-sheet, four-poster beds, certain scented flowers, a bed facing an open door, and the number four removed from the doors since they considered it bad luck.

The *whales* were the betters who thumbed their stacks of $500 and $1000 chips, and were guarded by lumberjack-brawny security guards in their hotel-issue coats.

Alex's mind was spinning. *Why would she surf the Internet of all places? Dr. Bennett Frank. That name rang a bell, but who was he? And why the names of two dead men—Frank and Darling, on the CIA's Book of Honor? What sense did it make?*

Alex was worried for Jo. Yet, he knew that she could pull her own weight. Then he thought about the dead man's clothes. They were in a heap on the counter in the autopsy room. They were not folded, but piled as if they were tossed there in a hurry. The suit, his shirt and pants and silk tie were expensive. "But why did this guy come to 'her' for an autopsy in his clothes? He *would have* if he'd just gotten there, at the hospital, if he *wasn't a patient* who had died there." Alex had a million questions that raced through his mind. Something was wrong, really wrong!

Alex knew there was big trouble when he opened the door to his hotel room. His room had been ransacked. Clothes were strewn across the bed and floor, his meticulously organized briefcase dumped open with his files poured onto the second bed's quilt comforter. Literature from the Consumer Electronics Show: from BetaTec, Cray Research, Pilot Software, SunSoft and more—as if someone was going through it when he walked in...

He didn't take more than one step into the room. His right hand was still on the door handle. In the ashtray on its glass rim, between the two queen-sized beds, next to the night-light and telephone, was a partially smoked cigarette, its tip still glowing. Alex knew that an intruder was inside—that he had no time to escape. What was Alex going to do?

Alex looked for a weapon, anything, and then he thought about the possible consequences of his act. What if he was to knock-out his prowler, and that intruder turned out to be a fed who was watching Jo, and then spotted him?

He quickly scanned the room. There was nothing that he could readily use. He was on the first floor. His room had a terrace that overlooked one of the hotel's two pools. There were two beds—one he slept in; the other he used as a catch-all for his clothing, briefcase and day planner. *What could he use? The intruder must be in the bathroom. He didn't bring an umbrella, he had no knife, nor fork from room service late last night. The room had been cleaned, the bed made, and the serving table removed—what?* Then it dawned on him: Why do anything? The sliding glass door had been jarred slightly open. It was cracked no more than a quarter of an inch. In the hallway, he had seen a maid's canvas cart. The cart had clean towels, sheets, cleaning supplies. Beyond it was a wall mounted two-and-a-half gallon fire extinguisher. It was enmeshed in the hall's motif. Alex knew what he was going to do.

In a howling voice he stormed out of the room, ranting that he was going to call the police. As he did, he deliberately slammed the door behind him.

The intruder, who had his silenced Makarov 9mm automatic pointing through the shower curtain, was prepared to kill Alex had the doctor entered the bathroom.

The intruder bolted out of the shower stealthy as a cat, and locked, then chained the door shut. He gave himself sixty seconds to finish his search of Alex's briefcase. He didn't find what he was looking for.

Then, as if he had never existed, he slipped out of the sliding glass door onto the poolside veranda.

However, the intruder had underestimated Alex. As soon as he stuck his head through the glass door he was done. *Bang!*

The man yelled as the fire extinguisher smashed into his head. A risky move, but Alex had no choice. Alex had concealed himself to the side of the wall, waiting for the intruder to leave. The man hit the veranda's Astroturf deck.

In the intruder's gloved hand Alex saw the silenced automatic. Alex kicked the gun away. Then he pushed the man with his other foot. He did not move. Alex knelt and pressed his index and middle fingers to the man's thick neck, and onto his carotid artery. The pulse was strong. "He'll live."

Spit, spit. Alex felt the whiz of two bullets zing past his head! They landed in the wall just above eye level, where he would have been had he not bent down to examine his assailant.

Again *spit, spit.* The missiles embedded into the low-rise stucco privacy wall in front of him.

Alex awkwardly grabbed the silenced 9mm Makorov. He quickly

shoved the sliding-glass door open, while bent low out of the line of fire. The sliding door jammed! He needed space to crawl into the room. *Crack!* the glass door shattered as Alex began to work his way back through the confined opening. *Crash!* another shot shattered the adjoining double-paned window. In the distance he could hear sirens. Someone must have called the police.

"I've gotta get out of here. I can't be here when the cops arrive." He didn't trust the situation, especially after he and Jo were followed on their walk outside the University Medical Center. And then, in an instant, his gut told him that he needed to search the man. Had he taken something out of Alex's briefcase?

Alex quickly checked his hands. Nothing! Then swiftly his pant and interior and external jacket pockets. There was no wallet, no ID, no business cards, nothing. Alex didn't have time. *Crack!* another bullet pierced the remaining glass portion of the door that hadn't shattered. Shards exploded everywhere.

There was nothing on him, he was clean. Then something quickly caught Alex's eye—a laundry tag pinned on the inside-collar label of his sports jacket. It read: "American Cleaners."

Spit. Another shot.

By the time the first of twelve cop cars arrived, the second assailant had carried off the intruder, who was just regaining consciousness. He had a goose egg on his head the size of Toledo. Initially, he didn't remember where he was—then he got mad and swore he'd get even. Alex had also disappeared.

There was only one place that Alex was going, and that was like a rocket back to the University Medical Center. Jo knew something that she had kept from him, and that something had almost gotten him killed.

If he could have driven any faster he would have. His brain was on fire. Why was the guy going through his briefcase? He didn't have anything of value, nothing worth stealing. Keys, notepads, a few files, literature from the electronics show, his Daytimer."

The intruder had a gun, and *was planning to kill Alex.*

But why?

Alex bolted through traffic. He zipped onto Sahara west to the expressway, barreled north down I-15 to Charleston, then west to the University Medical Center. By the time he reached the hospital it seemed like an eternity...and it was too late.

Ambulances with their flashing lights and four squad cars with officers were routing traffic around the Medical Center's front entrance. What appeared to be a woman was on a stretcher. Her face was partially covered and an IV bag hung from a pole attached to the head of the stretcher. Her hair was auburn and curly. "They've got her!"

Alex threw open his door and ran out. Officers tried to restrain him, but he pushed his way through. When he got to the ambulance, blood was everywhere. There had been a shoot-out. A jealous lover and his wife. She, not Jo, was on the stretcher. "Thank God." He had dispatched her in front of the hospital, then stuck the gun to his temple and pulled the trigger. There was a splay of blood on the building's front.

An ambulance driver on his way out of the Emergency Room to fill up with gas, at the I-15 and Martin Luther King Boulevard Chevron, drove past the hospital and saw everything. He lost his lunch—the Big Mac with fries and chocolate shake, onto his steering wheel and pants.

"Jo, Dr. Knight, is she here?"

"No," answered the staid nurse standing outside of the hospital's automatic double doors. Along with the gaggle of people, she watched as an emergency room doctor desperately tried to stabilize the gunshot victim.

"Do you know where she went?"

"I'm not sure," another voice answered.

Alex turned to face a physician. The doctor wore a plaid sports jacket. He had an expressive boyish face that crinkled around his mouth and muppet eyes. A stethoscope bulged out of his left pocket, with the earpieces twisted in a clasp. "Who's asking?"

"Dr. Alex Seacourt. Jo's a friend of mine. Do you know where she went?"

"I don't know...but she seemed to be in an awfully big hurry."

"Was she by herself?"

"Can't say."

"What do you mean?"

"I don't know."

"Was she with anyone?"

"I don't..."

"Look," Alex grabbed the pompous ass by his lapel, and pulled his body against his chest. "I'm in no mood for banter. Did she go willingly?"

"Hey easy. I don't know. "

"Well?"

"I don't know...she was just in a hurry. I wasn't really paying attention."

CHAPTER 11

There was a full-blown emergency on board *Mir-Kennedy I*. It was a "code red" alert. Code red emergencies were reserved for the dreaded piercing of the space station by a meteor, or most likely outer space junk—one of the tens of thousands of satellites and other debris that hurtled through space.

"God, help us," Jackson yelled into his VOX headset mic as he bumped and pushed from the observatory through the Kristall module to the Biologics Production Lab.

"Gregov," Maya screamed into her headset as she too ran closely behind Commander Jackson. "What's the problem? Gregov!"

"Code red alert."

"Code red? Did you have meteor penetration?" Maya could hear the distant crackling of inappropriate electricity over her headset.

"It's *LAV-10*," Pokrovsky said.

"My God, *LAV-10*!"

"That's correct."

"What going on?" Jackson demanded as he jammed his way down X-hoop docking module A, past Life Support Systems, the two Biologics Experimental Bays, and the Metallurgics Crystallization Lab to the Biologics Production Lab. Biologic Productions was sealed off. Through the clutter of wires, ducts, hardware, some of it held in place with bungee cords, they worked their way to the titanium sealed pressurization door.

"The main computer says that we've got one hundred percent containment in Biologics." said *Mir-Kennedy I* Commander Vrubel. (Technically *Mir-Kennedy I*, with its 270-day crew of eight (four cosmonauts, one Canadian, one Japanese and two American astronauts) was under the command of General Vrubel. Though Commander Vrubel was responsible for the operation of *Mir-Kennedy I*, Mission Commander Jackson was responsible for all souls on board. In four days Commander Vrubel was scheduled to return to earth to TsUP Control Center and Kaliningrad near Moscow, along with the five other crew members. They would be replaced by Jackson, Spacewalker/ Pilot Randall Smith, Chemical Engineer Stephen Cunningham, Jr. (the two American astronauts), Maya, and Tool Specialist Vladimir Budarin (the Russian cosmonauts). In one hundred hours, Commander Vrubel was to hand over the "complete" reins to Jackson.

"Pokrovsky," Jackson spoke to Gregov through the containment window, "talk to me."

"Commander..."

"Gregov," Maya pressed her face hard to the Plexiglas window. She firmly shook her head "no."

"Speak to me," Jackson reiterated as he quickly glanced at Maya, then back to Pokrovsky.

"I had...an electrical fire. I was working behind the glass when it happened. I lost power, and the isomer separator shorted out, then the emergency backup kicked in..." He was trembling. "I had a cooling systems malfunction. I might have had a spill."

"Of what?" Jackson demanded. He wasn't aware of anything that would cause a code red alert.

Maya was still signaling "no," but this time more ardently.

"What's your containment status, and how long until we can come in?" Jackson asked.

"You can't."

"Why?"

"Biologics."

"What do you mean biologics? We don't have containment level organisms on board."

Pokrovsky glanced at Maya, then turned to Jackson. "I'm sorry Jackson, but you can't come in. Ever."

"What do you mean I can't come in? This mission's my charge."

"I mean you can't come in, Commander."

"What's going on Pokrovsky? I order you to answer me!"

"Commander, I can't. You can't come in. It's not safe."

"I order you to answer!" Jackson cock-turned his head and faced Maya. Maya had been working with Pokrovsky at Kalinigrad, giving him ground support on the Draculase and 4TC project. Her job was to assist Pokrovsky on the perfection of the synthetic fast-acting clotbuster which was similar to TPA and streptokinase and 4TC, the anti-Alzheimer's drug. Pokrovsky was scheduled to return to earth in four days. Yet, yesterday, orders from Johnson Space Center Houston called for a change of charge. Flight Engineer Cosmonaut Nikolai Solovyev was to return to earth in lieu of Pokrovsky. This would have left the *Mir-Kennedy I* crew shorthanded in its crystallization projects, especially the zero-G silicon growth. In addition, that specific order was irregular since Pokrovsky would be habitating beyond his 270-day tour.

Maya did not answer. The alarms continued to blare. "Turn off those damn alarms," Jackson ordered. By now, Smith and Cunningham, two of *Mir-Kennedy I* replacements, arrived at the other end of the Biologics Lab. Jackson could see them through the six-inch Biologics window, also looking through Plexiglas.

"What the hell's going on, Commander?" Smith asked firmly.

"What the hell is going on?" an infuriated Jackson asked Maya again. She did not answer. Instead she looked past him to Pokrovsky.

"How long until you're out of oxygen?" she asked.

"My estimation…" Pokrovsky looked down at his twenty-four-hour watch, "72 hours."

"Are you sure about the spill?"

"Yes, positive."

Mir-Kennedy I continued its portentous orbit. Johnson Space Center, Houston, was notified of the crisis on board, along with TsUP Control Center direct to Kaliningrad. This second transmission was routed to Moscow. Maya was ordered to communicate with the Kremlin in tier 3 scrambled, Vyacheslav Code via the Sojuzkarkta observation satellite. At 14:57 hours, the crew of *Mir-Kennedy I*, except for Pokrovsky, met in the Command Center on Jackson's orders.

"Gregov," Maya spoke into her mic, "how's your hardware and respiratory monitor working?"

"Unremarkable."

"Do you feel any ill affects?"

"No."

"Any changes in environment?"

"None."

"Any increase in respiration or pulse rate?" She had been monitoring his breathing and heart rate through Command Center telemetry and was aware that there had been no objective change. She, however, wanted Gregov's personal interpretation.

"A sense of anxiety, I'd say. I'm hungry, but that's to be expected. I haven't eaten. No shortness of breath, double-vision, hallucinations—no early signs of gangrene."

"Keep me posted."

"I'll do better than that. I'll keep on working."

"Be careful Gregov. You understand the urgency of our mission."

"I understand." He signed off.

"Now what the hell's going on," Jackson asked Maya. Jackson mirrored Vrubel's anticipated questions. At control, huddled around a planning table for eight, were the thirteen crew members of *Mir-Kennedy I*.

"Gentlemen, comrades, I'm sure all of you are well aware of the classifications of biologics that we're authorized to work on in *Space Station Mir-Kennedy I*," Maya said.

"Class one and limited class two," Computer and Metallurgic Specialist Zvezda replied.

"We have a class four problem," Maya said in a business-like manner.

"Excuse me, if I'm a little behind the power curve," Spacewalker Holloway, the Canadian astronaut asked, "but what's the difference?"

"The difference is massive," Jackson interrupted.

"Let me explain." Maya replied, "The Centers for Disease Control in Atlanta has set international standards for the classification of research biologics. Class one is..."

"I thought we weren't carrying anything dangerous," Smith interjected.

"Yeah, that's what my understanding was. Is this some kind of Russian trick?" Cunningham asked with suspicion.

"No. This is not a trick! What this is...Let me first explain, then maybe we can come up with a solution, though I..."

"...Don't think there is one?" Vrubel interrupted.

She ignored him. "In traditional hospital settings, diseases are categorized by type of isolation and precautions required. Strict isolation prevents the spread of highly communicable diseases that can be readily transmitted by contact or airborne routes. All persons entering a room with a patient, for example, must wear gowns, masks and gloves; all persons entering and leaving the room must wash their hands with antiseptic soap; and all articles leaving the room must be given special handling to ensure their disinfection and proper disposal. These organisms, such as chicken pox, hemorrhagic fever, herpes zoster can vary from a class two to class four; and in some cases involve special ventilation, as in Lassa fever, and even surgical space suits as in Ebola."

"So what's..."

"Let me continue." Maya looked at Cunningham with an ill-tempered eye. "Thank you. There are also other levels of isolation: contact, respiratory and tuberculosis. They require varying degrees of precaution...

"Organisms, however, are also classified by work area level precautions. Biosafety Level 1 requires a work area with everything removed that touches skin: clothing, rings, contact lenses, etc. The investigator works in sterile surgical scrubs. Biosafety Level 2 is the same as Biosafety Level 1, but there is decontamination with ultraviolet light. Biosafety Level 3 involves working in ventilated space suits. Biosafety Level 4 is done in an air-lock and decontaminating showers are taken after working conditions. Ebola, for example, is a Biosafety Level 4 or Class 4 virus."

"You mean to say that we have a class four biologics on board?"

"Yes, sort of."

"Sort of? A class four—sort of? Who gave you authorization?" Jackson yelled at Maya.

"It's classified."

"Biologic Engineer Mukhina, I order you to tell me what we have on board and who gave you authorization for a class four!" Vrubel raged.

"I'm sorry Commander, I cannot tell you either."

"Is this some kind of fucking *glasnost* plot?" Cunningham angrily snapped

"On the contrary."

"Then what?" Jackson demanded. His face was splotched red.

"I order you, right now, to tell me what we have on board and who gave you authorization!" Vrubel reiterated. He stood up and slammed his Russian fist onto the table. The force of the blow propelled him toward the ceiling, but he caught himself with his knees under the secured meeting table. "Now!"

"What sort of game is this, comrade?" Computer and Metallurgic Officer Zvezda asked.

"It's not a game nor a trick. What we have here, gentlemen, is a serious biologic accident that is classified and, that needs to be remedied if possible."

"Let me get this straight. Theoretically, on board *Mir-Kennedy I* we're suppose to have Draculase, a synthetic clotbuster from vampire bat saliva; 4TC, an anti-Alzheimer's drug; and a spider-silk producing E. coli—and that's it? Is that correct?" Jackson asked.

"Yes," Maya answered as she looked gambler-hard into his eyes.

"But we also have something else on board. Is that correct?"

"It is."

"And the consequences of this mystery drug or whatever it is?" Vrubel asked.

"The consequences are that we'll *need to permanently seal the Biologics Lab* or risk losing the entire space station, and possibly our lives."

"Permanently seal the Biologics Lab!" Jackson howled. "What's in there? I want to know now!"

"Even if I was authorized to tell you, which I'm not..."

"Tell us!" Holloway railed.

"Easy!" Jackson grabbed young Holloway's arm and steadied him in his chair before he began floating away.

"So why seal the Biologics Lab? And, are we in any danger?" the levelheaded Flight Engineer Shoyo asked.

"The answer to that question is difficult."

"What do you mean, difficult ?" Jackson asked.

"With regards to the first part, 'Why seal the Biologics Lab?'—all I can say is that what Pokrovsky was working with is beyond deadly. The agent...is worse than your most appalling nightmares. It makes Ebola virus, the plague, small pox, dengue and hemorrhagic fever all rolled into one look like kindergarten stuff."

"A virus?" Solovyev asked.

"No."

"Bacteria?"

"No."

"Then if not a virus nor bacteria, then what?" Holloway yelled.

Maya continued. "With regards to why and when we permanently seal off the biologics module, I'm not sure. It may be..." She looked into Jackson's eyes. She remembered the words that she shared with him just a few hours earlier while looking at galaxy M100 in the observatory.

"You mean..." Vrubel said interpreting between the lines, "that there's a chance that whatever Pokrovsky was exposed to in lab could mean the decommission of the entire mission?"

"What are you talking about?" Smith asked.

"That's...right comrade," Maya answered, looking at Vrubel.

"Decommission means that we're all toast. That we're all going to die, doesn't it?" Jackson asked. He looked into Maya's face for an honest answer. He got it without her speaking a word. *He was right.*

"So, on whose orders do we have a level four biologics on board?" Vrubel asked.

It was then that an urgent message was received from CIA Headquarters, Langley, Virginia. "Mission Commander Jackson," a puzzled Communications Officer Hobbs returned from his ground relay terminal with a printout via Tracking and Data Relay Satellite System West. But instead of giving it to Jackson, he handed it to Maya.

"What the..." Cunningham asked.

The message was from the CIA—addressed to *"The eyes of Biologics Engineer Maya Mukhina only."* Except for the transmission heading, the communiqué was coded.

"Excuse me, gentlemen."

"Wait," Jackson demanded. "We've just begun our meeting."

"Sorry."

"Wait one second! We've not gotten any answers except that

there is a biologics on board that is neither virus nor bacteria, that Pokrovsky is going to run out of air in seventy-two hours, that we need to seal the Biologics Lab, and that we might need to *decommission* this entire mission."

"That's correct," Maya replied as she stood and began her weightless march back to her sleeping module and her Russian Paavo FCD Earth-Net Computer.

"Who are you?" Jackson asked.

"*The messenger of doom*," Maya said under her breath as she trudged her way to her cabin to decode the communiqué. "We'll need to reconvene in one hour. I might have an answer for you then."

CHAPTER 12

It took Alex just over twenty minutes to find Dr. Knight's house. It was a sanctuary. As open as she was with him, there was still very much a private side that she had not revealed.

It had been a dinosaur's age since he had been there. They were going to go jogging. She had forgotten her workout suit. She asked if they could stop by her house on the way to the Las Vegas Athletic Club. First they were going to lift weights, do a forty minute chest and arms workout, then drive out 159 to Red Rock Canyon and run the three-thousand-foot rising, thirteen-mile sheer sandstone escarpment trail.

She at times was almost a fanatic about her workouts. He was somewhat back then, but over the years he had slacked off—just like most of the doctors he knew who became consumed with their careers and the sixty to seventy-hour work weeks.

The house was off Valley View between Charleston and Sahara within a walled community called Vista View. It was on Plaza De Cielo. The lawn in front of her house was picture-perfect green. Pansies and azaleas were planted around two slim-trunked trees that sat back slightly from both corners of her front yard. The trees mimicked Chia pets on top of bark-covered pogo-sticks. Two sprinklers had just popped out of the ground, one in a clump of hydrangea shrubs, that sprayed in an umbraging mist.

Alex parked at the corner of Barnard Drive and Plaza De Cielo on the opposite side of the street. He got out and walked up to the house. Small children were riding tricycles and bikes in all directions. He dodged them on the way to Jo's driveway. He walked to the front door, got splashed on his left shoulder by spritzes of water, and rang the doorbell. There was no answer. He rang again. Still no answer.

In the back he could hear a dog yap as he rang the second time and thereafter. "Maybe she's just not home," he thought.

He walked back down the drive to the street. A child with brown pigtails nearly ran him over with her hot pink and white Stardust Schwinn.

"Mr., you looking for the doctor?" the six year old precociously asked as she took a comb out of her basket. It, too, was pink. The handle was broken and two teeth were missing. She combed through her bangs and cracked her gum.

"Yes, I am."

"She's not here."

"No? Do you know where she went?"

"Nope," she blew a bubble that expanded to almost the size of a grapefruit before it popped. With her dirty fingers she picked off the remnants that stuck to her cheek and the tip of her nose and put them back into her mouth. She peddled off. "She went with some bad men," she said.

"Wait a second," Alex ran after her. He caught her fifty feet down the road. "Wait a second." He was out of breath. "Who?"

She smiled and planted her legs. She blew another bubble. "Two men. She didn't look happy. They took her."

"Do you know what they looked like?"

"Nope."

"Do you know what they wearing?"

"Nope."

"Do you know what kind of car they had?"

"Nope," she said as she stood erect and balanced on her bicycle pedals.

Alex knew she meant that Jo had been abducted.

He trudged back to her house. Then he remembered that years ago, when they had to break in, she had had a dog run out back that led into the garage. She kept a key hidden over the garage door transom.

Jo's car sat in the driveway. It was a blue-black 318i BMW. He tried its doors. They were predictably locked. He looked through the windows. There was nothing of interest inside, just the remote to the garage door.

He walked around the garage to the rear. There was a garden with sweet tomatoes, chives, green peppers, asparagus, eggplant, and carrots. He walked past it. The dog run was still there, attached to the garage door that was one-half glass and the bottom half aluminum. The kickplate had been modified and the center portion was made into a hinged door for the dog to enter.

An Irish setter popped through the opening. Its orange-brown coat was neatly groomed. She barked and jumped up onto the galvanized fence, her paws pressed anxiously to the fence as she whined for attention.

"Easy girl," Alex petted her paw. She eagerly licked his hand. "Easy." He thought that Jo had a golden retriever, but that was years ago. This dog was too young.

Alex climbed the fence and hopped into the dogrun. The dog was all over him. He squatted in a catcher's position and patted the dog's head. She was starving for attention. He then tried the garage door. It was locked. He attempted to crawl through the door, but there wasn't enough space through the hinged kick-flap. He stood up and looked through the half-door window at the door handle inside. The lock was a metal switch that pushed backward.

Alex slid his head, left hand and most of one shoulder through the opening. While leaning on the ground and pushing with one knee, he leveraged his body upward. On his fifth attempt he was able to manipulate the switch forward and release the door. It swung inward and he spilled onto a garage stoop while jamming his shoulder into the bottom of the hinged opening.

He righted himself. The dog bounded onto him. But when he looked at her with disapproval, she got down. Alex walked over to the inside garage door. He stepped up onto a small stoop, and then felt above the transom.

"Old habits die hard," he said. On top was the key. Over the years its copper had faded to gray-dinge. He slid it into the door lock and deadbolt. He jiggled the key in the handle, then shook it into the deadbolt. The key hadn't been used in a while.

The dog followed him in. "Come on girl." But she didn't want to go out. Alex stuck his head outside the door to let the setter back into the garage. It was then that he noticed that her food bowl was nearly empty and her water almost gone.

"Jo definitely was taken against her will," Alex thought. "She wouldn't have left her dog without food."

Alex looked around the laundry room. He opened the closet doors. Inside was a forty-pound bag of dog food. He filled the bowl twice past it brink, and filled the two water bowls. It seemed that Jo made sure that there was always enough food and water, if for some reason she was gone on an emergency autopsy overnight.

Alex walked through a hallway and into the front foyer. It led to the kitchen, family room and living room. He walked into the living room.

"Jo. Jo you there?" He knew she wouldn't answer. "Jo?"

The living room had a somber framed pencil etching of a woman wrapped in a shawl. She was sitting at a sewing hearth, knitting a thigh-length sweater.

"Jo, are you there?"

A mahogany baby-grand piano with ivory keys sat in a corner. There was a metronome that was closed on the left leaf. A piano book was open to Shuman's 3rd Sonata in D Minor.

Across from the piano sat a sofa. It had flower autumn prints that were outlined in lavender. There was a walnut table that sat next to large French windows that were closed shut to the daylight by indoor shutters. The table was over-glossed with furniture oil and looked sticky to the touch.

Alex sat at the piano. The keycover was open. He lightly drummed "C,D,E...C,D,E." He paused, then repeated his disharmony, thinking.

What was that smell? Mothballs? Why an ELSIA test? He didn't look like he had AIDS. An adult male, about fifty who was, at least by the look of things, in perfectly good health. *ELSIA. What other diseases cause a positive ELSIA test? If positive you run a Western Blot Test, then what?*

Alex got up. He walked through the dining room. There were prints on the wall. All pencil sketches by Joseph Piccillo. All expressed a sense of melancholy.

Alex entered the kitchen. There was an enamel-worn refrigerator. It was the only thing in the house that was ancient. It dated back to the '60s.

"Jo?"

He walked through the family room.

"The only reason I'd run an ELSIA test is if I knew that it would likely be positive—at least run one on the CSF."

Alex looked at the bookshelves built into the wall on both sides of a pressed brick fireplace.

"Jo." No answer.

Alex walked upstairs.

He found a master bedroom that lay over the dining and living rooms. She had a mahogany four-corner bed with a headboard. She had two dressers of drawers, one next to the bed, and one kitty-corner. There was a small color TV that sat upon a tempered glass plate that covered the dresser. The room had drab window shades that were pulled shut and beneath nutbrown shutters that were closed.

Alex left the bedroom and walked into two guest bedrooms. The beds were fastidiously made, and dust covers were pulled tight. Choya and pear cacti and ice plants in clay pots were strategically arranged— and turned every other day to the sun. There were erudite books on shelves. Then he walked into her study.

The home office was the only room that looked lived in. Her desk was the focal point of her study. Above the antique rolltop desk was a faded color photograph. It was of what appeared to be a much younger Jo, and three men. One was wearing a peculiar suit. Alex didn't give it much notice. Next to it was an additional pencil etching. This one, too, had the same woman darning, but before a burning fireplace. This was the only rendering that manifested any kind of essence of life, that didn't instill a sense of desolation.

"You never really know someone," Alex thought.

The editor's rolltop desk was broad. It was a perfect working space for Jo, since it had so many cubbies. On top was a receipt from Federal Express that was written yesterday. It was made out to:

The Doomsday Kiss

Dr. Livingston Warner
USC University Hospital
1500 San Pablo Street
Los Angeles, CA 90033

The 8:00 a.m. delivery box was checked.
"Dr. Livingston Warner."
Next to the receipt was a tape recorder. The tape was partially used. Alex rewound the microcassette and played it. It was recorded in the voice-activated mode. Alex could hear sounds, as if the tape recorder had been set on the rolltop desk and then Jo had stood back, and walked and talked as she dictated.

"I'm in extreme danger," she began, her tone uncertain. *"I've thought that we were done with this kind of work. If I'm right, we're all going to die if—Inv..."*

Her message was interrupted with a thundering crash as the front door was kicked open.

"Get him, he's got to be in here!" the assassin yelled to four others. "Get him, now!"

CHAPTER 13
The Ricki Lake Show

Mahalia Hunt remembered the swallows. She thought about them as she combed her tangled blond hair in the dressing room mirror. She gazed deeply into her blue eyes. She was not an albino, but as close as she could come to being one. Her cheekbones were high and with makeup she was stunning. But without—as she had been called in her youth by those who were cruel and insensitive— she was a plucked chicken. Spider-red vessels pierced through her paper-thin skin.

"I remember," she mouthed the words into the mirror which was surrounded by twenty moonbeam lights. They knew her story.

"I remember the birds and the Old Mission San Juan Capistrano. The pond in front of it and the lily pads. I can see its reflection...the belltower and the cross that sat on top."

They had taken her there, beyond the arches, past the ruins and the Moorish fountain and the gardens that were reminiscent of Spain.

"The birds would come. One by one. The swallows would build their delicate mud nests, their funnels into the jagged stone cliffs."

The Doomsday Kiss

She took a thick brush and pushed back the unwilling tufts of her hair. She combed the strands from her forehead. It revealed a scar that was scantly visible, but only without makeup. It was on the left side of her forehead and ran vertical. She had cut herself when she was a baby and fell down basement steps while living in the two-story brick and mortar tract house. It was before Capistrano.

"*He killed her,*" she said trance-like. "*He killed her...and the baby birds.*" It was his fault.

In her mind's eye she saw in the makeup mirror the rock cliffs. She was young again. She was six and she had climbed down the escarpment to feed a lissome blue and green hatchling. "Why did you kill her?"

She reached out to feed the bird as it perched on the edge of its mud home. She had bread in her hand that she had ripped into small pieces. Then, from above, came a night hawk. It swooped down with its talons ready to snare.

"The screaming, stop the screaming!" she yelled. She looked beyond the mirror out at the Pacific ocean, away from the cliffs...and then she saw her helpless mother fall to her death. "You killed, you killed her!" she ranted.

"Five minutes," the pageboy knocked on the dressing room door. The three-beat tap was enough to momentarily bring her back to sanity. "Five minutes."

Then—again her reflection in the mirror began to fade. She could hear the tolling of the century-old bells that had worn its path in time. There was no serenity and peace amid the lush gardens and cool fountains, nor the cloistered adobe walls. She was at the Mission. It was two days before St. Joseph's Day. It was March 17. She was six. It was before all the visitors had come.

The legend was that the swallows of Capistrano came on March 19 to seek sanctuary from an innkeeper who had destroyed their nests. They had taken up residence at the old Mission—and then later the ocean cliffs and rock wall crannies.

Each year they returned to the same site to rook. They knew that their young would be safe within the Mission walls, and on the sheer ocean-rock walls.

That day, Mahalia had come to feed the birds—and her mother *died*.

"Almost ready?" the persistent page tapped on the door again. She had carefully chosen *this* show. Ricki Lake was the reigning queen of trash TV. Ricki taped two shows back-to-back at the Ricki Lake Studio on East 37th Street in Manhattan. She was the most popular daytime TV talk show host.

The arrangement was that Mahalia would go last. She would be the entire second show, and if she told her revealing story...it had to be live. Ricki agreed to that, but with a ten-second tape delay.

Ricki and her publicist badly wanted Mahalia. Ricki's ratings had stagnated and Oprah, whom she had topped six months earlier as the number one rated syndicated talk show, was back on the way to the top. Ricki needed a fresh, more controversial spin. Mahalia was it. Ricki was willing to take the chance with Mahalia—whom she thought compelling.

The eighth floor audience had already been warmed up. They were, as the trade called them, "the loudest audience in television history." Her fans roared on cue as Ricki bounced in wearing pancake makeup, red lipstick, a white turtleneck, a brown jacket, leggings, and clogs. "Go Ricki!" they chanted.

"How many of you came here today to get on TV?" she asked. They whooped.

The first show of the day was, "Surprise! I Want You to Be the Father of My Baby!" It led off with a pretty young woman who wanted her best girlfriend's boyfriend to impregnate her. "Lorraine, what kind of cockamamie idea is that?" Lake asked from the aisle.

In the wings, the executive producer scrawled questions in black marker on sheets of cardboard and held them up. Ricki largely ignored them.

Five young men were paraded out to be stunned by each woman's declaration. The audience was caught up in the drama. What they wouldn't do to be on national TV.

"You ready, Miss Hunt?" The pageboy drum-thumped on the door.

"I am."

It was time for Ricki to introduce Mahalia. The audience was warned that the second show was going to be live, and that the topic was a serious one: "Women Who Were Abused by Their Fathers."

Ricki had been pressured by advertisers and congressional investigatory committees to "clean up her act." It wasn't just her act, but all the trash TV talk shows that had over the last several years sprung up like weeds in a river of already polluted journalism.

Ricki was going to "experiment" with a serious topic, with one guest only, on live TV. She had screened Mahalia. Ricki had taken notes and was prepared for a heart-to-heart.

Ricki had cooled the audience down from its manic pace as a lone sofa was brought center stage. The show opened to its usual standing ovation. Burly security guards flanked the exits. Ricki changed into a new jacket, this one red. "Yes," she warned the audience, "what you are about to see may disturb you, but there are moments that I'm a little tweaked about the stuff that happens behind closed doors. It's time that we expose some of that."

She then introduced Mahalia Hunt. Mahalia, a twenty-nine-year old lanky, attractive wisp of a woman, walked slowly on stage. She wore short chalk-white Payless pumps and a red-and-blue checkered sundress that flared at mid-thigh. Around her neck was a cheap red-plastic bubble bead necklace.

Her hair was six inches past her nape and lay limp in over-hairsprayed waves. She chewed gum. Her lips were painted tangerine red, and her eyebrows plucked pencil-thin and smudged thick with Mabelline brown. This wasn't what she and the executive producer agreed that Mahalia would wear.

On cue the audience reticently applauded. They were taken aback.

"Mahalia," Ricki said. She was thrown off by her guest's appearance. "Before we start I just want to tell you how much I appreciate you coming forward and sharing your story with our audience. I know that the subject of molestation is a very serious one."

Mahalia sat with her knobby knees pressed together. She looked neither directly at Ricki nor at the audience. She saw the swallows of Capistrano again. Ricki continued to speak. Mahalia did not absorb a word. She just waited for her turn. Four minutes twenty-two seconds later, after Ricki's diatribe on the subject of child molestation, it was Mahalia's turn.

"...and so Mahalia, can you tell us your story."

"I remember a lot of fear. I remember being 7, 8, or 9. I was really scared. I felt like I had done something really bad. I remember the first time my father hit me. I was petrified. I was humiliated. I wanted to cry. I felt angry...more so today, than anything else."

"What happened, Mahalia?" Ricki asked. "Tell us, if it's not too hard, about you and your father."

"I would hear his footsteps...come down the hall. It made me fearful that I was going to again get punished for something that I didn't do. I was afraid of him..." She grimaced. "I wanted to strike back. I wanted to hit him before he hurt me. I wanted him to die. That's when I first started feeling the lump in my throat. I was around 11 or 12. I resented everything he said. When I disagreed with him...I was afraid."

"What did he do?" Ricki moved closer to Mahalia—she was honestly concerned, not just faking it. She and the audience had Mahalia's absolute attention.

"I'd get angry. There was nothing I could do about it. I remember the day he hit me in the face with a pot..." The audience murmured. "It was for looking at him like the way I did. I have a scar." She pointed to the one on her forehead that was hidden by the stage makeup. "I balled up my fists. I was so angry I couldn't see."

"Did you call the police? What about your mother? Did she know what was going on with your father?"

Mahalia did not answer Ricki's questions. "It first started when he was teaching me piano. He rubbed himself up against me. I could feel him, I could feel him grow. Then after our lesson he would hold me by my shoulders and bounce against me. I hated that. I wanted to get as far away from him as possible."

"That's...terrible. What did you do?"

"Then there were the bad times. The times that he told me that I didn't deserve to live."

"Mahalia..."

"He used to lock me in the closet."

This was not the story she had told Ricki earlier. "That's terrible...tell me about the closet..."

"He would leave me there in the day. It was so dark. I could feel the night." She paused and imagined the innocent blue and green swallows fly. "He left me there the first time for three days—in the dark without food and water."

"I'm sorry. I didn't..."

"Then he beat me and tied me up on the bed on my stomach." The audience was hushed. A pin could have dropped and been heard for miles. "He beat me more until I submitted. Then he entered me."

Ricki knew that she was beaten, but not locked in the closet, nor tied to the bed. This was going to be a story about a little girl who was abused emotionally, called names like "you good-for-nothing, lazy," and then slapped and pushed around. That was terrible enough. *But not this.* This was new.

"When I asked him why he took me, why he made me submit, he said that it was God's will and that I had it coming," she continued. She hadn't blinked while telling her tale. "He would tie me naked, in spread eagle with four point restraints. Then he'd want me to pray to Jesus for forgiveness...and then...after he plundered me..." She stopped speaking. The audience was in utter shock.

She turned her head ever-so-slightly and looked up at Ricki. Ricki put her hand to her mouth and murmered, "Oh my God." She was horrified. Then Mahalia looked into the camera.

"It was a flotilla."

"What?"

"There was a whole stream of them."

"'I'm sorry Mahalia...I don't...understand." For the first time in Ricki's run on nationwide television, she didn't know what to say.

"The men, it was as if one after another forced themselves into me." She stood. "But it was just him. When I complained, when I cried, he would beat me more until I took all of him inside of me. He ruined me. He tore me."

"I...I..."

"And then there were the whips and the fire and the burning. I would be in there for days, sometimes more. He made me bleed all over."

"I'm..."

Mahalia stood up, on nationwide TV. She slowly turned, then dropped her sundress over her shoulders. She pulled it to her waist in a rumple and exposed a toothpick bra that dug tight into her skin. From a distance the scars were clearly visible. They were deep, almost keloid. Six of them ran on the diagonal in parallel widest from her left shoulder down to her right hip. They were browner than the rest of her skin and were striated. They appeared to have been burnt into her back with a branding iron or a long circular grooved poker. Lines in diagonal, scarred thicker than the rest, spiraled in a barber-pole up her back.

There were also two smaller scars that were only half the length. These were perpendicular and ran from her right shoulder to just past the middle of her back. These scars were superimposed onto the six longer ones.

Two women in the audience fainted. One ran out.

Mahalia left her dress down for ten seconds. Camera two pulled in tight for a close-up. The director fed the ten-second delayed atrocity to Ricki's nationwide audience.

CHAPTER 14

Alex clicked off the tape recorder. "Get him!" The assassin yelled. "You two up there, you two down here, now! Kill him!"

Alex ran out of Jo's study in the only direction he could go—to the bedroom, the farthest room from the stairs. He bolted into the master bedroom's bathroom, and in an instant thought that he could leap out its two-story sliding window. He quickly looked out the window before flinging it open. Beyond were two armed men waiting for him.

Across from the bedroom was an eight-by-six foot closet. Alex ran into it. There were dresses arranged by increasing length hanging from one side; blouses and skirts from the other. Quickly he scanned his surroundings. He had no options. There was nothing that he could do.

"Get him," the assassin railed as he stormed up the stairs. The other snarled, "Did you hear something?"

They had their weapons primed. They stormed the first guest bedroom, then the second, then the hallway waiting bathroom, then the study. Nothing.

They plowed into the master bedroom. One of them slung the bathroom door open. The other flung the dust ruffle out of the way, and angrily looked under the bed. They both rammed into the closet. The uglier of the two posted cover as the tougher one ransacked the clothes.

From downstairs came a voice. "Anything up there?"

"No," the ugly one yelled. He sounded like a hyena. The merciless plunder continued throughout the house. The initial foray was just the superficial inquisition. Then the real game began. They were frenziedly looking for something. Bookshelves in the den were emptied of their volumes. Priceless first editions and other rare tomes were destroyed. The kitchen was torn apart, as well as each of the guest bedrooms. It was just about then that one of the men began his search of the master bedroom. He had gone through Jo's dresser drawers, ripping them out of their walnut slots. He had viciously disheveled the bed and had begun tearing apart the closet.

"I've found it," one of the assassins said. He was in the study.

"Let's get out of here," another contemptuously growled. "No one's here. It's been four hours."

By nine past nine they left. The house couldn't have looked worse if Jo had passed out fliers inviting every punk in town to come and take a crack at it. Her priceless Piccillo pencil etchings had been eviscerated. They were cut through from the rear and torn apart. Antique books had been defoliated at their seams, and irreverently separated at their bindings.

It began to rain. Thunder exploded in the distant Calico Hills.

At half-past midnight, Dr. Alex Seacourt, who only by the skin of his teeth had escaped the assassins, slid out of the rafters and through the crawl-space attic floor-plate that lay just past the master bedroom closet transom.

One of the men had tentatively looked up there. But not well enough. He shined his penlight through the murk and cobwebs, through the fiberglass insulation and wiring that snuggled into ceiling brackets.

But Alex had worked his way across the two-by-sixes into the only corner that offered shelter from the light. He had crouched down in a ball, and had pushed what was left of a roll of the spindly fiberglass between him and the cornice.

Alex had thought that he heard them leave, but stayed in the murk three hours longer to be absolutely sure. He didn't want to drop into a trap.

"What did they do to this place?" He was dumbstruck. Alex hoped that the tape recorder was still in the office. Carefully, he walked into the study. No one was in the house. The microcassette recorder was gone. The room was in shambles. On top of the desk, amongst papers and spewed junk, was the picture of Jo and the three others. It was upside down. The back had been ripped off. Alex could tell that there had been something hidden between the photo and the backing. There was the impression of what appeared to be a three-and-a-quarter inch computer disk.

"They were looking for a disk and me. Why?"

He didn't want to stay in the house any longer than he had to. He pushed the scattered desk papers aside. He couldn't find the FedEx receipt anywhere. But he remembered:

"*Dr. Livingston Warner, USC.*"

Alex worked his way downstairs carefully. He slid out the garage door. The Irish setter with the glossy yellow-brown coat was dead, shot in the head.

In front of Jo's house, down the street, he saw a man sitting in a car, patiently smoking a cigarette. He was watching Alex's rental car and the house.

Alex sneaked through the shrub rose and ajuga hedges that separated Jo's property with her backyard neighbor's. He crept through yards until he made his way to Decatur, off Sahara. There he found a pay phone near a 7-11. He nervously called White Cab.

He arrived in Los Angeles via Southwest Flight 247 at 8:10 A.M. He had hid out at an all-night bar, Play It Again Sam, a candlelight funky blues and jazz lounge that was a locals' hangout. It was a place that the show performers, grips and electricians, dealers, cocktail waitresses and keno runners went after work.

Alex took a no-name cab from LAX. They rattled down the Santa Monica Freeway eastbound to I-5/I-10/60 freeway, then the San Bernardino Freeway to Soto Street. From Soto they drove to Alcazar, and then to the hospital. At 9:23 A.M. he arrived at the Richard K. Eamer

Medical Plaza. Three staggered water fountains in front of the seven-story building welcomed him. Palmetto palm trees sat at ten-foot intervals next to the entranceway windows and rose two-and-one-half stories. The sky was a haunting azure.

"Dr. Livingston Warner?" Alex asked the receptionist. She sat behind a large, lavender marbelite desk. "Infectious Diseases." She looked at Alex with a pleated, funny face. Alex had a five o'clock shadow and he smelled like stale bar smoke.

"Thank you."

She gazed at him curiously, but didn't say what she wanted to.

Alex took one of three elevators up. The plaza was crowded. The elevator was thick with patients—all sorts, many unkempt. He fit in. By the time they arrived on the sixth floor many of them had already scurried off. He found Dr. Warner's office halfway down the hall.

"Dr. Warner in?" he asked.

"He's ...he's not in," the receptionist said. Alex could see that she had been crying.

"Do you know when he'll be in?"

"I'm sorry...but the doctor died this morning in a car accident."

"What?" A chill ran through Alex's body.

"It was a hit-and-run. The police think it was a sanitation truck."

"Dr. Warner is dead?"

She began to cry.

Alex walked around the reception counter. He tried to comfort her. He put his arm around her. "I'm sorry. What happened?"

"They...don't know. He was backing out of his driveway this morning and..." She couldn't maintain her composure. Behind her Alex saw a just-opened box of Kleenex on a vertical file cabinet. He got a handful of tissues.

"Thank you," she sniffled.

"I'm sorry. I'm Dr. Alex Seacourt. I've come from Las Vegas to see Dr. Warner." She cried more. He said nothing. He observed his surroundings. Dr. Warner's office was small. It wasn't for seeing patients. It was the heart and pulse of an academician's workplace. Somewhere where he'd churn out unchallengeable research papers like automobiles on an assembly line, where undisturbed he could theorize.

"Could..."

"More Kleenex?"

She nodded yes. He got her the entire box this time. Quivering, she pulled out three pieces and blew her nose. She tossed the tissue in a wastebasket under her desk.

"I'm sorry about Dr. Warner. I've come here from Las Vegas. A friend of mine—Dr. Knight—does her name ring a bell?"

"No," she sniffled.

"...was abducted. Two days ago she sent Dr. Warner a Federal Express envelope. Did he receive it."

"I don't know. He gets a lot of mail."

"Did Dr. Warner say anything to you yesterday about Dr. Knight?"

"No, not that I remember."

"Do you think...I don't mean to be rude, but...that his death wasn't an accident?

She sniffled more, then dispiritedly sighed. "I don't know. Why?" She thought that was a strange question.

"Do you mind if I take a look at the FedEx?"

"I don't know. I don't think I can."

"Look...I don't mean to be insensitive. But one of my best friends was kidnapped yesterday...and I was..." He stopped and contemplated.

"Kidnapped?"

"What kind of work is Dr. Warner involved in? Does he see patients?"

"No...not really. He's basically involved in research and chairs the Infectious Disease Department. Why?"

"Have you ever heard the name Dr. Joanna Knight?"

"No, not that I remember."

"Look, can we just see if Dr. Warner got that FedEx, and if he did—see what's in it? I won't take anything...please."

"I don't think I'm supposed to."

"What if they're connected—your boss's death...and my friend's disappearance?"

She thought for a moment and remembered what the police had said: "Hit by a trash truck while backing out of his driveway." But the truck driver didn't stop. They were still looking for the driver. It wasn't right.

They slowly, deliberately walked back to Dr. Warner's office. The door was locked.

"Does he always lock his door?"

"No, not usually," she replied with concern. "Just a moment, I have a key in my desk." She went back up front to her reception desk and returned with a ring of keys. She fumbled through several until she finally found the one that unlocked the door.

A hurricane might as well have hit Dr. Livingston Warner's office. Stacks of research papers that had been organized by date and subject were thrown from a credenza. His desk had laser-printed drafts of research papers, pencils, ball-point pens, rubber bands, paper clips of different sizes and shapes, and the contents of his punctiliously organized drawers—spilled on top of it. Books from a shelf next to an Escher lithograph were pushed aside and rummaged. The rear of the Escher had been cut open similar to the wall-mounted photograph at Jo's house. There was no space for a disk behind it.

"My God!" she exclaimed.

"Help me find the FedEx." At first the receptionist stood there confounded. Then she worked her way through the clutter to the seat side of the desk. She and Alex went through everything. There was no sign of any Federal Express envelope.

"Does anything come to mind. Anything unusual?"

She walked to the window and looked out onto the plaza's hypnotic fountain, and toward Norfolk Street and Hazard Park. She was in disbelief that Dr. Warner, who yesterday was very much alive, was gone.

"I don't...know," she replied. He could hear the tears in her voice. He made his way through the disarray to comfort her.

"Anything? Do you know any reason why someone would do this?"

"Nothing...really."

"What? You hesitated."

"Just...nothing."

"Just what?"

"He tried calling someone yesterday. He had me place the call over and over again...maybe, I don't know...ten times. It was probably..."

"What's the number?"

As if on theatrical cue, she sighed, took a deep breath, stepped through the jumble, and walked back to her reception desk. Alex followed. She looked for her "to do" notes from yesterday. That and her telephone log were missing.

"What's wrong?"

"My daytimer. I log all my long distance calls. It's gone."

"Did you write down the number anywhere else?"

"No."

"Are you sure?"

"Wait a second. She swung her chair over to her computer workstation and word processor. She had been typing the re-edits on Dr. Warner's research paper *New Quinolone Approaches to Synergistic Host Defense Mechanisms.* "414-235-3069." He had paged her with the number when she was working on one of her pages. She jotted it down on the upper right-hand corner.

"Could I use your phone for a second?"

"Sure."

With hope, and weary anticipation, Alex tried the number. There was no answer. He redialed it thinking that perhaps he miskeyed the first time. There was still no answer. Then he called the GTE operator. "Operator, what area code and city does 414-235-3069 belong to?" She went off the line for a few seconds then returned. "Oshkosh, Wisconsin."

"Thank you."

"What'd she say?" the receptionist asked. She had taken a compact from her purse and was looking into the small, rectangular mirror as she blotted dry her eyes.

"Oshkosh. Does the doctor know anyone in Oshkosh?"

"Not that I know of," she replied.

"Thank you," Alex said. He put both hands on her shoulders and gently held her. "It'll be okay," he said. Tears once again welled in her heavy eyes.

CHAPTER 15
Space Station Mir-Kennedy I

Maya typed the encrypted communiqué from CIA Langley into her work station computer. She deleted every other word, then alternatnatively every third word. She then entered the last ten sign-off numbers less the second and third to last, then pushed Cod-Shift-T Cir simultaneously on her keyboard. The message read:

LAV-10 not stable. Hughes Spruce G still viable.

Need to override isolation—press forward despite consequences.

Nikita

She could not abandon her mission. She had informed her superiors. She knew the risk when she melted into the dance. All chips were riding on this hand—and now...

"Damn them!"

"Maya," Jackson said as he gingerly, almost apologetically pushed opened her sleeping module door. "Mind if I come in?"

"No," she replied tersely. She hit the escape key and wiped out the message.

"Sorry if I was so hard on you, but we have a serious crisis —

code red. Maya, I need to get to the bottom of things. Please help."

"That's okay," she said pushing her short hair back off her face. "It's your job."

"Maya," he asked as he studied her cubby.

This was where he had spent last night, where he had made love to her for the first time—and where he too probably fell in love with her—but was unable to admit it to himself, let alone her. Now he needed to press those uncomfortable feelings aside. "What's really going on, Maya?"

"Scoop," she replied with genuine remorse, but said no more.

"Maya, what's the deal?"

"We have to break the seal."

"What are you talking about?"

"I have to go in."

"Maya...the Biologics Lab?"

"Yes."

"But it's class four."

"I know."

"You can't do that. You said yourself that Gregov was working with a..."

"I can go in if I enter through Metallurgics and then you seal me in permanently. You'll also have to seal off the Metallurgics Lab." She rubbed her eyes.

"Maya, talk to me. What was the communiqué all about? Why the secrecy, and why the hell from Langley?"

Her lips wanted to speak the truth, to tell him what she and Gregov were working on, but she was forbidden. Her directive came from the top. "I can't," she said. "It's classified."

"Shall we play animal-vegetable-mineral?" he rejoined sarcastically. He was angry. He did not anticipate a response from her. "Let's see," he said sarcastically, "is it mineral!"

To his disbelief she said, "Yes." It gave him the spook-house chills. He continued. "So it's *not* bacteria, virus, fungus, animal or human?"

"Yes."

"And it's *mineral?*"

"Yes."

"Do by mineral you mean *chemical?*"

She did not answer. He locked gazes with her

"Will this kill us?"

"Yes...and more."

"Is it a type of nerve gas, cardiovascular or respiratory suppressive agent?"

"No."

"How long has it been up here?" She would not answer. "Longer than 90 days?"

"No."

"You mean you goddamn brought this stuff up here with us on the shuttle?"

She looked him hard into his truth-probing eyes. "Yes, some."

"Goddamn you!" He grabbed her and shook her violently. "Tell me what's going on!" She would not reply. He let go of his grip and she floated back a foot toward the wall. Scoop walked to the cabin door, then turned.

"What does the CIA have to do with this?" She wouldn't answer. "Did they give you orders to bring whatever the crap we have on board up here?" He, the consummate poker player, read her. The right corner of her mouth twitched ever so slightly when he got a correct answer. "Does the KGB have anything to do with this?" There was no twitch. "Maya, please, tell me what's going on." She still didn't respond. Her eyes seared into his at an unyielding even keel.

Then she said, "We have 72 hours...or this whole planet..."

"Whole planet! What the hell's going on Maya?!"

It was then that the code-red alarm rang a second time. Overhead the flashing emergency lights blazed.

"This is Jackson," Scoop toggled on his VOX headset, which he had turned off for their encounter, "What the hell's going on?"

"Commander," Holloway replied from *Mir-Kennedy I's* Control Center. "We have decompression in Biologics!"

"Jesus!" Maya yelled. "Gregov." She too went back on VOX line and screamed into her headset, "Gregov! Gregov, answer me!" She and Jackson ran, bounced and flew through the space station.

"Maya, you understand," Gregov despondently said in a shallow voice with his space suit on. He had decompressed the Biologics Lab, expelling all of his contaminated air into outer space. "Maya...I know..." he coughed, "that you would have done the same if you were me. It's for..."

She arrived as he abruptly stopped his telegraphic explanation mid-sentence. She looked through the six-inch Plexiglas window with Jackson, Solovyev and Zvezda at her side. Through Metallurgics, at the other end of the lab she could see Vrubel, Budarin and Shoyo.

"Please Gregov, this accomplishes nothing. You don't even know that you've been affected." She, however, even from a distance saw through his reflective space suit visor that his skin had turned an ashen white—she presumed that the beds of his fingernails had already transmorphed into a turpentine green.

"You'll need to get in your space suits," Gregov hacked. "I'm afraid that it's possible that there may be contamination of the..." He coarsely coughed again, "the rebreathers."

"Our air?" Solovyev asked.

"I'm going to purge," Gregov said.

"Gregov don't, please!" Maya implored. "You can't. I can help you."

"No, you can't."

"Gregov."

"Do I have any choice? My hands...The gangrene...it's worked...it's working its way up to my elbows."

Maya knew how fast it moved. "Gregov, listen to me. You have choices. There's no guarantee that you're going to die. I can help you."

"You know the statistics."

"What are the statistics?" Jackson interrupted.

Maya looked at Jackson and pushed her VOX mic away from her face—and in a foreboding voice replied, "one-hundred percent."

"One-hundred percent," Gregov said. "And within twenty-four hours. It hasn't even been two."

"Gregov, listen," Maya implored, "I'm going to suit up and come in. I've already been talking about this with Commander Jackson. I've also had contact with our *friends*. I'll enter through the Metallurgics Lab, after I first depressurize."

"There's no use. Besides I'm concerned..."

"Concerned about what?" Jackson cut in.

"Concerned that...it might have *geometric affinity*."

"What does that mean?" Jackson asked.

"That it...sticks to our space suits," Maya replied.

"So what you're telling me is, that if you go in there, through Metallurgics, space suit or not, you can't come out?" Jackson asked.

"That's correct," Maya said without reservation.

"Maya, don't," Gregov warned. "You know the stakes. I knew them when I decided to..."

"And if I don't—what about...Do I have any choice?"

Gregov looked at her with his strained eyes. "It was my fault. I screwed up. I didn't take proper precautions."

"No you didn't, there was a short," Jackson said.

"Not exactly," Gregov replied.

"Gregov, did you not work from behind the shield?"

"That's correct."

"Why Gregov, why?"

"Because...it was too hard to handle. The reverse ion-field mircoflux equipment was awkward...and in zero-G's. I needed to try something with the freon—the molecular manipulation. I couldn't get the cylinder tip in proper position from behind the shield. It wouldn't fit. So I took it out."

"The..."

"Yes. But it was contained." He coughed. This time blood tinged sputum came up. "I needed to try and bend the molecules...with the cyanide-bond chlorofluorocarbon." Then he hacked up twiney crimson and fell to his knees. He wobbled, and in reaction to his weightless state floated to the ceiling. His upper body lost its rigidity, and he flailed.

Maya shoved her way past Jackson, Solovyev and Zvezda. She ran and bumped into docking module A. By the time Jackson caught up, she had stripped off most of her anti-G space jumpsuit and was in the process of shimmying into her space suit.

"Maya, you can't do this. You heard what Gregov said. Once you go in you can't come out!"

"I have to! I have no choice."

"Maya. I'm ordering you to tell me what the hell's going on."

"I can't. Monitor my vitals from control. Get Johnson Space Center on standby. I'll be in in five minutes."

"Maya," Jackson said as she slid into her Russian Orlan-III DMA space suit. He double-checked her redundant oxygen system, sublimator for cooling and water vapor removal, lithium hydroxide cartridges to remove carbon dioxide, and her caution and warning systems.

"Good to go," he said with regret. "I don't..."

"Good to go," she replied.

He kissed the polycarbonate faceplate of her 231-pound Russian space suit. She had geared-up in seven minutes, less than half the usual time. It was then, at that awkward moment of crisis that he wanted to tell her he loved her.

"Do you have oxygen cartridges?"

"Four."

"That's twelve hours for the one on your back, and twelve times four—sixty hours total airtime, plus a thirty minute emergency reserve."

"It'll have to do."

"You know there's no coming back."

"I'll maintain contact via control. You'll have video once I'm in. Also, set me up for video/audio simulcast with Houston."

"Yes." He looked at her. He adored her. He wanted to tell her, to utter those sacred words, but...

Fifteen minutes later, Maya was in the Biologics Lab. Equipment was wafting in a free-for-all. A centrifuge had escaped its mounting with the decompression. The Draculase experiment and spider-silk growing E. Coli that were behind the air-tight glass had exploded into the vacuum .

An IBM SP2 minisupercomputer chess set, with its white and black pieces that sat next to Gregov's work station, was floating in disarray. The SP2 chess computer was part experiment, part leisure from the Big Blue. Test tubes, serum acrodisc filters, a vortex microrotary evaporator, Naleene safety wash bottles, a gel-drying film kit, micro diluting pipettes and slides, whizzed willy-nilly across the room in perpetual momentum.

A bubble stretcher (portable biocontainment pod) had come loose from the counter. Fluid oozed from two glass-filled sealed tubes. A faceplate on a console that measured the effects of cosmic rays on the E. Coli bacteria-producing spider silk, had broken loose and was ricocheting off the lab's walls.

Maya found Gregov's body. He had decompressed his rear entry Orlan-III space suit by releasing two internal latches. His blood had boiled—and he had exploded into a million fragments—droplets of flesh and tissue, some of which seeped out of the adjustable space suit. Maya turned her head.

"What is it?" Jackson asked viewing the flicking video monitor in Control. Gregov's body was out of camera-angle view. It was floating near the ceiling.

"He decompressed."

"Jesus."

"It was intentional."

Maya looked around and found the counter where Gregov was working. A stainless three-liter freon container was on top of his titanium work station platform. She skimmed through his ill-defined notes.

Commander Vrubel got on the horn. "Mukhina, what do you have?"

"He was right! *Everyone needs to get into their space suits now!*" she yelled in shock. "We've got an emergency." Then, using the relay that was preset on hold, "Johnson Space Center, Houston—Houston Control, over."

"Roger, this is Houston Control, over."

"Houston Control this is Biologics Engineer Maya Mukhina. I need..."

"Mukhina this is Flight Director General Oliver Peterson. I've been briefed of your situation. I need to speak to ..."

"Buzz off, Houston. Tie me in with CIA Director Harlon Gates, now!" she ordered.

"What the..."

"You have less time than you think. Before it's too late, give me Gates!" The terror shook her voice.

CHAPTER 16

"**W**hy Oshkosh?" Alex was thinking to himself as he was driving his rented Astro Minivan. The van was all they had left. It had a used-up pinetree car freshener hanging from the rearview mirror. He wished he had an intermediate-size car.

He was heading north on I-41, past Menomonee Falls, then Hartford, Fon du Lac and finally to Oshkosh. He had already made his pit stop in Waukeska, just west of greater Milwaukee. Oshkosh was on the western shore of Lake Winnebago. He had heard of Oshkosh from flying. He'd heard about the Air Show, but he always imagined it somewhere that was landlocked, like in Iowa settled among farm-tilled rolling hills. Instead, it was situated on the banks of a large inland lake that was twenty miles on the north and south.

The Oshkosh EAA Fly-In was touted as one of the most significant events in aviation—an opportunity to showcase sport aviation. There were daily airshows and hundreds of planes and exhibits: the ultra light/light planes, the homebuilts, the antiques and classics displays, warbirds, the EAA Mini-Museum, Burt Rutan's Varieze, the

Fly Market, the North and South Exhibit Hangers, the Main and North Aircraft Display, and more.

As he drove his right foot continually fell asleep. He had the radio on, but had no idea what he was listening to. Everything had happened too fast. *Lock-n-load.* That's what the men did as they walked up the stairs at Jo's house...as if they knew that *he would be there.* "Kill him." Nothing made sense. Not the FedEx, not Dr. Warner's death, not the autopsy. Not one damn thing.

Why call Oshkosh? What's in Oshkosh?

At 9:10 in the morning, he walked into the telephone company on N 17 and W 24300 Riverwood Drive in Waukeska. There was no Ameritech office in Oshkosh. Waukeska was the regional Ameritech center.

"Remember," they taught him in his anti-terrorist training, "things are never what they appear to be. Look deep into a situation. The meaning may be entirely different than you suspect."

"May I help you?" the clock-faced clerk asked as Alex stood, pressed to the phone company's information desk. The chest-high countertop was marble blue with dull moon beam streaks. The room was stark white. "Is there anything I can do for you?"

"Yes."

"Excuse me?"

"Oh, I'm sorry. I was thinking."

"Can I help you?" she asked, this time a little irritated, but still wanting to be agreeable. This was the Oshkosh Fly-In and all of Wisconsin had more people than ever who needed assistance.

"I have a problem. I'm wondering if you can help me?"

"Yes."

"I mean this is real stupid, sort of, but I'm supposed to meet some friends, and I've been calling them all day, and no one answers the phone." Alex was winging it as he went along.

"Uh huh."

"The telephone number is 426-4877. I've lost the address."

The unassuming clerk was chewing gum, and had pushed the piece to the side of her mouth, between her molars and cheek so as not to be rude.

"I lost the address. I can't find it," and then Alex lifted up his left forearm and noticeably glanced at his watch. "Shoot."

"What?"

"I'm going to be late. Man, I hate that. Don't you?"

"I guess."

"You ever miss a real important..."

"Ah..."

"You know..."

"Yeah...last weekend I had to go to my Aunt Dorothy's after church. I forgot about the whole thing."

"Yeah."

"Had to bring my kids and everything. Boy was she pissed. I showed up nearly two hours late. The family had been there forever."

"I've done that before. Were they mad?"

"Mad? That's not the least of it. I heard about it every day for the last week. Missed the apple struedel. She was mad."

"I'd imagine." Alex paused and waited for her to continue.

"Yeah, sometimes she's a jerk anyway."

"I bet."

"I'm sorry. I didn't mean to ramble."

"No, no," Alex said looking at his watch. He wanted to remind her that he was late. "I just need the...address." He looked up with sad eyes. He spoke from his heart.

"I'm really not supposed...You know Hill Donnelly prints a reverse directory. You can get it from the library."

"She was angry?"

"Oh...you can't even imagine. Angry, that's not even the word. Dorothy was yelling at the top of her lungs in front of the kids and the whole world."

Alex smiled. He empathized with her.

"You know," she shook her head. "I'm not supposed to..."

"I'd really appreciate your help. I just," he glanced down at his watch again, "am going to be..."

Five minutes later, the affable clerk returned from the back room with a print-out of the name and address. The right hand corner was ripped on its edge. "Enjoy the air show. I hope you find your friend."

"I will. And you don't be late again."

"Yeah..."

The name and address on the print-out was:

Robert Charles Davis

Terminal Velocity Wingwalkers & Skydiving
3200 Eide Road
Oshkosh, Wisconsin 54903

With the help of the Texaco gas station off Oregon Street, as he drove into Oshkosh, Alex found 3200 Eide Road. It was north, northwest of the airport.

There was an old hangar with walls made of wind-whipped concrete. It had rusty corrugated sliding doors. The building needed a fresh coat of primer and paint.

Three cars were parked next to the structure—an old Buick Skylark; a Bronco with a dent in the driver's door, and paint flaked off long ago; and a Ford Ranger truck outfitted to transport hay.

Alex got out of his minivan and walked to the door. It had a glazed, wire-reinforced security window. He knocked hard. There was no answer. Then he noticed the sign. It was below the smudged window. It read:

"Out for the week. Find us at North Aircraft Display 547N."

Below that was another sign, this one on the door instead of the glass. It read: *"Lessons in Skydiving."* And then below that, *"Pepper Knight, Proprietor."*

"Pepper Knight. I didn't know that Jo had a brother—Pepper? Why was Dr. Warner trying to call Pepper? Was it Jo's cousin, or brother?"

And then Alex remembered what *they* had said, *"Things are never what they seem."*

CHAPTER 17

It was the stench of the autopsy that he couldn't get off his mind. It was one thing to be a doctor and to take care of his patients. He had done that a million times, and he could do it in his deepest sleep: the ear infections that the kids got, the diabetics, the asthmatics, the hypertensives, the epileptics, the angina patients, the lacerated, the kidney diseased—all of them—it was cake. He had done it so many times before. Their treatment he had memorized, and he responded with computer-fast accuracy.

But the autopsy room. The cadavers. He had never liked that, never gotten used to it. Maybe he had never come to terms with *his* eventual demise. Maybe he saw himself there, lying on the cold steel slab—waiting to be cut open and dissected. It made him squeamish.

"Trust your gut," that's what they told him in D.C., Rio and Moscow. Don't depend on anyone else but your instincts. He had to do that now. To trust his intuition. What was it in particular that bothered him about the autopsy? Was it what Jo had told him—that the cadaver had a face of horror, a look of abject terror? Was it the smell of mothballs that imbued the autopsy room and oozed out of the "C-cut?" Was it the exposure of the brain and the gelatin-like color and consistency of the cerebral spinal fluid? Or...was it more, was it the non-obvious. Was it what he immediately sensed: that Jo was hiding something—and now she was abducted and Dr. Warner dead?

After walking briskly, and twining through tens of thousands of spectators and numerous planes, Alex found the Terminal Velocity Wingwalkers exhibit.

"Pepper Knight. I'm looking for Pepper Knight," he asked.

"In the plane," the man said, pointing toward the air show from behind the booth. His spindly finger directed Alex to the horizon. He stood underneath a red-and-yellow striped tent that was open at all four sides and sat on ten-foot poles. The pavilion was 30 feet square, and was propped highest by two frontage poles that lifted three feet above the tent's brim.

From the west, in the direction the bony man pointed, screamed a red-and-yellow experimental Spacewalker. It raced just barely over the runway as it exhaled billowy white smoke from two exhaust ports under the engine's belly. As the plane gunned over the tarmac it cocked a ninety-degree pitch with the right wing barely above the runway and on the left, with head propped above the aileron, was Pepper Knight waving to the crowd. It was coronary time.

Pepper was going to scare the hell out of everyone, to thrill the fans with a truly unique act. After twenty minutes of a death defying, low-altitude routine that many swore left the biplane with grass-stained wingtips, and after a series of low spins that seemed as if they were going to terminate in someone's basement, it was time for sheer excitement.

Two volunteers from the crowd got to be some of the foolhardy few who stood in the middle of the Oshkosh runway holding two willowy poles. Between them was a streamer of ribbon, fifteen-feet wide and only six feet above the tarmac. Pepper's smoking stunt biplane was going to flip upside down and at 110 miles per hour, with Pepper's head only inches above the ground, his body would slice through the ribbon.

"Who the hell is this idiot?" Alex said aloud. "He's got to be related to Jo." Or so he thought, along with thousands of others.

A breeze had snaked in. An afternoon thunderstorm that the EAA had hoped wouldn't arrive was about to. Downdrafts had begun to waggle in from the south in a swirl of early gusts. The sun disappeared behind the gray mush clouds. The air that had been calm had abruptly turned bumpy.

On the first pass the red-and-yellow experimental Skywalker quickly flipped from upright to upside down near the end of the runway, as if done by robotic switch and not pilot dexterity. With smoke streaming from its undercarriage and Pepper using his body as a lancet, they bore down on their mark.

Suddenly, a gust of spiraling wind twisted up under the biplane, billowing it up first ten feet, then slipping it four feet right and down eight. The pilot, Jimmy Tucker, corrected immediately. They were too near the ribbon and their gutsy volunteers. Jimmy pulled up to avert imminent disaster.

The crowd "awed" as they boldly zipped past.

"Pepper, I think that it's too dangerous. Let's just do a vertical hesitation Four Point Roll and a Reverse Cuban Eight with smoke, and call it a day. Whata you say...there's too much turbulence. The storm's rolling in."

Pepper heard every rattled word through his two-way radio system. However, his helmet mic had shorted-out from the premature high-altitude drizzle during an Immelmann, then Cloverleaf Loop-roll combination. Pepper nodded his head an exaggerated "no." Jimmy clearly saw him in his cowling-mounted mirror that was forward of his cockpit—their back-up way of communicating during Pepper's routine.

"Come on pal, let's call it a day."

Again Pepper signaled a hard "no."

"Come on. A day, okay?"

A final no, and that was it...Pepper was the boss.

The disturbance was coming in fast, and their ride became even bumpier. This go-around would be it. No aborted bumps—only the lancet-clean cut.

Then, suddenly from the west, came what appeared to be the North American Team. There were three T-6 single-wings, brown-camouflaged except for two wrathful eyes painted behind the single-engine propeller; and snarling shark's teeth with gaping jaw and fiery tongue below the eyes—World War II fighters—that were flying in tight "V" formation. They, too, were pluming white smoke.

"I'm going to get as close as I can," Jimmy keyed his mic and said to Pepper as he snapped the biplane into inverted flying. "I'll gun it up to a buck 35, that should give us more stability."

Pepper nodded as the surging wind buffeted their upside-down craft.

"Ladies and gentlemen it appears that Pepper Knight will be making one final approach at the ribbon before we have to call it quits for the weather. Keep your eyes on this one folks. It's a sight you won't believe." The Oshkosh tower announcer boomed.

The three T-6s split as they quickly approached the north/south runway. The one in the center punched straight, heading just south of the FAA tower. The one on the right went high and forked down toward the deck. The fighter on the left went high about eighty feet from the ground. From left to right they formed a wedge at altitudes of eighty, sixty and forty feet respectively. They were dashing straight for the ribbon cut.

Pepper saw them, but Jimmy didn't. No one was supposed to be infringing on their aerobatic airspace. The FAA had strict regulations that governed stunt exhibitions. There was no reason that Jimmy should have been looking for interlopers. He was focusing on the stunt.

One hundred fifty feet from the ribbon. They would either be run into the ground, or the ribbon holders would be injured or killed. Another light buffet nudged the Spacewalker downward. Pepper flagged his hands at Jimmy, signaling the impending danger. The marauding T-6s were going to collide with them in midair!

"We're going right in for the ribbon. We've got it square on," Jimmy yapped. He nudged the throttle forward, inching the biplane up to 138 knots. Pepper frantically signaled him, while sliding quick glances between the ribbon, Jimmy's mirror and the three warbirds.

One hundred ten feet, one hundred, ninety, eighty, quicker than the speed-of-light, they were doomed—and so were the two volunteers holding the poles.

CHAPTER 18

"Son-of-a-bitch!" Jimmy yelled. He was scared to death. He had never been frightened before. However, at the very last second he saw the three demonic WW II fighters and what they were attempting to do—and that was run them into the ground and oblivion.

Jimmy Tucker gunned the throttle full blast. At the same instant Pepper froze rigid to the stabilizing strut that was mounted on the center of the top biwing just above and to the right of the pilot's head. Pepper braced for the ribbon cut, which was like smashing barefoot into concrete from a twenty foot drop.

Slam! The experimental red and yellow Spacewalker and Pepper Knight, which were only inches from disaster, rocketed through the ribbon.

Then Jimmy stuck the Skywalker hard right while jamming the rudder left. He scraped the left wingtip onto the tarmac. He just barely avoided a collision with the WW II fighters. The fiberglass-coated wingtip chaffed—and sparks flew in orange and red bursts as the wing spars folded into the smashed endlet.

As quickly as the three warbirds appeared, they converged into a tight-flying, low-altitude pod and disappeared to the west.

"Who the bejesus is in their flight path!" a fuming controller yelled at two controllers in the FFA tower.

"Get those idiots outta here!" another barked as he woke up from his decaf trance. He wanted to avoid a disaster, an FAA investigation—and the bad press.

But the tribulation was not over for the Skywalker whose right aileron jammed into a level-locked position. It made flipping back into normal flight level out of the question.

"Mother son-of-a—" Jimmy yelled to Pepper, raising his fist.

The crowd applauded like they had never before. They were enthralled by the sight that they had seen. They didn't realize the electrifying debacle wasn't part of the show.

The two helpless volunteers—a young bride who had come to Oshkosh for her honeymoon, and a McDonald Douglas quality control engineer early retiree, had the thrill of a lifetime. The engineer grasped his heart after the fly-by and the incredible ribbon–cutting. Not normally faint of heart, the bride keeled over in a heap.

"Pepper, do you read? Pepper?" There was no answer. Jimmy looked into his mirror. Shaken, but not stirred, gutsy Pepper signaled Jimmy to push the stick forward to gain altitude. He tried to loosen the right aileron but it wouldn't. "Pepper do you copy?"

Pepper signaled again. He waived his hand.

"Tower to Spacewalker 1, tower to Spacewalker 1, over."

"Spacewalker 1, to Tower—son-of-a-bitch tried to kill us."

"Tower to Spacewalker, that was an unauthorized fly-by, repeat, that was an unauthorized fly-by. Spacewalker, we've tried to hail the culpable idiots, but so far no response. Was this stunt your lamebrain, publicity-seeking idea?"

"Are you crazy!!!"

"Sorry Spacewalker...had to ask."

"Roger."

"Any damage, Spacewalker?"

"Well, let me put it this way: you can't kill us until you kill us."

"What?"

"Nevermind. Tower, my right aileron is stuck. I'm trying to work it free. I don't have any ability to turn."

"What's your plan Spacewalker, are you declaring an emergency?"

"Negative, tower. My plan is to fly on heading one zero to five thousand feet. At five I'm going to loop over to level, then try to shake the aileron loose."

Jimmy looked into his mirror and saw Pepper nodding in confirmation of his design. Jimmy gave the plane several kicks of right and left rudder, then powered up and powered down in an attempt to shimmy loose the aileron.

"No dice tower. Just tried jiggling it. Tower, I'll fly three miles out, then back. With my rudder and throttle I should have enough control to land, once I flip the bird over."

"To repeat Spacewalker 1, you're going to fly heading one zero, three miles to flight level five thousand, then do a 180, then power down and land rightside up."

"That's affirmative tower." What Jimmy didn't realize was that the storm front approaching from the south also had a small cell that had bifurcated from the building system and was now descending in a second prong from the north. As they reached flight level four thousand and began their 180-degree turn to normal level flight, the turbulence picked up strongly. Without the ailerons, which were used to steer the plane from right to left—as opposed to the rudder whose function was to point the plane's nose, and assist in crab landings—they essentially piloted a craft that Jimmy couldn't control.

Firmly Pepper held onto the off-center support pole. Buffeted by the swirling winds, Jimmy leveled out at fifty-two hundred feet. The fiberglass fabric tip of the right wing began to unravel and the biplane's stability decreased.

"I'm going to power down quickly and then back up, kicking the rudder, so hang on tight," Jimmy radioed. Pepper shot Jimmy the thumbs up sign. But before he could do that, a downdraft thumped into the biplane, shimmying it instantaneously toward the ground. At 3,700 feet, Jimmy leveled off. He kicked the rudder and powered up and down, and jammed the stick from side to side. No change.

They were quickly heading toward the airport. It was only one-half mile away. Pepper knew that there was no second chance at this maneuver. Because of the impending storm they had to land now or ditch the plane. Ditching, though, was not an option for Pepper, since there were too many people on the ground. They could be injured or killed.

"Oshkosh tower, this is Spacewalker 1, this is Spacewalker 1."

"Spacewalker 1, over."

"Tower we have an emergency. We're going to have to ditch. Tower we've got an emergency. I repeat...we'll have...Jesus!"

"Spacewalker 1, over."

Looking into his rattling mirror, Jimmy could see that on top of the right wing of the Spacewalker, despite the unpredictably fierce buffeting, Pepper Knight was walking precariously to the leading edge.

"Son-of-a-..."

Out of the corner of his eye, Jimmy could see Pepper walking precariously on top of Spacewalker's right wing, despite the wind's buffeting gusts.

Bump! The biplane was thrown up fifty feet by an undertow of convulsive wind. Pepper had worked his way nearly to the aileron's edge, and began manually working the flap free when *slam!*

Another microburst updraft crashed into the biplane, rocking it in a yo-yo yaw.

Pepper wiggled the wing flap, bending back the rigid plate that had been smashed into the wing's end. Another blast of wind hit, but this time from the left side.

"Skywalker 1, this is tower, over. Skywalker 1, Skywalker!"

"Tower, this is Skywalker..."

Boom! A large downdraft slammed onto the plane. It threw Pepper over the wing's edge in a reverse somersault.

"Skywalker 1, this is tower. Skywalker, this is tower, over!"

CHAPTER 19

Pepper had been catapulted off the upper wing, but like superglue clung to the flap's edge. By doing so, and using the momentum of his fall he nearly broke loose the aileron.

"Pepper, Pepper..."

With one last effort, Pepper kicked upward in a bucking pike, putting all of his weight into his contact point. He cracked free the aileron, thus allowing the Skywalker to roll and bank. It was then that Pepper lost his grip and plunged to the earth in a backward delta dive, aiming straight toward the airport and the point of the ribbon-cutting below.

Twelve-hundred feet above the ground, in his bright-yellow nylon jumpsuit, he flared his body to slow his descent, then manually threw out his pilot chute. With a panache that made Pepper Knight a heart-stopping showman, his main chute deployed 150 heart-pounding feet above the ground—and Pepper glided onto the exact spot of the ribbon cut.

The crowd, the spectators from all over the country, burst into the loudest applause that he had ever heard. The tower announcer didn't give away the potential tragedy. "And let's give another round of well-deserved applause for daredevil and wingwalker Pepper Knight."

A light sprinkle began to fall. The clouds had risen in a smoky, threatening anvil head—and in moments, sheets of rain would tumble down.

Alex had pushed his way to the front of the throng, many of whom were patting Pepper on his back. "Thata boy." "Great job." "Unbelievable." The daredevil was surrounded by his admirers and autograph seekers.

"Pepper, Pepper Knight." Alex anxiously spoke. Pepper pushed his way past him as he headed in a beeline for the tower. "Pepper, Pepper." Alex grabbed him by the back of his flight suit. "Pepper Knight, I need a word with you."

Pepper was in no mood to slow his march to the FAA tower to find out who the hell had tried to kill him.

"Pepper, hold it!" Alex grabbed him this time, clenching the jumpsuit in his hand. This slowed Pepper's progress. Alex's force of will was not enough to stop him. Pepper's anger was focused.

"Goddamn you!"

"That's it," Pepper barked. He ripped off his helmet and shoved Alex's hand off his shoulder. He was not a he. He was a she. Pepper's below shoulder-length hair spilled in a ratty heap onto her shoulders.

The drizzle turned to rain. Those around her, her fans, began to disperse. Pepper was in no mood to sign anything.

"Get your hands off me and out of my way!"

Alex was shocked. "You're a woman?"

"No kidding!" She stormed to the tower.

"Wait a second."

"What?" She wasn't about to stop walking. The wet tarmac smacked under her determined steps.

"Wait a second. Dr. Livingston Warner."

She slowed, but not much, "What about him?" She didn't turn.

"He's dead."

She stopped fast in her tracks, spun and faced him. "Dead?"

"Yes."

"Dead. My father's dead?" She didn't move a muscle, except for her lips. Her face turned sober. "What happened?"

"Hit and run, but I don't think..."

"When?"

"Yesterday. The police said it was an accident."

"How?"

"Look, do you want to sit down and talk about this somewhere out of the rain?"

"How?"

"A truck, or a garbage truck ran him down."

"Where?"

"As he was leaving for work. He was backing out of his drive-way and was hit in the driver's side door."

"Do they know who did it?"

"No."

"Was it an accident?"

"I don't think so."

"What do you mean 'you don't think so'?"

"Can we get out of the rain?"

"My God." She put her hands to her face and out of character, the iron-nerved, deliberate Pepper Knight began to cry. The rain pounded the tarmac.

Forty-five minutes later Alex was waiting at the Terminal Velocity hanger per Pepper's instructions.

The inside of the hanger looked like the out. The building's tattered zenith was held in place by splintering two-by-eight pine-wood trestles that attached at each end to the top of an A-frame. The ceiling was vaulted and forty-five feet high. At one time, in the late '30s, the structure was a military bivouac.

Parachuting gear was strewn throughout—some meticulously displayed: jump, CRW and free fall awards, parachutes, tandem jumping equipment, sliders, brakes, canopies, ripcords, friction adapters, helmets and goggles in two huge glass enclosed cases; others on three-foot high packing tables, or ready for inspection.

The airplanes, several that were out of view, were berthed past a fiberboard petition. On the wall hung a twenty-foot wide by fifteen-foot poster of two skydivers in skintight spandex jumpsuits plunging out of a twin-engine Queen Air into the pristine clouds below.

He was there alone, except for Regis, Pepper's chief mechanic, who had let him in on Pepper's telephone call. He was grizzled, chewed

Red Man tobacco, had three quarrelsome ex-wives, and was a man of few words. Now, however, he spoke like a whirlwind.

"There was no excuse. Those T-6's weren't on the agenda. There's no way those World War II birds could have...Someone tried to kill them."

"What do you mean, kill them?"

"Pal, the airspace is restricted. No one is allowed to fly over Oshkosh during a performance, period! At least not without the tower's clearance. And I can tell you that never happened."

"Who were they?"

"Don't know!"

"What?"

"The EAA doesn't have 'em logged."

It was then that Pepper stormed in. Her eyes were riotous. Her wrath had just begun to show. "Scum!"

"What did they say?" Regis asked impatiently.

"No idea. No one's got 'em. Not registered, not exhibitors, nothing."

"That's impossible."

"No kidding."

"What's the deal?" Alex asked, confused.

"The deal? What's the deal?" She stormed through the gear room into her office. Chutes and harnesses were in different stages of preparation, along with a multicolor, ram-air canopy that was deployed from the ceiling. It hung from its pilot chute, then the bridle cable attached to the canopy. Nine Dacron cells lined horizontally along the long axis of the chute. The suspension lines, slider and riser, all came to a point at a mannequin dressed in jumping gear. He was strapped into a harness with a safety helmet on, his hands in the steering toggles. The dummy was smiling.

"Finnegan," Regis said. He noticed Alex looking at him.

"Who?"

"The dummy. As in Finnegan's Rainbow. Idiots..." he ranted.

"Oh."

Pepper sat at her desk, boots kicked up onto the metal surface. She reached into the top left-hand drawer and took out a bottle of Jack Daniels and a pack of Marlboro Lights. She fumbled through the top drawer, and then nervously searched through the two on the right, looking for a lighter.

"Smoke?" She stopped and gazed up at Alex as he walked in. Her eyes were full of lament.

"No."

"What are you looking for."

"Nothing." She threw the cigarettes back into the top left drawer and slammed it shut. She took a slug of whiskey out of the bottle. "Want some?"

"No."

"I don't smoke," she said.

Alex watched her drink up the Jack.

"Have a seat," she said, wiping her face on her sleeve. She wore the dirt and char from her flight in a raccoon stencil below the white skin where her goggles had snugged. She had smudge on her flying suit. It was not skin-tight but baggy, and gave a dramatic impression for the air shows.

"Bastards, tried to fly me into the ground."

It was then Regis stuck his head into the office. "Idiots. Everything okay?"

"Yeah," she replied as she eyed the bottle of Jack. She decided not to have another hit.

"Spoke with Jimmy. He's still with the FAA. He'll be there for at least another hour. They're investigating."

"If he calls, and I'm sure he will, buzz me."

"Will do...those pin-brain bureaucrats are scared of their own shadows." Regis left.

She stood and went to a file cabinet behind her desk. She slid open the top drawer. On top of a dictionary and several jumpmaster log books dating back to 1979, was a framed glass picture. It had dust on it and a corner of the glass at the bottom edge was cracked off. The photo had faded to dull green and off-color red. She gazed at the picture and then threw it down on top of her desk. It landed face up.

Alex looked at the photo. Pepper decided to have another shot of Jack after all. He studied the faces as Pepper unscrewed the pint bottle. She deliberated this time, before slugging down two large mouthfuls. She did not return the screwtop to the bottle head.

"Is this..."

"There's no way that those bastards couldn't know who tried to run us into the ground! No way!"

Alex continued to study the photo, looking into the little girl's eyes. A young child, maybe six. Her cheeks were chubby. Her nose was turned up. Her smile was innocent. Alex looked at Pepper. The girl was her.

The woman had sandy-brown hair like Pepper, but darker. The eyes and the lips were the same. The woman was about the same age as the adult Pepper Knight. It had to be twenty years ago that the photo was taken. He looked at the face harder. The hair was curled and tight. She wore lipstick. The red coloring was darker than he had seen before. He studied her jaw line.

"No way! No way! No one comes into this airspace without anyone goddamn knowing. The FAA, the tower, all of them have to get clearance for the EAA Fly-In. Someone's covering up! Someone tried to kill me and my pilot!" She stopped her ranting and looked at another photo, this one on the wall. It dated back to 1973. There was a 450 Stearman biplane similar to Pepper's. The pilot had inverted the plane similar to Pepper's stunt today. The wingwalker appeared to be a man. He too was flying a ribbon cut, just feet above the ground. Two volunteers were holding a twelve-foot streamer that he was just about to slice through. The volunteers couldn't have been more than feet in front of him. The photo was signed "With love, Bill."

"My father," she said.

"Father? I didn't know Dr. Warner was a pilot."

"He isn't." She eyed the bottle of Jack. Her adrenaline was still flowing. She barely felt the effects of the whiskey. "He is and he isn't."

She walked back to her desk and sat down. She blankly stared past Alex.

"Is this you?" Alex asked as he returned the framed photo to her desk, facing her in an upright manner.

"Yes. And that's my father also."

"The one on the plane?"

"No. Let me explain... idiots!" She had begun to collect her senses. She realized that she didn't need any more of the booze. She screwed on the cap and returned it to the top drawer that she had purposefully left open. "My real father is in the photo on the wall. He died before I was born. It was an accident. It was the same trick that I was doing today, that I've done a hundred times before, as he did."

"What happened?"

"It...was on ABC's *Wide World of Sports*, nationwide, on Sun-

117

day. He was perfect at it. It was a routine stunt. He had the best pilot, everything. They decided to use a shorter ribbon for TV. Coming in on the approach he went lower than normal, maybe a foot off the tarmac. He wanted to be a real show-off. Anyway, right after he carved through the ribbon there was a gust of wind. An unexpected downdraft. It came out of nowhere. It was supposed to rain, and the clouds were moving in. The downdrafts were starting. Normally he would have bagged the stunt. But the whole world was waiting to see the Great Billy Knight, wingwalker, the fearless Billy. Anyway, he did it. Despite his better judgment, despite the weather, despite the advice from his pilot. He did it for the cameras.

"Over a million people were watching TV that day. The downdraft hit right after the ribbon cut. Decapitated him." A new tear swelled in the corner of her right eye. She pushed it back. "That was a long time ago. My mother, the one in the photo, and my step-father, Dr. Warner, raised me. That's Livingston when he was young."

"I'm sorry. I didn't know."

"Don't be."

"Who's your mother?"

"Dr. Joanna Knight."

"Jo, Joanna Knight?"

"Yes, why?"

CHAPTER 20
New York City

The therapists called it delusional psychosis. She called them crazy. The pills that she took, the different funky "zines" didn't do anything. She didn't need them anymore. She was sane—and she proved it by her very deliberate actions on the *Ricki Lake Show*.

"I love you," Katrina said.

"I love you, too," Mahalia replied. She gazed deeply into Katrina's eyes.

They lived in a brownstone in lower Manhattan near the site of the first Dutch settlement in 1625. To Mahalia, New York was a snapshot of her life—the diversity, the symbiosis of the city, the paradoxes and the coexistence between life ascendant and life descendant—chess next to pornography, a book and a beggar. It was the English horn music moving on the air like a transparent streamer, as much a part of the urban atmosphere as oxygen. It was the sinology and sculpture; poetry and particle physics; the rich and polyglot marketplace of galleries, museums, plays, concerts and libraries. It was Thomas Wolf stalking the streets of Brooklyn, Sonny Rollins practicing his saxophone on the Williamsburg Bridge—it was the osmosis of culture.

But there was a dark side to The Big Apple, a seedy mien that was the addiction which made her cling to the city and come back. Time after time, this was where she ended up.

It was in the evenings and on the weekends when much of the city was deserted—it was then that the sinful element emerged from the slimy bottomlands. It was the cauldron, the feeding ground for harlots and the hedonists. It was the cesspool of greed from which the estuary of immorality was sprung.

She and Katrina would work the debauched corporate culture and twist the number-crunching egghead minds to reel whatever jig they wanted them to dance.

They cajoled the Wall Street bankers, the Fortune 500, the CEOs, and the New York Stock Exchange movers and shakers into doing exactly what they wanted them to do—and parting with their tainted Benjamin Franklin's.

"Kiss me," Mahalia ordered. "Kiss me hard." Mahalia was sitting at an ostentatious vanity mirror. She was looking at the red-and-blue checkered sundress that flaired at mid-thigh and the red-plastic bubble bead necklace which she had worn on *The Ricki Lake Show*. Katrina obeyed. She reached around the wall-lit mirror and laid softly, then pressed hard, her cherried lips to Mahalia's.

"You were so good," Katrina said.

"Thank you," Mahalia replied. She looked into the foreboding mirror as she sat on her round, 19th century side chair. The mirror curved inward at its ends in a teardrop shape. It gave her a panorama of her face.

"What a show. I was great, wasn't I?"

"Yes, you were," Katrina replied. She stood above Mahalia, behind her, to her left. She placed her right hand on Mahalia's shoulder and began kneading the muscle. She looked down at the scars on Mahalia's back.

She had perfume: Beautiful, Chole, Chanel No. 5, 24 Faubourg, Joy/Jean Patou; some of which were in Baccarat crystal fragrance decanters. There was a widebrimed glass vase holding freshly cut flowers: daisies, pansies, irises, tulips and morning-glory.

She had multi-vitamin moisture supplement, mascara for sensitive eyes, Eau de Toilettes, cover creme makeup, antiwrinkle cream with Vitamin E, Gel Eye, makeup remover, Le Vernis nail color and a large container of cold cream.

"Hand me the envelope."

Katrina stopped rubbing Mahalia's shoulder and walked to a white sofa that sat in an anteroom between the bathroom and the master bedroom. Next to it was a Louis XIII table above which hung an oil painting—part of Francis Ferdinand's extensive collection of European art. Mahalia had acquired it from a dubious rare art importer. Later, she had it appraised by one of her special clients from Sotheby's. He said that it was looted from the Frederick R. Koch Austrian collection.

On top of the high-glass table sat the vellum envelope. The letter had already been written. She had scribed it in Indian ink with a quilled pen.

Katrina opened the top drawer of the Louis XIII table. Within was red embossing wax and an 18th century British Empire Indian seal. She removed those and brought with her the letter and envelope, the wax and seal, and a bayberry candle that was melted into a pricket. She returned to Mahalia, who was removing her makeup with the Gel Eye.

"Do you want me to do your back?" Katrina asked.

"Yes."

Mahalia took the letter from Katrina and opened it. In very ornate and meticulous calligraphy the note read:

"The Kiss of Death is upon you."

She then carefully folded the deckle-edged paper into thirds and slid it into the stiff envelope. She took a gold cigarette lighter that she had on her makeup counter, and lit the candle.

"It smells good."

"Yes."

She waited momentarily, then took the stick of embossing wax and warmed it over the candle. She worked it in a circle until the tip grew soft. Then she dripped five drops onto the envelope at the apex of its closing flap. While the wax was still soft, she took the seal and pressed it into the wax. Two turtledoves appeared. They were embossed into a carved lover's heart. They were kissing.

"It's ironic."

"It is," Katrina said as she kissed Mahalia's cheek, and then tauntingly nipped on the lips. "Shall I do your back now?"

The Doomsday Kiss

Mahalia gently blew out the candle. It left the room with an aromatic smell. She then kissed the back of the envelope just below the wax seal. She left an exaggerated imprint of her lips—with their plump furrows and valleys.

She set the envelope on the corner of her makeup counter, but far from the cosmetics and perfume. She gazed at the letter. It made her remember. She hypnotically looked into the mirror. She could see the swallows of Capistrano again.

"Should I begin?"

"Please."

It did not interrupt her vision of the swarming birds.

"I remember the swallows and the Mission San Juan Capistrano."

"Yes, my love," Katrina said in a soothing voice as she sponged several sheets of tissue into the large cold cream container.

"The lilies lay in a cluster floating on top of a pond next to the cattails in front of the mission. Azaleas and calendulas lined the water's edge. I remember the palm trees and the willows, and the bell that hung from the steeple tower and the white cross on top. That was when the swallows came." She looked at Katrina.

"One by one they'd come. He told me that they spit mud into the walls, regurgitated it to build their nests. They were funnels set on their side…The birds came back to their home each year because they knew that it was safe. *Is it safe?*"

"It's safe," Katrina replied.

Mahalia swept her hair back with a boresbristle brush. She stared into the mirror, into her own deep blue eyes. Katrina had a splotch of the cold cream in the Kleenex but stopped to also look into the mirror and listen to Mahalia's reflection tell her.

"Then the night hawk came. The swallows had built their nests on the stucco walls in crevices and on the jagged rock cliffs. That's where we were, by the ocean. I could see the Pacific. I could smell the salt water. Little droplets drifted in the breeze.

"Thousands of the swallows came. They built their nests. And then they laid their speckled eggs. The eggs were so small. The birds were so graceful. They would float in the air when they fed their hatchlings, like hummingbirds. Did you know they can hover in space in one spot?"

"No."

"They can, just like hummingbirds. In one spot. And there was this baby. My mother and I had gone to the ocean, to the cliffs. We had parked on top, on the drive. There were picnic tables and barbecue grills. I climbed down the rocks, down the cliff face. I was only six...I think. I wasn't supposed to go. I remember it was a clear day. The sky was blue—like baby's eyes.

"I had come before to feed the birds. To feed the hatchlings. I would watch them perch on the rims of their nests. They wanted to be brave. They weren't sure if they could fly. They would huddle in threes and fours. There were thousands of them."

"Did you feed them?"

That brought back the powerful memory. She saw it, clearly in the mirror. She was there on the rocks. She was six again. She had bits of bread. She climbed to the nest's edge to feed them. The rocks were dagger sharp. She could feel the gravel skid from under her feet as she squeezed down a ledge to the nearest nest. The mothers and fathers had a fit when she fed the hatchlings, but they didn't abandon the dependent babies like her mother said they would.

There was one hatchling she tried to feed. That was when the yelling started from the hummock above. *It's your daughter! It's your responsibility! I know that you don't want her, you don't care about her!* She blocked out the screaming. She put her hands over her ears when it got real bad. She almost lost her footing. The ranting didn't stop.

Then she reached out with the long piece of bread that she was trying to coax the hatchling into eating. "Please baby bird, take it. I won't hurt you."

The hatchling propped itself on the edge of its earthen nest. "Please baby, take it."

Suddenly, from above, there sounded a slap and violent shouting. "Stop it! Stop it!" Mahalia begged with her hands covering her ears. But she had implored just as the innocent hatchling had gotten enough courage to reach for the food. "No!" she screamed as the baby fell out of the mud nest. With lightening speed, the nighthawk came thundering down with its razor-sharp talons poised to rip the swallow apart. "No!"

The hatchling struggled. It fell toward the rocks and breakneck ocean spray. Out of instinct it frantically fluttered its downy, untested wings. The uncoordinated flapping momentarily stopped its descent...then gradually, as if by force of will, the baby swallow began to rise. It was mirthfully chirping.

"No!" came a frightful scream from above. At the same time, as if in preordained synchronicity, the nighthawk mercilessly snatched the baby swallow in its claws. "No!" Mahalia yelled, "No!"

At the exact instant that the nighthawk clamped down onto the hatchling, crushing the life out of it, Mahalia's mother plunged to her death—*before Mahalia's eyes.*

"No! No! No!"

"Are you all right?" Katrina asked.

Mahalia shook her head and snapped out of her uncanny trance. She again saw her haunted image in the mirror. San Juan Capistrano and the oceanside cliffs were gone. "Yes.... Please do my back."

"I'll rub it as I take off the makeup. It'll feel good."

Mahalia looked into the mirror at Katrina. She answered with her saccharine eyes. Katrina began stroking the cold cream into her back. At first it nipped her tender skin, then it felt good. Mahalia took a sip of white wine that Katrina had poured for her earlier. The wine tickled her tongue.

"There," Katrina said as she began smudging out the stage makeup. She threw away the sticky, dirty tissues into a waste basket under the vanity counter. It was thick with crumbled liquid latex body putty and spirit gum. She pulled several more tissues out of the Kleenex dispenser. "There's no way they could have known."

Mahalia looked at the right-hand corner of the mirror. The theatrical scars were perfect. Katrina rubbed deeper this time. The prismatic bands dissolved into the cold cream, turning the tissue an ugly brown-black.

"Ricki Lake, the audience, the whole world doesn't know. It was perfect," Katrina said.

"It was, wasn't it?" Mahalia looked at Katrina in the mirror then back at her own reflection. "Perfect." Then she remembered the hatchling's feather that floated down from the nighthawk's beak. It came to rest in her palm. Magically, she caught it.

She kept the feather. She would never forget the hatchling or the nighthawk, or her mother—*or him.*

CHAPTER 21
CIA Headquarters
Langley, Virginia

Fifty-three-year-old, six-foot two-inch Director Harlan Gates wore his thick gold and platinum framed glasses with a scowl. Despite his many medals—Distinguished Intelligence Cross for extraordinary heroism, Distinguished Intelligence Medal for outstanding service, Intelligence Star for courageous action and Career Intelligence Medal for exceptional achievement—Gates was afraid.

His office was near the cornerstone of the new CIA building which was completed March 1991. On his desk sat a twelve-inch bronze sculpture of the American bald eagle. A Biblical verse which he thought characterized the intelligence mission in a free society was engraved on its base. It read:

And ye shall know the truth and the truth shall make you free
    —John VII-XXXII

But today the truth wasn't making Gates free. He had come from the dome-shaped Headquarters Auditorium via an underground passage. He stood in the rear, unobserved behind the 350 that sat listening to a lecture on cryptography. Some heads were bobbing as the ambitious took notes. Gates paid particular attention to the industrious pens.

He stopped at the permanent museum in the new Headquarters building to take his mind off his conundrum. He casually studied the artifacts related to the career of DPI Allen Dulles and OSS founder William Donovan. He studied the first flag to fly over the original CIA Headquarters, several items from Operation Desert Storm, a three-hundred-pound chunk of the Berlin Wall, and a cipher machine used by Germany during WW II.

His mind, however, was predictably elsewhere.

Gates had not been back in his office more than ten minutes when Deputy Director for Intelligence Henry Dulles came in. He wore a stiff white shirt and a red power tie.

"Harlan, may I have a seat?" Dulles asked.

"By all means." He gestured Henry to one of two burgundy half-clubbed chairs across from his *too* proper cherrywood desk.

Henry Dulles was 43 but looked 50. He had a beagle face and wore spectacles that slid down the bridge of his pointy nose, leaving indentations in his skin when he took them off. He had an orange-brown Scottish beard that was trimmed to two-weeks growth, but was scraggly and should have been buzzed shorter. His height was medium, though he appeared lanky, and he had Rus ears on both sides of his thinning hair.

"I've got Matheson, McWillis, Kincaid, Dr. Johnson at Mills Farm, General Simpson at NORAD and Arms Control Intelligence in on this. We have no option but to advise the President to terminate *Mir-Kennedy I.*"

"What about General Peterson at Houston Control?"

"He's not in on it yet."

"And by terminate you mean—decommission?"

"Eradicate, sir. Arms Control tells me that we've got a small window of opportunity to proceed in—and if we don't decide within the next twenty-four hours, there's a chance that the Russians might get wind of what we've been up to—and they might choose *not to terminate.*"

"What about the FSB (KGB)? Do you have any feedback through our usual channels?"

"No, just that Chief Directorate Yezhov is extremely agitated over the Ambassador Perov and Aeromexico Flight 900 incident. Personally, I don't blame him."

"Do you think he's aware of what's really going on in *Mir-Kennedy I?*"

"Well, it would be hard for him not to be cognizant of the shenanigans, especially in light of the fact that it is one of their own cosmonauts, Gregov Pokrovsky, who's dead."

"How many on board?"

"Thirteen, counting Pokrovsky. Five American, six Russian, one Canadian, and one Japanese. Their names are," he flipped through a leather-bound dossier setting on his lap. Inside were long sheets of yellow legal paper with handwritten notes that Dulles had organized just five minutes before the meeting. "American: Mission Commander Scoop Jackson, Spacewalker/Pilot Randall Smith, Chemical Engineer Stephen Cunningham, Communications Officer Roy Hobbs. Russian: of course Biologics Engineer Pokrovsky, Commander Anatoly Vrubel, Flight Engineer Nikolay Solovyev, Computer and Metallurgic Officer Petrov Zvezda, Biologics Engineer Maya Mukhina and Tool Specialist Vladimir Budarin. Canadian: Spacewalker Rusty Holloway. Japanese: Futabatei Shoyo." ·

"I see. What about Perov?"

"Our divers located his body thirty miles off Cabo San Lucas, Baja, Mexico—1,210 feet down just above the Cedros Trench. *It looks like LAV-10.* Though that wasn't the cause of death."

"What was?"

Heart attack, probably due to the explosion and the fact that he survived the bomb—and then Flight 900 plunged 33,000 feet to the Pacific."

"Did you recover his briefcase?"

"We did."

"Nothing yet makes sense. I'm sure the Russians are going to want it back."

"Do they know that we salvaged the flight?"

"Are you kidding? With their Sojuzkarkta and Bukashev spy satellites—I'd be surprised if they didn't record our divers' conversation."

"Yeah, that's what I figured." Gates looked again at the bronze statue on his desk. He mouthed the words: *"And ye shall know the truth and the truth shall make you free."*

"In one hour," Gates said, "I want everyone involved to have a full report on my desk. I especially want Reinerson in on this. I'll review the findings and we'll meet at 0900, then I'll contact the President with a full accounting."

"One thing, Harlan."

"What's that?"

"Peter Reinerson is missing."

"Missing?"

"That's correct."

"How long?"

"Three days."

"And this has gone unnoticed?"

"He's Associate Director of Chemical and Biologic Weaponry."

"That's not his style. He's not involved in any field work?"

"No."

"Is it personal?"

"Not that I'm aware of."

"Is he sick?"

"No."

"Have you spoken with his wife?"

"Yes, and she said that he said that he was going to Nairobi for the agency."

"Kenya?"

"Yes, that's what I said."

"Was he?"

"Ostensibly."

"Nevertheless, I want him on line in one hour."

"I'll see what I can do."

0938 Hours
The White House

President Climan was sitting at his desk in the Oval Office. He looked beyond his mahogany desk to a set of four oversized leather chairs arranged around a dark mahogany Louis XIV table. On top, sat a lighter encased in scrolled Baccarat crystal. Next to it was a matching crystal ashtray. Both were gifts from Queen Elizabeth. Between the two chairs seated farthest apart sat a patterned pedestal table; behind it, a Louis XV marquetry table dyed gold-and-black.

"Mr. President," his whip-snapping secretary Rose Fairweather said, "I have Director Gates on the line."

"Put him on video," Climan said. The President had a virtual ATT scrambled V-2001 video telephone on his desk. The rose-tinted camera lens portrayed him in the most affable political light.

"Harlan, talk to me."

"Mr. President, I'll cut right to the quick."

"Go on."

"With regards to Ambassador Perov's death, I think that it's pretty safe to say that he was the victim of the Islamic Hamas' revenge for Russia's plan to build a private enterprise nuclear power plant in Tel Aviv..."

Climan abruptly cut him off. "Is there any relationship to the *Mir-Kennedy I* incident?"

"We're not sure Mr. President. But I can assure you that we're looking into it." Gates paused for a moment to review his notes before conferring with Dulles, who was seated in the room with him. "Mr. President...I'm distressed to say...but you need to know...it looks like Perov might have been a victim of *LAV-10*."

"But that's impossible."

"That's what we said. Also, prominent South Korean industrialist Kim Young Mun, CEO of AFI Amalgam Federated International, died yesterday morning—also from what appears to be *LAV-10*."

"What's...the connection?"

"Mr. President," a gravely concerned Dulles spoke, "it gets worse."

"How so?"

"We suspect that Perov and..."

"Mun are linked," Climan intuitively finished. "How? *LAV-10* is top secret!"

"*The Armory.*"

President Climan hadn't heard that name in years. The Armory meant bad news—and worse, it meant that if Perov and Mun were involved, then so were others.

The Doomsday Kiss

Federal Security Service, formerly
Komiter Gosudarstvennoy Bezopasnosti
KGB Headquarters, Moscow

The day was overcast and gloomy in the "Great Tank-for-Chicken" trade society. Mikhail Gorbachev had thrust Russia, yawning and blinking, into capitalism. But to the ultimate chagrin of both the country and its leaders, no one had any idea what to do with the bear once it was roused. A totter, a hesitation, then a crash amongst flying rubles. Gorbachev surely paved his countrymen's descent with the best intentions. He envisioned a sound economic future—way into the future. But his hesitant steps toward a free-market system only plunged the stagnant Soviet economy further into its own morass.

That meant that the corrupt and treacherous, in search of their all-mighty fortune, soon rooted deeply into all aspects of Russian society—including the FSB.

"How long has there been a problem with cosmonaut Pokrovsky?" Chief Directorate Laventy Yezhov asked Associate Director Dmitry Korazhinshy. Yezhov was pensive.

"I suspect, Chief Directorate, that since last October we might have had a breach."

"How long has he been up on *Mir-Kennedy I?*"

"Since January."

"Who else?"

"We believe that we have four wildcard agents working under the code name IVANOV. Also...Comrade Director...the tentacles of corruption extend beyond the FSB."

"How deeply entrenched?"

"We're still early in our defrocking process, but my information points to the French Direction Generale de la Securite Exterieure, the MI-6 and possibly the CIA."

"MI-6 and the British are involved?"

"Yes comrade...and also possible civilian entities."

"What about our countermeasure?"

"*It's been planted many harvests ago. I'm waiting for the tree to bloom.*"

"And when will that be?"

"Soon."

"It better be soon."

CHAPTER 22
Terminal Velocity
Wingwalkers & Skydiving

The rain came down in sheets. Alex could hear the clamor on the tin roof. The storm would pass in an hour. It was a typical midwest downpour, furious at its onset, then ending as quickly as it appeared.

"She's my mother. After father was killed, she finished medical school. She paid for it as a wingwalker."

"I didn't know."

"She met father, Dr. Warner, at Stanford. He raised me as his own. I loved him." She paused to think. "Are they sure that it was an accident?"

"I don't know."

Then she suspiciously asked. "Why are you here?"

"For your mother."

"My mother?"

"She's missing."

"Missing. What do you mean?"

"Four days ago I was in Las Vegas."

"Las Vegas?"

"Yes, to see your mother. Actually, I was there at the Consumer Electronics Show. I hadn't talked to her in years. I thought I'd stop by and say hi. We're old friends. Did you know that?"

"No. I hadn't spoken to her for a while."

"Why?" Alex asked. He leaned back in the worn Naugahyde chair.

"Why?" Pepper thought about taking another hit from the bottle of Jack Daniels, and then angrily looked at the faded photo in front of her on her desk. She slung it into the wall. The glass cracked inside the brass frame, breaking free a large wedge of glass, which slid across the worn carpet. It scraped a line across Jo's Kodachromed face.

"She left me when I was four...for her job. She didn't love me. She never cared about me. She took a job with the government. Livingston raised me. He's my father.... She's a bitch!"

"She's missing."

"She didn't care about me. I was an *inconvenience*," she snarled under her breath.

"Why did you become a wingwalker?"

"For my father. To be like my *real* father."

"Mind if I have a drink?" Alex didn't want one, but he thought it might help cut the tension.

"No." She pulled open the drawer and returned the bottle to the desk, but this time she also removed two smudged shot glasses. She poured one for each of them. Alex looked down at the shattered photo, then back to the shot of Jack. She followed his eyes.

"Sorry 'bout that," she said. Pepper got up, picked up the photo, and the dagger-sharp shard of glass. She fit the broken fragment into the photo and set it on top of her desk.

"I've been out of the country for three months at a seminar..."

"What kind?"

"Training. Nothing. Anyway, on my way back to my practice..."

"You're a doctor?"

"Yes. Anyway, on my way back home to Salt Lake City, I stopped off in Las Vegas for the Consumer Electronics Show. I thought I'd also see your mom. I did my residency with her."

"Yeah."

"When I got to the hospital, she was doing an autopsy without her resident. We used to be real good friends, Jo and I. Well...Jo was freaked out. She was acting real funny. The body wasn't right."

"What?"

"The cadaver...it smelled like mothballs. Then, when Jo opened the cranial vault, the CSF fluid was wrong."

"What's CSF?"

"Cerebral spinal fluid. It was like purple Jello, but clear."

"So."

"It's not supposed to be like that."

"And?"

"Well, your mom kicked me out when her resident showed up. Two days later, she called me frantically afraid of something. I met her at the hospital and she was freaked out. She told me that the feds came in, kicked her out of the autopsy room and seized everything."

"Did she know why?"

"No. She said she was being watched. She also told me that her resident was missing. I told her to call the police."

"Did she?"

"No, she wouldn't. I think she was hiding something."

"That wouldn't surprise me," Pepper said as she shot her stout Jack. It seared. She looked at the luring bottle that she had left on the desktop. She wondered about taking another chug.

"I went back to my hotel and someone was in my room, waiting for me. They'd gone through my papers."

"What papers?"

"My stuff from the Consumer Electronics Show."

"What happened?"

"The guy was probably hiding in the bathroom. I left the room, grabbed a fire extinguisher in the hall, and cold-cocked him when he tried to escape out of the terrace sliding-glass door. Then I was shot at. I got away and I went back to the hospital. Your mom was gone. I went to her house and apparently she was abducted. A neighborhood girl saw two men take her away. I broke into Jo's house and found a Federal Express receipt and a microcassette player with a tape recorded message *left for me*."

"*You?*"

"Yeah. Anyway, I had just started listening to it when men entered the house."

"Who?"

"I don't know, but they wanted to kill me. They had guns."

"Why?"

"I don't know."

"What did you do?"

"I hid."

"Did they find you?"

"No. I'm here, aren't I?"

"What was on the tape?"

"I don't know. I didn't have time to listen to it. She said something about "Iv." I don't know. The FedEx was sent to Dr. Livingston Warner, Chief of Virology at USC. So I went there. When I arrived, his office had been ransacked and he had been killed in a hit-and-run. There was no sign of the FedEx.

"I spoke to your father's secretary. He tried calling you eight or nine times the night before he was murdered. She gave me the number, so I came here."

"Murdered?"

"I don't know what else you'd call it. Too much coincidence for me."

"So you came here?"

"Yes."

"Did you call the police?"

"No. I've had a bad feeling about this whole thing, especially after your mom and I were followed outside the hospital.

"Followed?"

"Yeah, when I met her at the hospital. We walked around the hospital and talked. Two cars, a Taurus and a Lumina. There were two men in each, and they followed us. Watched us with binoculars."

"Jesus."

"Yeah. Do you have any idea why your father may have called you?"

"No."

"When did you speak with him last?" Alex thought about drinking his Jack. He really didn't want to. He lifted the shot glass halfway, then processed what he had just told Pepper. He stuttered, then slugged down the whiskey.

"Regis." Pepper punched the page button on her telephone.

"Yeah."

"Any messages on the answering machine?"

"No, actually...its broke. Someone was messin' with it. The cover was smashed into the tape. Damn thing wouldn't work...idiots!"

"That's strange." Pepper released the button and picked up the pint, then twisted on the top and returned it to her desk drawer. She looked behind her at the photo of Fearless Billy.

"Do you have any idea why he might've called?"

"No. Why do you think this is happening?"

"I don't know. Your mother wouldn't tell me. She was keeping something very close to her chest. I do know, however, she did run an ELSIA test on the CSF and *it was positive.*"

"What's an ELSIA test?"

"It's an AIDS test."

"Do you think the dead man had AIDS?"

"No. He didn't look like any AIDS patient I'd ever seen.... Why'd you say man?"

"I don't know."

"No. He was in his late fifties, maybe early sixties. Looked healthy as a horse except for his smell."

"So why," she asked, "would someone kill...my father, try to kill me and kidnap my mother?"

"Are you sure someone tried to kill you?"

"Absolutely. Especially since the tower and FAA can't tell me who piloted those three T-6s that tried to fly me into the ground. It has to be a cover-up. Besides, do you know how *rare* T-6s are?"

"No."

"Let's put it this way...you just about gotta be *God or the military* to own one...and three of 'em? Bullshit! Come with me." She walked out of her office through the shop and hangar, and past a Sukhoi SU-29 and a Pitts Challenger that her mechanic was working on. She walked to the front desk and looked at the Phonemate answering machine. It looked like someone with a large hand had smashed a fist into it. She then sat down at a metal desk and began going through her paperwork.

The files had obviously been gone through. They weren't rifled, but papers that she would notice were tampered with were not put back in their proper place. Some of the mail on the desk, in the bills stack, had been rummaged through. There was a fresh bundle bound by a thick rubber band that had just been delivered. It had not been gone through, she noticed, as she pushed back the elastic.

"So how was the electronics show?" She was making small talk while she was flipping. She didn't want to discuss her mother or father. "You want to talk about the show?"

"Yes. Okay. Bigger than I expected."

"That's good." she said indifferently as she thumbed through the stack.

"There was Rogaine," he said sarcastically as he thought about a stupid looking professorly colleague.

"What?"

"Oh, I ran into a doctor friend of mine from medical school at the University of Miami. You know it was funny, but he, at least as I remembered, had lost his hair."

"Doesn't that stuff help you grow hair or something?"

"It's supposed to."

"Maybe you should..."

"What?" he said. He was obviously sensitive to the proposition of losing his hair.

"You don't have to be defensive. Your hair...looks mostly okay."

"*Mostly*?" he flagged his eyebrows and gingerly touched his scalp.

"Wait a second," she said.

Alex was still feeling his scalp. "What?"

She pulled out a letter that was postmarked three days ago. The return address was the University Medical Center, which Jo wrote in blue ink beneath the printed return address. She opened the envelope. Inside was a brochure. She unfolded it. There was no handwriting nor message inside, nor on the brochure. Just the high-gloss brochure.

"What is it?" Alex asked.

"The St. Louis Zoo."

CHAPTER 23
"The Kiss of Death Is Upon You."

Mahalia Hunt thought that her choice of words was particularly dramatic. She looked at the rear of the vellum envelope which she was holding between her delicate fingers. The impression of her lips had long since dried, yet it was full of today's life and the morrow's lust. Then she slid it back into her Verucci purse.

This was the last envelope she'd mail. There was one more after this. It would be delivered by a courier. All of them had *her seal* and *her mark*, her butterfly kiss: *The lips of Mephistopheles*.

"New York is where I have to be." She wished she knew why. It was a function of her contradiction and complexity. It was the energy and animosity, the clutter in contrast to its great charm. It was the root of all evil.

"What, sweetheart?" Katrina asked Mahalia as she brushed her long hair out of her face.

"Oh, I was just thinking how I love this city."

"Yes. Me, too."

Audaciously, Mahalia was going to deposit the envelope at the post office next door to Pennsylvania Station and Madison Square Garden.

"What time's our clients?"

"Two," Mahalia said as she looked at her 18-carat gold Cartier watch. Mahalia was wearing a bright red *postiche*. She had gaudy Gucci silver-dollar-sized sunglasses that transmuted from dark to clear when she left the sun. Her lips were ruby-red, and her cheeks were over-blushed. Her dress was V-cut past her bosom line and was tawny gold. Her hem ended below the knees and had a thigh-high slit on both sides that was lined with ostrich feathers. She wore nothing underneath.

"Overnight Express, please."

The postal clerk, a 272 pound civil servant, whose platinum blond hair had tones of green and gray throughout it, smacked her lips together in disapproval. She looked down her ski-slope nose. She recognized Mahalia for what she was—a cheap, two-bit hussy parading in a thousand dollar outfit. "So."

"I would like to send this letter overnight please," Mahalia requested in a more commanding, yet mannered tone.

"Did you fill out the form?" the clerk rudely asked.

"What form?"

"The form to send your package Overnight Express."

"I thought you did that at the counter."

"No, they're there," she indignantly pointed to a linden-wood counter opposite her station, next to the Madison Square Garden-facing plateglass window.

"I'm sorry."

"You'll need to fill out the form, and get back in line."

A small tick became apparent in Mahalia's left front neck muscle, just below her jaw. "Excuse me...I didn't know that there was a form."

"You'll need to fill out the form. Next." There was a line of at least thirty. Mahalia stood her ground. Behind her, devoted Katrina was anxious. She put her hand on Mahalia's shoulder and said. "Come on."

"Next," the clerk snapped as she looked past Mahalia.

The twitch became more prominent in Mahalia's neck. Her vision sharpened. She withdrew a Hoyo De Monterey Excalibur 6- inch cigar from her purse. It was in its own yellow with tobacco-brown tube. She removed her Cartier lighter and fired up.

"Can't you see, *No Smoking*," the crude postal clerk retorted as she pointed to a faded *"No Smoking"* sign on the wall beyond Mahalia's left shoulder. "Next!"

Mahalia culled several puffs into her mouth, then tongue-licked them. The next person, a shy gray-haired, bald man stepped up behind Mahalia. Mahalia blew the cloud of smoke into the clerk's pug face. She then lunged over the counter, and grabbed the clerk's hair with her left hand, and put the fiery end of the Habana within an eighth of an inch of the clerk's left eye. There was a volcano within Mahalia waiting to explode.

"I want my form now or I'll jam this fucking cigar into your eyeball, and then rip your throat out! Understand?"

The clerk peed in her pants.

"Really, it's no problem," said the man behind Mahalia.

Mahalia quickly spun her head without releasing her grip on the horrified civil servant and growled, "Butt out!" She then reaffixed her stare on the clerk, "Understand!" The cowering civil servant nodded her head in horrified affirmation. "Good." Mahalia released the woman's hair, taking with her several strands, and tauntingly took another puff on her stogey.

The clerk reached into a drawer underneath her station and pulled out an Express form that she had had all along. Five minutes later, Mahalia had finished filling out the blank. In the spot marked Sender she wrote: "Your lover." For the address she deleted the road but wrote, *"Old Mission Street, San Juan Capistrano."*

When she finished she said, "Thank you," reached into her purse to pull out another cigar, and slid it into the mortified clerk's left ear. *"Take a tip from me...smoking can be bad for your health!"*

Mahalia and Katrina took a cab to Central Park. Mahalia wanted to feed the ducks, then go window shopping before their two o'clock at the Plaza Hotel. She had the cabby drop them off in front of the Metropolitan Museum of Art at Fifth Avenue and West 84th. She wanted to see what was on exhibit. It was the *Splendors of Imperial China, Nicholas Poussin/Works on Paper Picturing Paradise—early Samoa and People, and Fabergé in America and Enamels of Limoges.* She wasn't interested.

They sauntered into Central Park, beyond glades, copses and

rock outcrops, south past Cleopatra's Needle and down a tree-lined driveway to the Loeb boat house and then Bethesda Fountain. The sky was luminous blue, and the radiant heat soaked into their husks.

"Why did you do that?" Katrina asked.

"Did you know that Salinger wrote *Catcher in the Rye* here?"

"Mahalia, I'm serious. Why'd you do that?"

"This is where Holden Caulfield came. Actually, it was to the Conservatory Pond. He searched for ducks and sardines."

"Mahalia?"

There were a hundred or so people surrounding the fountain. Some were on lunch, others were tourists. They all had their special itineraries in mind. None of which mattered to Mahalia. They were bothersome gnats that needed to be shooed. "I wanted her to remember me."

"That was a pretty powerful way to get her attention."

"Wasn't it?"

"Mahalia," Katrina grabbed her velvety hand and softly stroked it. "I love you. Please, let's follow our plan."

Mahalia looked at Katrina with *those* eyes. They were glassy, and held secrets of her infected youth. "Let's feed the ducks."

They bought Cheeze-Its and for an hour they fed the mallard and broad-bills in the algae-defiled pond. Mahalia was preoccupied. She was not in Central Park. She found herself at the Old Mission in San Juan Capistrano.

She was six and she was standing in front of the church pond. The green and yellow lily pads floated next to the cattails. She saw the sole rattan palm tree and the azaleas and bluebells. Before her was the steeple and the bell and the white cross above it.

Then she was on the cliffs. She was standing on a craggy rock ledge. The blue and green swallows were flying furiously. Something had scared them. At first she thought that it was she, but it wasn't. It was the fighting above on the knoll.

"Don't you dare hit me, you son-of-a bitch. You're a good-for-nothing piece of dirt. I'm going to make you pay, and pay through your greedy, pious nose."

"Please, please. Calm down," he said. "Let's just talk about this rationally."

"She's your daughter and you know it. It's your fault. You're a good-for-nothing."

"Please, get hold of yourself, please."

"You're going to pay and you're going to pay dearly."

Mahalia saw the dancing blue and green swallows. They were flying in a frenzied swarm. There were hundreds of them. She covered her tender ears with both hands and worked her way out on the jagged granite ledge to feed the hatchlings. She didn't want to hear them fight.

"Pay me now!" she ranted.

"You can't do this to me. You'll ruin everything. Let's just talk about it calmly. Please. We can work everything out."

"Pay me!"

Mahalia reached out with her long bread strip to feed the naive hatchling. The baby swallow had worked its way to the lip of its nobby mud nest. From above, a nighthawk dive-bombed with its talons spread out for its unsuspecting meal.

She had tried to feed it. It wasn't her fault that the hatchling fell. Mahalia looked at the baby bird as the life was mercilessly crushed out of it. Then, from above, she heard her mother's scream. Simultaneously, the nighthawk consumed the hatchling in one gulp. The baby swallow's tail and one leg jutted out of the hawk's powerful beak as the predator jerked its head and forced down the rest of its meal.

Simultaneously, Mahalia's mother plunged past her. Down she tumbled in a flail of arms and legs to the dagger-sharp boulders and ocean wash. "*Noooooo!*"

"Mahalia, Mahalia…"

Mahalia snapped out of her stupor and back into the world of the tortured, as fast as she had gone into it. "We need to go."

They walked past The Sheep Meadow. The grass was still limpid green and was dog day vibrant. It smelled of fresh cuttings. They wandered beyond the Tavern on the Green of Central Park West to an out-of-the-way travel agency where they had two first-class tickets waiting for them. Mahalia picked up the tickets and their printed confirmation for the Adolphus Hotel.

"Is it nice, the hotel?" Katrina asked.

"It's the best."

"Scotch?"

"If they don't have mine, then they'll get it."

"How long will we be there?"

"Just a couple of days."

"Who are our clients?" Katrina asked, thinking of work and the possible role she would play this time: temptress, seductress, schoolgirl, dominatrix.

"Some Meryll Lynch types."

"What are they paying us?"

"Five thousand."

"They want the girl-girl act?"

"For five thousand, that's what they get."

"Shoot, Mahalia," she cooed into her courtesan's ear and said with a Southern drawl, "I'd do that for free."

Mahalia smiled and kissed Katrina on her tender lips. "I know, sweetheart."

Mahalia withdrew another Hoyo De Monterey Excalibur from her purse. She studied its phallic-shaped yellow cover tube. She had used it before as a rectal dildo on Katrina. Katrina liked that, it gave her the chills. Their clients loved to watch.

They made their way back to Fifth Avenue and browsed Saks, Cartier, Fortunoof, Bigan and the twin Gucci panache near 54th Street. They window-shopped the stores at the glitzy Trump Tower. Katrina liked the five-story waterfall and corner terraces. This is where she and Mahalia would sometimes make out just like high school lovers.

They went into Tiffany & Co. and studied the crystal and jewels. "Should I get this one for you?" Katrina asked. It was a five-carat marquise flawless diamond.

"Next week, my tender."

Finally, they shopped Bergdorf Goodman which was located at the former site of the Cornelius Vanderbilt mansion. It was more like a collection of small boutiques than a department store.

By 2:10 P.M., they arrived at the Rainbow Room on top of Rockefeller Center. It was a bit campy and very expensive. The eating was in a 1940s style dining room. Jacket and tie were required.

The big-money entrepreneurs were getting the best money could buy. Mahalia and Katrina had copulated with royalty—they had taken sheiks and ambassadors, senators and powerful diplomats on "round-the-world" tours. They had bedded fifteen of the Fortune 500 CEOs.

Their clients didn't know who they were. Mahalia would find them though. They would wear a white rose in their lapels. When she found the two johns, they were sitting at a table that faced Central

Park. She smiled.

"Good evening, gentlemen," she said devilishly. They were older businessmen, men of unequivocal substance. "I'm Cinderella and this is Little BoPeep." She and libidinous Katrina took a seat. The men had little-boy smiles on their faces. The one who sat next to Mahalia wore platinum bank teller glasses. He slipped her the money in an envelope under the table. She discretely looked inside. All the bills were hundreds. There were seventy-five.

"Oh, for the bonus round?"

"No, to show you our appreciation in advance."

Mahalia smiled and got that seductress look in her eyes. She thought of the Capistrano swallows and the hatchling. He was the nighthawk. *She was revenge.*

CHAPTER 24
St. Louis, Missouri

"You ever skydive?" Pepper asked as their ABC Cab bumped along on blown-out shocks south on 170, then east on 40/64 toward Illinois, en route from the airport to the St. Louis Zoo.

Alex and Pepper were sitting in the back seat of the banged-up Impala. He looked into the driver's rearview mirror to see his hair. Murky clouds covered the sky, causing his reflection to appear clearer, devoid of any glare.

"Rogaine?"

"You need some." She teased as she pointed to a nonexistent widow's peak with her taunting index finger.

As they drove, he studied his jiggling reflection.

"Why are you so sensitive?" she asked.

"Nothing."

"I'm sorry. I was just kidding."

Alex pouted. To him going bald represented his vulnerability, his aging, his fight against that relentless Grim Reaper. Just the thought of it gave him an uneasy feeling. It was stupid. It was the same reason he didn't like the autopsy rooms.

"So you said you went to a seminar. You were gone for three months."

"Yeah," he said as he watched the gray sky pass by his window.

"So what kind of seminar?"

He looked at the sky and thought. He remembered what they taught him in Moscow. The two rules of dealing with a terrorist situation: *"Don't trust what you see,"* and *"Go with your gut."* They were simple enough. "Seminar?" he said rhetorically.

"Yes."

"I took three months off my practice. It was to train physicians globally on how to deal with a terrorist germ warfare situation."

"What did they teach you?"

"Some I can talk about, some not. But basically how to handle situations with anthrax, botulism, Ebola and the like...and how to deal with terrorists."

"Where was it?"

"Washington, D.C., for a month. A month in Rio and a month in Moscow."

"Sounds interesting."

"Yeah."

"Were you able to take the time off work?"

"Yes and no. I work with a group in Salt Lake City. They covered my patients. But I missed them."

"So why the Consumer Electronics Show?"

"It was on my way back from Moscow. It was arranged by Oleg Shlyapnikov, Assistant to the First Directorate KR Line of the FSB, or Federal Security Service, which is the new name for the KGB."

"The KGB?"

"Yeah, you know with détente and all. It was just part of the training."

"But the KGB?"

"Yeah. Anyway, I thought that I could get some ideas for the clinic...at least in the abstract."

"That's strange."

"Isn't it—*since that's where all my problems started—looking for a nonexistent software.*"

"Nonexistent software?"

"*LAV-10.*"

Pepper was apprehensive about the zoo. She wasn't quite clear why they were going. But she knew her father was dead. She was angry with her mother, yet felt a sense of obligation to come to terms with her feelings. Her mother had sent her the map for a reason.

As they neared the zoo, they passed Clayton Road and a number of limestone granite and dryvit buildings, one designed in 1896 by Henry Ives Cobb. Next to it was the 1986 *Trompe l'oeil*. Out of the corner of his eye Alex saw what he thought was a dry cleaners. "Stop here!" he abruptly said.

The cab driver slammed the vehicle to a grinding halt, then quickly pulled out of traffic to the road's edge. Alex jumped out of the cab and ran back sixty yards. Pepper had no idea what he was doing. She slid to the rear door, nearest the curb, and stuck out her head.

"What do you want me to do ma'am?" the taxi driver asked.

"Wait here."

She opened the door, got out, and ran down the asphalt-patched concrete and caught up with Alex, who was frozen solid in his tracks.

In Alex's mind he was no longer in St. Louis. He was back in his room at the Desert Inn. The papers spread out on his bed, the intruder in the bathroom, then Alex surprising him on the veranda...Going through the intruder's pockets looking for I.D. Nothing...until he spotted the laundry tag inside his jacket: *American Cleaners*.

He looked up at a ten-by-twenty foot clapboard billboard that sat on top of a two-story brick building. It bore the same name: *American Cleaners*.

"What is it Alex?"

"We're in the right place."

He walked deliberately back to the cab. "Let me see the map," he said. She had it in her dufflebag purse. She pulled it out. They had both been through it a hundred times, and again on the plane from Oshkosh—the answer was in the brochure.

The St. Louis Zoo. Alex vaguely remembered it was supposed to be one of the best zoos in the world. At least that was what his mother said when he was a kid growing up in the suburbs of Detroit, and was watching Marlon Perkin's *Wild Kingdom* on TV.

It was supposed to be the biggest in the world. That was when he was eleven. He was forty-one now. Things change.

They pulled up to the south gate off Hampton and Wells Drive.

It was big. There was no doubt about it. There were six thousand animals, many of them endangered species. There was a twenty-four gauge, twelve-pound rail train, the "Zooline" that buzzed between four stations in its round-trip tour of the park. It was just like the Detroit Zoo where Alex had made many a pilgimage as a youth.

They didn't know what they were searching for, but there was no doubt this was the right place.

Why would she send Pepper, her estranged daughter, a map of the zoo? Why lead Alex on a quest? Jo called Alex because she wanted him to know something just in case. She was too smart, too calculating, and too deliberate. The map was meant for Alex to find. Alex knew it. He paid for their admission and unfolded the brochure.

He and Pepper had already looked at it too many times. There was no writing, no clues, not a hint. Yet...it had to be there.

"Do you have any ideas?" she asked.

"What's up with you?" he asked as they walked north past the Herpetarium. Alex sensed her exasperation.

"I haven't heard from her in more than two years and then she sends me a map, no note, nothing. And then someone tries to kill me at the air show."

"All the more reason to find her."

"I suppose."

The zoo was surprisingly crowded for a weekday. There were young couples intimately holding hands, kids with one of their parents, teenagers on the lam from their chores, and senior citizens with not much else better to do except take advantage of their Zoo Friends membership. Alex and Pepper walked past a large man-made lake bordered with centipede grass, bugle weed and wintercreeper. In the center was a flowered island full with rhododendrons, tulips and azaleas. Two donut-pulsating water fountains framed the isle. North of the spritz was a snowcone and Oscar Meyer footlong hot dog stand.

They passed the sea lion basin. A black, thick fur seal with large ears and blunt snout stood on its tail. It clapped its flippers, brapping for another silverfish from its caretaker.

"It'll just come to you. Open your mind. Let it happen. It'll come," they taught him. It was the *doctrine* of dealing with terrorists. *That's* what he should do. He should free his mind and let thoughts enter when they were ready. He wouldn't force them. *"Think unencumbered, let it flow. Why the zoo?"*

They walked past the stir at the Small Mammal Pits and the Jungle of the Apes. The chimpanzees, orangutans, baboons, and gibbons were howling and play slapping, or screeching in jabbers as they scrambled up fake tree limbs, staking out their territory.

Then they passed the Bird House. He could hear birds trilling, enigmatic courting songs as they approached.

Pfff. Pfff. A lady in front of them screamed as her six year old daughter fell to the ground in a rapidly birthing pool of her own blood. *Pfff.* Another silenced shot screamed past them.

"Run!" Alex grabbed Pepper's hand.

"Bravo team this is Delta, I've got subjects under surveillance."

"Affirmative Bravo this is Charlie..." the man with the 18mm HT-7 day/nightscope binoculars looked more carefully. "Christ someone's opened fire on them!"

"Bravo, Charlie, Delta, which one of you sons-of-a..."

"*Alpha, it's not our men!*"

Another shot, then a volley of four rang out in a hiss! Two more zoo-goers tumbled in their own crimson to the ground—one, a man shot through the heart, and another, a teenage girl with home-made Daisy Duke shorts and a torn rock t-shirt, was shot through the lower right leg.

"Run," Alex yelled as they scrambled into the Bird House. Two men, different than the shooter, were hot on their tracks. Alex and Pepper disappeared into the curving exhibits. They slipped past a high-humidity rain forest, and through sandy shorelines. Resonant voices and brilliant colors had nothing to celebrate as the two shoved others out of their way. The visitors inside the aviary had not heard the shots, so were unaware of what had occurred outside.

Alex and Pepper ran beyond a rare lyrebird with its peacock-like tail and bright red body plumages. Beside it, in a eucalyptus tree, were two oblivious king birds of paradise.

They dodged passed delicate wires that separated them from the exotic birds: golden-winged sunbirds, waxbills, paradise whydahs, honeycreepers and others.

"Shoot 'em on sight," the first man said as he ran into the Bird

House, barely hiding his ready automatic under his flapping slicker.

"They're toast," wheezed the other, a two-pack-a-day smoker, as he followed.

In an electronics van outside the zoo's north parking lot, the sortie leader was frantically on line with his four penetration teams.

"Who the hell gave you orders to shoot?" he yelled to Alpha as the insertion team leaders were all paying heed with bristling ears.

"No one, sir. It's not our men."

"I don't give a damn whose men they are, our orders are explicit. You're not to interfere unless we're code red."

"We have red!" Bravo interrupted as he saw Alex and Pepper dash out of the east shrub-lined exit of the Bird House.

"Then you know what to do!"

"Affirmative big brother." Alpha paused for a second while he was handed a note from one of his men who was monitoring the police frequencies. "We've got more problems. This deal is going to blow out of control! The zoo has called the locals...they're en route."

"Pull the draw strings shut! Now!"

"Done."

That was the code for Alpha's men to converge. They, too, would take *no prisoners.*

"Follow me," Alex yelled over his shoulder, as Pepper stayed just barely abreast of him. Alex thought about Moscow, what they had taught him. "*Do the opposite of what they'd expect,*" they said.

"In the bushes now." They made a bolt for the dogrose and hedge laurel just opposite the east railroad station.

"Change shirts with me!" Alex had on a green long-sleeve dress shirt with two pockets in front. She wore a white oversized blouse, which hung loose outside her black leggings.

"No."

"Shut up and take off your shirt!"

Close to where they were hiding Pepper could hear two men screaming at the faceless others to move, and she could see guns in their hands. Sirens wailed in the background, and more people were screaming as the panic spread like a ripple in a wave pond.

Alex slung on her shirt, which fit him poorly, and she begrudgingly tried on his. Her bra slid halfway down her right shoulder in the tussle to rip off her blouse.

"Roll the sleeves up and tie it in front."

"What?"

"Just do what I say!" She did. "Now give me your sunglasses and hat." They were black Vuarnets. Her hat was straw and full brimmed. "Now change your hair," he further demanded. She removed an elastic red tie that held her hair in a conservative short ponytail. She finally figured out where he was going with all this.

She rolled up the shirt and turned it into a halter. He put on the sunglasses. The hat wouldn't fit so he threw it into the bushes.

"Hey," she protested. He looked at her. She knew better.

"Take my hand." He pulled her. They got lost in the panic-stricken crowd. They walked slowly, deliberately through the hysterical, undulating mass—to the railroad station. They hopped a two-foot high white picket fence and got onto the narrow gauge track. The track took them from east to southwest, into a faux granite cavern under Big Cat Country and the Sea Lion Show. They passed a siding track and a reserve train, and a grungy maintenance grotto. There was a signal light next to the track. Its lens shone green.

"Wait for me." Alex left her standing in the shadows. He looked both ways to be sure that no one was following them. She stood next to a crisscross steel girder support that had been partially covered with wire mesh and dolomited. It looked like real rock.

Three long minutes later she heard a faint, echoing crash. Then, in five minutes he returned with a blue-denim work jacket and a green-vinyl raincoat.

"Where'd you get that?" she asked.

"Stole it from the maintenance shack." He had wrapped her shirt around his elbow and had made a large padding, and then broke through the pane-glass window door. There was blood oozing through the makeshift wrapping.

"Ouch!" he said. There was a two and one-half inch cut, and several splinters of barbed glass had embedded into his skin. He ripped the blouse into four strips with his teeth, and then made a stopgap bandage with the smallest remnant.

"Will that stop the bleeding?"

"For now," he said. He took a medium-sized strip from a portion of the blouse and folded it over several times onto itself, then into a square. Then, he pressed it into place and tied the bandage over it.

"You need stitches?"

"Yes."

"What are we going to do?"

"Get our butts out of here."

She looked into his eyes. They masked the fear that she knew he must have felt. She gazed at his chest. It glistened in the darkness. He was hairy, some had turned to dull grey.

Alex put on the denim jacket. It smelled of grease and hydraulic fluid. She already had on the raincoat.

They walked along the track on pumice gravel toward the zoo's entrance. They emerged facing east just next to the Primate House. As they exited the tunnel and climbed a gentle ridge, the next train, the Lewis and Clark, steamed passed them and quickly penetrated the opening.

They cautiously walked up a slight mound, past two maple trees and through a low-rising Russian privet, and then a honeysuckle. They deliberately walked along the crowded footpath toward the Herpetarium and the South Gate.

"Got 'em," the assassin said as he squeezed the trigger.

"Be sure not to miss this time, you idiot!"

CHAPTER 25

"In here," Alex said, firmly tugging Pepper toward the opening to the immense Herpetarium.

"Look," she grabbed his hand, "no one's at the front entrance. We can walk right out."

"No," he insisted and pulled harder. "Follow me." He directed her into the reptile and amphibian Herpetarium. "Whoever shot at us will be waiting."

She wanted to leave, but she followed Alex's instincts.

Pfff, the shot landed off its mark as a sortie commando from Bravo team scaled the rooftop of the Zoo Parents Kiosk, and planted his own silenced bullet into the back of the assassin's head. The killer, with his high-powered Belgic FN 30-11, had within his striking range nearly any spot inside the park.

Two different men entered the Herpetarium shortly after Alex and Pepper did. One man—250 pounds and six-foot-six had a blonde military crew-cut. The other man was Asian, five feet ten inches tall, and thick like a fire hydrant. Alex spotted them as he and Pepper subtlely pretended to mull in front of a king cobra exhibit.

"Don't look now, but there're two of 'em," Alex whispered. The Herpetarium was relatively calm, since most of the zoogoers, especially those inside the renovated exhibit, were unaware of the turmoil outside. There was a button in front of a display for the cobra that said, "Push me." A little girl in white sneakers, black pants and a red sweater pressed it.

"The king cobra, the largest venomous snake in the world, can grow to as long as fifteen to eighteen feet. This seven-foot rare youngster was captured in the Siwalik Hills of Punjab, India..."

"Let's walk," he said as the ominous men approached. They were looking in all directions for their prey.

Alex and Pepper moved to the next exhibit. The little girl and her classmates followed. She pushed the button again. Alex pretended to look in. Blood began to drip down his blue-denim sleeve.

"The Fly River turtle is a rare aquatic reptile from New Guinea. These pig-nosed turtles feed on tropical fruits that fall into the water from nearby trees, thus aiding in seed dispersal..."

They moved on again. The school-aged children followed. The men with the menacing guns came closer. They were inspecting everyone.

The girl, no more than eleven with a cherubic face, pushed the button.

"Another fascinating addition to the Herpetarium is the frilled lizard." The blood began dripping onto the tile floor as the makeshift bandage slid off Alex's elbow. A trail of drops followed him. "This Australian reptile boasts an amazing defense mechanism in the wild. When threatened by a predator, it fans out the large flap of skin around its neck like a collar, stands on its hind legs and runs at its enemy with its mouth open in an aggressive posture..."

Alex tried not to be too obvious. He studied the exhibit, and then assayed the Herpetarium's architecture which was decorated with sculptures depicting reptiles and amphibians.

The determined blonde man walked past Alex. He didn't notice either Alex or Pepper since they were not acting unusual. Pepper, however, was on edge. But Alex's nonchalance made up for her nervous demeanor. The stout Asian man was not that far behind.

"Hey, Mister," another of the girls said. She also wore white tennis shoes and a long pink oversized jacket. "Hey, Mister," she said again, but this time more concerned as she tugged at his sleeve.

The teacher, a cocoa-skinned Hispanic woman in her mid-thirties, interrupted. "Sarah, it's not proper to talk to strangers."

"That's okay," Alex said. He didn't want to draw attention to himself. He turned toward her, careful to avoid the Asian man's glance.

"You're bleeding." She pointed to the trail of droplets on the floor. The blonde man ahead of Alex and Pepper couldn't hear the exchange. The Asian man was right on top of them. He looked down at the trail of crimson, then lunged toward Alex.

Alex saw the assassin coming. He half-squatted back on his foot, then grabbed ahold of the Asian's left hand as it landed on his shoulder. Using the speed and momentum of the his nemesis' powerful burst, he rotated him over his hip and into the frilled lizard's Plexiglas display window.

The assassin's head went "clunk" as his face slammed into the unyielding window. He then fell headlong onto the tile floor. His limp knees hung over the usher's guard rope. He was out cold. The little girls screamed. And so did others.

The blonde man heard the shrieks and ran toward them.

"Let's get out of here!"

Alex and Pepper walked quickly with the unsuspecting schoolgirls and their chaperone. Alex tried to blend in. There were fourteen of them. They were all from St. Mary's Catholic Summer School. "Mister," the proper child said, tugging at his sleeve as Alex was quickstepping. She wasn't afraid. "You're bleeding."

"Shhhh, it's a secret," he said as he and Pepper walked briskly. "Can you keep a secret?"

"Yes."

The blood had seeped through Alex's jacket sleeve. The other assassin spotted them. They were two exhibits, with no more than fifty feet in front of him and his prey. He pulled out his weapon, a silenced Tokorov TT-33, and let off a round.

The shot pierced through the left side of Alex's jacket, grazing his rib cage and the overlying muscle. It exited the denim and shattered the giant king cobra exhibit plate glass window.

Everyone screamed. The blonde man stormed at Alex.

"Think fast," they taught him, *"Do the unexpected. Do what*

no one would think that you would do. Do the opposite."

Alex crossed over the guard rope and reached for the dead ashen branch that the deadly cobra had been roosting on. The yellow snake perched on its tail and spread its hood. Alex knew the way cobras disabled their victims—spitting poison into their eyes and blinding them. Then they'd strike.

The cobra spit its venom. It landed on Alex's newly-acquired sunglasses. Alex quickly pinched his eyes shut. He then grabbed a stick and quickly swung it under the rare king cobra's body. Simultaneously, the assassin pushed his way past the people and over the guard rope.

Alex turned with stick and venomous snake in his hand. "Catch." He flung the cobra onto the blond-haired giant. The man screamed as the cobra's fangs pierced through the skin of his face, and into his meaty cheek. He aimlessly fired a volley of six shots into the walls and ceiling.

Alex threw off his sunglasses and wiped the venom that had landed on his face onto the sleeve of his jacket. "Find me a drinking fountain, quick."

There was one just past the entranceway, inside the Herpetarium. Pepper swiftly guided him there. He buried his face into the stream of rousing cold water until most of the angry sting vanished.

"Mister," the intrepid little girl said through the rife screaming. The zoogoers were all terrified of the snakes. "Are you with the government?"

"No, not really," he answered. Alex slowly, deliberately opened his eyes. His lids had been momentarily stuck shut by the water. He then looked around for the little girl's chaperoned group. They were gone. They had run out in the midst of the lethal serpent panic. "Where're your people?"

"I don't know," the girl answered as she, too, looked for them.

"Give me your hand." Alex said.

"I'm not supposed to talk to strangers."

"You're right," Alex said as he quickly scanned the Herpetarium for additional adversaries. He knew that they had to get out of there. "My name's Alex. What's yours?" He extended his hand to shake. She grasped his paw and squeezed with all her might.

"Brenda."

"There, you see we're no longer strangers."

"I'm Pepper."

"Here." Alex lifted Brenda to his shoulders to keep her safe from snakes he hadn't seen. The three of them quickly marched out of the exhibit. They sprang with the hundreds of panic-stricken others under a railroad track bridge and out the South Gate. They blended in with everyone that was fleeing the St. Louis Zoo.

"Where's your group parked?" Alex asked the child once they crossed Wells Drive and entered the South Parking Lot. She looked around for a few moments among the exodus. Then she pointed to the far southeast corner, to a school bus. Brenda had been taught that if she got separated, that she should meet at the St. Mary's bus in the parking lot.

Alex, Pepper and Brenda slowed from a trot to a fast walk through the parking lot. Automobiles, converted vans, campers, pick-up trucks, motorcycles, and four-wheel drive vehicles were pulling out everywhere. Cop cars were ubiquitously arriving, with Alpha, Bravo, Charlie and Delta in a desperate hunt for Dr. Alex Seacourt and Pepper Knight from the skies above.

"Are you a spy?" the child asked.

"No," Alex answered as he slowed down.

"Why were those men trying to kill you?" she asked.

"I don't know."

"Men just don't try to kill you unless you're bad," she said.

"But I'm not bad."

"Then you must be a spy," she concluded.

"You watch too much TV."

"Are you?"

"No."

"Then they must have a reason."

"That's true."

"What's the reason?"

"I don't know."

"What do you think?"

"I wish I knew what to think."

They walked almost to the bus, which was churning in idle, when she asked her final question. "Are you James Bond?"

"No," Alex replied. He almost laughed.

"You look like him."

"I do?" he asked with a smile. Alex could see that the girl's St.

Mary's classmates had clustered around the lumbering school bus. So were the driver and Brenda's teacher.

"I do?" he asked again.

"Almost, except."

Heedfully he let her down, she had bucked, indicating that she wanted to walk the rest of the way, to show that she was brave and not afraid of "ugly" snakes.

"Oh, except what?"

"You have less hair," she replied.

They arrived at the bus. The thankful teacher was near tears.

"She's all right," Pepper said.

More cop cars arrived. Their sirens howled.

"We've gotta go," Alex said as they continued walking briskly, past the school kids as Brenda peeled off. They did not stop their march.

"Thank you." the teacher said.

In the backdrop Alex could hear the little girl say, "He's James Bond, he's James Bond, but without the hair. I saw him in action!"

That pissed-off Alex more that he'd like it to. Pepper could sense his aggravation.

"I think she meant that it's different."

"Different?" he railed.

"Your hair."

"I've got plenty of hair. Lots of hair." Alex ran his fingers through his meager tuft. "Leave my hair out of this."

"I think that she meant that it's…"

"It's what?"

"You know…different."

His face still stinging, now his ego was bruised.

CHAPTER 26
Space Station Mir-Kennedy I
245.49 Miles Mean Orbit

"Biologics Engineer Pokrovsky is dead. He suspected contamination of the rebreathing system, though initially I thought his concerns were overblown. How wrong I was," Maya told CIA Director Gates and Dr. Perry Johnson, Biologics Warfare Director, Mills Farm, Virgina. They'd carefully, uncompromisingly monitored the situation.

"Are you aware of the possible jeopardy?" Dr. Johnson asked.

His educational background and achievements in civilian and governmental life were unparalleled. He had schooled at Yale, Harvard and Columbia. He was Chief of Staff at Massachusetts General Hospital, then later Associate Director of the Centers for Disease Control (CDC). He had published or been an assistant or associate editor of every important medical and professional journal: *The New England Journal of Medicine, Annals of Internal Medicine, Journal of Medical Virology, Viral Immunology, Immunogenetics, Communical Disease Report*. He was the authoritative fount. He was also the CIA and NSA's top go-to man.

"Yes."

"Have you checked the lithium hydroxide crystals?"

"Already done. No signs of integrity compromise."

"Is the crew in extravehicular gear?"

"No, just me."

"I'd recommend immediate EVM."

"Consider it done," Jackson and Vrubel chimed. They were monitoring the communication from the Command Center. They got the ball rolling poste-haste.

"How much do you want me to tell..." Maya began to say.

"Tell?" Jackson garbled into his earphone with clip and microphone VOX mic as he interrupted the terse conversation between Maya and Dr. Johnson, "Goddamn everything!"

"Who's that?" Johnson asked.

"Fair question?" Maya replied.

"This is Mission Commander Scoop Jackson, and *we the hell* want to know what's going on up here!"

"I'm sorry Commander Jackson, but that information is classified," Gates said.

"This is my space station, and I'm responsible for the lives of the twelve souls up here. We've already had one death. So what's on my station?"

"The attendant condition," Gates sternly warned, "is classified. At *this time* you'll be on a 'need-to-know' basis. All I can say is that you've had an accident that has unequivocally threatened the integrity of your mission..."

"Integrity?" Jackson growled.

"Yes..."

"I'd call it murder!"

"...integrity of your mission. I, however, believe that Dr. Johnson might have a solution...but..."

"But what?" Jackson demanded.

"Dr. Johnson, explain what your premise is."

Dr. Johnson got back on line. "We've done some tests in normal Gs at Mills Farm, and I can't say that this is going to work, but we suspect that an admixture atmosphere of 10 percent nitrogen, 70 percent helium and 20 percent oxygen may abate the effects of *LAV-10*..."

"*LAV-10?*"

"Yes."

"What do you mean abate?" Jackson asked.

"By abate I mean that it should buy us another week maybe...while we work you through this...situation."

"What do you mean a week?" Maya asked.

"I mean..."

"You mean you don't have a solution, do you?" Jackson intuitively said.

"Yes....Can you do it."

There was scratchy, cryptic mumbling in the background over *Mir-Kennedy I's* TDRS uplink with Flight Engineer Shoyo and Environmental Engineer Crux.

"It'll take some jerry-rigging, but we can have it on line by 1400 hours. Is that soon enough?"

"It's gotta be," Dr. Johnson replied. He was gravely concerned.

"Do we need it space-station wide, or do you want us to localize it in X-hoop only?"

"Systematically!"

"We might have one problem," Crux said as he punched up his preliminary calculations on his IBM integrated 9Com computer, then rechecked his input numbers.

"What's that?" Johnson asked.

"I don't know how long we can hold the helium at 70 percent. I don't know if the scrubbers will handle the load for more than three hours."

"Do whatever you need to do, but do it now!" Dr. Johnson ordered.

By 1400 hours, the entire crew of *Space Station Mir-Kennedy I* was in space suits—the American, Canadian and Japanese astronauts in their NASA Extravehicular Mobility Units, and the Russians in their 231-pound Orlan-III DMAs. They each had four bottles of oxygen, each good for twelve hours. Because of the extra power requirements of releasing and maintaining the gas admixture, Jackson decided to form two teams, and to power down to bare minimums the rest of the space station. The first team would work in the Biologics Lab with Maya, and assist her in whatever research she was capable of doing. This team would consist of Shoyo, Budarin, and Smith. The seven others would work in the *Mir-Kennedy I's* Command Center.

In the interim, three pair of *asapornis persorata* birds were carefully monitored. This University of Alabama space procreation project, due to laboratory overcrowding, was moved from its original location in the Biologic's Lab to the Hydroponics Greenhouse. Plus, the crew thought that the idea of the lovebirds in the greenhouse, at least psychologically, made *Mir-Kennedy I* an aesthetically better place to live in. They were right.

It was auspicious for the space station's crew, and for Dr. Johnson and his team of clandestine Mills Farm scientists, who carefully monitored the space station for signs of contamination. The birds turned out to be a control bonus.

At 1600 hours Shoyo became ill. His first signs of sickness were nausea and dizziness, then tingling in the tips of his fingers, his toes, and in the area around the mouth. At 1657 he was too sick to stand, and a makeshift thermoplastic foam bed was made on the zero-gravity floor in Biologics. He was strapped down with bungee cords. Shivering, double-vision and vomiting began shortly after 1712 hours.

"How's Shoyo?" Jackson asked.

"Done," Maya replied.

"How much longer?"

She walked over to the jerry-built bed, and looked through his breath-fogged faceplate. His complexion had already turned turpentine-green.

"Maybe half an hour."

Shoyo overheard their conversation on his VOX microphone headset. He turned it off and looked at her concerned face. "*Yurushite agamas*," he said. She did not know that he told her that he forgave her in his ancient Burakumin tongue.

Then he died.

At 1810 hours, the first of the three sets of love birds became ill. They were a hardy species of small parrots. These particular birds were from Madagascar, and were an affectionate, close-sitting pair. They were five to six inches long, chunky and short-tailed with red bills and prominent eye-rings. Two of the sets of the lovebirds had not procreated. The last had just laid six eggs eighteen days ago. They were due to hatch in two days.

The faltering bird began squawking loudly. Then it fell backward off its birch-branched perch onto the bottom of the cage. It bounced toward its mate, gasping for air.

By 1835 hours, five of the six love birds were infected.

At 1937 hours, Solovyev alerted both Jackson and Maya that five of the six birds were dead. The last appeared to have no ill effects.

CIA Headquarters
Langley, Virgina

A disturbed President Climan was on the phone with CIA Director Gates. Dr. Johnson was on alert and his dedicated pedantic team was working feverishly on an antidote.

"Tell me what you've got," Climan said.

"It's all crap," Gates said honestly. The disappointment rang true in his voice.

"Well...how bad is all crap?"

"To start with, Mr. President, the situation on *Mir-Kennedy I* is worse than hopeless."

"What do you mean? Are we going to be able to save our astronauts?"

"No."

"Why?"

"Unless Dr. Johnson comes up with something at Mills Farm—and let me remind you Mr. President, that no one has been able to come up with *any solution* to our conundrum in the last twenty years—then we might be facing the..."

"Speak up."

"The end of the world."

"Excuse me, but did I hear you correctly? Did you say 'the end of the world'?"

"Mr. President, if Dr. Johnson doesn't come up with anything within the next twenty-four hours we need to make preparations to terminate *Mir-Kennedy I* or face possible earth contamination."

"Terminate?"

"Blow it out of existence."

"Is President Cheka aware of this situation?"

"Yes, Mr. President, Moscow is well aware...in fact it was FSB Chief Directorate Yezhov who suggested this scenario." Harlan wasn't telling the President the entire truth.

"What about the 'Armory'?"

"We've got possibly as big a problem there."

"What?"

"Well, as you know Mr. President the 'Armory' is pretty much coming down to what we had anticipated—in part a '*CIA within the CIA.*' Some of our early intelligence called it the 'Inner Circle,' but they preferred to call themselves the 'Armory'."

"How so?"

"I'd venture to say—because that's where they first started meeting—in an old National Guard Armory on the East Side of Detroit on Eight Mile Road in the early '60s."

"Who're the players?"

"It's not just CIA. At first the Armory was strictly a group of gung-ho, ultra-rightwing patriots who wanted to work outside the parameters of our directives to meet the ends of their own agenda."

"Murder for hire?"

"Later on maybe, but I think that initially they really wanted to go after bad guys like Castro and Noriega; at least after Noriega doubled-crossed them, which in turn indirectly caused us to turn up the screws on Noriega and pull the plug on his regime. Except we didn't know that it was the 'Armory' who was really behind our invasion of Panama."

"However, in the early '80s, it became apparent that there were other players that weren't of U.S. origin. It got to be big business—and my guess is they ran with whomever was willing to pay the most money. The American 'Armory' worked through the CIA. Others—the French DGSE, Korean Mafia, some KGB, some MI-6 and Chinese Foreign Intelligence Department."

"How many all told?"

"At least ninety-two. We had a contact that was playing both sides of the fence. He helped supply the Afghani rebels with arms during the Soviet-Afghanistan war."

"What happened to him?"

"Garroted four months ago."

"Why?"

"I think that whoever is behind the 'Armory' sensed that we were getting close."

"What about *LAV-10*?"

"We've got three confirmed kills, possibly a fourth."

"Who...and where?"

"Russian Ambassador Perov, Tanzania Serengeti National Park game warden Abeid Nyerere, South Korean industrialist Kim Young

Mun and a possible in Vegas not to mention Biologics Engineer Gregov Pokrovsky—and now Japanese Flight Engineer Futabatei Shoyo."

"And the tie in?"

"Mr. President, I would suspect that they're all 'Armory'—and that they've all been screwing with something that they don't know that they have. My guess is that Nyerere might have been a way point for their smuggling operations. As for the others, possibly distributors, or at least players."

"Do you think that someone is killing them off?"

"Very possibly."

"Who's the head man?"

"Don't know. My information is still very sketchy. I'm going to be meeting face-to-face with Chief Directorate Yezhovin in," he looked down at his gold Rolex with burdened, tired eyes, "three hours."

"What about Ambassador Perov and the Aeromexico Flight 900 bombing?"

"My gut is that the terrorist incident was coincidence, dumb bad luck. I know that might be a hard pill to swallow. Possibly Perov was dabbling in some shenanigans with Qaddafi and his buddies."

"Harlan...let's just suppose that you're right about Perov, Nyerere, Mun and the kill in Vegas; what if it is *LAV-10*, then what? How bad?"

"Pray it isn't, Mr. President."

CHAPTER 27

Mahalia Hunt slouched lazily in her plush United Airlines first class seat. Katrina had fallen asleep. They had been flying for nearly an hour. Mahalia had ordered a Martell cognac and had the glass brandy snifter in her right hand. She sloshed the golden French brandy in concentric circles.

The voices were gone now—at least most of the time. The doctors said that she was stuck in the narcissistic stage of her psychosexual development. They said that as a child she preferred to obtain sensual satisfaction from her own body; pleasure gained from her anal stimulation during her defecation and masturbation. They said that they couldn't determine if her problem was purely biological or partly sensual. They said that it was a form of her self-expression in which she perceived herself in a biological sex role. Other doctors said that she had a sexual ambiguity. That because of premature weaning from dependency of her mother, the culturally prescribed difference between boys and girls became blurred. Her psychosexual-stage was a muddle. Then later, there were the deeper issues and *allegations* and *recriminations* that surfaced. She told them that they were money-grubbing, parasitic charlatans. They said that she had a rare type of disintegrative psychosis. That she had a period of vague illness and mood change, and irritability with marked regression and loss of developmental landmark achievements previously acquired.

Soon after, the delusions and indications of violent behavior, even minor aggressive outbursts, were gone. They disintegrated as wafting ocean fog in the light of day.

"I have no problems. I am perfectly fine. Everything is fine. It's all behind me now."

Mahalia opened her Louis Vuitton purse. She bumped her umbrella with her Nair-slicked shin and looked out the window. Thousands of feet below was her lost life, the life that she could have had, and *would soon reclaim.*

She removed a Hoyo De Monterey Excalibur from her purse. The pale yellow tube for the handmade six and three-quarter inch cigar had the likeness of a cigar band printed on its stubby end.

The cigar was, in her mind, the best that was available. It was a marriage of English Market wrapper with Claro. Each was carefully, richly handmade and filled with precious long-filler leaf. They came in a Spanish cedar box to enhance the seasoning and taste, or in individual tubes. She preferred the tube. She also fancied her phallic cigars with her twelve-year-old Cragganmore Scotch.

The brown seal on the end of the Banquets had been broken. She worked the tube between her delicate fingers. She placed it in her left hand and with her right she raised her brandy snifter and took a sip of the cognac. She closed her eyes and remembered. Playing with the cigar tube prodded her recollection of rolling the bread pieces into balls and long cylinders to feed the hatchlings. The swallows of Capistrano. The hatchling.

"You're a good-for-nothing, piece-of-shit," Mahalia's mother screamed. Scared, six-year-old Mahalia had pressed her hands over her ears. They were clamped tight, but she could hear her anyway.

"You're worthless."

"Calm down, please calm down," he said self-assuredly.

"You're nothing. I've had your daughter for you, and now you don't want to admit to your responsibility...you scum!"

"I've never said that. Please calm down."

"You can't fool me. You might be able to deceive everyone else in this whole goddamn world, but you can't fool me!"

"Please, just settle down and let's talk this over rationally."

"*I'm going to expose you* for who you are to the entire world, and then you won't have anything. Your empire won't be worth a beggar's pot to piss in. I'm going to ruin you. I'm going to bring you down!"

"Please, please I beg you. Please reconsider." He was becoming unnerved.

"You're through!"

It was *then* that the hatchling fell out of its nest. It was *then* that the vile nighthawk swooped out of the sky with its razor-sharp talons, and engulfed the baby swallow. *Mahalia was the baby!*

It was *then* that her mother plunged off the cliff—screaming, crying, flailing for her life. Mahalia gazed down the jagged cliff's face. Her mother lay crushed below. The angry waves crashed onto the rocks, and relentless spray beat onto her rag-doll body. Blood oozed from her mouth and eyes, and a notched crack in her crushed head. Her dress, where her stomach was, was impaled with a granite spike. Her eyes were wide open, her mouth was agape. Her fists were clasped shut in rage.

Mahalia awoke from her nightmarish trance. The brandy snifter had shattered in her hand. She was bleeding. Two pear-shaped glass shards had embedded into her palm.

"Are you all right?" a stewardess asked.

"Just a little accident."

Katrina stirred, but did not awaken. They had a busy night with the software company CEO and his haughty European CFO counterpart. They had given them a show they wouldn't soon forget for the $7,500 plus a five grand tip.

"Let me get you a washcloth."

"No thank you, I'm fine."

"Please, let me..."

"Noooo!" Mahalia snarled. "Here," Mahalia said cheerfully in immediate paradox, "I've got it." She took the paper napkins on her tray top and cleaned off the blood. She removed the two glass fragments with her long french-tipped nails, and took a patterned burgundy and red Hermes scarf that she had wrapped around her neck, and tightly looped it three times around her crimson palm. She smiled at the stewardess. "Can I get some fresh napkins please...and another cognac?"

"Sure."

Mahalia looked at the tube. She had crushed it slightly. She again began working the cigar cylinder with her fingers. She knew that she was like the Buddhist...that no matter what happened to her she would be reborn, reincarnated. Her life would go from one human form to another until she reached nirvana. *It was just a matter of time.*

"What's all the fuss?" a sticky-eyed Katrina asked. She yawned.

"Nothing. I cut my hand."

"Let me see."

Mahalia crossed her right hand and placed it into Katrina's lap. Katrina was sitting in the aisle seat. Tenderly she unwrapped the Hermes scarf. Blood began to flow from Mahalia's life line in rivulets, from between her thumb and index finger to the plumb of her wrist.

"Let me kiss it."

Mahalia looked into Katrina's jeweled eyes. Katrina pressed her lips to Mahalia's palm and kissed, then vampire sucked the blood from her laceration. This aroused Mahalia. Katrina steadied Mahalia's palm. Mahalia quivered in her seat. Then Katrina gently reached over her with her left hand and ran her index and middle fingers along the inside of Mahalia's thigh.

Katrina buried her fingers into a slit Mahalia had in the dress. She worked her hand up Mahalia's naked skin to her pubic mound—and then with two fingers into her vagina.

Mahalia moaned.

Katrina delicately, tenderly played with her swollen clitoris with the nub of her thumb as she twisted and thrust her fingers into Mahalia's throbbing vault. Mahalia tremored in shuddering orgasm. Then, after Mahalia was repeatedly satisfied, Katrina rewrapped Mahalia's palm. Mahalia slid back in her plush first-class seat, and lay content. She quivered, then began kneading the cigar tube between her good fingers.

"Feel better?"

"Yes."

"I love you," Katrina said.

"I know."

Mahalia turned her head and gazed out at the flocculate clouds below. She flew in astro projection to the alabaster puffs.

Mahalia looked down at the Hoyo De Monterey tube. She pressed her cheek against the cold plastic cover over the jet's window. She tapped it on the tray top in front of her.

In her purse she had a book, *Thinking Body, Dancing Mind.* It was about positive mental perspective and good focus for a clear mind—unconscious and conscious. There was a speck of blood on its gray cover. She opened it to the prologue:

"The Great Tao extends everywhere.
All things depend on it for growth
and it does not deny them...
It clothes and cultivates all things,
and it does not act as master...
In the end it does not seek greatness,
and in that way the Great is achieved."

She was the Tao. Tao was the way, and the power.

Mahalia opened the lid to the Hoyo De Monterey. She slid onto her bandaged palm a sealed vial. Inside the double-walled test tube was a pinkish liquid. It had the consistency of maple syrup.

"I have the Tao. I have the Kiss. I have the Power."

CHAPTER 28

"So what do you think?" Alex asked as they sat down at a table far from street view at Imo's Pizza Shop on Clayton Road, two blocks from the St. Louis Zoo. He readjusted the makeshift pad that had slipped down to almost his forearm, and tightened the shredded blouse bandage.

"Are you just crazy? Let's just get the hell out of here!" Pepper growled. The day was gloomy and the overcast perfused a melancholy that increased their desperation since their escape from the zoo.

"No."

"Look Seabreeze..."

"It's Seacourt, Dr. Alex Seacourt."

"Whatever. Someone tried to kill...kill me twice now... and you lollygag over to this stupid pizza shop..." she stopped her tirade. Their server arrived.

Alex looked at the college waitress. Her make-up base was too sheer and red mounds of bee-bee shot zits sprouted through like weeds.

Alex put the finishing touches on his bandage. With the renewed pressure and the proper positioning, the bleeding stopped. "Two coffees please," he said as she handed them menus. The waitress noticed that a portion of Alex's left cheek was reddened. It looked like he had been slapped. It was from the toxic yellow cobra venom.

"How would you like them?"

"Black," he replied and then glanced at Pepper who ordered the same.

"Will there be anything else?" the waitress studied him, more curious about his combination denim jacket with no shirt underneath. Of course, all types came into Imo's.

"No, thank you."

The break was what Pepper needed. She was ready to vent and she knew better than to do it in a public place, though sometimes her emotions got the best of her.

Imo's was crowded. There were about thirty tables and all but two were occupied. The restaurant doglegged in a reverse "L." They sat all the way in the back, next to the last table. Across from them were two restrooms whose doors occasionally squealed open and shut. Behind the last table were two automatic doors with cruise ship round eye-level windows in the center. They led to the kitchen. Imo's was not really a pizza joint, it was an Italian restaurant that sold pizza.

Alex could smell the fresh garlic bread and the drifting aromas of the sizzling pizzas hot out of the brick ovens. He could savor the olive oil, the alfredo and the tomato sauces that were poured over the linguini, rotelle and tortellini. He could almost taste the fettucini, ricotta, mozzarella, and romano cheeses.

He looked at the glass dispenser with parmesan cheese that sat on their table. Its metal top had smaller than eraser-sized holes. He picked it up and shook the nearly full container. He studied the way the cheese flaked together and then separated, like late-autumn snow-flakes.

"What are you doing?"

"Thinking," he replied. The cheese was fresh and had not yet congealed into a ball. "Let me see the map."

"Sure." She pulled it out of her purse and dropped it onto the table.

Alex spun it around and scrutinized it.

"They knew we were coming."

"What?" she asked.

"The way I figure it, whoever shot at us at first was posted on top of one of those structures." Alex pointed to several buildings: the Herpetarium, the Jungle of the Apes, the Zoo Administration Building and Kiosk. "So let's assume that they were waiting for us. Why kill me?"

"Don't you think you're being a little presumptuous?" Pepper asked sarcastically. "Did you so quickly forget that someone tried to fly me into the ground?"

"Maybe, or maybe so that *I* can't talk to you or to anyone. Maybe I know something and I don't even know it."

"What do you think it is, Mr. Smartypants?"

"I don't know." And then in the recesses of his mind he flashed back to Moscow. He saw himself in the Federal Security Service Headquarters, three stories underground. He was watching a film that was translated into English on espionage techniques and terrorist tactics. He couldn't get it out of his mind. *Always anticipate the unexpected. Things are never what they seem.*

He looked past Pepper. "Maybe it's not the zoo at all. Maybe it's something different."

"Like what? The moon?"

"Let's suppose that your mail had already been gone through— then whoever tried to kill us *knew* that you had a letter from your mother with the St. Louis Zoo map. But maybe they didn't know what it meant."

"It wasn't opened. You saw the mail. It was untouched."

"Suppose I'm right, that the bad guys figured that that's where we'd go once we got the zoo brochure from your mother."

"Okay, so."

"Suppose something's in here; something's in the brochure that your mother wanted you to see, to trigger your memory."

"Yeah, like what?"

"I don't know. You tell me. Maybe...they wanted you to show them...the bad guys." He handed her back the brochure. One quarter of it was the actual map of the zoo. Another quarter was a welcome to the St. Louis Zoo with a list of attractions and a description of each exhibit and the Animal Pond and Children's Zoo show schedule. The bottom right-hand portion had a pitch to join the Zoo Friends Association and the Zoo Parents Program for forty-five dollars a year.

Inside was a description of the Herpetarium and a picture of new reptiles and amphibians on exhibit, along with a schedule of events and holiday gifts, T-shirts and animal-themed gifts that were for sale. There were creepy crawlers, slithering snakes, leaping lizards and more. There was also a photo of the Painted Giraffe Cafe in the upper rotunda of the Living World.

"Got any ideas?"

"No."

Alex closed his eyes.

"What are you doing?"

"Shhhh."

"What's with this closing your eyes stuff?"

"Shhhh." He tried to visualize Jo's house. What he saw when he was there. Nothing much was out of the ordinary. It was clean and too orderly. Everything had its exact place. The furniture was early American and didn't strike Alex as Jo's taste. Everything looked unused. It was more a museum than home.

In his mind's eye he saw himself in her study. There were photographs on the wall. It was the only room that had them. He hadn't paid much attention to them before. He tried to focus. *To be there.* There were four of them above her desk.

"Alex," Pepper said softly as she looked behind and through the restaurant to a distant street window. Two men who appeared *very government* got out of a nondescript car and walked into Imo's. They wore long trench coats and carried stern looks. "Alex," she turned and said in a louder voice.

"Shhhh." He looked at the cryptic photos. The images were blurry. There were four photos. Jo was younger in all of them. There were many men with her in three of them. They were at a University or in a hospital. The last...

"Alex!" The foreboding government types began walking through the restaurant, checking the tables. "Alex!"

The last photo was of Jo and three men and *a little girl.* One of the men was wearing something funny over his head, *something peculiar.*

"Alex!"

He opened his eyes and saw the government men.

"Let's go."

They snuck through the kitchen. They pretended that they belonged there. Abertelli, a hard-working, portly chef, said something to Alex. Alex ignored him. They exited into an alley. The buildings surrounded them in late roaring '20s terra cotta and pressed brick.

There was water in the narrow alley and full dumpsters reeking of food scraps—mostly garlic, fetid tomatoes, onions and moldy pastas. Flies buzzed overhead. The rainwater that puddled early yesterday had a film of oil that reflected the murky light.

Alex took Pepper by the hand. "Tell me about your mother," he said as she dodged divots in the alley, but slipped into a still-water puddle.

"I don't know. I really didn't...haven't talked to her for two years."

"I saw a picture in her study, when your mother was young. I presume it was with you."

"I don't know. I was raised by my father until I was 18, then I left home."

"You mean Dr. Warner."

"Yes."

"Tell me about her."

She kicked into two plastic milkcrates. She stumbled, but kept her footing. "I don't know. I saw mother a couple of times when I was very young...at work. I don't remember where. We had to drive several days though."

"Do you know who the picture was with?"

"I really don't remember."

They came to the end of the alley. They waited in the shadows at the edge of Washington Drive until a cab drove by. Pepper hailed it. They got in and drove toward Illinois. The cab was new. At least its back seat wasn't refurbished with black electrical tape.

"Beeman."

"Beeman?"

"I remember a beeman. I think I was three or four."

"Where to bub?" the cab driver asked as he approached Lindell Boulevard.

"Keep driving," Alex curtly replied.

"It's your dime."

As they drove, Pepper stared at the dingy city. It gave her the feeling that it was dying, despite the city fathers' efforts at revitalization. It brought back memories as if...I caught one on a dandelion, in my hands." She mystically showed Alex her left palm. "I got stung."

She pointed. "They were all over, the bees were everywhere."

The driver couldn't help from hearing. He looked at them in his rearview mirror with a sour smirk.

"He was an apiast?"

"A what?"

"A beekeeper. That's what I saw in the photo." Alex could dimly remember the framed snapshot above Jo's roll-top desk. The man had a white beekeeper's suit on and a netted hood that was crunched back, exposing his face. "Pull over at the first pay phone."

At Grand Boulevard and Olive Street they stopped at a pay phone. Its Yellow Pages were missing. They went down a block and found another with Yellow Pages that were intact. Alex looked up beekeeper. He found seven listings. He tore out the page and returned to the cab.

"Give me the zoo brochure."

"Sure." Pepper handed him the crinkled brochure. Alex opened it to the map and News, and then to the reverse side to the schedule of events. He scanned down the list.

"Bingo," he said.

"What?"

He pointed to August 1 through September 25. It read:

"*Honeybee Exhibit*. Visit the nation's only domesticated *Apis mellifera* exhibit. See a cross-section of their complex hive. Catch a glimpse of the three castes: workers, drones and royal honey-fed queens. Discover eggs hatching into grubs, and queens emerging from pupae."

"Take me to the nearest rental car place."

"Okay," the driver replied.

CHAPTER 29

The rocks looked like ostrich eggs. Some were covered with moss and crisscross seaweed. Their surfaces were worn except for those nearest the cliffs which were jagged granite and craggy limestone, and protruded in prehistoric spikes. Orange- and yellow-flowered iceberg plants climbed the sloping edge of the cliff as it met the spiny mono-liths. This was where she died.

In the distance, spirited elephant seals perched on two fingery outcroppings, a hundred yards into the swirling surf. A lone hoary albatross landed on its forty-foot chimney.

The seals barked like taunting dogs and rubbed whiskers in court-ship. Their coastal domain had not been ruffled by Mahalia's dead mother. Tranquility and solitude were undisturbed. Sycamore and oak trees from the hummock above cast shadows on her body. Rocky tide pools absorbed her blood without care—it was life completing its circle. The thread of her mother's epoch had come to a conclusion.

Mahalia read:

"Those who identify with the Tao

are likewise welcomed by the Tao.
Those who identify with Power
are likewise welcomed by Power
Those who identify with failure
are likewise welcomed to failure."

"I am the Tao." She said to herself. "I am the Power." She held tight the Hoyo De Monterey Excalibur tube. *"I am the Power. I am the Kiss of Death."*

He looked like a rock star type and sat in A-3 across the aisle from Mahalia and Katrina. He had an Elvis jaw with plump lips and beady eyes. His white shirt was herringbone and studded with emerald inlaid silver cufflinks. His only collar button was undone and the brim of his neckband was pulled up and bent inward slightly at his Adam's apple.

He wore a black cashmere jacket and black tweed pants, with a thin black alligator belt and silver buckle. He had blue emerald inlaid silver cufflinks. His hair was thick brown-black, cut in a ducktail, with long, mocking sideburns. The ducktail ended in a three-braided ponytail that hung over his jacket.

He had been watching them. He saw Katrina plunder her, arouse her to climax. It turned him on.

"You want to fuck me?" he said as he nudged out of his seat and bumped into Mahalia after first letting Katrina brush past him. Mahalia looked at him with vixen eyes.

"I saw you," he said. "You know."

She smiled wickedly.

"I want you." He pushed his body next to hers.

"You want to taste my cunt?" She trembled.

"Yes," he moaned.

She grabbed Katrina by her left arm and spun her around. She lifted Katrina's hand to his nose. Katrina reflexively obeyed.

"Smell her fingers."

He did. Then he planted a soft, inviting kiss on Katrina's salty index and middle fingers. He stuck out his tongue and gently lapped off Mahalia's dried essence. His bulge against her thigh grew powerful.

"I need you to take me," he said.

First class travelers got out of their seats. Some pulled down their clumsy bags from the overhead storage compartments. Others had the stewardesses bring their jackets or carry-ons to them. The coach fliers pushed forward into first class.

She reached down to his groin. She gently stroked the outline of his pulsating organ.

Then, suddenly, in an unexpected vice-grip, she seized his penis and squeezed down on it as hard as she could. She strangled the life out of it.

"Ahhhhh!" he winced in pain, his eyes flew open in agony. With both hands she clamped tight onto his organ and pulled him face-to-face. Her nose touched his, and the stale cognac on her breath passed into his mouth.

"Next time..."

"Ahhhhh!" he grimaced, his knees buckling.

"...mind your own business!"

Then she released him. Wincing, he fell back into his seat and onto the rigid armrest.

"Is there a problem?" a stewardess asked as she came over to assist them.

With a naive smile, Mahalia looked at the rock star. "No. Only a case of mistaken identity."

"What was that all about?" Katrina asked as they walked through the boarding ramp to the terminal.

"Busybody."

"Oh."

"I know this club..." she said, changing the subject. "Deep Ellum. We should go there tonight. Mance Lipscomb's playing."

"Who? What?" Mahalia's abrupt segue threw Katrina as usual.

"A blues musician. He's famous. He studied under Blind Lemon."

"Who's...Blind Lemon?"

"Never mind."

"*I thought I knew everything about you.* I didn't know you liked the blues?"

"No one knows everything about me."

Aspen, Colorado

CIA Deputy Director for Science and Technology Peter Rinerson's winter retreat was modeled after the old ranches of Colorado with a porte cochére which straddled a turn-of-the century logging road. The cedar-clad main house mellowed naturally. Hickory and cane chairs surrounded a cherry dining table, which was the first obstacle that CIA Director Gates plodded into when he entered the house through the breezeway door. The ceilings were an expensive pressed tin and something that even the Director of the CIA couldn't afford—and Deputy Director Rinerson did not come from a well-bred family.

The house was set in a heavily wooded exclusive area located in the heart of the White River National Forest, Aspen—with few neighbors, mountain views to the east and west, and an old logging road running through it. It was 10,000 square feet, and had to have cost Rinerson at least two million.

Nestled in the woods, the three-story main house was flanked by two connected cabins. The house was constructed on stone bases of a combination of board and batten and beveled horizontal siding. It looked unlike any other. The main abode had communal living spaces, while the two end units each had a suite.

"Mr. President," Gates said.

"Talk to me Harlan, talk to me."

"It's Peter Rinerson, Mr. President. He's dead."

"Where."

"At his Aspen retreat."

"How."

"Same as Perov, Mun and Nyerere."

"*LAV-10?*"

"Yes..." A self-realizing chill ran through Gates' body. He knew that if Rinerson was in on this, it was bad. Real real bad. "They have a vial."

"Jesus!"

"I've got a team on it now," he said as he walked around the front of Rinerson's logger's desk. "We've got a neighbor who ID'd Perov, Mun, Nyerere, and an unidentified man and woman in Rinerson's house three days ago. His name's Travis Clark. He's a country music singer of some repute. Seems reliable."

"But wasn't Ambassador Perov in Mexico City then?"

"Yes, that's the kicker. But it's possible Perov could have doubled back here by private jet and used Mexico City as an alibi. Also, Clark admits he did some wild partying, did some serious boozing. So his times might be screwed up."

"How much could he be off?"

"Well, he's still got alcohol on his breath, and apparently had a big weeklong Hollywood shin-dig during that time. So in reality, it could have been as long as six days ago, which could have put Perov in Aspen and then later in Mexico City. In any event, I'm tracking down his guests. Apparently half the city... and Tinsel Town was here."

"See what you can come up with."

"Yes, Mr. President."

"What about the unidentified man and girl?"

"I'm still working on that, but I've got a hunch on the man."

"And the girl?"

"Nothing."

"My agent's feeling on Clark's take is that she was a hooker. Younger than the others."

"Hooker?"

"Maybe, but I'll talk to Clark myself."

"What about *LAV-10?*"

"In Rinerson's study we found a *Hoya De Monterey* humidor, in a safe behind a Renoir."

"Cigars?"

"Yes, a humidor, but with a false bottom. It had two compartments. In one was a double-sealed glass vial labeled X23 *LAV-10B.*"

"What does that mean?"

"It means, as the name implies, a sealed, fracture-proof test tube with X23 *LAV-10B*—which in turn was resealed in a second fracture-proof test tube."

"Two vials?"

"Yes..." Gates regretfully said. The cederwood cigar box in the hidden compartment had a green felt interior, and was divided in two by a wooden half-height riser. "We suspect there was also an A, as in X23 *LAV-10A* and X23 *LAV-10B.*"

"What about the Mills Farm records of TTLV-1?"

"We've still tracking them down, but our records indicate there's no shortage at Mills Farm—but if Rinerson's involved, I wouldn't be surprised if he walked out undetected with a vial or two."

"Then how..."

"*Mir-Kennedy-I.*"

"Shit."

"Yeah, that's what I say."

"The deaths?"

"My guess is that *X23 LAV-10B*'s outer seal was violated."

"Any problem with exposure?"

"No. If the outer seal was violated, and subsequently resealed, the exposure window would have been immediate—at least that's what Dr. Johnson thinks at Mills Farm—that *LAV-10B* is fomite or vector borne."

"Vector borne?"

"Vector borne means that it spreads via object contact."

"I thought all *LAV-10* was airborne."

"I'm not sure. But either one of two things—*X23 LAV-10B* might be different than A. There is a possibility the B self-extinquishes after twenty-four hours, or there was direct contaminate on the outside of the inner vial. I don't know. However, we're pretty sure if there is an *LAV-10A, it's airborne.*"

"What's the bottom line?"

"*LAV-10* has two problems: The first is immediate death due to organic cyanide bonding within twenty-four to forty-eight hours. I think that that's what we saw in Rinerson, Perov, Mun and Nyerere. To be frank though, Mr. President, this is all just a guess. We really don't have any definitive data on what the hell happened—at least why there was no airborne exposure and all of Aspen wasn't wiped out."

"And Dr. Johnson agrees with you?"

"Like stink on shit."

"And the second problem?"

Gates inhaled deeply through his flaring nostrils, then sighed. "If there's another vial out there, and my gut tells me there is...and if it's ever opened...aside from within a Biosafety Level Four lab, it's *our Judgment Day.*"

CHAPTER 30
Outside St. Louis, Missouri

This was the last stop that Alex and Pepper would make. They had hit six of the seven beekeepers in the St. Louis area. They had traveled north to the shores of the Mississippi to Alton in Illinois, then rambled west to Troy, motored south to Defiance and Chesterfield, and then spun farther west to Mount Sterling, Ownsville and finally to Cuba.

Cuba, Missouri was on Interstate 44, twenty-six miles east of sprawling Rolla, where the University of Missouri was nestled on the return trip east to St. Louis. They had driven nearly 150 miles over the last several hours, not to mention their fruitless pit stops at each apiast. Nightfall was quickly approaching as the sun huddled beneath the resplendent Ozarks.

The cogs within Alex's muddled brain were rapid-fire clicking as he studied the Budget Rent-A-Car road map.

They had procured the vehicle in downtown St. Louis. It was the second one that he had rented this day—but for this car he paid cash, so that there'd be no record. Still concerned about being discovered, they shopped at a secondhand store and bought a pullover and baggy pants for Pepper. Alex found himself a faded lumberman's shirt with a torn pocket.

Something about the erudite University of Missouri and nearby Cuba seemed to have an ironic twist about it. "I don't remember a thing," she said. She was already weary. "It was so long ago. I was just a child."

"So why didn't you see your mother more often?"

"She didn't want me."

"I don't understand."

"What do you mean?"

"I just don't read her that way...as not wanting you."

"No, Alex...I do!"

It was nearly sunset when they rolled up to the last beekeepers. It was south of Cuba on State Road 19 toward Onodaga Cave. They followed a gravel road for another two miles until they came upon Tate's Honey Farm.

A lumbering oak stood midway between the country road and a decrepit two-story farmhouse. The white picket fence that enclosed only the house and small yard was chipped and faded. Slats were missing, or were windblown and cracked. A brown and white cocker spaniel was yapping on the porch. Matted hair covered its face, and burrs were embedded into its scruffy underbelly.

In the distance was a three-wheel tractor in disrepair. Attached to it was a twelve-arm till rusted solid. A small drive wandered beyond the tractor toward row upon row of manmade hives, with honey-filled "supers" resting on top of each hive. The lower hives were where the bees entered and left. Young were raised in the bottom level or "broad chamber" and honey was stored in the upper food chamber. There had to have been at least 400 hives.

A six-wheel semi-truck and large flatbed was parked on an angle on the dirt drive. Wooden, grooved "fit-tights" had been mounted into the flatbed. The honey hives would slide into the horizontal slots and were lashed down. Tate's Honey Farm would ship the hives throughout Missouri and Illinois, and sometimes into Texas to pollinate apple orchards, cherry trees and cotton cash crops.

An old man with short black hair, a shaggy dark brown and gray beard, and a pear-shaped body in tattered overalls, was hammering at a honeybee hive. He stood next to the barn that was equally in disrepair. He had several three-penny nails in his mouth.

"Is this Tate's?" Alex asked. Pepper stood behind him but was tentative as the bees danced too close to her in the tepid early evening air. The thick prairie grass and dried fameflower stalks brushed against her legs at knee-level, and made her nervous—as if they were a swarm of bumblebees ready to sting.

"It is..." he mumbled with nails in his jowl. He spit them onto the board that he was pounding, which lay perpendicular on a saw-horse. He stood up instead of hunching, and extended his grimy paw to shake. Alex did so reluctantly.

"We're looking for someone who might have known Dr. Joanna Knight, about twenty years ago. She might've worked here."

"Can't say that I do."

"Tall lady, 'bout five-seven"..."

"Had long brownish-blond hair," Pepper interjected. A small ladybug landed on her forearm. She jumped and brushed it off.

"Not been here twenty years," he said as he spit a disgusting wad of Bandit chewing tobacco in front of Alex's feet. The gesture was hostile. Tate carefully eyed the girl. "That would have been my brother. Died of a heart attack 'bout...six years ago. I took over then...me and the Missus." He spit another bullseye wad at Alex's footing. "Now if you don't mind, I've got work to do."

"Yeah sure. Sorry for bothering you." Alex uncharacteristically backed off. He turned and began walking back to his car. Pepper followed him. Tate reached into his pocket and pulled out the long-cut tobacco. He removed a fresh squeeze of the chew, rolled it in a cigarette butt-size wad, and packed it between his cheek and lower teeth on the right side.

Alex had a feeling Tate wasn't telling him the truth. Halfway to the car he stopped. He turned and reapproached Tate. He had planned his move. Pepper slowed her stride and started to turn, but then came to an unexpected standstill. A forty-five year old oak tree's branches spread over the weed and wild grass infested lawn. A rope swing hung from a convulsing branch. Bark had engulfed one of the rope ties. It had overgrown it twenty years earlier.

"Uh, uh," Alex cleared his throat deeply. "Is it possible...that your brother might have mentioned or said anything about a Dr. Knight?" The gruff beekeeper turned to only partially face Alex. He continued working. "Could there be any records, anything in your files? Maybe she was a client? You rent bees for pollination don't you?"

"Look bub, I said no." He spit.

"I'll pay," Alex said now even more sure that Tate knew something. "It's worth a couple hundred."

"Leave!"

"You want more. This is a matter of..."

The man put down his hammer a second time. "I got a 12-gage, Mister. It's loaded and this is private property. Get my drift?"

Alex stared at the man. Undaunted, Tate chewed his tobacco more fiercely. He spit again. He adjusted the super he had been working on, and then walked toward the house. Alex followed him.

"I'll make it worth your while." Tate did not answer. "Name your price." Still no reply. In his peripheral vision Alex saw Pepper fixed where he had last left her. "How much?"

Tate bumped briskly through the foxtail, in a short-cut to the rickety house. He clambered up the creaky porch and flung open the screen door.

"It's important." Alex did not follow Tate into the house.

Tate did not answer. Noises from inside echoed through the screen door. Alex heard sounds of a man's hands fumble through a tool drawer, recklessly searching for cartridges.

"I know you know," Alex yelled. He listened for a response. Then he heard the drawer slam, and the metallic sound of a shotgun being breached. Tate had found his shells. Alex ran to the car.

Tate emerged with the Remington pump action under his left arm. It was cocked open at ninety degrees. Dual barrels bore down on the plank deck.

By the time the first shot was fired Alex had nearly reached the car. Buckshot pelted in a tirade, but was low and right into the dirt.

"Come on, let's get out of here," Alex yelled at Pepper. Her gaze as well as her body was planted on the oak-tree swing. "Come on," he yelled as he ran past her.

The gun's report startled her out of her trance. She turned to look at Tate, who was more than a hundred yards away. She could just make out the surprise on his face that he had missed. She then twisted and ran to the car.

Pepper jumped into the Buick at the same time Tate fired his second round of buckshot. Several pellets struck the hood, denting the brushed metal. Others cracked into the upper righthand corner of the windshield just above Pepper's head. It left a crack in the glass that spread instantaneously in a spider web to the rearview mirror mount, and then down to the center heater vent.

Alex quickly started the engine and threw the vehicle in reverse.

"I've been here," she said out of breath.

"What?" Alex yelled, more immediately concerned about their retreat and safety, than her past-life recollections.

"When I was a child," she said. "I swung in the swing. I remember."

Alex quickly scanned his rearview mirror. He jammed the car into the first leg of a "U-turn," then threw it into drive and slammed his foot all the way down on the accelerator. Gravel spit up in a dust cloud.

Tate had reloaded and let out two more volleys. They fell short of their mark.

"When I was a child, maybe four, I swung on it. I remember the rope creaking and catching a bee. It landed on the lawn, on a dandelion. It was green then, there were no weeds. I caught it between my hands, and picked it off the dandelion. It stung me. I remember."

Alex glanced at her quickly as he steered a sharp left, swinging the car onto the paved road. The rear wheels slipped around, then waggled even.

"He knows something."

"No kidding."

"We were at the right place?"

"Yes."

"I know, I know that man..." she said.

Alex looked at her without a fraction of doubt.

"He was younger, without the beard. It was a long time ago, but I know him."

As they barreled at 90 mph, Alex saw it whiz by. It was two miles down the road in the opposite direction from which they came. He slammed on his brakes. Wild wheat and thistle hid a corner of the paint-chipped sign. It sat forty yards past a three-stranded barbed wire fence. A small metal placard hung from the top line of barbed wire. It swung back and forth in the wind, "*Do Not Trespass. Violators will be Prosecuted.*"

A corner of the metal sign bent down on itself. It was twisted and weatherworn. Wind rustled Johnson grass and fescue against the faded letters. Set back nearly three-quarters of a mile, was a ponderous, two-story factory with no windows, save for a few on the smaller second story. They appeared to be offices. The plant along the road for nearly a quarter-mile. Isolated in its northern Ozark farmland oasis, the peculiar building was an albatross.

Fate had sent Alex scurrying down the highway in the *wrong direction*. Haste to escape the crazed Tate in the opposite direction from which he came, led him to his kismet: *Inveco Chemicals*.

"This is Tate," the tobacco-chewing apiast snarled over the telephone to the man in St. Louis. "I tried to stop the bastard, but he got away."

The man on the other end barked orders to Tate. "Don't worry," Tate said in reply, "I know where they went. And just remember one thing...nobody's ever gotten away."

Tate slammed down the receiver and placed two more calls. One was to the east coast, the other to the sheriff's office in Cuba.

CHAPTER 31
Space Station Mir-Kennedy I

There was still hope that the astronauts might survive. Commander Jackson worked his way from Control Center through the Kristall module and into X-hoop and Biologics. He had acclimated better than most to the weightlessness. It was second nature to him.

"So what's the scoop, Scoop?" Maya asked in a sardonic Moscovite voice as she bent over her video monitor. She studied the computer-generated results of a classified reactant that she had chemically combined with *LAV-10*.

"Nothing," he replied. "Switch to T/R (transmit and receive) intercom two."

She toggled a rocker switch on the communications control unit attached to the wrist of her Orlan-III DMA space suit, and went to channel two. "Where, I've gotta ask, in all seriousness did you get that name, Scoop?" she asked as she continued to carefully watch the video screen, while simultaneously manipulating two robotic arms behind the previously hermetically sealed biologics chamber.

"It's not what you think."

"Then let me guess. High school at a soda fountain. You were a *jerk*," she said with a touch of sarcasm. "You were the king ice cream scooper."

"No, not really."

"Where, then?"

"Don't be coy."

She stopped working for a moment and turned to face him. The glare of the overhead light bounced off his visor, and into her discerning eyes. Only his nose, mouth and chin were visible.

"Were the words too strong?" she said.

"Earlier?"

"Yes, earlier."

"Love?"

"Yes..." he said with deliberation. "Maya, I just think that it's hard for me to...express my feelings," he said as he pensively placed his glove on her shoulder. The aluminized mylar space suit wrinkled with his firm touch.

"Not me." She continued her gaze. She imagined his reticent eyes beneath the reflection.

Uncomfortable, he turned and faced the video screen. "I was editor of the *Warrior Update*. I broke a story that I shouldn't have."

"How so?"

He remembered with regret. "I was eager to make a name for myself. There had been a long standing rumor that the Food Service Director was taking kickbacks. You know it was one of those dumb things that cadets complain about. I think that everyone disparaged the food, all the time, even though it was really pretty good. Anyway, there were some money problems one year when Congress was late in passing its military appropriations bill. A secretary had been fired from Food Service for ineptitude and chronic tardiness. She had been written up several times, and finally after her fifth write-up she was canned. Well, this was before the days of the E. E. O. C. and there wasn't much that she could do...."

"What?"

"...so..." He stopped to reflect. "I spoke with her. She was bitter and would have bad-mouthed anyone. She told me that Lt. Col. Palmer, that was his name—Palmer something... I don't remember—had taken home a couple of whole hams on Christmas. No big deal, huh?"

"I suppose not. But it was stealing wasn't it?"

"Yes it was. Well...I ran a story without further looking into the veracity of her accusations. Front page that Palmer had been pilfering from Food Service. And as a result of which, there was a serious investigation and he was terminated and brought up on charges. He almost ended up going to Leavenworth prison. He lost his family and house over the whole ordeal, and ended up moving out of Colorado Springs. The story was later picked up by the wire services and papers across the country.

"The funny thing is, that sure he took the hams and he shouldn't have, but he had given them to the Salvation Army to feed the homeless. They were surplus. They would have been thrown out. That never came out in the press. Also, after the military tribunal concluded their investigation, it turned out that Palmer had run a tighter shop than anyone had imagined—and had actually saved the Academy money."

"So you screwed up."

"I did."

"And that's how you got that name, Scoop."

"Yeah. Everyone thought that I was the big hero. In reality, I probably ruined an honest man's life."

"But he shouldn't have taken the hams?"

"No, he shouldn't have. But his motives were unselfish and good."

"How could you have known?"

"I couldn't."

Behind him, several minor components of scientific equipment, laboratory tools and hardware floated past him, including an electromagnetic inducer, Ku-band communication adapter, a zero-G three-axis wimble brace, a carbide beam kinetic energy discharger, and a tungsten inert gas, handheld plasma arc vacuum accelerator, among others. Though the equipment in the Biologics Lab had been secured earlier, with decompression they had been liberated. Tool Specialist Budarin and Spacewalker/Pilot Randall Smith were securing the last of the errant apparatus.

"So what's the prognosis Maya?" Scoop asked.

"No better than before."

"Are you making progress?"

"No."

"Has the artificial atmosphere helped at all—the 10/70/20, the nitrogen, helium, oxygen?"

"No."

"So what's the plan?"

"I don't know."

"Are you going to tell me?"

It was then that Flight Engineer Nikoloy Solvyev broke in on VOX intercom channel two from the *Mir-Kennedy I* Command Center. "Comrade Mukhina, I've got General Peterson at Houston Control on line, and he's tied in with Dr. Johnson at Mills Farms, Virginia. They want you now."

"Thank you, Nikoloy." Maya toggled her communications rocker switch to VOX air-to-ground channel one.

"Houston Control this is Biologics Engineer Mukhina, over."

"Biologics Engineer Mukhina, this is Dr. Johnson at Mills Farm, Virginia. Do you read me?"

"I do. How are you Dr. Johnson? Any progress?"

She switched her Biologics Lab real-time video monitor to split screen with Johnson Space Center Houston Control on the left, and Dr. Perry Johnson at Mills Farm, Virginia on the right. "Any success with the tri-gas atmosphere?"

"None. In addition, I tried amyl nitrate, Kelocyanor, amantadine, ribavirin, interferon, acyclvir, and PAM (Pralidoxine Chlorided). Nothing. Do you have any suggestions."

"What about the love birds?"

"Five of the six died. The sixth doesn't show any imminent signs of illness."

"Is that a good sign?"

"It's too early to tell."

"Have you thought about an autopsy on any of the dead birds."

"Yes, but I'm afraid if I do that I might cause another nexus for contamination. Plus, I don't have the equipment up here."

"What about a blood sample from the healthy bird."

"I'm ahead of you on that. Already ran one and nothing. No signs of cellular lysis, heterophil agglutination, elevated differential WBC count, or bright red venous blood."

"Biologics Engineer Mukhina, we have reason to believe that *LAV-10* might, though only in microscopic amounts, bind with the mylar on the space suits."

"I know, that's what Pokrovsky thought."

"Good, at least we're thinking along the same lines."

"And that would be the NASA suits only?"

"Yes, but we have to assume similar contamination of the Russian Orlan-III DMA's, though I know they're not constructed out of mylar, but rather semi-rigid latex-rubber and monopolymer synthetics."

"I see."

"So..."

"So," Jackson broke in, *"you're saying that we can't come down. Is that correct?"*

"I'm not *exactly* saying that, but I am saying that we have priority concerns about earth environmental contamination."

"Do you realize that we're living off the oxygen packs in our space suits—and that we only have roughly," he did some quick calculations with a wax pencil on a plastic note pad on his left sleeve, "Twenty-two hours?"

"Yes."

"So you're telling me/us, that if we can't resolve the situation with the 10/70/20 nitrogen mix, or whatever solution or reactant we come up with...then this is our grave."

Dr. Johnson reluctantly cleared his throat and succinctly answered. "Yes."

"So," Jackson said in an upbeat demeanor to Maya, "guess that we need to come up with something."

"That's affirmative," General Peterson replied. Houston signed off and the screen went dark. Maya switched back to her microscopic field.

"So what are our chances?" Jackson asked. He knelt down next to Maya, who was sitting. He took her by both shoulders and turned her to face him. He held her tight. He wanted to say that he loved her. He wanted to badly.

"Between slim and none," she said.

His mind was on fire. Jackson would not accept "slim and none." He stood and said, "That won't happen." This time he repeated his pronouncement to the entire crew on the T/R channel one VOX mode. "This is *Mir-Kennedy I* Mission Commander Scoop Jackson, and you bastards heard what the man said at Houston Control. This *ain't* going to be our goddamn grave. We *ain't* going to quit, and we *ain't* going to die! And that's an order!" There was no immediate response—except for silence.

"Commander Jackson," Smith said, "switch to two." Jackson

bruskly did. "Commander, what if...and I'm just saying hypothetically, that we decide to abandon the space station and return to earth? All of us."

"Randall, we're not..."

"Please hear me out Commander."

"Go on."

"Let's just suppose, hypothetically, we decide to abandon *Mir-Kennedy I*. We have the Soyuz TM29, which can be used as an ERV (Emergency Reentry Vehicle). Three cosmonauts can return in it. The shuttle *Orion* has a flight capacity for seven. We can jerry-rig it for one more astronaut easy. I can do the modifications."

"And where would we go if what Houston Control says is true...that we have *LAV-10* on our space suits?—that if we land we'll contaminate earth?"

"Just hypothetically, let's say that we *can land* at one of the remote landing sites, for example the second alternative landing site at White Sands Space Harbor, New Mexico. It's isolated enough."

"It's a possibility if..." Jackson replied. His wheels began to turn. There might be an alternative.

"What about our space suits?" Maya asked. She had been listening in.

"What about them?" Tool Specialist Budarin interjected. He too was on channel two.

"What? Is everyone eavesdropping on our conversation?" Jackson asked.

"I guess so," Vrubel replied in contemptuous Russian.

"Well," Jackson said, "let's just all go to fricking channel one and party this one out—and come up with a goddamn solution."

"Sounds reasonable to me," Maya replied. "But there are a lot of problems. First we would need to land in a completely isolated area. White Sands Space Harbor might not be the place..."

"Then where?" Spacewalker/Pilot Smith interrupted.

"I don't know. Let me continue."

"Sure," he replied sarcastically.

"Second, we'll need the cooperation of both Russian and American governments to ensure that we are immediately placed into Biosafety Level 4 Decontamination. For example, the shuttle *Orion* and *Soyuz* can be shrouded in an airtight Kevlar 29 or Cordura vinyl-only Level 11A tent. We can be given oxygen refills, and I'm sure some sort of airlock can be arranged so that we can get out of our contaminated space suits. I think by..." Maya rattled off a litany of scenarios and solutions. They all seemed vaguely possible.

"Well," Commander Jackson said, "we've got a mandate to save our lives. Let's get to work on a solution. Now!"

However, Jackson knew different. He had been with the Air Force and NASA long enough. He had worked with the *unyielding political types*. Those in political power would never let them come down, no matter how "airtight" their solution. Nevertheless, the crew of *Mir-Kennedy I* needed to solve the *LAV-10* mystery in space...*or die*.

CHAPTER 32

"What do you think?" Alex asked Pepper. They had about a half-hour of daylight left. Already the sky was fading and streaks of golden evening were transforming into surreal night.

Entry into Invenco had been a puzzle at first. Alex supposed that the guard had been let down once the building had been abandoned. Fifteen years had passed since the structure had last been occupied.

After twice walking the circumference with no apparent way in, he found a drainpipe affixed to the building's rear wall that looked climbable. They scaled the wall using the pipe as a ladder. Once on the second floor, they worked their way on a narrow ledge to the building's front. That's where the only accessible windows were. They entered a second floor office by breaking a double-paned window using a jack handle Alex brought with him from the car.

"I don't know what you expect to find," Pepper said as she checked for a light switch. She found one, but there was no power. "I don't remember this place at all, nor my mother ever mentioning an Invenco."

"I'm sure that's what she was telling me on the tape. '*Iv*' something was Invenco."

"Are you positive?"

"Yes... and you said you remember the swing?"

"I do."

"Tell me about it," Alex said as he walked from a large vacant office into another. The floors had lift-up panels. Underneath, at one time, ran throaty-gauge computer wiring. Thousands of miles of cable had been laid. It was gone now. Several panels, in what appeared to be random locations, were either missing or pushed away from their resting place. The remains of an evisceration were all that was left: connectors, conduits, females for male-to-female plug connectors.

In the next room, covering at least four-thousand square feet, there appeared a semicircle-shaped impression sticking out four feet from under the wall. There were no windows. Alex was able to see the impression only from what fading light remained of the day. More places for panels in the floor were coverless. Most terminated at the head of the "C." At least four panels were removed in a cluster at the very center of the "C."

In the middle of the room he could see two faint parallel indentations that were six feet in width and twenty feet long. "What was this place?"

Pepper tapped Alex on the shoulder. He jumped.

"I found something," she said.

"Look at those dents," Alex pointed. At first she couldn't see, but after her eyes accommodated they became obvious. "Computers. There were massive computers in here." She agreed.

"Come with me," she said.

They walked down two hallways where it was brighter than where they had been, then down a stairwell. The light was extremely dim, but enough came in through a dingy skylight in the chamber they were about to enter, that their trek was navigable.

"What do you make of this?"

It took Alex a few minutes for his eyes to readjust to the different degrees of light and darkness.

The chamber was enormous. It looked like they were inside a nuclear reactor, but it wasn't. The vaulted room rose the entire two-story height of the building, then descended at least four stories into the ground. It occupied most of the circumference of the structure. In the center was a huge pendulum device that rotated 360 degrees and was at least forty feet in length. The base of the pendulum resembled an oblong two-story building set on its side.

Porthole windows, at two different levels, peered out of the bizarre container. The end that was farthest from the axis meshed with the curvature of the wall, and rode on two sets of massive black parallel wheels that ran flush with the cylinder.

"What the hell is that?"

"I have no idea," Alex said.

"It looks like something out of an outer space movie."

Alex studied the puzzling structure. "It looks like a room set on its side and centrifuged." He looked more carefully. Wires and cables egressed the top of the container and worked their way up the pendulum axis. There was also piping that left the structure and fed into the axis.

Alex looked for a way down the parapet, but there was none. Apparently, he surmised, the entrance into the room was at the base where the pod had came to rest. "Any way down there?"

"I'd imagine, but I can't see in this dark." Night was quickly approaching. They had only minutes of daylight left.

When the first of two Hellfire ATGMs (air-to-ground missiles) fired from one of two Bell 04-58D Kiowa Warrior attack helicopters, it blew the roof off the 100,000 square-foot building, and a hole the size of Cleveland out of the rear wall. They were thrown eighty feet into a water-recovery slush pond that was immediately behind the rear retaining wall. Had that tarry cesspool not been there, they would have been dead.

Alex was stunned. He had shrapnel embedded into his right shoulder, but the wound was only superficial. It was the air pressure wave of the percussion blast, and not the fiery explosion from the Hellfire ATGMs, that had propelled them.

Pepper, who had flown farther and landed harder, had momentarily lost consciousness, but quickly came to after a slap on the cheek from Alex.

In the past Pepper had skydived to within microseconds of her death, she had pushed her mortal envelope to its absolute limits—but those risks were at her own beckoning. They were calculated. Being hurled nearly one hundred feet by an air-to-ground missile designed to vaporize them, terrified her.

Yet...as a pro, she wasn't going to show Alex her vulnerability. She was "Pepper Knight," nothing scared her. At least until now.

"Run!" Alex yelled as he dog-paddled in the rancid mush, and pulled her with him as they swam out of the polluted recycling pond.

Two more rocket blasts engulfed the building and annihilated it, incinerating the remnants of Invenco.

The night and the crematory flash were their allies. They scrambled through the waist-high quack grass and mullein, and stumbled onto a rutted dirt road overgrown with foliage. Inactivated trip wires and sensors were all that stood between them and freedom.

Pepper stumbled across the first of the low-lying strands. She lurched forward and fell onto the palms of her hands. Small rocks and pebbles scraped into her flesh. A few embedded themselves into the skin. It was by the grace of God that she had fallen.

The first reconnaissance Bell OH-58D Kiowa Warrior helicopter, with its mast-mounted sight housing TV and IR optics and laser designator/range finder, was blinded by the conflagration. However, as the inferno subsided, the Bell OH-58D scouted for survivors. Alex was still out of visual range due to the continuing structural flames. Pepper was not.

When the spotter had scanned her position she had just hit the deck. He dismissed the image as "insignificant" nocturnal wildlife. Her "down on all fours" image gave her the appearance of a predatory quadruped as opposed to human, at least until the incendery glow subsided.

Alex, who was twenty feet ahead of Pepper when she had fallen, could hear teams of men with high-powered sniper and assault rifles scouring the debris and grounds. Though they were over three-thousand feet away, he estimated that there had to have been at least twelve vehicles, and at the minimum twenty men. Two of them, for sure, were police cars. He could faintly see the red-and-blue lights mounted on the vehicle's roofs—and that was only on the east side of what was left of the blazing building, not in front.

"They've sent the whole fucking world after us," she said as Alex helped her regain her footing. He quickly cleaned off her hands, and

removed several stones embedded in them. She stood passively, looking into his exhausted eyes. "What did you do Alex? What?"

"And you?"

"Maybe I have nothing to do with this," she said as she faltered
to her feet and brushed herself off. "Maybe it's because of where you
were going with what you know, but don't know."

That got Alex thinking again. In an instant he remembered the
autopsy. He saw the cadaver and the large from-neck-to-pubis "Y-
section" Jo made. He remembered the mothball smell and Jo pulling
back the scalp and cutting open the cranium and removing the brain.
gelatin-like translucent cerebral-spinal fluid had leaped into his senses.
"Why an ELSIA test? What does this have to do with AIDS? Then it
dawned on him. The sludge pond, *it smelled like mothballs!* He lifted
his hands to his face. Pungent odors penetrated his cerebrum. The
smell was different but very similar to the cadaver.

"Over there," one of the men yelled, as he scanned the vast field
looking for survivors. "Over there." He pointed to 3,260 feet north
by northwest and the infrared silhouettes of two humans. He barked
orders into his palm-held radio. Spotlights beamed in Alex and Pepper's
direction.

"Let's get out of here," Alex shrilled over the roar of the helicopters.

They ran three-quarters of a mile. They flew over a wooden fence
to the nearest farm. The two helicopters and all-terrain vehicles rapidly converged. The cars split into two contingents. Half followed as
far as they could through the field, the other half doubled back to the
main road and were directed by radio.

When they arrived at Mortenson's Dairy Farm, Kaleb Mortenson
had just finished supper. He was standing on the porch with his fifty-
year-old, cow-milking wife to see what "the racket was all about."

The sky was luminescent with flames, which leapt 150 feet above
Invenco's previous roof.

"What the hell's going on?" the missus asked as she stood dumbfounded from the stoop beyond her porch, then stepped down onto
Mother Earth. Four sedans squealed up to the house, then slid to a
halt, swirling dust in a cloud.

"Come out," a man commanded through a megaphone. Four

men, each in flack jackets, stormed out of each of the sedans. M16 A1 assault rifles were brandished.

The leader and two thugs rushed the house. "Where are they?"

"I have no idea..." Kaleb said as a man slammed his M40 rifle butt into his stomach. Kaleb bent over in agony, gasping for breath.

"Where are they?" the sortie leader demanded. He wore Ray-Ban sunglasses, even in the twilight. Two other men arrived. They pinned Mortenson's wife's arms behind her back. The leader lifted up Kaleb's head and again asked, "Where are they?"

"I have no idea what you're talking 'bout."

The leader backhanded Kaleb. The man wore rings that were deliberate weapons that had been crafted with vicious, tearing points. Bloody grooves left their mark in a mangle on Mortenson's face.

"One more time...Where are they?"

"I have no idea who you're talking about. I swear to..." But before he could finish, the leader gun-butted his wife in the jaw with the barrel of his silenced Tokorov-TT.

"Over here," a man yelled in the distance. One of the plunderers had spotted the two with their infrared heat detectors.

"Hold 'em!" the leader ordered.

"Jesus, they've found us," Pepper said, peering through the cracks of the wooden barn that was adjacent to the house and was connected by a maplewood breezeway. All lights converged on them. Alex knew that they were not safe, not safe anywhere until they took some kind of action. He needed to make them...

"What are you doing?" Pepper frantically asked.

"I'm getting us out of here," Alex replied as he began pumping kerosene out of a 95 gallon cylinder that was strapped to a support wall. He handcranked the fuel into two five-gallon gasoline containers that stood next to the kerosene tank. "Give me a hand."

Bullets ricocheted into the barn. Alex filled the plastic containers to their brim, then stuffed a rag down the top of one. In the center of the barn was a John Deere tractor with a glass-enclosed driving cab. Alex spilled the kerosene in the unclosed container onto the cab floor, then set the sloshing receptacle upright onto the floor next to the clutch pedal. The other he strapped into the center-mounted driver's seat.

"Find me some matches, quick."

Pepper knew what Alex had in mind. Alex quickly scanned the instrument panel, the engine throttle, three-point hitch, electrohydraulic SCV's, PTO's and sixteen-speed power shift transmission—and fortunately found a key in the ignition. He tried to start the Deere. It wouldn't fire up.

Bullets rained through the barn's walls. Wood-cracking pops filled the air. The driver's windshield was penetrated four times, but did not shatter.

"Got it," she said. In her hand she had a welder's striker. Alex shoved the makeshift wick into the five-gallon's opening, then pulled out the kerosene drenched rag. On first flick sparks flew from the flint. The rag burst into flames.

Alex turned the ignition key again. The tractor wouldn't start. "Damn!" he yelled as he watched the fuse burn down. Again he tried it. Nothing.

Men had arrived at the barn's entrance. He could hear bloodthirsty voices through the gunfire. A second, then third time... then he figured out that he needed to push the clutch in to disable the ignition override. The tractor fired up.

Alex threw the mud and rain-spattered John Deere into second gear and jumped off the running platform searching for cover. The tractor rammed the barn doors into a hailstorm. Less that ten feet past the wooden entrance it was hit by an M47 Dragon tube-launched missile that blew its left front wheel off. Within a quarter of a second the kerosene bomb exploded. It rocked the barn and killed six sortie agents. The front of the structure was demolished, and what was not blown up was set ablaze.

The evil leader gazed through his Ray-Bans and smiled as he saw the cropland tractor disintegrate into a molten heap. He looked at the Mortensons that his men were holding. "Kill them," he said.

CHAPTER 33

Alex and Pepper hid in a corral with the cattle. They were crammed in with 181 Guernseys in a ninety-by-ninety pen. The sortie team's ANIAVS-8 GEN III "near" infrared heat detectors were not effective amongst the cows. All they picked up were radiant bodies. Alex and Pepper were temporarily safe.

They stayed until daylight. Even if they wanted to fall asleep they couldn't. They were beat-up, fire-singed and their thighs were raw with wear from the pushing cows. Manure and bovine reek had absorbed into their clothes. Standing in place, propped between shank and flank bone, was not the worst thing they could have done for twelve hours. It was, however, the safest.

Daylight was on the brink when the last two sedans left the farm. The morning was foreboding. The air was brisk and the taint of smoldering wood, metal and chemicals was fetid. The bloodied bodies of the Mortensens, he with his head blown to bits and she with two automatic rounds into her gut, were in a jumble. Blood in copper streams had worked its way through the grass and dirt to the edge of the door stoop. The sight sickened Pepper.

"Why?" Pepper asked in disgust as she looked in disbelief at the two.

"Let's get out of here," Alex said. He brushed off the stench that had sponged into his denim jacket. Though he didn't think that he had slept, he must have while standing, but dreamt of being awake.

He looked up at two crows perched on a lower limb of amaple tree. They were cawing woebegones at the last remains of the enkindled barn.

"Where to?" she asked. He pointed out of instinct. They made their way through a cornfield. Husks slapped across their faces. The waxy leaves stung in beat to their steps.

They emerged from the field onto a meadow that was the first in a series of gentle rolling hills. Prairie grasses, fameflower, poppy mallow and larkspur nudged through their legs as they walked to safety. Ambient heat slowly warmed their bones as they headed north.

At 9:03 in the morning they came upon an old German family rambling along in a faded '57 Chevy pick-up. They were heading east— where Alex and Pepper needed to go.

"Goin' to Sullivan?" the German asked when he stopped to pick up the two "thumbers."

"Where's that?" Alex asked.

"Toward St. Louie."

"That's where we want to go. Thanks," Alex said.

They hopped into the back and sat on boards that were pounded into the rusty metal frame and balanced on top of each wheelwell. Pieces of hay and cardboard made soggy by two-day old rain water were scattered on the truck bed. Six snot-nosed kids wearing hand-me-down clothes sat with them, as they pealed off the shoulder and drove with cool air blowing through their hair.

A sliding-glass window was open. The maw held a baby wrapped in a home-made quilt. She breast fed the infant. The baby was fussy and squirmed to suckle its breakfast as they bounced forward. Next to her was a two-year-old boy. He looked like a girl with his muffin hair.

"You see the fire last night?" the maw asked as Alex gaped through the slat at their progress.

"Yes."

"I told Pa that that place was no good."

"You did?"

"Never liked 'em," pa said.

"Liked who?" Alex asked and stuck his head as close as he could to the window.

"I said I never liked 'em. That damn Howard Hughes. To hell with him, and to hell with the *Goose*."

"The goose?"

"Common knowledge 'round here — that cursed place. They were 'spose-a be working on some high-level fantsy-smansy research for Uncle Sam, but everyone knew what they were really doin'."

"What was that?" Alex asked.

The maw looked at him. She grimaced slightly as her baby snuggled into her bosom, and gummed her nipple. "They were working on the *Goose* for Mr. Hughes. They were working for him."

Aspen, Colorado

An exacerbated CIA Director Harlon Gates got on the scrambled NSA Vista II satellite line with President Bill Climan. Climan had been wearing a hole in his Oval Office carpet. He had paced back and forth enough times to walk to China. Or at least that's how he felt.

"Mr. President," Harlan said with gloom sown deep into his rock-steady voice.

"Yes, Harlan. Tell me the best, 'cause I'm expecting the worst."

"This is how bad it gets...and it gets worse than a..."

"Cut the shit."

"Sorry, Mr. President. Here's the skinny as best as we can piece it together. X23 *LAV-10A* and X23 *LAV-10B* are two different versions of *LAV 10*..."

"Two different versions?"

"Yeah."

"You're positive."

"One-hundred percent."

"Meaning?"

"Meaning it's what we thought."

"The difference again?"

"*LAV-10A* can be spread via *airborne* release. *LAV-10B* is spread by surface contact, or fomite/vector contact, as in object-to-object."

"And the *LAV-10B* that you recovered was fomite?"

"That's correct."

"Then there is an 'A'?"

"That's what our sources tell us."

"What about the unidentified man and the girl?"

"The man was Roscoe J. McMahon III. He's a California industrialist and CEO, and on the board of a number of national and international companies. In addition, McMahon is the CEO of BetaTec Electronics. Mr. President...McMahon is dead."

"How? Where?"

"*LAV-10B*, and in Las Vegas."

"What about the girl?"

"We're not yet sure what her involvement is. We've traced some telephone calls from Rinerson's place to New York. Two of them trace back to that girl, who we now think was a high-priced hooker, to a voice mail answering service. It's registered to a Katrina Lee. We're running her down right now. It may be a dead end."

"Any luck with the neighbors?"

"No. Rinerson kept pretty much to himself. There were always a lot of people coming and going when he was in town—both men and women. Also, there was nothing else new from the country western singer Travis Clark, or any of his Hollywood guests, so far. I spoke to Clark myself."

"A fuck house?"

"I'd say so."

"So that lead in New York might work out to something?"

"Could be. In any event, I'll keep you posted. But Mr. President..."

"Yes."

"I'm just thinking out loud...but for argument's sake say that *LAV-10A*, the airborne stuff, was ripped off by the hooker. That maybe Rinerson or McMahon slipped and told the girl too much one night in a drunken stupor...Suppose that maybe the broad thought that she could shanghai one of the vials and sell it for a bundle. Maybe back to Rinerson or on the black market. Maybe she didn't realize what she had and how dangerous these men were?"

"It's possible. You think she's dead already?"

"I don't think so. We probably would have heard of it by now. I've already run down all the coroner offices in New York, as well as locally, and in each town where one of our 'Armory' guys died."

"So, it's plausible that these traitors might have been exposed to the *LAV-10B* 'fomite' agent, and not the girl."

"It is. Certainly, her death by now would have been imminent had she been exposed. Plus, the deaths were in and of themselves so bizarre, it would be extremely unlikely that they would not be reported to the CDC (Centers for Disease Control)."

"So what about the 'Armory'? Motive?"

"My guess is that you have to look at their history. First formed in the late '60s and then known loosely as the 'Inner Circle', and later of course the 'Armory'—originally their mission was to preserve the integrity of the Central Intelligence Agency. An intelligence Star Chamber of sorts. Their idea was to clandestinely, outside the scope of the CIA, take care of problematic geographical areas, particularly third world leaders. We think they've been directly involved in the assassination of Algeria's head of state Muhammad Boudiaf and killing the head of the pro-Iranian Hezbollah movement, Sheikh 'Abbas al-Mussawi in Southern Lebanon.

"Later, the 'Armory', as they became known by their own constituents, began stockpiling strategic projectile and biologic weaponry. The thought was to use it, *when* necessary.

"However, as the world changed, so too, did the 'Armory'. They became international, and as I mentioned to you earlier, included high-ranking agents from the KGB, MI-6 and DGSE, among others and certain global industrial leaders. Their mission had transmutated, as the world's purpose had changed. Now they were in the strategic projectile and biologic weapon *sales business...*"

"To the highest bidder."

"Yes. Also industrial secrets, exotics such as the esoteric: highly technical computer viruses to sabotage commercial networks, clandestine high quality intelligence information. Whatever a buyer was willing to pay for. For example, if I was the President of Intel and I manufactured Pentium microprocessors, a several billion dollars a year business, and Toshiba in Japan was ready to leapfrog me with a next generation CPU chip—how much is that worth for me to get that information?"

"Hundreds of millions. Are they?"

"No. I was just using that as an example. Nevertheless, with the Russian Cosmos 2,305 fifth generation imaging vehicle, Dezhurov

Gals, 'Rosto', and New Express heavy imaging reconnaissance spy satellites and high-resolution listening and photographic techniques available, not to mention our litany of satellites, our Intruder intelligence satellite network, Counter Drigg BBS covert spy satellite series, etc...just about anything is possible."

"I see your point," Climan said in disgust. He disdained people who lacked integrity. Thinking of the espionage made him vilely angry. "So where do we go from here?"

"Well, I'll work through the New York lead, since I think that when we find the girl we'll find the *LAV-10A*. I'll keep you posted. Oh..." Gates said as he was almost ready to disconnect his satellite up-link, "the terrorist on board the Aeromexico 747-400 flight...we were able to nail that one down. He was Khalifa Ali Al-Megrahi from the Muslim Fundamentalist Hamas, the organization aimed at wiping out Zion. Seems that Ambassador Perov had some deep business ties with Israel..."

"Armory?"

"Possibly. But Al-Megrahi's motives were in retaliation for Russia's détente and the firming of ties with Israel. An attempt to unsettle the already unstable region."

"I thought that with the self-rule of Palestine and the formalization of relations with Israel and Yassar Arafat's Palestinian Government and autonomy, that things were smoothing out."

"Yes, in general that's the consensus. However, some extremists saw the murder of Perov, and a hundred plus innocents, as an opportunity to make a political point. This especially in light of Perestroika and Russia's desire to share nuclear technology with Israel."

"I see your point."

"I'll keep you posted."

"Harlan..."

"Yes."

"Don't be discouraged. Just keep up the good work."

"It's not being discouraged, Mr. President...I just hope that it's not too late."

En Route to St. Louis

Alex and Pepper chugged down the road back toward civilization. They were in the land of the Ozarks, of antebellum residences, of "Boone's Lick Country" where Daniel Boone and his sons moved from Kentucky to make salt, where planters from the South settled to cultivate cotton and soybeans.

What do I know? Think Alex, think.

Alex sat tight to Pepper, his thigh pressed to hers. She looked at him sideways, and then at the autumn foliage. Some trees had been split, and others cracked as they had lain in the path of "Tornado Alley." They drove beyond a river bluff, then dipped into a valley. Elk and bison had once roamed freely here.

"Long Beach," Alex said.

"Long Beach?"

"Howard Hughes had an experimental eight-engine flying boat, the *Spruce Goose*. It was flown only once in the late '40s. It's in Long Beach next to the Queen Mary. It's a tourist attraction. I remember...about four or five years ago one of my nurses went to Disneyland with her kids or something. They went to Long Beach to see the *Spruce Goose* and the *Queen Mary* on their last day. They had nothing else to do."

"Long Beach?" You think we should go all the way to Long Beach...are you kidding?"

"Do you have any better ideas?"

"No."

CHAPTER 34

"You idiot!" Spacewalker/Pilot Smith said, "I'm as goddamn helpless as a shoeless Appaloosa on a macadam road!"

"What'd he say?" Tool Specialist Budarin asked Maya.

"He said he was frustrated," Maya replied as she continued to manipulate microscopic droplets of *LAV-10*, this time with Enivorchem. "Nothing."

"Commander Jackson, this is Commander Vrubel, over."

"Over. What ya got?"

"I've made the calculations we've discussed…"

"Go on."

"I suggest that if we decide to land at the second alternative landing site at White Sands Space Harbor, New Mexico that we don't use the ERV."

"Why's that? What's wrong with using both *Soyuz TM 29* and *Orion*?"

"Several things. First, assuming that we are contaminated, that is, that our space suits have this 'sticky' *LAV-10* chemical attached to the mylar, then I think that we would be increasing the risk to earth by coming down in two different vehicles."

"That doesn't make sense," Smith gruffly said.

"On the surface I would agree with you. However, I think that it would be important that we land as close together, or in reality, at the same spot, so that whatever decontamination processes need to be done can be performed simultaneously. If, for example, we land several hundred kilometers or even several kilometers apart, the logistics of decontamination, and even shrouding our reentry vehicles in a Kevlar 29 or Cordura Level 11A Biosafety Level 4 environment, can be overwhelming."

"I see some logic in that," Jackson said.

"Then there is the question of extricating two separate crews out of two sealed environments versus one environment, such, as in *Orion*. No...I think that if we abdondon *Mir*, then we all need to return in the *Orion*."

"Commander," Smith asked Jackson, "what are the possibilities of that scenario?"

"I don't know. There are eleven of us, and maximum seating on *Orion*, with modification...for nine."

"What about the storage, or our experimental or equipment storage bays? Couldn't we strap in two of the astronauts in one of the bays, or jerry-rig something?"

"I don't know. Why don't you, Hobbs, Holloway and Zvezda work on that right away."

"All right," Hobbs replied, as well as Holloway and Zvezda.

"Cunningham, you need to figure out the rough weights of the additional eight hitchhikers and whatever jerry-rigged equipment we'll need, and pound 'em through the computer."

"Pound 'em through?" Commander Vrubel asked.

"I'm already ahead of you, Commander," Cunningham said. "We should be able to escape this Houdini death chamber by the skin of our teeth. Don't worry."

"Now," Jackson addressed the crew, "as you all know we only have eleven hours of oxygen left. Biologics Engineer Mukhina has some ideas that we're going to work through. We're going to try a reverse approach. We'll first flood *Mir* with a hundred percent nitrogen."

"Can do," Environmental Engineer Crux replied.

"We'll hold the nitrogen for thirty minutes, purge and try one hundred percent helium, hold for thirty minutes then purge and try one hundred percent oxygen. Can you do that?"

"I can, but what about the love birds?" Crux asked.

It was then that Holloway returned from the Hydroponics Lab. "Dying. I don't think it's going to make any difference."

"Should we go ahead with the one hundred percent nitrogen?" Jackson asked Maya.

She nodded her Orlan-III DMA helmeted head.

"According to my calculations Commander, we have until 2300 hours to abandon the space station," Cunningham said as he looked into the computer screen. "That'll give us a cushion of three hours to return to earth."

"Then what?" Maya asked.

"I don't know." Jackson replied. "NASA will come and get us out of these space suits, or at the worst give us a reload of our O^2."

"Do you really think," she said sarcastically, "that they, either the Americans or Russians, will actually let us land?"

"I don't know Maya," Smith interjected as he turned to face her, "It depends on what we have on board, doesn't it?" He was menacing as he approached her. Jackson stepped between them. "What is it Maya? What do we *really* have on board? If we're going to die, we have a right to know at this point what's going on."

"Comrade Mukhina," Commander Vrubel barked. He, too, was feeling the stress. "Comrade, I direct you to tell us what we're dealing with regardless of your clandestine orders from earth."

Maya was torn between her orders from earth and her loyalty to those with whom she was serving on board *Mir-Kennedy I.*

Morally and ethically she should disclose all. She could hear the 20-70-10 nitrogen/helium/oxygen load vent out of the space station. It made an eerie hissing sound.

She thought about the Cat's Eye that Scoop had told her about earlier, and she imagined their thirsty bodies touching, naked in space, making love, being one, he recklessly inside her. She felt human, she felt unpretentious and vulnerable.

"I suppose," she said hesitantly, "you all need to know."

Jackson grabbed her by both Orlan-III DMA arms. He brought her to her feet. They began to gently float towards the ceiling. He wanted to say it more than ever, that he loved her. But, he still couldn't make himself. She knew he wanted to, needed to.

"Nine months ago when Biologics Engineer Pokrovksy came on board *Mir-Kennedy I* for his tour of duty, he brought with him something that he wasn't supposed to. He had smuggled on board a vial of TTLV-1."

"What's that?" Smith asked.

"TTLV-1 was an experimental chemical."

"*Not a virus?*" Jackson asked.

"*No.* It's a proreagant... A proreagant that is a viral *deactivator.*"

"So..." Smith again interjected, "we don't have any viruses up here."

"And why bring it to outerspace?" Jackson asked.

"Because it wasn't safe to work with on earth."

"You said that it was a viral *deactivator?*" Vrubel asked.

"True. The problem, however, is that when not handled properly the viral *deactivator* had deleterious side effects. The problem that we were having on earth was that TTLV-1 at normal Gs caused cyanide bond formation in the body within twenty-four hours."

"And thus the deaths of Pokrovsky and Shoyo?" Crux said.

"Exactly. When Gregov had a spill with *LAV-10* he liberated, though microscopic amounts, the chemical which in turn caused his own death, and that of Shoyo."

"Wait a second. I'm a little confused Comrade," Budarin said. "You said that Pokrovsky brought on board TTLV-1, but it was *LAV-10* that we were exposed to?"

"That's correct. We've known for a long time, that though TTLV-1 was a *super viral deactivator*, the downside of working with this chemical was too severe to risk manipulation on earth at normal gravity."

"So in a sense," Jackson said, "you had a *super remedy* for the common cold, chicken pox, the measles..."

"And AIDS," Maya said with certainty.

"A cure-all?"

"No, not really, but it cured AIDS forever—or so we initially were led to believe."

"Then why so secret?"

"I can't tell you," she said. "But..."

"So," Commander Jackson said, "TTLV-1 was smuggled on

board by Pokrovsky and since he was now working in a zero-G environment, he could bend and twist, manipulate TTLV-1's molecules."

"And that's how he made *LAV-10?*" Vrubel surmised.

"Yes."

"And he was going to perfect TTLV-1's imperfections, make it safe, then sell it on the black market. The cure for AIDS to the highest bidder." Smith said. "Eradicate the disease, but for a price."

"Yes."

"You were involved in this?" Vrubel asked.

"No," Jackson answered for her. Immediately the communication from the CIA came to mind. "She was sent *to stop the people who were involved with Pokrovsky.*"

"Something like that," Maya said.

"So what about it Maya, why's this chemical sticking to the mylar on our space suits, and if it only works for twenty-four hours, then why do we have to worry?"

"I said that *LAV-10* kills within twenty-four hours. How long it *remains active* is a mystery."

"So why the gas mixtures?" Jackson asked.

"Dr. Johnson and myself, and the others that have worked on this project, and the previous research on TTLV-1 feel that there is a possibility that we can force disabling or twisting of the cyanide bonds with *LAV-10* using high concentrations of nitrogen, helium and oxygen."

"But?"

"It probably won't work."

"Oh, that's positive." Smith said sarcastically.

"Why?" Jackson asked.

"Given more time, I could answer that question, but basically because of TTLV-10's flipping ability."

"Flipping? What's flipping?"

"It's instability. *This is the real problem.* The cyanide bonding is incidental. 0.05% of the TTLV-1 and *LAV-10* molecules flip to the isomer opposite form. From 'd' to 'l,' or *dextro* to *levo.*"

"What's 'd' and 'l'?"

"'D', or dextrorotary means turning or rotating the plane of polarization of light to the right, or clockwise. 'L', or levorotatoly means turning or rotating the plane of polarized light to the left, or counterclockwise. They're mirror images."

"And so the oxygen or nitrogen won't bind with the 'l' isomer."

"Yes."

"Is there any way to make all the isomers uniform? All 'd'?"

"Not that I'm aware of."

"So that's the predicament we're in?" Jackson asked.

"Yes, in a nutshell."

"So I presume that we need to move forward and anticipate the worse scenario—that we're going to abandon the space station?"

"Yes, but..."

"But?"

"They won't let us land," Maya said honestly to all.

No one spoke.

"Maya," Jackson asked, "Pokrovsky had been up here for nine months. Has he sent any *LAV-10* back to earth?"

She hesitated in her reply. "We...think so."

"We?" Jackson asked.

"I believe that Gregov had sent at least two vials back to earth on the Progress-Newstar robotic resupply transport. One is a fomite form of *LAV-10* and the other airborne. You see, he thought that if *he* didn't solve the problem with TTLV-1 in space in its conversion to *LAV-10*, then the rest of the work could be done safely by scientists on earth, at normal Gs."

"And your job was to find out who those scientists were, who Gregov's organization was?" Jackson asked.

"Yes."

"And to stop him."

"Yes."

"But the situation got out of hand."

"Yes."

"How were you recruited?" Commander Vrubel asked.

"By Gregov. We had worked together for years, since the Academy of Sciences of the USSR. He knew my initial anti-Communist sentiments, long before *Perestroika*. He recruited me four years ago."

"Four years?" Jackson asked.

"Yes, but I hadn't worked with him that long. I was later enlisted by *other sources* to..."

"KGB?" Vrubel asked.

She did not answer. Commander Vrubel knew what the answer would be.

"So what's the difference between fomite and airborne?" Smith asked.

"Fomite," she said "is not spread through the air, but needs to come in physical contact with an object in order to be effective."

"And airborne," Jackson finished, "is spread via the air."

"So..." Vrubel said, "we've got a lot of number pounding to do to get off this place."

"We do," Jackson replied.

Outside Cuba, Missouri

What was left of the barn was smoldering. The bodies of Kaleb and LaRue Mortenson were unaccounted for when CIA Director Gates arrived.

The stoop beyond the plank-board porch had melted into the gravel driveway. The clapboard farmhouse, with its dormers and gables and gingerbread trim and maplewood breezeway that connected to the barn, was destroyed. The remains of a molten-green, John Deere tractor glowed. There was coagulated blood between the end of the drive and the burned-out house.

Gates placed an encrypted NSA Vista II satellite linked call to President Climan via real-time video. It was near 6 p.m. in Washington when President Climan took the call.

"Mr. President, Harlan Gates."

"Give it to me Harlan."

"I'm calling you from South of Cuba, Missouri on State 10 toward Onodaga Cave."

"What are you doing there?"

"We have more problems."

"What?" Climan said perturbed.

"*Dr. Alex Seacourt.*"

"That's a new name in this game. Who's he?"

"Dr. Seacourt is a Salt Lake City physician who just got back to the United States four days ago. He had participated with a contingency of 150 United States physicians—a total of 440 doctors worldwide—in an anti-terrorist germ warfare training program in Moscow, Washington, D.C. and Rio, for the last three months. His training included simulated biologic emergencies with botulism toxin and sarafan nerve gas, schooling of others in responses to such emergencies, and modalities of direct confrontation with terrorists."

"So, what's the connection?"

"Apparently Dr. Seacourt was routed to the Consumer Electronics Show in Las Vegas, to the BetaTec booth. He was told to ask for Roscoe McMahon and for a demo software copy of *LAV-10*."

"*LAV-10*?"

"It was our FSB friends who pointed Seacourt to BetaTec and in particular Assistant to the First Directorate KR Line Oleg Shlyapnikov."

"Shlyapnikov?"

"Yes."

"Shlyapnikov...do you think he was using Seacourt and Seacourt didn't know it?"

"Yes."

"And the connection?"

"I think that Shlyapnikov wanted to use Seacourt to see if he could get him to make a *LAV-10* connection, without the doctor knowing it."

"Ingenious."

"Yeah. We'll, it gets a lot juicier. Turns out Seacourt's connection is dying when the doctor shows up at the BetaTec booth. And then, by serendipity, Seacourt turns up at McMahon's autopsy."

"So the bad guys think that Dr. Seacourt had something to do with McMahon's death."

"Bingo."

"So what about Missouri?"

"Seems that Dr. Seacourt's friend, Dr. Joanna Knight, a pathologist at University Medical Center in Las Vegas, was the one who performed the autopsy on McMahon...and she was abducted."

"Why?"

"Well...I believe that the bad guys, the 'Armory', have been after Dr. Seacourt. And Seacourt is no fool. When he becomes the hunted he puts two and two together. He tracks down Dr. Knight's ex-husband in L.A. Apparently Dr. Knight sent him an autopsy specimen, a slide. Seems that Dr. Warner, her ex,is killed the morning Seacourt arrives, gets run over in a hit-and-run."

"Seacourt involved?"

"No. however, Seacourt discovers that Dr. Warner had made a

number of calls the night before—to Oshkosh, Wisconsin where his stepdaughter, Dr. Knight's daughter, lives. Then Seacourt makes his way to Oshkosh and finds Pepper Knight, her daughter. Turns out Knight is nearly murdered in a biplane mishap.

"Next, Seacourt and Pepper Knight show up in all godforsaken places—at the St. Louis Zoo. That's where they were both shot at...and where we came into the loop. Then we lost them, until they turned up outside of Cuba, Missouri...at the old Invenco plant."

"What's Invenco?"

"*That's where the early experiments on TTLV-1 were done*, before the project was abandoned due to safety concerns."

"So what's the link?"

"Dr. Joanna Knight, twenty years ago, was one of the original TTLV-1 researchers."

"...and so a dead man, of all the ironies, ends up on her autopsy slab...and he died of *LAV-10*, or for all intents and purposes TTLV-1."

"Yes."

"Where's Dr. Seacourt now?"

"We don't know. But I'm sure wherever he turns up, so will our bad guys."

"How long do we have with *Mir-Kennedy* I?"

"Ten and a half hours. Otherwise we need to decontaminate."

"Are you sure about that...that we have no alternatives?"

"Positive. I've been working hand-in-glove with Dr. Johnson at Mills Farm. If they come down there's too big a risk of contamination."

"How would you decontaminate?"

"One of our SR-71A's is on alert at Edward Air Force Base. We anticipate that the astronauts will disobey Houston Control's directive and land the shuttle at the second alternative landing site at White Sands Space Harbor, New Mexico. To be honest, I'd do the same if I was them. In reality there's a fifty/fifty chance they can come down and safely enter Biosafety Level 4 without contaminating our environment."

"And..."

"And if they come down?"

"Yes."

"The public will think that it's an accident. We can blow them out of the sky at seventy thousand feet with our Betsy ASAT antisatellite missile. It'll be another *Challenger*-type accident."

"Don't let it come to that Harlan. There are too many brave men up there."

"I don't want to, but we probably won't have a choice."

"I know."

CHAPTER 35
Long Beach, California

"How much more melodramatic could the name have been than *Spruce Goose Suppliers*, a Hughes Corporation." Alex had found it when he and Pepper returned to St. Louis. The company was listed in a 1975 St. Louis Yellow Pages he found on microfilm at the main St. Louis Public Library. Were the feds just living larger than life, did they think that they walked on water, that they were untouchable? Or was this just a "wild goose chase."

All Alex knew was that the *Spruce Goose* was somewhere in Long Beach. At least that was what he remembered. The plane was displayed next to the *Queen Mary* in 1982. It was an eight-engine albatross that flew just once. It was the world's largest flying boat. Alex had always wanted to see it. He was fascinated by the thought that something that substantial could be built that would turn out to be totally worthless.

Long Beach was as Alex expected. The day was cloudless and a glib breeze swept off the Pacific while surfers and sailboats decorated the waves in the distance. The sun smacked on their faces.

Alex and Pepper drove along the beach and watched sea kayaking, sailing, windsurfing and jet skiing. Roller bladers, joggers and bicyclists zoomed past them. Though for all intents and purposes they were in the grit of a big city, the sprawl disappeared when they approached ocean's edge.

"So, where to?"

"To the *Queen Mary*," Alex replied. Pepper was a little confused. Alex had deliberately not taken the Harbor Scenic Drive to the *Queen Mary* when he got to the heart of Long Beach and at the end of the 710 expressway. Instead, he followed the highway to Shoreline Drive. He wanted to get a sense of the city.

He drove past the World Trade Center/Long Beach Area Convention and Visitors Bureau and then to the downtown shoreline Harbor Marina. He needed to see the ocean, to smell the salt water and taste its brine. Across the Queensway Bay he could see the *Queen Mary* and the dome. They got out of their car and walked through the Shoreline Village and the marina. There was a historic waterfront collection of restaurants, shops and bookstores.

"Alex, I don't understand, why are we stopping here?"

"I don't know." He could see the three red, black-tipped smokestacks loft out of the *Queen*. Their view was fettered by hundreds of masts bobbing in the marina. Behind the *Queen* was the monstrous dome that housed the *Spruce Goose*.

"Something's not right."

"I don't understand Alex."

"It doesn't make sense."

"I know."

"Your father's dead, your mom was kidnapped, and worse—we were almost murdered."

"Yes."

Then he flashedback to Moscow, his anti-terrorist germ warfare training and Sambo—it was an FSB fighting technique that involved lifting an opponent and throwing him down, often on his head. That was what they had endeavored to teach him, amongst other things. But Alex was not made of steel, nor had he training in karate nor jujitsu, nor any of the other exacting disciplines.

They would tell him to *slow down* when split decisions were needed in a crisis. But slow down *didn't* make sense to him initially. Then, finally, he understood. Slow down meant to not panic, to think through a situation, even if the time for reaction was only microseconds. And then, if all else failed, let his *inner* voice speak to him and nine times out of ten, it would give him the right answer.

And now, Alex's inner voice told him to slow down. He had come a long distance on a hunch, and a few minutes would not make a difference.

"What's wrong?" Pepper asked.

"It's not here."

"What do you mean not here?"

"I screwed up. The *Spruce Goose* was moved a few years ago. Evergreen Aviation bought it and moved it to Oregon."

"When did you find this out?"

"When we rented the car at the airport," he said.

"Why didn't you tell me?"

"Because this was where we had to come. I could feel it."

"Bullshit!"

"I know, this is all bullshit. This isn't about the zoo, this isn't about the bees, this isn't about you or me...*it's about the autopsy.* It's about *LAV-10.*"

"Screw you, Alex! Why didn't you tell me when you found out. We're in this together! You and me, bucko!"

He closed his eyes and listened to the ocean—and the freighters in the distance. As the vessels passed the Queens Gate Breakwater into the Outer Harbor en route to the Port of Long Beach and the Southeast Basin they would sound their horns.

"Why an ELSIA test? What about the *LAV* demo?"

"What are you talking about Alex? One of your delusions?"

"An ELSIA test, the AIDS test your mother ran on the dead guy in the autopsy room."

"So?"

"Do you remember anything at all about your mother's work when you were young."

"No. Just the swing...and birds."

"Birds? Why...did you say birds?"

"I don't know. I just thought about it."

"What kind of birds?"

"...Turkeys?"

"She talked about turkeys?" Alex shook his head. He was even more perplexed. Turkeys made no sense. Then he thought, *now it's goddamn turkeys?*

"What?" Pepper asked. She heard him mumbling to himself in a low voice.

"Let me ask you a question. What if this whole deal doesn't have anything at all to do with you, but with your mother...the *LAV-10* software...and then my association with your mother?"

"I don't get you. You're confusing me."

"Forget it. Let's get out of here."

"Fine!" she huffed.

They doubled back down Shoreline Drive, then over the Queensway Bridge and to Queensway Drive and the dome. It was white and gigantic, and foreboding. They parked in an immense lot at the Queen's Marketplace just north of the dome. Alex looked at the mammoth boat. He was magnetically drawn to it.

They walked to the dome where once was housed the *Spruce Goose*. It was locked tighter than a drum.

"Alex where are you going?" she asked as he walked towards the ticket booth between the dome and the entrance to the *Queen*.

"Let's get on board."

"Alex, are you nuts?"

"Very much so. Let's do it."

"Okay...jerk."

Alex paid their fare for a guided tour. They hiked up the long walkway toward the art deco vessel. The *Queen Mary* had been built with all the pride of Britain's seafaring tradition by John Brown & Company. Three hundred thousand workers and contractors participated in its construction. On September 26, 1934 it was launched. It spoke in a remote dialect to Alex.

From the Queen's Walkway they went down a staircase to the lower decks and the engine room. The guide began speaking. "Today we'll begin our tour by viewing this video presentation of the *Queen Mary's* construction, launch, maiden voyage, and service in World War II as "The Grey Ghost'." There were at least sixty people in the clutch. Alex was oblivious to all of them.

They walked into the engine room exhibits. There was a mini-museum depicting the history of the *Queen Mary* and other maritime events. There was an exhibit honoring Clydebank District, Scotland, where the ship was built and launched in 1934. Then they walked into the two engine rooms that housed the turbines. Alex felt overwhelmed. From there, the group took an escalator up to the observation bar, out onto the bow, and up into the officer's quarters, the bridge and wheelhouse. Alex didn't realize how big the *Queen Mary* was until he was actually on it. It was stupendous.

"You got 'im?" a man said into his hand-held radio.

"I do," he answered as he removed the safety-tip of his poison gun. One push of a button and it was instantaneous death. "Give me three minutes and then the girl will be ours."

The weapon was a metal palm-held cylinder, one half inch in diameter, with a tube of prussic acid. Upon detonation of a small charge, an ampule was crushed, spraying poison into the victim's face. Instant constriction of blood vessels produced death that resembled a heart attack. With swift post-mortem realization, the evidence would be literally wiped out before autopsy. It was the same one used to kill Lev Rebet, a Ukrainian activist leader in Munich on October 12, 1957, and Stefan Bandera, also in Munich, in October 1958. However, then authorities found traces of prussic acid in the victim's stomach, along with flakes of glass on his face from the exploding ampule. *But that was just what the killer wanted—something to throw the police off track*. Something very European and very old "Cold War" exotic.

"So what do you think?" Pepper asked.

"I have no idea," was what Alex was about to say when a flash of light bounced off an object palmed by one of two men rapidly approaching him through the spacious bridge. Alex knew that whatever was in the man's hand was in store for him and Pepper. But, before he could push Pepper out of the way, the first man grabbed her from behind, and the second flung his palm into Alex's face. With the thumb he pressed back on a trigger causing the prussic acid to break. In a short burst, the poison blasted out of the weapon.

CHAPTER 36

"Duck!" Alex yelled as the man pushed the trigger releasing the poison into his face, while at the same time clutching Alex by the neck.

Alex had seen it coming. He pushed his way free and fell to the floor and down to his left side. He closed his mouth tight, and shut his eyes. He knew not to inhale. He held his breath as long as humanly possible. A man in front of him had set a large Coke on a wheelhouse ledge.

Alex pushed through the tourists to the counter. An innocent man next to him had not been so lucky. He too had been struck by the spray. He fell to his knees, grasped his chest and wheezed for air.

Alex desperately wiggled his hand and forearm onto the ledge and felt for the cup. He ripped off the top of the two-thirds full container and threw it onto his face. It was enough to wash off the deadly prussic acid, and what wasn't washed off was neutralized by the pop. Just a feel away was a restroom. He had remembered seeing it when he came onto the bridge. With one eye squinted open, he ran

ran to it. The "Woman's" was on his side. He flung the door open to screams. He found a sink and ran cold water, full blast. He then buried his burning face into the basin.

His hair, face and shirt were drenched. The lethal poison stung, and should have been enough to kill him. He ripped off his shirt.

Down the hall were more screams. He could hear a woman cry in agony, "Don't die, don't die. I need a doctor!"

It had been nearly thirty seconds, and Alex was just regaining his composure. He had to go after Pepper, but whatever was sprayed in his face, scorched like hell, worse than the cobra venom.

"Help, I need a doctor." she yelled again.

Alex had no choice. He glanced down the crowded sports decks walkway. Pepper was nowhere. He couldn't even recognize the man who abducted her if he had to. It all happened too fast.

He ran back to the wheelhouse. Men, women and children surrounded the fallen victim. A woman with blond hair and sunweathered face knelt next to the man. A little girl in a blue shirt and white shorts, and a small boy with a red T-shirt and golden tuff were crying over him.

"My husband, my husband."

Alex pushed them aside. He knew he had to give the man CPR, but was leery of what had been sprayed onto his face. Alex struggled to lift the victim.

"Help me." The others did. Three men, with Alex, rushed the man into the Women's bathroom. They rapidly drenched his face and then they ripped off his shirt. It burned to the touch.

After a burst of cleansing water, Alex tilted the victim's head back and performed CPR. He gave him six cardiac compressions and one breath in alternation. Then he was helped by two other men. They performed CPR until two tourist physicians arrived, a cardiologist and pediatrician. They futilely took over. The pulse that had been strong when Alex started the man's resuscitation was beating slower.

"Goddamn them, goddamn them! Where did they go!" Alex bolted out after he felt the man's agonal carotid. Alex stood up half-naked. He wrung out his partially ripped and drenched T-shirt, and put it back on.

He scrambled down to the Sun Deck, past the Sun Deck exhibits. He ran to both port and starboard sides of the ponderous vessel looking down the Queen's Marketplace and the bay. No Pepper.

"Maybe they're still on board."

He ran past the Sun Deck Deli and Bakery, down to Sir Winston's restaurant, and pushed his way through the crowd. Down to the Promenade Deck through the Piccadilly Circus Shops, through the fifty thousand square foot Queen Mary Exhibit Center where there was a trade show with nearly 180 exhibits. It was a convention for Independent Indemnity Insurance Brokers. He pushed two booths over in his frantic effort to find Pepper and the abductors. They were nowhere.

Then he stormed through a vast conference room. There was a wedding. The bride was cutting her five-tiered cake. He charged through the tuxedos and rented formal wear. He rammed into a serving table full of appetizers and entrees: chicken Jerusalem, chicken Catawab and North Atlantic Salmon. Two chefs who stood behind in their white-starched outfits, bobbed aprons, and foot-high *toque* hats swore at him as they tried to save their masterpieces.

He charged out onto the Promenade Deck and bowward to the Observation Deck. Again he looked toward the street-level Queen's Marketplace shops. He quickly scanned down at the English seafaring shops. Between the Cockney gas lampposts he searched for Pepper. He didn't see her.

He ran to the starboard side and peered into the low-pitching Queensway Bay. There was nothing. Pleasure craft, sailboats and wave runners. The only thing that could have possibly made any sense was a small runabout that sped away from the vicinity of the *Queen Mary*. It was halfway to the Queensway Bridge, nearly a half-mile off. It was heading up the bay into the mouth of the Los Angeles River.

Alex pushed through the tourist crammed stern, down the Promenade Deck toward the exit. By now an ambulance and police cars had arrived. Regrettably, it was too late for the poison victim in the women's bathroom. He lay nearly lifeless on the tile. The two vacationing doctors did their best work, everything that they could to save him.

As Alex hurried down the escalator, sliding down the brass banister, harried Long Beach policemen ran up the entrance ramp. Alex slowed to a normal walk. He didn't trust anyone: not the cops, not the FBI. Who was it that tried to kill him? *Certainly in Missouri it was two Cuba City Sheriffs.* Or was it?

Alex headed toward the wharf. He quickly and nonchalantly

combed the marketplace shops. He knew he wouldn't find them there. He walked through the parking lot, looking for what?

More cops had arrived, these from the Long Beach Port Authority, and a second ambulance. Alex got into his rental car and pushed back his seat. He started up the vehicle and thought. *"All has been lost."* He studied his face in his rearview mirror. *This was the second time in the same number of days his "mug" had been attacked.*

Alex stared at the commotion in the parking lot: the blaring red and blue bubblegum lights, and then the paramedics who rushed the poison victim on a stretcher.

He looked again at his face. His cheeks and the top of his right eyelid, and the bridge of his nose were beet red. His skin was on fire. "I screwed up." He sat silent, dejected.

Then he thought of Moscow. The words they told him stuck deep in his memory. *Think, slow down.* Something in the back of his mind was bothering him. Something real bad, but he didn't quite know what it was. Then he remembered...It *wasn't Jo's office.* It was the *Consumer Electronics Show.* The stricken man and a woman. *A hooker.* In a flash he saw *her face and the side of his.* The ill man had thick gray hair like, *...like what? Where?* He knew that he had seen him before. He began to fully picture the woman. She also looked familiar. And then there was a third man, a man in dark sunglasses with jet-black hair, smoking a cigarette in his right hand. A bodyguard?

Alex looked at his watch. Night was approaching. Where was he going to go? He started his car and headed back towards Long Beach. He stopped at the first service station he found and approached a pay phone.

There were both Long Beach and Los Angeles GTE telephone books. They were ragged and the Los Angeles book was especially thrashed. He looked up Invenco in both volumes. Nothing. He slammed shut the Long Beach directory. He called information, using the 310 area code.

"Do you have a listing for Invenco?"

"One moment please." After what seemed like an eternity, the answer came in a persnickety voice: "No, sir."

"Do you have a listing for a *Spruce Goose* Enterprises, or a Hughes Enterprises?"

"You're allowed two requests per call. Which will it be?"

"*Spruce Goose.*"

She paused for a moment, and then returned. "No, we don't."

"Do you have..." She curtly hung up.

Alex was irritated, but calmed himself. He called information back.

"May I help you," a different, more pleasant operator asked.

"Yes, can you please check to see if you have the telephone number for a Hughes Enterprises."

"One moment please." She came back in ten seconds. "No, we don't."

Then Alex thought, why not? and he asked her, "Do you have the number for Tate's Honey Farm?"

She paused for a few moments and then said, "We don't. Thank you and..."

"Look, can you please give me one more number?"

"I'm not supposed..."

"I'm just wondering if you have Yellow Pages information."

"I'm sorry sir we don't. I can give you my supervisor."

"Please."

Within a little over a minute an understanding supervisor came on the line. "May I help you?"

"Yes, I've got this little problem."

"Go ahead sir."

"Well, I'm from out of town and I'm looking for something, and I'm at a pay phone here near the Queen Mary with the telephone books. I've got Los Angeles and Long Beach, but there aren't any Yellow Pages."

"I'm sorry sir, but we don't provide Yellow Pages information."

"I know, but it wouldn't be any big deal...and I'm an hour late for an appointment. I've stopped by three different pay phone booths and all of them have the Yellow Pages ripped off. You know what I mean?" He was ad-libbing.

"Yes, I do sir."

"Well...anyway, if you could just do me this one small favor; I just need you to look up beekeepers in the..."

Under her breath she snickered. "Sir, did you say beekeepers?"

"I did."

"Sir, is this a joke?" She could barely keep a straight face. Obviously Alex's chances of getting help had immediately improved.

"No kidding. I'm serious. It would be under beekeepers in the Yellow Pages."

"Do you have the name of the business sir?"

"No, ma'am, I don't, but how many beekeepers can there be in Long Beach or L.A.?"

It was all she could do to keep from laughing. "One moment sir." She was away from the phone for nearly five minutes. When she came back on line she spoke quizzically. "Sir there is one bee-keeper in Long Beach, well...not exactly a beekeeper but a merchant."

"Do you have the number and address?"

"It's Missouri Apiary Suppliers. The number is 435-5620. The address, I'll be a son-of-a-gun..."

"What?"

"It's on the Pier. Right near the *Queen Mary*...at 253 Pier C Street."

CHAPTER 37

Sandy white beaches and eclectic neighborhoods, the flavor of the smile on a child's face as he sees a migrating gray whale, the sweet aroma of fresh apples rolling off a farmer's truck at an open-air market, the vibrancy of the Pacific breeze—these were *not* the smells nor the sights that Alex encountered at 253 Pier C Street.

The place stunk like crap. Stale backwater had delivered garbage and flotsam that had stagnated in a sordid swirl. The Cerritos Channel that bifurcated at Turning Basin into Channel No. 2 and the Inner Harbor was the dregs of the industrialized society.

Terminal Island and the U.S. Naval Station Long Beach were two miles away. In the distance loomed the Long Beach City Hall, the World Trade Center, the International, the Breakers Hotel, and the Villa Rivera. This was the heart of industrialized commerce.

Alex drove down Pier C Street beyond stacked, rusted C-Line train containers that were piled ten high and eight deep. The gloomy, yellow sky painted every aspect of the horizon, choking its environs to one hundred feet above the ground.

Alex drove past the warehouse to the end of the dock, and then into a parking lot kitty-corner from his destination. He found a spot where his car disappeared with others as he watched the warehouse's entrance. Missouri Apiary Suppliers sat off Channel No. 2 in the midst of the industrial clutter.

The building was four stories. It was constructed of aluminum and concrete corrugated walls. In front were a pair of two-story sliding doors that hung exactly in the center of the edifice. On the side nearest Alex was an entrance door. In the rear there was a corroded crane that sat on lurching stilts and rolled down an old railroad track. The derrick had the words "Hughes Industries" painted on it. Alex knew that he was in the right place.

Alex waited nearly a half hour, then a man arrived. He wore not the ordinary longshoreman clothes that Alex would have anticipated, but a conservative suit with stern white shirt and burgundy-red power tie. It spelled government.

The man was alone and drove a fed-issued, gray Taurus, but without the civil service emblem on the driver's and front passenger's doors. The tires were blackwalls, and the wheels hubcapless.

The man reached into his suit. He removed his billfold and took out a keycard. He slid the card into an electronic scanner that was mounted next to the door, just above the handle. Then he punched in a set of numbers into a keypad next to the scanner. The door popped open. The man entered, and then shut the door behind him.

Alex waited another thirty minutes. Two cars pulled up. These were also Tauruses, but one was white and the other dark blue. Two men got out of the first vehicle, and one from the second. One from each car went to the door. They repeated the routine that the man had gone through earlier to gain entrance. The last man waited outside. He took off his jacket, and though the driver's window was rolled down, he opened his car door and set his coat on the front seat.

When the man left his car, in his right hand he had a cigarette that he had lit up inside, but had not smoked. He stood in the pungent air and puffed. He paced and walked to the rear of the warehouse, then returned. He glanced down at his watch and rolled up the sleeves of his white shirt.

Night had begun to ease in. The glow of the cigarette became more prominent. The man paced back to the car, inhaling lonely drags, then blowing out smoke rings.

He was heading back toward Channel No. 2 when he finished his cigarette. He flicked the butt onto the asphalt and watched it bounce, then land in a greasy puddle. He then briskly returned to his car. He got in, glanced at his watch and then removed another cigarette from a pack on the front seat. He fired up with the car lighter. He got back out of the vehicle and began walking.

"I gotta go for it," Alex said to himself. He had been lucky. He had parked in a lot where apparently all the cars from West Coast Machine Works—a machinery shop, parts exporting business—had been either left out overnight, or were from workers who were on the afternoon shift and had not yet gotten off work. Alex found the switch inside his car. He turned off the inside light so that when he opened his door it wouldn't go on. It didn't. He quietly closed the door, then squatted between his car and a two-toned Impala.

Alex watched as the cigarette-smoking man started his march back to the waterfront. The dash across the street in the sparse traffic would leave Alex out in the open for no more than fifteen seconds. From there he saw a spot behind a telephone pole and several dumpsters. He would have a vantage point to the second Taurus between the two trash bins. He would wait until the man got as far as he was going to walk to the channel, and then he would make a sprint for the car. He would squat on his run, reach over the car door to the man's jacket and into the inside pocket. Hopefully, he'd find a keycard.

Alex knew that Pepper had to be in there. He had to risk it.

He watched the man walk back and forth twelve times before his cigarette died. It took him nearly forty-five seconds to walk to the far end of the property, up to a chain-linked and barbed wire fence that separated him from the Channel No. 2 loading dock and the crane. Then the man returned to the Taurus, got another cigarette and repeated his routine.

Alex waited until the man made his pivot near the Taurus, then he made his move. He ran as swiftly as he could, in nearly a duck waddle to the car. He glanced above. There was a video camera pointing down at the vehicle. "Shit!" But he had to go through with it, he couldn't stop now.

Alex reached into the car. He was unable to get the jacket, it was too far over. *Son-of-a...what do I do now?* he thought. He quickly glanced at the man, who had nearly reached the water and was about to pivot back.

The driver's side window was open. Alex had only a split second to decide. He dove into the vehicle through the window, over the backseat and onto the floor. He knew he'd be out of sight.

He listened carefully. He could hear the gravel underneath the man's feet as he slowly paced back toward the car. The man made grunting sounds as he got closer to the vehicle. Then he stopped, and pivoted on his heels. Alex could hear him walking away.

Alex reached up into the man's coat. There was no wallet, no billfold, no keycard.

"Goddamnit I told you we should have brought the other car," the first man said to the other as he slammed open the warehouse door and straightened his jacket to fit over his holstered, silenced Tokarev-TT.

"Son-of-a-bitch, I told him also."

The door slammed back nearly shut when the last man, the despotic leader stormed out. He was still wearing his Ray-Bans. "Look you assholes, let's get this thing done and get the fuck out of here!"

The man who had been pacing walked briskly back toward the car. Enroute he threw the two-thirds smoked cigarette to the ground. "Where do you want the bodies dumped?" he asked.

"Look, I don't give a fuck how you do it," the Ray-Banned man said, " I just want it done tonight. As far as I'm concerned you grind 'em into chopped liver, but not in the building."

"Isn't that what you want us to do?" the one with the Ray-Banned man asked.

"No, you fuck! It's set to blow at midnight. They'll blame it on a gas leak. I don't want them in there when it blows. Now get the rest of the files out of here."

"So let's just blow 'em with the building," the smoker said.

"Look, we can't leave anything behind."

"Boss," the other said, "with all that C-4 there won't be a trace of them left. Poof,"

"Fine, fine. Just be sure...not a trace. Now go get the van and we'll load this shit up and get our asses out of here."

"Whatever you want," the smoker replied as he walked over to the car. Alex smashed down flat onto the backseat floor. The man opened the door, but did not look into the government vehicle.

"Joe, you and Marty help me," the Ray-Banned leader said.

"Frank, you go over to the Naval Yard and procure one of the Aerostars. We'll have the files ready for you when you get back."

"Whatever you want," Joe the smoker replied. He grabbed another cigarette, fired up on the pop-in car lighter and slammed his door. Sweat rolled down Alex's brow. He was nearly a dead man.

The boss decided to post Joe the smoker on the door, and he and Marty would bring the files down the office stairs and leave them outside for Frank.

Two minutes later Frank was gone in the other Taurus. Joe posted guard at the keycard door, and Marty and the Ray-Banned leader brought out white cardboard banker's boxes.

Alex knew that if he didn't do something quick he'd be caught. The men had brought out six boxes. Then he overheard, "Joe give me a hand. These are too fucking heavy." Joe looked around. No one was there, so he propped open the door with a box. He looked around again and said, "What the fuck," and went upstairs.

At that moment, Alex heard the van coming. He looked up above the seat and saw an Aerostar bearing the U.S. Naval Station Long Beach insignia pulling into the warehouse's parking lot. It drove in nose first, then the driver realized that he wasn't thinking. He figured that it would be easier to load the file boxes if he backed in. So he put the truck in reverse and backed out.

This was the only chance that Alex had. He threw open the car door, then quickly shut it as quietly as he could. Then he dashed for the warehouse door. At the exact instant that he made it into the doorway, the van driver looked into his rearview mirror. He thought that he might have seen someone.

A few seconds later the Ray-Banned leader, Marty and Joe climbed down an observation office stairway. They were carrying an awkward aluminum-strip reinforced file box that was nearly the size of a small steamer trunk, and three times the cardboard thickness of a normal banker's box. They were in eyeshot of Alex. However, they were too busy maneuvering the unwieldy box to notice Alex sneak in back of the door and behind several 105 gallon drums.

"Hey," Frank yelled as he ran into the immense warehouse with his gun drawn.

"What the fuck's up with you?" the Ray-Banned leader snarled as they finished descending the last step, and nearly rammed into Frank.

"Sorry, I thought I saw...nevermind." He holstered his weapon, then gave them a hand.

The leader's instincts told him different. "Let's get these boxes loaded up, then I want one of you to give this place a good once over."

"No problem," Marty said.

CHAPTER 38

It took the men nearly an hour to load the boxes. The light inside the warehouse was dim, and only one of three sets of overhead fluorescent lights was on. Alex was crouched behind a three-wide and three-high 105 gallon black drum escarpment. He remained as motionless as possible. As his eyes adjusted he tried to make sense of his surroundings from his narrow vantage point. He saw barrels upon barrels of the three truss-ribbed drums. The stenciling on them was faint and hard to read in its bleached-out script. It said something about "U.S. Army Experimental...."

"Let's get the fuck out of here," the Ray-Banned leader said to the others as he readjusted his sunglasses. A head injury in Vietnam left him sensitive to light and he wore sunglassses even after dark.

"Frank and I'll take the van. Joe, you take one of the cars. Marty you give the place one last once-over, then I'll see you in Dallas."

"Dallas?" Alex thought. He got one last look at the leader. He was sure that he had seen him recently. But where?

The three men left and the metal security door clanged shut.

This left only Marty inside with Alex. Alex had noticed that Marty had a gun holstered inside his jacket. On one side he had a gun belt that slung over his shoulders in a figure eight. The weapon was holstered on the right. On the other side was a portable secure-cell phone, uplinked to the CIA Intruder satellite network.

Marty hit a panel of lights, eighteen switches in all, and illuminated the wharf facility. He looked over the one hundred thousand square-foot warehouse. Alex had not realized the enormity of the building, nor the total number of U.S. Army Experimental drums. There were thousands of them.

Alex could hear Marty's footsteps as he walked the cold concrete warehouse floor, and then up a flight of stairs to an observation office. The solitary office was forty feet above the stacked barrels and protruded outward fifteen feet. It provided a view of the entire complex except for a blind spot beneath its belly. There were six glass windows in the front and one on each side.

When Marty reached the office, he flicked the lights on. At one point Alex thought that he heard stifled voices. They were distant. Then the sound became more clear—it was only one voice. Shortly thereafter, the lights cut out. From his vantage point, he could see Marty, but Marty could not see him.

Marty returned to the wall outlet switches next to the security door and killed all the lights. Then he left through the keycard door.

Alex waited until he could hear the Taurus drive off, then he got out of his crouched position. His knees were stiff and his back ached.

Through brine-dirty windows at the top of the four-story building came in the only light—that after awhile was sufficient to let Alex find his way.

"Pepper had to be there," he thought. "Plus hadn't he heard them say...they?"

Alex headed for the stairs that led up to the observation office. When he got to the top he noticed that there was a dim light coming from inside. He hadn't noticed it before. The glow emanated from twenty black-and-white monitor screens. He walked into the office and saw a huge, security panel. Monitor after monitor provided different views of the warehouse, both inside and out. There were a number of alarm lights on another, more elaborate panel. Some of them were labeled "motion detector," others had initials. One switch had been kicked down to the "sound mute" position. Below two of the motion detectors were red set lights that were flashing on and off.

Alex scanned the office. Five-drawer file cabinets that appeared to have housed important documents were pulled open. Inside he saw nothing but empty space and hinged metal file-holder skeletons.

There was a door that led to another room. He cautiously opened it. Within were Pepper and Joanna Knight. They were bound and gagged to a plastic container. On top was an electronic device with a digital read-out. The display read: "*2 min. 20 sec.*"

Alex gazed down at Pepper. She had fear in her swollen eyes. Her face was bruised plum purple, especially under her right cheek. Again he looked at the device. It read: "*2 min. 07 sec.*"

"Shit!"

Pepper and Jo's hands were tied to one another with clothesline cord , then duct-taped to the drum that sat between them. Their feet were secured to one another in a similar manner.

Alex ripped at the duct tape around Pepper's right arm. She mumbled furiously. Alex quickly glanced down at the timer: "*1 min. 40 sec.*" He then looked at the menacing device. Three wires came out of the mechanism: one red, the other white and the last blue.

"Hmmmm, hmmmmm!"

Alex stopped his efforts on Pepper's hands and worked free her gag. The timer read "*1 min. 13 sec.*"

"Get your ass out of here, this whole place is going to blow!" she yelled at the split second he released the gag from her face. This statement, however, brought Jo back to life, and though she appeared drugged and her almond eyes were lifeless, they burst wide open. She too frantically began to mumble. Alex quickly glanced down at the timer. "*0 min. 44 sec.*"

"How do I undo it?"

"You can't," Pepper yelled, "It's booby-trapped."

At that moment, in the observation office, a third red flashing light illuminated on the motion detector board.

"Tell me what to do!"

"You can't do anything. They said it would detonate if it was screwed with. Run Alex!"

Alex swiftly looked down at the mechanism. There was a keycode board with the numbers zero through nine and the pound and star signs.

"Alex run!"

"No!"

"You can't pull out the wires, it'll blow!"

Alex rapidly studied the mechanism. He knew he had to do something, pull a wire...anything. The board read "*0 min. 30 sec.*"

"Put your hands up!" Marty ordered from behind him. He had doubled back. Better to let them flush themselves out, than risk being shot in the back. "Up to the sky, fucker!"

Alex quickly glanced down at Pepper. She had terror in her eyes. Then he looked at the device. It read: "*0 min. 19 sec.*" He rapidly glanced at Jo who was in a drugged craze, mumbling the same thing over and over again. "You have fifteen seconds to disarm the device," Alex said calmly as he stood up from his hunched position, glancing down at the bomb. "Twelve seconds."

The man made his way over to Alex, his eyes bouncing between Alex and the bomb. "Seven seconds," Alex said.

A frantic Marty shoved Alex back toward the door, then kneeled to punch the numbers into the keyboard. It read "*3 seconds.*" He furiously punched in the sequence. 3, 4, 7, 1 then "pound" "star" at the same time. He miskeyed. "*2 seconds.*"

Quickly Marty hit 3, 4, 7, 1...*1 second*," then "pound" "star" simultaneously. Click—*zero seconds*. The device was disarmed. Sweat wielded on Marty's face.

"Now you're going to die, Seacourt. I've been waiting for you."

Marty squeezed the trigger. But Pepper had broken free and shoved Marty's firing elbow forward. The bullet missed its mark.

Before Marty could get off another shot, Alex lunged onto him. He slammed the killer into the C-4 drum. "Ahhhhh!" Marty moaned as his back dug into the rim of the explosive container. He fired off three shots from his Tokorav-TT. The bullets flew widely and ricocheted off the room's floor, wall and ceiling. One buried itself dangerously close to the explosive barrel.

Alex knew that he had to grab for the gun. In an instant, he grasped the killer's gunhand. That was enough to free Marty's left knee from Alex's block. Marty threw the full-force of his extremity into Alex's groin. "Uhhhhh!" Alex groaned with the delivery of the impact. Despite the blow, Alex held on tight to the gun. They tumbled to the unyielding floor and struggled for the weapon, the killer for control, and Alex for his life.

Shots spit out again and again from the Tokorav. Then Marty nailed Alex in the jaw with an uppercut. "Uhhhhh!" Alex moaned as he felt his lower teeth loosen and blood come from his mouth. Again deadly shots railed until...*click, click, click.*

With the Tokorav-TT empty, Alex could let one hand off the killer's gunhand, and fight back. But when Alex did this, that was enough to allow Marty to break Alex's grip of his right hand. With the gunhand free, Marty railed a blow of cold-steel against Alex's forehead. Alex lost his footing and fell backward to the floor.

"That's it! You're dead!"

Alex looked up. He was disabled. He saw double. He could see Marty standing over him, ready to bash in his brains with the butt of his Russian-made automatic.

Smash!

Behind Marty was Pepper Knight, who had worked herself free. She had in her hands the disabled electronic device that she had pulled from the top of the bomb. She cracked it over Marty's head. The henchman stood there for a moment, dazed and confused. Then, he looked down at Alex as blood began to drip out of his mouth. Like a fallen two-hundred year old redwood, he toppled face first to the floor in a bone-smashing crack.

"You okay?"

Alex was disoriented from the blow, but was coming to his senses.

"Alex, are you all right?" she asked as she reached down to give him assistance. He took her hand and tried to stand up. He was woozy. He got halfway to his feet and then teetered backward onto his buttocks. The room spun. He felt for his forehead. The blow had landed just into his hairline. "Uhhhhh," he rubbed his scalp.

"You all right?" She asked again.

"Uhhh...yeah."

"Be careful," she said smiling. "Don't rub too hard...you might lose some more hair."

Alex gained more of his wits and looked at her with burning eyes. "Watch it." He slowly righted himself and shook the cobwebs out of his brain. "Who's he?" Alex asked as he looked for some duct tape. Alex found a roll on a shelf along with security wire and other odds and ends. "Help me tie him up."

"Sure," she said, as she kicked Marty as hard as she could in the ribs.

"What was that for?"

"For this." She pointed to her face with her index finger.

They taped his arms, and then his legs behind his back. Then they tied all four extremities together in a cradle position. Marty's chest bowed into the floor. They did all this while Jo hypnotically gazed at Alex. She wanted to be untied.

Alex then began working on Jo's gag. With some difficulty, he cautiously untaped her mouth.

"They drugged her," Pepper said.

"I...can..." Joanna Knight hesitated before she answered. She tried to get the grit out of her mouth. "Wa...ter."

"Get some," Alex ordered Pepper as he finished untying Joanna. Pepper returned a few minutes later with two paper cups full. There was a bottled-water dispenser in the office.

"They wanted...ya...you."

"Take your time," Alex said patiently.

"They gave me thiopental or some kind of truth serum to make me talk. They wanted you Alex."

"Me? Why me?"

"Are the... containers safe?" Jo asked in a confused slur.

"The drums in the warehouse?"

"Yessss."

"Take your time," Alex said as he propped her head up and she drank more water. Then Pepper took over, cupped the back of Jo's head with one hand, and helped her drink the second glass with the other. He went to the office and got her a third. There were no files left behind. Alex scanned the room and the monitors—nothing. Then he realized that the black and white monitors were *not* just video but audio also. He looked further at the panel. There were playback controls. Alex tried one of the monitors. After a few minutes he had figured out its operation.

"Those idiots forgot their tapes."

"No they didn't," a voice came from the other room. It was Pepper, who had come to see what was keeping Alex. "They were going to blow everything to hell." Behind her, on wobbly legs, was Jo. Alex helped her into a swivel-back chair. He gave her another glass of water.

"Why did they want me?"

"I don't know," Pepper answered for her.

"Because of the grill?"

"The grill?"

"...girl." Jo replied. "More wa...ter, please." Pepper got her another glass.

"What girl?" Alex asked.

She cud-chewed her mouth. "I don't...know. But they know you know the girl."

"I don't know any girl." Then he glanced down at the sophisticated controls. The video recorder started its playback. Alex had selected the monitor in the office. Nothing. He fast-forwarded images of four men bringing Pepper and Jo into the office, then the explosive device being brought in, then the men packing up the file boxes. "Wait a second." Alex freeze-framed the tape. He could see the man with the Ray-Bans take out a three-by-five photograph from his jacket pocket. In the photo was the Ray-Banned man, another man who also looked familiar, and the girl. The girl's face was circled with a wax pencil.

"It's...the autopsy." Jo said as she viewed the video while weakly forcing herself to stand. She looked over Alex's shoulder.

"That's it, it's the man in the..." a chill went through his body. Alex turned and faced Jo. "Who is he? You know who he is!"

"I don't," she replied.

"This is the man we performed the autopsy on, goddamnit!"

"Dallas, tomorrow," Pepper interrupted. "They're going to Dallas."

"Who is he?" Alex asked Jo sternly.

"I don't know, and *I can't tell...you if I did.*"

"Bullshit you can't!" Alex railed. He wanted to grab her by her shoulders and shake the sense out of her, but he didn't. "I've been shot at and have traipsed all over this goddamn country trying to find you, and now you tell me that you can't tell me what this is all about!"

Jo looked down, then hesitantly up at Alex, "That's right."

"*No Jo, that's wrong!* That's dead-to-rights wrong! You're going to tell me! You're going to tell me everything!" Then he looked back into the monitor. Another chill resonated through his body. He flashed back to the Las Vegas Convention Center. He knew where he saw the man with the dark sunglasses. He had bumped into *them,* when *they* were coming out—the man had nearly fallen to the ground, he was sick. He was wretching. He didn't see his full face, but it had to be the same man that Jo performed the autopsy on. Alex just didn't get the connection at that time. *It was him!*

"The man with the sunglasses, there!" Alex said, pointing to the video frozen in midframe. "He was watching us at the hospital wasn't he?"

"Yes," Jo replied, timidly avoiding Alex's glare.

"They killed Dr. Warner. They tried to kill your daughter and me. Tell me!"

"No...Livingston, not Livingston!"

"Yes! Who's your goddamn loyalty to?" Alex exploded. "They were going to kill you!"

Pepper took Jo's hand and carefully placed it between her own. This was the first time in years they had any type of physical contact. She tenderly, and with genuine forgiveness, looked into Jo's eyes. "Mother, please."

Jo began to cry. "You haven't called me 'Mother' as long as I can remember."

"I know. I'm sorry."

"Jo," Alex begged, "Please help me, help us. Tell me what you know."

She paused, then raised her head and looked Alex square in his eyes. "Livingston Warner, he's dead?"

"He was run down by a trash truck while he was leaving his house...after he received your FedEx."

"My God."

"Tell me, please," he implored.

We're all going to die because of me. It's my fault.

CHAPTER 39

"It all started with the KGB...and a *turkey virus*."

"What do you mean?" Alex asked. He anticipated the worst.

She had been drugged, yet she found that she could force the words to come out in some sort of semblance of order. "Do you remember Alex...publicity that spread like wildfire a number of years ago...about the origin of AIDS?"

"Somewhat."

"Actually, it wasn't that far from the truth..." She needed more water. Pepper filled another cup and gave it to her. "In 1983...Service A, which is a subdivision of the KGB, by a mixture of...both overt propaganda and covert action, attempted to blame AIDS on American biologic warfare."

"*Oleg Shlyapnikov Assistant to the First Chief Directorate, KR Line—FSB*," Alex thought, "*had arranged for him to go to the Consumer Electronics Show. Did he cause Alex to run into the dead man?*" Shlyapnikov had arranged his tickets to the states and his itinerary at the Consumer Electronics Show and for him to go to BetaTec, and ask for the demo *LAV-10* software.

"We actually caused AIDS?" Pepper asked in shock.

Jo took an unsteady sip of the water and looked up at her daughter. "Yes and no." She was making her drugged mouth work.

"Yes and no?" Alex asked incredulously. "Like 'yes and no' pregnant?" He sarcastically said.

"Yes Alex, like 'yes and no' pregnant."

"Tell me."

"First the Soviets..." she drank some more, smacked her lips and continued. "A lie...you see sometimes is very much based on the truth. In the summer of 1983, an article was published in the Soviet Indian newspaper *Patriot*, alleging that the AIDS virus had been 'manufactured' during genetic engineering experiments at Fort Detrick, New Jersey...no Maryland. Initially...the story had little impact, but it was revived with great effect by the Russian *Literturnaya GaZeta* in October 1985.

"In its resurrected form, the AIDS story was bolstered by a report from a retired East German biophysicist, Professor Jacob Segal... Segal sought to demonstrate through circumstantial evidence that the virus had been artificially synthesized at Fort Detrick from two natural existing viruses: VISNA and HTLV-1. Thus, assisted by quasi-scientific jargon, the AIDS fabrication not merely swept through the Third World but also took in some of the Western media."

"Did we or didn't we cause AIDS?" Alex nipped.

"To continue...In October 1986, the conservative British *Sunday Express* made an interview with Professor Segal the basis of its main front page story. In the first six months of 1987 alone, the story received major coverage in over forty Third World countries. At the very height of success, however, the active AIDS measure was scuttled...ostensibly by Gorbachev's 'new thinking' and '*Glasnost.*'

"Gorbachev and his advisers were clearly concerned that Western exposure of Soviet disinformation threatened to take the gloss off the new Soviet image. Faced with official American protests and the repudiation of the AIDS story by the international scientific community, including the leading Soviet AIDS expert, Viktor Zhdanov, the Kremlin for the first time showed signs of public embarrassment...at a successful active measured campaign. In August 1987, U.S. officials were told in Moscow that the AIDS story was officially disowned... Soviet press coverage of the story came to an almost complete halt."

"So did we or did we not cause AIDS?" Alex provokingly asked.

"Do you need some more water?" Pepper asked in anticipation as she walked to the dispenser.

"No, thank you." Jo sat up more rigid in her chair, then she stood on wobbly legs.

"Do you need a hand?"

"No," she told Pepper who helped her anyway. She slung her arm around Jo's back. Jo walked to the monitors and looked at the flickering freeze frame of the man with sunglasses, and the three-by-five photo, of the victim, himself and the girl. Something was written in wax pencil on the photo, and the girl's face was circled.

"Continue," Alex said impatiently. He tapped his foot in an uneven patter.

"Can you read what it says?"

Alex looked into the monitor and tried to make out the indistinct writing on the photo.

"Can you blow it up?"

"I doubt it, but let me try. Keep talking." He began playing with the knobs and switches on the intricate panel.

"In 1993 we began working together." Jo paused to think. "They contacted me. The Russians were now working with the CIA to try...and find a cure for AIDS."

"The CIA? Why would they contact...You worked on the original AIDS project twenty years ago at Invenco, didn't you?"

"Yes."

"Jesus Jo, why? What did you do?"

"It's not what you think. Let me explain..."

"That was when I was a child," Pepper interrupted. "That was when I came to see you. The beekeeper."

"Yes. The project was too dangerous. I couldn't have you around. I was afraid that if I ever got unknowingly infected, I could infect you.... So I had Livingston raise you."

"Mother," Pepper had tears in her eyes.

"People had already died. It didn't dawn on me at first but that's how Dr. Frank and Lansing Darling died!"

"The names on the CIA Roll of Honor?"

"Yes. They worked on the original project with me. It was so long ago, the names escaped me."

"Tell me Jo," Alex said. He was beginning to feel an urgency to leave the warehouse. "What happened twenty years ago?"

"It started with a turkey virus. We didn't cause AIDS, at least not as we know it. No one really knows what happened, how AIDS came about. But I can tell you my story and what pieces I've put together...In 1973, just after I finished my joint residency in pathology and my Ph.D. in virology at USC, I was recruited by the Deputy Director for Science and Technology at the CIA for a covert...and very important project. It was a dream come true. But I was not allowed to bring my daughter with me because of the unknown dangers of working with a new virus the Government was investigating."

"You're serious?"

"Yes. You got to remember this was back in the early '70s, I was stupid back then. My career meant everything to me, so I thought that it wouldn't make much difference. I rationalized that I'd be back in L.A. within three months, then six months passed...It turned out to be nearly four years.

"We had come across a turkey virus. A mysterious infection was killing millions of turkeys, and left a million others severely underweight and threatened turkey farmers in six states."

Alex listened intently while he played with the video panel. There were no enlargement adjustments, just zoom controls. He did find a switch to print a hard copy.

"Just two weeks after Memorial Day in 1973, we discovered a disease that was wiping out the turkey industry. The disease was thought to be transmitted by turkey droppings and possibly some insects. It had spread from North Carolina, Virginia, South Carolina, Georgia, Indiana and New York. An estimated two million birds had died since the summer."

"The Government stepped in and eliminated nearly twelve million turkeys," Alex said, "I vaguely remember reading about it."

"I never heard anything about that." Pepper said.

"You were too young, and besides it was all kept quiet. Later a virus was implicated. Which I suppose now in my infinite wisdom...I understand what the Government was really doing."

"The experiments were to develop a biologic weapon?" Alex conjectured.

"In a sense we did. It was also just about the time that the first case of AIDS was identified."

Alex pushed a button and a hard copy spewed out of a laser

printer. Alex walked over to the printer and looked at the image. It was twice as large as the video screen. Alex studied the photo of the three. He tried to make out the wax pencil writing.

"Jo," Alex said as he scrutinized the black and white, "I thought that the first case of AIDS was discovered in about 1983, not 1973."

"*That's not true.* What I'm going to tell you has been classified until now...but...if I don't, it may be too late for everyone." She moved away from Pepper's supportive arm, and sat back down in her chair. She felt woozy and the room spun.

"You have to find the girl."

"The girl?" Alex asked.

"Yes. They were going to...."

"Dallas," Pepper interjected. "I overheard them talking."

"Me, too," Alex said.

"This is what we really know. It is commonly believed," Jo continued, "that the origin of AIDS is from a monkey virus. The French scientist Montagnier...discovered a human retrovirus in a remote Mande tribe in West Africa in 1983. This HIV-2 provided a partial answer to the fundamental question raised by the AIDS epidemic: How could AIDS have appeared without warning, and then spread so rapidly from one part of the world to another?

"Speculation is that the human AIDS virus might have resulted from the very recent introduction of a monkey virus into the homosapien population. In addition, biologists had numerous examples of infectious agents that appeared relatively benign in their natural hosts, but became highly virulent when introduced into a new species. The progression from a benign infectious agent in African green monkeys to a virulent killer in humans seemed relatively straightforward. It's thought that the time of divergence between the human virus and the monkey virus is forty to eighty years ago."

"Forty to eighty years? But the first cases of AIDS weren't reported until 1983," Alex said as he quickly crunched the numbers.

"Putatively," Jo answered with authority. "But testing for HIV wasn't available until 1985. You need to remember that."

"But..."

"Let me continue. It is believed that HIV may have been limited to small, relatively isolated populations in rural Africa. The social mores of those populations may not have been conducive to rapid spread of the virus. The few cases of AIDS that did develop could have escaped detection against the backdrop of multiple life-threatening infections common in the region...The major factor responsible for changing this pattern appears to have been urbanization. African cities grew dramatically during and after World War II. As in other parts of the world, urbanization was accomplished by social changes that affected the lives of millions."

"So what you're saying is that AIDS has really been around for forty to eighty years."

"That's correct."

"And the government knew about it..."

"That's right."

"So the government knew that one day there would possibly be an epidemic that would threaten the world, and that whoever controlled AIDS, whoever had *the cure to AIDS*, had the power—and had *an incredible weapon*. You...they...could release AIDS on their enemies...and eventually in five or ten years there would be no more bad guys."

"That was it."

"How could you have worked for them, Mother?" Pepper asked in disbelief.

"At first, I didn't know what I was getting into. The turkey virus was thought to be benign to humans, but highly deadly to the turkeys. In fact...it turned out that the virus was indigenous to the *poule d'Inde*...a French turkey. However, the virus was missing snippets of genetic material, including a key gene called *nef*.

"The turkey virus, called TTLV-1 was not able to reproduce effectively in humans. We thought that if we could develop an attenuated, or heat killed TTLV-1, we could cure AIDS."

"So you developed a cure to AIDS?"

"Yes and no. We could have stopped AIDS dead in its tracks before the outbreak in '83...had the funding been in place. *But we were shut down.*"

"Whose decision was that?" Alex indignantly asked.

"I don't know. You see, back in the early and mid-seventies, we didn't have the technology we have today. There were deaths during the project. We didn't understand how the researchers got contaminated, but they did. And some of them did *not* directly work with the virus. That's why I couldn't take Pepper with me."

"I thought you said TTL wasn't toxic to humans?" Pepper said.

"It's not. But we were working with the AIDS virus and we didn't understand how the virus worked back then. There was still a lot of mystery about how it spread, whether it was airborne, or vector borne, or blood borne."

"So researchers died?"

"Yes, and not just a few. What we had developed with TTLV-1 attenuate..."

"You mean heat-killed virus?"

"In a sense, and also chemically modified. Anyway, what we had developed with TTLV-1 attenuate was a *super 'on-off' switch*." Alex did not like what he was hearing. "At first we thought that TTLV-1 attenuate would stimulate human helper lymphocytes, as a vaccine to make antibodies to fight HIV or the AIDS infections. However, soon we discovered that the TTLV-1 attenuate bound with the normal HIV and formed a mutant HIV. In actuality, it *turned off* HIV."

"So that was great wasn't it?" Pepper asked.

"Initially it was. But then we discovered that the new mutant virus would turn back on in rare instances. But it wouldn't turn back on in the usual way. Normal HIV can only become transmitted by fluid to fluid modality. *The mutant HIV was capable of airborne transmission.*"

"Jesus Christ." Alex stopped looking at the photo. "That explains how the researchers died, the ones who weren't directly involved with the AIDS research."

"Yes, airborne transmission, but it wasn't the combined virus though. We later learned that it was due to a *'flipping'* of the TTLV-1 attenuate. In the combined heat and chemically treated form, TTLV-1 in part, in the *nef* gene, came in a *'d'* or *'dextro'* form. The *'d'* form turned off the virus. However, about .5 percent of the attenuate that was bound to HIV formed a mutant HIV flipped to a *mirror image* form, or an *'l'* or *'levo'* form. The *'l'* form conversely *supercharged* the AIDS virus. It changed HIV's properties, turned it into *an airborne killer.*"

Alex looked out the control room windows. He gazed down at the stenciled drums. He squinted, focused, then studied the distant markings underneath the "U.S. Army Experimental" stenciling. They read: *TTLV-1 A.* "That's the goddamn attenuate down there!"

"Yes. And if they blew this place up, chances are *it wouldn't all be destroyed.* The viral attenuate, though in only minute amounts, might survive. That's been our experience. For example, at the Nevada Proving Grounds we found that even after atmospheric nuclear detonation at ground zero, some virus and primitive life forms survived—in microscopic amounts. *That's all you need. One microscopic droplet...*The only safe way to dispose of this stuff is to bury it in a salt mine, miles beneath the earth's surface, as far away from civilization as possible."

"That's what the room was at Invenco—it was a gravity room?" Alex asked.

"You mean the room that was at the center of the huge centrifuge?" Pepper asked.

"We tried working in a 2-G environment. The thought was that if we could develop a TTLV-1 attenuate at a twice normal gravity, it might not flip in normal G's."

"Did you have any success?" Alex asked.

"We weren't allowed to complete our work. One day, we were just shut down. By then...I was so disgusted with the whole thing that I just picked up and moved to Vegas. I lost my husband, my daughter, everything. I wanted to get away."

"So you went to Sin City?" Pepper said.

"Yes, to pay for my sins."

"So what did the dead man on your autopsy table have to do with all of this?" Alex asked.

"The people who died twenty years ago from the airborne mutant AIDS virus *looked very much like him*. I knew it when I saw his face."

"That's why you did the ELSIA test?"

"Yes."

"Then why aren't you and I infected?"

"The airborne strain only survives outside the body for twelve hours. Once a person is infected they are communicable for another twelve hours. After that, the virus loses its airborne capabilities. One still has the normal fluid to fluid infectivity, but the airborne characteristic is negated."

"So what about Russia?"

"In a sense, their disinformation campaign was correct. Though we didn't create AIDS, we could have prevented it if we continued our research."

"But you didn't?" Pepper interjected.

"No."

"But you said you were contacted?" Alex asked.

"Yes. First by Dr. Gudayer at the CDC, then later by a joint Russian-American scientific team spearheaded by a Dr. Mikulas Petrovich at the CIA's Mills Farm research center. It turned out that we had a Soviet 'mole' scientist working in our original group twenty years ago. The Russians knew about our research all along."

"And no one found out?"

"As it turned out, the Russians have been working on solving the AIDS problem for the last four years on *Space Station Mir*. They have taken the inverse approach and are trying to develop a TTLV-HIV mutant at zero G's that wouldn't flip in normal gravity. With the advent of the joint *Mir-Kennedy I Space Station*, the project has been moving forward at full throttle. Dr. Petrovich wanted me on the team."

"To be an astronaut?" Pepper proudly asked.

"Yes, something like that. Their derivative TTLV, *LAV-10*..."

"Did you say *LAV-10*?" Alex asked angrily.

"Yes, *LAV-10*. In early testing it appeared to be the direction to go in..." She had a doleful face.

"Those sons-of-bitches."

"Who?" Joanna asked.

"The FSB!"

"The who?"

"The KGB!"

"What about the KGB?"

"Just go on, please Jo...any luck with *LAV-10*?"

"No, not so far."

"So why kidnap you?" Alex asked. He was infuriated at the *scam* they pulled on him.

"They..."

"Who are they?"

"I don't know. *They* have access to everything. They're feds, but I'm not sure whose side they're on. Anyway, 'they' apparently were responsible for locking me out of my autopsy room. The mere fact that I did an autopsy on the John Doe was coincidental, and nothing more."

"You mean that you didn't know who he was."

"That's right...Alex, *they wanted you!* You were talking to the girl."

Alex had accidentally run into them at the Las Vegas Convention Center at the Consumer Electronics Show. The man was bent down. He was wretching. Alex had shared words with the girl. He had asked the girl if he could help the man. She said, "No." Then the man fell to his knees and Alex helped him up. Alex had said something else to the girl, but he couldn't remember. Then the other man—the man with the dark sunglasses—helped the sick one to his feet... And Alex had been sent by Oleg Shlyapnikov *to ask for the demo LAV-10 software, which really wasn't a software at all, but an AIDS super on-off switch.*

"How long after you get the mutant AIDS virus do you get sick?"

"There's one more thing Alex."

"What's that?" He was enraged.

"Not only is the mutant HIV airborne, but it also acts much more quickly."

"How much?"

"Not the normal five to ten years...*but twenty-four to forty-eight hours!—and it's a thousand times more virulent!*"

"Christ." Alex wondered if he was exposed, then he thought about the infective window and realized that if the man in Las Vegas was sick, he was already past the communicable stage.

"Alex, they must have seen you with me at the hospital. And then they saw you with the girl. They think that you know something, or that the girl gave you something."

"Pepper, you heard them also say they were going to Dallas?"

"Yes, first thing in the morning."

Alex looked intently at the photo. On two lines he barely made out the letters 'Te' on the top line, and 'Sta' on the other. I know where they're going. We need to get out of here!"

"I agree," Pepper said.

"I can't come with you," Jo interjected—out of a sense of duty.

"Why?" Alex asked.

"Because I have to make sure I take care of these," she pointed to thousands of the deadly 'U.S. Army Experimental' government stenciled 105-gallon drums outside the office windows.

"The TTLV-1?"

"Yes. Don't worry about me. I still know the right people."

"Are you sure?"

"Positive." She took another sip of her water.

"Alex," Pepper asked as she, too, looked at the grim black-and-white laser print and the photo within. She studied the girl's face, and the cut-off words: '*Te*' and '*Sta*'. Then she said, "I've got it!"

CHAPTER 40

The Adolphus Hotel had undergone a $45 million restoration. It was built by brewer Adolphus Busch in 1912 and was now marketed as "The beautiful lady with a past." The rooms were lush, and though the hotel was not in a particularly southern city, its ambiance imbued such.

The one-bedroom suite that Mahalia Hunt procured was extravagant and at the same time historic. Their living room had an Italian hand-blown glass chandelier; their bedroom, Chippendale and Queen Anne furniture, and Williamsburg paneling. There was also a sense of the city and the state's independence in the taunting 19th century oil paintings that hung on the ornate stippled walls.

"So what's with the blues?" Katrina asked quizzically.

"I don't know. I like a little of everything. Before I met you, for about a year, I worked in New Orleans out of the French Quarter..."

"Before New York?"

"Yes. I was at Mardi Gras. There's something sensuous about New Orleans. It's a ritual...of watchers. The Phunny Phorty Phellows."

"Who?"

"A group of anonymous people that runs the Carnival. The captain is the president. There is the parade and Rex the King of the Carnival. The revelry lasts until midnight. They all wear masks. It's an observance, a love story for the Southerners. And then, as the streets cleared and the men with funny gold masks and foil teeth, and women with dazzling sequined bead work drifted their ways—I heard it. It was a piper's call."

"Heard what?"

"A white stallion pranced past me. There was a man with a bug's face and brilliant yellow fly wings, and pink clown hair and two stick antennas with gold balls on top. Behind him was an old Negro man. He had a Duzzenburg stubby hat on, that was bent at the brim—and a gray-blue shirt. His face and hands were timeworn. He was playing a guitar that he had strapped around his shoulder. He had a sad look on his face, and he sang the blues. He told me that he was *Steelhead*. But later I found out that he had died years earlier.

"He sang of death. Of clay-cold bodies on the surf...of a journey that never ends except in the corridors of hell."

"That sounds...morbid," Katrina said.

"It wasn't. It was a love song. It was a dirge of life."

And then Mahalia was there—at the New Orleans Jazz Festival. Robert Cray, B.B. King and Eleanor Ellis were holding court in the Jazz tent. The crowd had poured into the Fairgrounds. They were eating crawfish po-boys. Tomatoes and cheeses, and the crawfish clampers, were falling out the edges. They were all there at once, looking at her, serenading her under the gospel tent.

The chairs they sat in were white willow wicker wood, and they rested their bare feet on the cozy grass. Slippery blades of sward stuck between her toes. Some people stretched out on the lawn between the chairs and the stage, which rose only six inches above the fescue. They were dancing the *fais do-do*.

"*Mahalia you are responsible. You are the sinner,*" they warbled in bluesy twang. "*Mahalia you killed her. It's your fault. You are the one.*"

Then she was back on the blustering cliffs with the blue and green metallic swallows of Capistrano. She was an adult. She was wearing a bright-orange dress with gaudy multi-colored plastic beads that hung from her neck. There were three rows and they were the size of grapes: green, red, yellow, and blue. She had an orange headband which pulled her hair back, and she was wearing dark sunglasses.

Below, on the jagged rocks, lay her limp mother. Copper blood spilled from her mouth. The swarthy nighthawk that had gobbled up the innocent hatchling, swooped down from the ominous sky. The predator was not yet satiated. It dove toward her mother with its razor-sharp talons spread wide.

"No!" Mahalia screamed, "No!"

With its keen-edged claws the nighthawk scooped out her mother's heart. It was still beating, pulsating, pumping blood as the nighthawk ascended. "Caw, Caw."

"No, No!"

"Mahalia, Mahalia, " Katrina shook her. "Mahalia!" Mahalia let loose her grief. Her brow was sweat drenched and her hands trembling. "Mahalia?"

"I'm fine," she said stoically

"Mahalia. Do you think that you need to see...a doctor?"

Mahalia gave Katrina *the same look* that she bestowed on the victim rock-and-roll star. "Tomorrow," she said, "Tomorrow morning I need to take care of business and then we go back. It's through."

"Are...you going to need me?"

"No sweet thing," Mahalia said. She kissed her sychophant on the cheek. "They're all booboisie," she mumbled to herself.

"What?" Katrina tentatively asked.

Mahalia walked to the commode where Katrina had placed her clothes. She had a particular outfit selected for the occasion. She was going to wear something special for "him." It was unforgettable. The dress was black and long, nearly to her ankles. She would wear black hose and shoes. She had a black hat with a veil. She would wear saturnine lipstick—a red that was nearly night. She would line her lips with a dark lip liner. She would paint one tear under her eye— with a red lipstick pencil—and then line it with brown.

Katrina did not know what her final plan truly was.

Tao said:

"Perceive purity;
Embrace simplicity;
Limit desires. "

Mahalia was Tao. She had the Power. She had come full circle.

The Doomsday Kiss

"I'm not his bastard child! He will pay! All men will pay!"

Mahalia removed her severe hat from its box. She walked to a mirror and tried it on. It fit perfectly. She pushed back the fine net veil and looked deeply into her tortured eyes. *You left me at the orphanage to die. You abandoned me. I cannot forgive you. You will pay.*

She walked back to the dresser and returned the hat to its drawer. Next to it lay a long silver and gold antique jewelry case. She opened it. The inside was lined with brushed red velvet. It was for pearls or a diamond lavaliere necklace. Instead, there was a single two-toned blue and green feather. It was a swallow's feather. It was the hatchling of Caspistrano's feather that she had saved. It was the one that had floated down into her hand twenty-two years ago. It was untainted. Each barb of plumage that extended in a vein from the center tapering shaft was perfect.

There was a knock on the door.

"One moment," Katrina said. She was in the living room of the pompous suite. She looked through the peephole. They weren't expecting anyone. "Who is it?"

"Gardener."

"I don't know any Gardener," she said. "Mahalia did you call a Gardener?"

"Yes. Let him in."

She did.

Mahalia walked into the living room. "Have a seat," she said matter-of-factly.

"Thank you, but no." The man was nondescript. He wore a smug leather jacket, and worn-at-the-knees blue jeans. His scraggly flap-top hair was unevenly cut, and greasy. He clutched an aluminum briefcase.

"Do you have it?"

"Do you have the money?"

"Yes," Mahalia curtly replied and handed him six crisp one-hundred dollar bills.

"Who's she?" he asked.

"She's fine. Do you have the gun?"

"Yes," he replied with a suspect look. "She's not a cop is she?"

"No. Let's see it."

He set his briefcase down on the coffee table in front of a mottled sofa. He opened it. Inside were three guns, all tightly packed in charcoal foam cut in an outline of each weapon. There was a burnished Colt 45, a Beretta 92, and a Swiss Sig Sauer Pistol 75.

"For six hundred bucks you get the Beretta. No serial numbers. If you want exotic, the Sig Sauer 75 chambered in 9mm is my recommendation. I, however, would steer you to this nickel-plated Colt 45 automatic for overall stopping power. It's not as accurate at longer ranges, but up close, it's as deadly as they come..."

"Mahalia, what's this for?" Katrina asked, concerned.

"Protection."

"But we've never needed protection before."

"Don't worry about it," she caustically replied.

"So what will it be? Do you want the Beretta, the Sig Sauer, or for an extra four bills you can have the Colt? And let me tell, if you really want, for an additional seven, I can get you a silencer for the Beretta or Sig Saver. Its a 'G' plus two for the Colt. What do you think?"

"The Berretta will do...as is."

"Are you sure? For a couple bills more you can have the Colt or a silencer."

"No, just the Beretta."

"Okay." He handed her the automatic. "Pleasure doing business with you." The slimeball closed his case. "Oh, before I forget," he reached into his inside biker-jacket pocket and withdrew two fifteen-bullet clips. "You know how to use 'em?"

"Yes."

"You ladies have a nice day." He stood up, nonchalantly tossed her the clips and left.

Mahalia took the Beretta 92, loaded one of the clips into the magazine with winged poise, and walked back to the bedroom. She carefully set it into the commode with the safety on. Katrina followed.

"Mahalia, what's the gun for?"

"Nothing."

"Mahalia?"

Mahalia had that unpredictable glaze in her eyes again—the psychotic, obsessive, desolate look. Katrina knew better than to say anything, but she did. "Mahalia what's going..."

Mahalia angrily slapped Katrina, then she kitten-cordial smiled. Her eyes beamed with *simpatico*. "Sweetheart, it's for nothing."

A tear welled in Katrina's eye. She raised her hand to her beet-red cheek. Mahalia bent forward to kiss it better. Katrina pulled away. "No," Katrina said.

Mahalia stared at Katrina with that quivering, lunatic look. Then Katrina let Mahalia kiss it, nurse it, suckle it. Then, Mahalia ordered Katrina on an errand.

One hour later Katrina returned from the gift shop. She had green foil wrapping paper, an eight-petal bow, a card, and a throw-away dispenser of Scotch Tape. Mahalia carefully swaddled the Hoyo De Monterey Excalibur cigar tube with the festive green paper. She wrote her last note on the card. In exquisite cursive calligraphy she scribed:

"I am Tao. I am Power. I am the Swallow."

An hour later, a messenger in a crisp delivery boy outfit arrived. He had epaulets on his dark green shoulders and wore a courteous cap. He took it off when he entered the suite.

"I want this delivered at exactly 8:00 a.m., tomorrow." She had the address written on a piece of Adolphus Hotel stationery. "And make sure you give it to him in person." She handed the delivery boy a hundred dollar bill.

"Yes ma'am. If it was the president himself, I'd make sure he *personally* got it."

"Good boy."

He left with a silly grin.

Mahalia would be through with everything after tomorrow. Life would have come full-circle. *"I am Tao. I am the Power. I am the Swallow. I am the Hawk. I am child to the father of the demon."*

CHAPTER 41

The Reverend Joe-Bob Jones was a strong man. He was firm in resolution. His name, no doubt, along with that of his departed wife, will waft on the lips of the titillated or the genuinely scandalized for years to come. His historical standing as fallen evangelist will rise with time and regale the lilted rebuke of the scandal consumed.

Former President of Christ's Divinity College in Atlanta and the New Christ Divinity Church, prodigy, visionary and builder of the Lord's theme park—Inspiration Village, on 2,900 rolling acres outside of Savannah, Georgia—Joe-Bob Jones had relentlessly declared his innocence, especially while he was hospitalized at the Fort Worth Medical Facility.

It was there in Texas, while in prison, that Joe-Bob first began reclaiming his empire and eventually his fleeting sanity—from behind the double barbed wire fence.

He had built Inspiration Village for good clean Christian fun. It was a combination resort and religious headquarters. It offered everything from camping in the woods to neck-risking on the Inferno, a sixty-foot water slide. Inspiration Village was open seven days a week, all summer, and nowhere did religion get a harder sell. It was there, in the 3,532-seat auditorium that morphed every Sunday into the sanctuary of the New Christ Divinity electronic church, that the faithful would pray and he would preach to his mesmerized worldwide television audience.

Inspiration Village was for Bible-believing, Christ-loving people. Above the registration desk at the gilt-encrusted Inspiration Grand Hotel, golden gothic letters proclaimed "Jesus Christ is Lord." Mornings began with a wake-up call reminding guests that "This is the day the Lord has made." Rooms were decorated with pictures of Jesus and Mary. The New Christ Divinity Bible was readily at hand on the table—not hidden, Gideon-like, in a drawer—and on television, the day-long schedule of New Christ Divinity programming was already in progress. No alcohol or tobacco was allowed, but there were plenty of other diversions: spiritual counseling in "the Heaven Room"—Jones' version of the place where Jesus hosted the Last Supper—baptisms every Tuesday afternoon in the hotel swimming pool, a Christian dinner theater, a high-tech passion play in the Inspiration Amphitheater, and, for night owls, a wafers-and-grape juice communion service at two in the morning.

In autumn of 1989, the New Christ Divinity Church needed cash desperately. The television ministry had built up an $11.2 million debt to the builder of Inspiration Village. Joe-Bob figured that he needed to do something fast, so he decided to hold a telethon to raise at least one million for the builder. He made this decision on a feeling of faith. "Well, Lord, I know I felt faith," Joe-Bob said to God and then to his studio audience. He explained to his followers that the Lord seemed to speak in his heart, saying, "You're on television all day; just mention it to the satellite people, the need, and do the special that you were doing with the studio audience all week long, to be able to raise that million dollars."

The special offer was a steal: for $1,500, Joe-Bob gave his viewers a package of lodging and free recreation that had once cost four thousand dollars. The New Christ Divinity Church disciples grabbed at the deal and contributed $25 million in just fifteen days. There was only one problem: all the money did not make it to the Inspiration Village coffers. Twelve and a half million dollars of it ended up in a Swiss bank account under a pseudonym used by Jones' wife Colleen

Winslow. In reality, Joe-Bob had no knowledge of the embezzlement.

Joe-Bob Jones and his wife Colleen, had for the obvious public purposes of the ministry remained married. It would have been immoral for him to have gotten a divorce. It could have brought down the New Christ Divinity Church.

Joe-Bob, however, was like any other desirous human being. And, despite his devotion to the marriage, a union that had soured into separate bedrooms and separate bathrooms, and regardless of the fact that in public she accommodated him and glorified his testimonial to the institution of marriage, he had an affair.

She never forgave him. As anger grew to rage, and eventually dementia, Colleen began to maliciously and secretly blackmail him from behind the scenes.

In reality, she despised the Reverend Joe-Bob Jones from the start. She had come from Springfield, Missouri where her father was a minister for the Assemblies of God Church. Their marriage, as her cane-carrying, butt-whipping father said "was ordained." She had no choice.

She married Joe-Bob out of trepidation of her inquisitorial father, but she remained chaste and emotionally distant from him. When she discovered his indiscretion, she found a vehicle to act out her anger toward her husband and father both. She stole the $12.5 million and planned to disappear.

However, federal investigators, who had already once looked at the question of financial irregularities and dropped an investigation back in 1987, were again hot on their heels.

Charges and recriminations came flying when Joe-Bob was indicted on bilking his followers out of the $25 million. By the time of the indictments, Colleen Winslow Jones had fled the country to Luxemburg, where she was eventually detained, and after a year and a half of legal proceedings, was extradited to the United States.

Prosecutors knew that the Reverend Joe-Bob Jones was not the mastermind, but for reasons of political gain and self-righteous indignation, wanted to overthrow his ministry. They felt that, morally, Joe-Bob was corrupt like the rest of the TV charlatans—Jimmy Swaggart, Jim Bakker—and that Joe-Bob siphoned money from the gullible lower class who couldn't afford their tithings, but fell victim to his hypnotic charisma.

Colleen Winslow Jones eventually made a deal with the feds to testify against her husband. Then later, while in custody, she was diagnosed with terminal ovarian cancer. By the time it was diagnosed it had already spread to her lymph nodes, pelvis, periaortic region and lungs. This would be her ultimate revenge.

Colleen Winslow owed a payback to her husband—holier-than-thou Joe-Bob Jones, for his indiscretion fifteen years earlier. She cast all blame on him. She said that he *"made"* her embezzle the money, that *he* had masterminded the whole affair.

Joe-Bob denied the allegations, but with twelve and a half million missing and the Inspiration Village Theme Park on the verge of financial collapse, and thousands of lower class faithful who had tithed their life savings up in arms—the feds and the press had a field day. They said he was the Caligula who stole from the religious Disney World—from people who trusted him—and that he should be sentenced to the same time as a bank robber.

Others said that Joe-Bob was not a preacher at all, but a show biz charlatan who intentionally weeded big words out of his vocabulary. That he used tears, humor, righteous anger, and gentle ministry to touch guileless viewers in their living rooms.

Joe-Bob was overwhelmed by the allegations. He knew he was innocent. The proceedings were more a tragic comedy than a criminal trial. First, a Government witness fainted on the stand, then Joe-Bob suffered a nervous breakdown during the stilted testimony of his wife. He had to be carted out of the federal courthouse.

Eventually, he was convicted of fraudulently raising $186 million in contributions from his adoring flock. Joe-Bob, the smooth-talking, scandal-plagued televangelist, drew a stunning forty-two year sentence and a million dollar fine from the U.S. District Judge.

Three years later, with the expiration of Colleen Winslow Jones, new facts began to surface: Joe-Bob may have actually had nothing to do with the Swiss bank account, but rather his signature was forged on documents by a yet unidentified accomplice of Colleen. The female cohort, some alleged, went so far as impersonating Joe-Bob in order to open a bank account at Union Bank of Switzerland.

But the clincher was a bank surveillance video of the putative Jones in Zurich at Union Bank, correlated with a dinner Joe-Bob had with Louisiana State Senator Clifton Chenier in Baton Rouge, at the same time. Joe-Bob couldn't be in two places at the same time—halfway across the ocean and in Louisiana.

Despite this, Joe-Bob's conviction was not overturned, but the 4th Circuit Court of Appeals struck down the original sentence and ordered Joe-Bob resentenced by a new federal court judge.

Due to the increasing skepticism concerning Joe-Bob's guilt and the inequity of his prolonged internment as compared to other white collar criminals; Joe-Bob Jones was, after five grueling years, adjudicated to time served.

With renewed belief in the benevolent, and his commitment to a policy of less flamboyance and full disclosure, Joe-Bob Jones who had served his sentence in the Fort Worth Prison Medical facility, had birthed the New Christ Divinity Foundation in Arlington, Texas.

This new ministry was the result of a ground swell of popular support by followers who were undaunted by the allegations and what they termed malicious prosecution and false conviction of the Reverend Jones.

Upon his release, Jones was determined to clear his name. First, as leader of the New Christ Divinity Foundation, he would not take a salary except for a stipend to be administered through an independent trust which would pay for Joe-Bob's mere subsistence: food, home, minimal clothing. The stipend was $24,000 per year—a far cry from the nearly $300,000 he took before.

Second, Joe-Bob agreed to have the New Christ Divinity Foundation's books audited monthly by the Evangelical Council on Financial Accountability. The Evangelical Council would ensure donors that New Christ Divinity's house was in order. Also, New Christ Divinity Foundation would comply with all financial disclosure rules of the more than seven hundred member National Religious Broadcasters Association.

The New Christ Divinity Foundation would be one hundred percent accountable. There would be openness and full financial disclosure in the form of income, assets, salaries, retirement benefits, housing, automobiles, hospitalization, etc.

Today, the Reverend Joe-Bob Jones had received an anonymous gift. It was wrapped in green foil paper with an eight-petal bow. It was shaped like a cigar tube and it was light as a feather.

He did not open it. The note particularly intrigued him. It read: "I am Tao. I am Power. I am the Swallow."

The Doomsday Kiss

It was delivered by messenger at 8:00 A.M. sharp.

"It can't be from..." Joe-Bob uttered with a penitent bray as he looked into the mirror. He had been up since five rehearsing his sermon. It would be powerful, bombastic—magical.

"She couldn't...have?"

He again looked at the card. It stirred deep-seated memories, memories that he had long since supressed. "The swallows..."

He breathed deep through his nose and smelled the freshly-cut flowers in his dressing room. Lilies, daisies, daffodils and gladiolus — nothing he had purchased himself. They were gifts from the hearts of his faithful. And after today, they would go the Children's Medical Center of Dallas to brighten the days of the bedridden.

The five bitter-hard years had taught him a humanity that he had once lost.

He looked at the reflection of his face. He still had his boyish cheeks, his broad-bream smile, his thick tomboy hair with only traces of gray streaked at his ears.

In his whole life, aside from his one indiscretion, he had only one other vice; a craving really—his once a month 6-3/4" *Hoya De Monteray Excalibur cigar*. It came in a yellow and tobacco-brown tube with a stout cigar band printed on the cylinder. He smoked the cigar in private. His habit was known *only* by Colleen.

He looked at the foreboding gift.

CHAPTER 42
Space Station Mir-Kennedy I

"What about dihydroxy-organopyrethrum-Zeta-4?" Chemical Engineer Cunningham, who had been all too quiet, asked.

"What's dihydroxy-Zeta?" Commander Vrubel inquired. Cunningham was working in the Command Center with Vrubel when he radioed Mission Commander Jackson.

"Commander Vrubel," Jackson said, "we have three hours forty minutes until we run out of oxygen, which by my readings gives us roughly forty minutes on board *Mir-Kennedy I.*"

"What's dihydroxy-Zeta?" Vrubel asked again.

"When," Jackson asked Vrubel, "do you suggest we inform Johnson Space Center Houston of our imminent descent?"

"Directly. They'll tell us to screw off, but we'll come down anyway," Spacewalker/Pilot Smith interjected. "Then they'll have to Biosafety Level 4 quarantine us at the second alternative landing site—White Sands Space Harbor. They'll give us oxygen, we'll be safe and not infectious to anyone, and that's that."

"What's dihydroxy-Zeta?" Vrubel asked again. He was not sidetracked by Jackson's deliberate skirting question, and furthermore, Vrubel wasn't aware of any dihydroxy-Zeta on *Mir-Kennedy I's* manifest.

"It's a cross between a hypnotic and psychometric drug," Cunningham replied.

"Go ahead," Jackson said. "There aren't any more secrets."

Jackson was speaking on VOX mode on intercom channel one. He, along with Budarin, Maya, and Smith were in the Biologics Lab—hopefully working toward a solution to their impossible problem.

The temperament on board, though they were all professionals and used to working in confined, perilous places for prolonged periods of time, was testy.

"It has effects on the cardiovascular system, causes reduced heart rate and blood pressure, and some hypnosis along with smooth muscle relaxation," Cunningham said with reluctance. "In addition, it has psychometric properties that produce central nervous system depression and somnolence."

"It's nerve gas!" Maya exclaimed.

"That's right," Jackson replied.

"I see you too, also wanted to build a better mouse trap?"

"Yeah. It..."

"It's benign. It doesn't kill, it disables the offender..." Cunningham continued mechanically.

"You mean enemy," Maya said.

"Maya," Jackson said, "that wasn't the purpose of dihydroxy-Zeta. It was designed to control crowds in mob situations, or to instill calm in the face of a riot."

"Kind of a new generation Mace?" asked Vrubel. He understood the chicane politics of détente diplomacy.

"Yes," Cunningham replied.

"Just as Biologics Engineer Pokrovsky came up here to work on TTLV-1, we, too, found a need to refine dihydroxy-organopyrethrum-Zeta-4. Our government just didn't think that it was politically correct to advertise our intentions. There wasn't anything diabolical about it. It just wasn't politically propitious," Jackson said.

"So two can play at the espionage game?" Maya asked rhetorically.

Jackson did not respond. Cunningham spoke. "One of the problems that we were having with dihydroxy-Zeta was that in its gaseous state it had an abnormal tendency to bind with water vapor, to 'lock up' if you will. It's hydrophilic. This can be 'good' or 'bad', but certainly bad from the point of view of its governmental use. You can't use it, for example, on rainy or high-humidity days. My thought, however, is that in this 'water-free' environment, Zeta might bind with *LAV-10*, especially since cyanide bonds have a high proclivity to bind with H_2O."

"Possibly."

"It may be *LAV-10*–loving like it's waterloving, or hydrophilic," Cunningham said.

"So if we try it, then how do we know if it works?" Vrubel asked.

"That's a real interesting question Maya. Tell me, we only have forty-minutes."

"I don't know...We can expose dihydroxy-Zeta directly to a sample of the remaining *LAV-10* that I've been working with. Pokrovsky has a reverse-mirror, threshold inducer spectrograph. I can take a reading on *LAV-10* before I expose it to dihydroxy-Zeta, and then one with dihydroxy-Zeta alone. The combined chemical, if they bind, will have an altogether different spectrographic picture."

"Like a fingerprint."

"Yes. . . "

"And if they don't?" Jackson asked.

"Then we'll have two separate pictures indicating the difference between substances. If they do, then we'll have a third completely new picture."

"It's worth a shot," Cunningham eagerly said.

"Let's do it," Vrubel concurred.

The remaining crew continued preparations on the jerry-rigged space shuttle *Orion*. The ship, which had five permanent crew deck seats, had its experimental bay and sleeping berths modified to accommodate four more. The positioning of the last two travelers was enigmatic until Communications Officer Hobbs came up with an ingenious but uncomfortable idea: disengage the alpha X-hoop docking module, pad it with corrugated polyurethane-coated foam, and install makeshift zipper and bungee cord belt and shoulder harnesses, and the last two astronauts can theoretically ride safely to earth. The alpha X-hoop docking module, external to *Mir-Kennedy I* was made detachable by Smith and Zvezda from within *Mir-Kennedy I*.

The docking module, which had been permanently installed by space shuttle *Neptune,* required moving of some of the core *Mir* solar panels and a 9.53 degree attitude adjustment of the Kristal stack. The 4.5 ton docking module, however, could only be withdrawn into the shuttle once the *Orion* had disengaged from *Mir-Kennedy I.* The potentially serious problem was, that there was no way to secure the module. There was genuine concern that whoever rode to the second alternative landing site at White Sands Space Harbor in the module, could be jettisoned out of the *Orion* if the shuttle was subjected to unexpected re-entry turbulence.

For that reason, two of *Orion's* emergency escape-chute harnesses, in addition to the zipper and bungee-cord belt and shoulder harnesses, which were utilized after the *Challenger* explosion, were secured into the docking module. The astronauts would precariously strap in, but the chance of survival in the event of a mishap would be between slim and none.

Maya positioned herself behind the cracked tungsten and gold-layered reaction shield, and pulled a sample of dihydroxy-organopyrethrum-Zeta-4. She began by first manipulating a zinc-cadmium vial labeled "Desiccated Inert Pituitary Extract," which in actuality was dihydroxy-Zeta-4, and added 0.001 ml of *LAV-10* to 1 cc of the 1:1000 dilute dihydroxy-organopyrethrum-Zeta-4, while under the 32,000 hertz inducer spectrometric lamp. She had already run her baselines for both reagents, and had the bar-type monochrome graph printed out. It demonstrated two chemicals.

"So if this works," she asked Jackson, "and we get our asses out of here alive—your government is probably going to continue its experiments with dihydroxy-Zeta, but this time not clandestinely?"

"Yes."

"Great," she said sarcastically and rolled her judgmental eyes.

Almost immediately, with mixture, the spectrograph demonstrated a new, individualistic reading. Maya was excited. She hadn't anticipated anything. She pushed and pop-floated her way down the aluminum-alloy lab bench. She quickly ran a laser print hard copy.

"What do you think?" Jackson asked.

"It's too early to tell."

"We don't have much time," he said, as he looked at his external watch on the rigid left forearm of his NASA space suit.

"We're ready any time you are," Smith radioed Jackson as he re-entered the recompression chamber from outside the space station.

"Commander Jackson," Vrubel asked, "do you want me to notify Houston Control now, or should we wait until we begin our descent? It's your honors."

"Let's just see what we get from Zeta-4 first, before we commit. Maybe we'll get lucky and have an answer for Houston that both they and we want to hear." Then he said facing Maya, "Go to two."

She toggled to the second intercom channel band on her VOX system. "What?"

"You know that they're going to blow us out of the sky if we try to land."

"Yes, I know...and?"

"I think you have no choice. If we don't go, then eleven crew members are going to die."

"And if we do, then I might expose the whole world to *LAV-10*? Is it worth the gambit, or is my thinking process wrong?"

"Not necessarily. If we all come down together as we've planned, no *Soyuz TM 29 ERV* in *Orion*—then NASA can quarantine us, let us in Biosafety Level 4. I'm fairly confident of our success."

"Confident enough to gamble the lives of billions?"

"Yes."

"But then the government would have to explain *LAV-10*. There'd be too many questions with the press: Why is *Orion* quarantined? Why did we land at White Sands Space Harbor instead of Kennedy Space Center, or Edwards Air Force Base. What about Biologics Engineer Pokrovsky and Flight Engineer Shoyo? It would be easier, and *probably safer* for them to blow us out of the sky."

"I agree."

"So why go along with my plan?" Jackson asked. He knew their desperate, but well thought out solution was probably for naught.

"Because it makes sense, and it's the right thing to do. We've got too many great minds on this mission to flush them down the toilet. Plus, what we've learned up here, with *LAV-10*, can be invaluable on Earth, and can potentially save millions of lives once *LAV-10* can be stabilized in the 'd' form. It'd be the long-awaited cure for AIDS and other medical scourges."

"But does my plan to abandon *Mir-Kennedy I* make sense? We both came up here with clandestine secondary agendas. Mine, in part, to work on banned nerve gas, you on *LAV-10*. We're both culpable. No one tells the truth anymore, do they?"

She looked deep into his eyes. She knew he was a good person. "I do, Scoop. When I told you that I love you, I told you the truth." She expected no response. He embraced her. He loved her, he needed her. Their suits, his NASA Extravehicular Mobility Unit and her Orlan-III DMA Space Suit smacked together in the reckless abandonment of weightless *Mir-Kennedy I*.

They each had one more operating oxygen tank, and then their thirty minute emergency life support systems. That was it. All the chips were on the one roll of the dice.

"Maya..." he said with painful thought, "Maya..."

"I think that we've got something," Tool Specialist Budarin excitedly interrupted on VOX intercom channel two. Budarin was observing the 32,000 hertz inducer spectrograph's video monitor. The picture of spikes and valleys was changing. "Maya!"

Maya rushed over to the screen. She quickly looked under her third-generation, plate wafer microscope at the combined chemical. "They're changing. Transmutating." She gazed at the tenuous, glare-tinted screen. She swifty pushed her way down the corrugated alloy lab bench counter, and printed out a hard copy. She studied it. The laser print rang a bell—somewhere in the not too distant recesses of her mind. "It's different. They've reacted in some...*Mother Russia, we gotta get the hell out of here!*" she yelled

CHAPTER 43
Dallas, Texas

They had hopped, skipped and jogged from one end of the United States to another. Dr. Alex Seacourt and Pepper Knight had been to hell and back. And now they were again heading into the lion's den.

"It was strange," she said, ill at ease as they were preparing for landing on board the American Airlines flight 1804.

"What?"

"I didn't feel right leaving my mother. After all these years, I've borne such hate for her. I didn't know. Am I just crazy?"

"No, I don't think so."

"I think that I don't know anything anymore. I mean was I the one who was wrong? Was I obsessed so much with my anger at her that I let it get in the way of my love?"

"I don't know. Do you mean that you're angry at her for abandoning you when you were a child?"

"Yes. That and more...I don't even remember her ever wanting me. I don't remember much. I don't..."

"She was afraid for you. Afraid of what was going on with the

273

experiments, with TTLV-1. And remember, she had already lost her first husband—your real father—in that horrific stunt plane accident, on TV, on *The Wide World of Sports*, before millions. Maybe she didn't want to lose you."

"Yes, now I know that. But I didn't realize it all these years. I grew up contemptful. I grew up angry. I hated her guts."

"I don't blame you. I might have felt the same."

"I mean, Alex, I really hated her. I didn't tell anyone I had a mother. If I was asked I'd say that she died..." Alex put his arms around her, and comforted her. "I mean dead. And now..."

"And now?"

"I don't know how I feel. I feel betrayed by my stepfather, I feel abandoned by everyone for not telling me the truth."

"Don't be so hard on Dr. Warner. He was just doing what your mother wanted him to do. She wanted to protect you. You know they both loved you?"

"No."

"Your mother did, maybe in her strange way. Dr. Warner...he raised you all those years, made sure that you had a roof over your head, fed you, gave you an education."

"Yes, but that's not love."

"Then what is?"

The 757's flaps were lowered, then the reluctant speedbrakes deployed. Several seconds later the landing gear was extended. They had traversed miles of plains, canyons and desert scrub. They had crossed Arizona, New Mexico and descended over Llano Estacado and Cap Rock, down over the prairies and cross timbers. They approached over Abilene and the Llano Uplift, then descended over smaller plains, prairies and former woodlands that ran in north-south strips toward the Colorado River. It was fifty-eight degrees when they landed at the Dallas/Fort Worth International Airport.

Alex had never been to Dallas before, but Pepper had. He was overwhelmed by the sprawling metropolis. "It's kinda the Manhattan of the Southwest," she said.

"What do you mean?" he asked as he snuggled his coat while waiting for the rental car van to take them to their vehicle.

"Cowboy capital, temple of consumerism, Sun Belt suburbia."

"Oh. That's a lot to say in one mouthful."

"Yeah, the 'Cadillac of Texas towns,'" she said with a Southern drawl.

It was nearly one in the morning when they got into the city and found a room. They had driven into downtown Dallas east on 183, past where they needed to go in the morning. Alex wasn't quite sure why he was going to stay downtown. From the airport he called the hotel and got a room, the last one available. He would sleep on the couch, or on the annoyingly uncomfortable sofabed.

Alex paid cash for the room, and registered under a pseudonym: Fred Smith. The front desk clerk gave him a knowing wink.

He hadn't planned on making love to her. It just happened. She had gone to bed. He had snuggled in the living room's pullout sofabed. The anticipatory crossbar was there. He could feel the grind under the small of his already-sore back. In disgust, he turned on the TV and watched CNN with the volume down. Though he was dog tired, and his face burnt and his joints ached, he couldn't go to sleep. Over and over he envisioned the man sprayed with the poison on the *Queen Mary*. How he died. The prussic acid had been meant for Alex.

He tried watching the news. Then he flicked through the channels. There was nothing he wanted to watch: a rerun of a 1930s *Thin Man* with William Powell, an English black and white dark comedy from the early '50s, an irksome infomercial selling some tarnish-removing disc, a rerun of *An Officer and a Gentleman* on HBO that he hadn't seen in years.

At two in the morning, she walked in. She was wearing a silver and blue Dallas Cowboy's T-shirt that swayed at her sexy knees. She had bought it downstairs at the hotel gift shop, just before it closed.

"Can't sleep?" Pepper asked as she sat on the corner of his sofabed. She set one bare foot on top of the mattress. The other was on the floor for balance.

"No."

"What are you thinking about?"

"Everything. I can't get it out of my mind."

"What?"

"I didn't tell you about the boat."

"No."

"On the Queen Mary they tried to kill me. If I hadn't seen them, the man with the spray…He was killed." He told her the story—how the man was shot in the face with the poison, and the horrific death that ensued.

She got onto the bed and put her arms around him, and held him tight. "It'll not...I..." he said. "I don't know if I can take this much more."

"Shhhh," she gently kissed his neck.

"I just tried to do..."

"Shhhh," she kissed his neck again. Then she took both of her hands and ever so tenderly grasped his face and turned it into hers. She delicately kissed his lips. He couldn't stop babbling.

"I don't trust anyone..."

"And then the Sheriff," he thought about the older farming couple outside of Cuba, Missouri.

"Shhhh," she slid her tongue gently into his mouth and worked it between his lower teeth and lips. She slipped it deeper and blew ever so softly.

Almost desparate for peace, for the warmth of a connecting touch, he embraced and finally kissed her. With her assistance, he glided his hand under her T-shirt and caressed her smooth stomach. She wore no underwear. He could feel her heat. He worked his way up to her nipples. They were firm and her breasts were supple. With her help, he slipped her T-shirt over her head and kissed her bosom.

They made love passionately until the dawn. Then they lay naked in bed and watched the starlight and city's electric glow waft through the dusky hotel window. It was hypnotic, yet he still couldn't get the merciless killings out of his mind.

"Alex."

'Yes?"

"It'll be all right."

He looked at her, into her gazelle eyes.

"It's okay if you don't say anything."

"I don't know what to say," he said. He didn't see her now. He saw the innocent, hardworking farming couple outside Cuba, Missouri being relentlessly mowed down by the man with the Ray-Ban sunglasses.

CHAPTER 44

Alex had slept soundly for three hours. Time had passed in an instant. He stood up, naked, and looked at his reflection in the television. He ran his hands through his hair, and slid on his slacks. He could hear the shower pound in rapt droplets. Then it stopped. He walked to the bathroom and knocked on the door. Steam seeped from under the door crack, and rolled onto the carpet in a marshy mist.

"Good morning," he said reticently. "Can I come..."

Before he could finish she was at the door, wrapped in a thick white terrycloth towel. Her hair was brushed back and sopping wet.

"About last night," he said.

She kissed him on his lips, and then placed both hands on his head and tickled him with her tongue. She tasted of peppermint. "About last night," she said as she pulled away.

"I didn't..."

"You have a problem with it?"

"I...no."

"Good."

She gently kissed him again, but this time without her tongue. Then she picked up the hotel's two-speed hair dryer and blew the condensation off the mirror before blowing dry her hair. The fluorescent light was uncaringly harsh.

"I don't think that you need it." She could see that he felt vaguely uncomfortable about making love, like a schoolboy who had morning second-thought guilt.

"Need what?"

"That stuff."

"What stuff?"

She set down the blow dryer, put both her hands to his head, and began rubbing his scalp with her fingertips.

"What stuff?" he said.

"You know...*that stuff.*"

He didn't get it at first, of course, still obsessively preoccupied with thoughts of Cuba, Missouri and the *Queen Mary.* Then he got it. "That stuff? I don't need that stuff." He looked into the steamed mirror. His reflection was mired in gossamer ringlets of condensation.

"I like it the way it is."

He pushed away from her and uncomfortably scrutinized his hairline. "I don't need that stuff."

"You don't need to be so *masculine* about it." She troll-smiled. Then she peck-kissed him on the neck and said, "I like you just the way you are."

She restarted the blow dryer and finished drying her shoulder-length hair. "So what's the plan," she asked.

"The plan is to find the girl."

"That's it?"

"That's it."

Alex showered. All the while he felt conscious of her presence. He thought that he shouldn't, but he did. Then she finished with her hair and left the bathroom and dressed in the other room. At twenty minutes after 8 A.M., room service arrived with the *Dallas Morning News* and two continental breakfasts.

Their hotel room was a generic pastel clone of every other place he had ever stayed: The Marriott, Doubletree, Embassy Suites, Ramada. They were all agreeable and lived by the "patron always comes first" mentality.

"Coffee?"

"Yes," he replied as he stepped out of the shower. She was in the TV room already pouring him a cup. He dressed in his slacks and turned inside-out underwear and sat down with her. She was eating two under-cooked sunnyside-up eggs. She dipped her buttered toast into the yolk after she first ate the runny eggwhite around it.

He had his morning coffee black. He wasn't hungry for the eggs or bacon, but ate a piece of white toast and had a sip of orange juice. It was then that he began looking through the morning paper.

"Felony Preacher at it Again."

The article read:

"Reverend Jim-Bob Jones, the high-flying one-time televangelist of the Atlanta-based New Christ Divinity Church and President of Christ's Divinity College in Atlanta, is holding his first televised 'megaworld rally' at Texas Stadium today. Reverend Jones, who was convicted of stealing millions from the people who trusted him, had been deemed the Caligula of evangelists."

"She's going to be at the rally!"

"What rally?"

Alex read more. *"Reverend Jones had been convicted of 32 of 41 counts of fraud and conspiracy. Jones, who had proclaimed his innocence, was sentenced to 42 years for defrauding supporters of his New Christ ministry. In September 1992 the 4th Circuit Court of Appeals overturned U.S. District Judge Mike Boyce ruling that he had made biased, unsuitable remarks about 'money-grubbing preachers' while handing down the sentence. Jones was subsequently resentenced.*

"Jones' wife, Colleen Winslow Jones, was also tried in a separate trial and convicted of fraud, conspiracy and money laundering. Colleen Jones was sentenced to 26 years. After losing her appeal, she died at the Rochester Prison Medical Facility of ovarian cancer."

"She's going after the Reverend Joe-Bob Jones," Alex said. "She's got TTLV-1 and she's going after the Reverend."

"Oh my God!"

The rally was scehduled to begin at 11 a.m. A crowd of 110,000 was expected to fill Texas Stadium. The rally would be beamed worldwide on Sat Com 5 in cooperation with the Christian Miracle Broadcasting Network and Jones' New Christ Divinity Foundation. Sixty-five thousand had galley chairs placed in eighty rows on the football field, and a 5,000 square foot stage with a state-of-the-art podium had been erected. Three twenty-by-thirty foot bi-directional plate-screen monitors were positioned on the stage in a cresent— one directly behind Jim-Bob's pulpit, and two on 45 degree angles.

CHAPTER 45

The throng had begun to swell with a sense of divine anticipation. It was only 8:30 A.M. and the Reverend Joe-Bob Jones would not begin his sermon for another two and a half hours.

Mahalia *could have killed him by then*, murdered him dead in the dressing room with her 9mm Beretta 92. She could have drilled him between his beady, weasel eyes. But that wouldn't be as *dramatic*. She had stolen the cure to AIDS, and for that matter possibly the cure for *all other viruses. She had the only vial in the world. There were two, but the other one didn't work!*

She had heard them jabber in inebriated stupors in Aspen, after they got drunk and she slept with all of them. She had taken the *only vial*—the one that worked. It would be poetic justice. She had the cure for AIDS and she had the plan. She would walk in at the height of the rally. *Then she would kill him*. It would be live on Sat Com 5, before a ten-million person, worldwide audience.

Mahalia had donned for the occasion, the long, black, requiem dress that brushed against her vile ankles. She wore black shoes and midnight-black hose. Her hair was dyed India-ink black and covered with a veil that she draped over her malevolent face. Underneath, she wore somber lipstick—a red that was haunting. Her lips were defined with a dark, bestial lip-liner and she painted an onerous tear under her right eye with a garnet lipstick pencil, then lined it with sepia brown.

She waited patiently in the first row as they all filed in—thousands of them, all anxious to see their rebirthed savior. It had come full circle, and she was going to make life complete. *She was the Power, not the Reverend Joe-Bob Jones. She was Tao!*

Joe-Bob Jones sat pensively in his ready room. He was preparing for the biggest performance of his life. He harbored anger and contempt, as any human would for what he had gone through—yet he knew that he had to be a paradigm of both unconditional love and forgiveness. After five years of incarceration, it was difficult at times to let the resentment go.

He looked into the mirror. He had aged. He had slight wrinkles and inching crows feet, frown lines and a sagging husk that weren't on his face five years earlier. However, he had grown wiser, he had grown stronger. He had tied a tauter knot with his compassionate God—who did work in mysterious ways.

He gazed into the mirror. He studied the lines that had grown from the corners of his eyes since his hiatus. He studied his hands and the scraggy wrinkles that were new. He looked at his neck and the wizened folds that he hadn't noticed before—the creases of despair and sorrow, from his crying and private torment.

His speech would be a powerful one. He would overwhelm the skeptical and convert the curious. He had always been able to do that anyway, because he had *that gift*. But it was different now. He had been given a chance to make everything right with his topsy-turvy world.

He had to be honest with himself, though. He had gotten caught up in the trappings of his opulent ministry. He had a $450,000 house in Palm Springs and the New Christ Divinity Church Board had paid him an exorbitant annual salary of $300,000. Then, he didn't look at it like he was stealing from his devoted flock.

Federal prison for five years gave him a chance to renew his misplaced faith and to seriously reflect. Like Eve, who was tempted by the snake to eat the apple, so was he seduced. And the worst part, he hadn't even known it.

Now the serpent was more crafty than any of the wild animals the Lord God had made. He said to the woman, "Did God really say, 'you must not eat from any tree in the garden'?"

The woman said to the serpent, "We may eat fruit from the trees in the garden, but God did say, 'You must not eat fruit from the tree that is in the middle of the garden, and you must not touch, or you will die.'"

"You will not surely die," the serpent said to the woman. "For God knows that when you eat of it your eyes will be opened, and you will be like God, knowing good and evil."

For the Reverend Joe-Bob Jones, it took the slap to his pompous face that he received with his wife's embezzlement. Maybe he was paying for his infidelity twenty-three years ago. But that was the past—and this was the present. He couldn't do anything to change what had happened, just what will be. In the now and the future he could shape a glorious new world—a universe of unconditional love and heartfelt forgiveness.

There was a knock on the dressing room door.

"Come in," he said. He was expecting no one.

In walked an unpretentious woman. She was taller than ordinary. Her hair was light, textured brown and her eyes were restrained. Her skin was milk white. She was tentative and he could sense that she was deeply troubled.

"How did you get past security?" he asked tenderly.

"It doesn't make any difference. I have a note for you." She did not look at him when she spoke, but rather down at her feet. She handed him a vellum envelope. There was no writing on it.

"Sit, my child."

Katrina had strict orders from Mahalia: She was to pay off the security guards with a hundred dollars each, then hand deliver the letter. She was to carefully watch him read it, and then to go back to the Adolphus Hotel and wait for her. She was to memorize his expression, and then tell Mahalia every detail.

But Katrina was visibly upset. They had never needed, nor used a gun before. In addition, over the last several weeks, Mahalia's behavior had become more erratic. She had become maniacally obsessive. *The Ricki Lake Show* was one thing, but a gun was something else.

"What is it my child? You look troubled."

Katrina had been in Mahalia's trance for the last two years. She was Mahalia's sycophantic lover; but no matter what the Reverend Jones did to her—it wasn't right to...

"Speak to me," he said in a reassuring, melodic voice.

She sat on a chair near him. Her hands were shaking. She, too, wore a black dress that hung to her ankles. She had also donned black hose and swarthy shoes. But she did not have the burning desire *to murder*.

Katrina Lee had been pushed as far as she was willing to go. Despite everything—and her robotic love for Mahalia—she was not going back to the hotel. She didn't know where she was going, but she knew the Beretta was wrong—and in her heart she knew Mahalia's intent.

"She's...going to kill you," Katrina stammered. "She's going to kill you. I know."

"Who?" Jones asked.

"Mahalia, Mahalia Hunt."

"I'm sorry child but I don't know a Mahalia Hunt," he said, barely moving his lips. Then he carefully opened the envelope. His fingers were delicate and solicitous like Mahalia's. They could have been cloned.

The envelope had been sealed with crimson red wax, and had the print of a lover's heart with two turtle doves kissing inside. Over that was the exaggerated imprint of a woman's vulgar lips.

He opened the envelope. There was a sheet of double-edge crown paper folded into thirds. In very ornate and cursive calligraphy, the note read:

"Tonight you will pay for your sins...FATHER!"

"Father?" he said.

"Father?" Katrina timidly asked.

"Father."

"I don't understand," Katrina said. "You're the one who beat her...raped her?" She vividly remembered the horror stories Mahalia had told her about a very bad man. But...him?

"No."

"You're Mahalia's father?"

"My child I have no daughter. The only daughter that I had...I lost a long time ago, when she was six."

"Six?"

"She was institutionalized."

"But Mahalia said that she was abused and repeatedly raped by her father, beaten and tortured by him until she ran away when she was sixteen."

"It wasn't me, my child."

"I...I...think it is." In an instant Katrina scrupulously studied his lithe fingers, his fine-featured face, his wispy lips. It was obvious.

"No. The...only daughter that I ever had was taken from me long ago, when she was barely six. I haven't seen her in twenty-two years. I do not know who is sending me these letters, these threats. I assume that she's your friend?"

Mahalia had told Katrina that he was a monster. But she didn't know that *he* was the Reverend Joe-Bob Jones. Even Katrina, a doubtful nonbeliever, had seen Reverend Jones on TV. She was inspired by him, overwhelmed by his innate kindness, the tears in his eyes, the pathos in his voice. This couldn't be the man that Mahalia said had abused her, raped her. "She wants to kill you. She has been planning it for a long time. She'll be out there in the audience, waiting for you. Did you take her...tie her down...beat her...?"

"No, my child. I haven't seen my daughter since she was six."

Then he remembered the last day he had been with his daughter. But, her name wasn't Mahalia, it was Tammy Savannah Jones.

It was overcast. The storm was approaching and the swirling ocean breeze was culled. They had come to the Old Mission San Juan Capistrano to feed the birds. Each year the swallows came. They traveled thousands of miles from Brazil, and there were tens of thousands of them. It was one of his favorite miracles. It was a cloistered place, a quaint town located above the shores of the Pacific, halfway between San Diego and Los Angeles, along the old Camino Real.

The swallows were mesmerizing. They had slender bodies with long pointed wings and large mouths for capturing unsuspecting insects in flight. Their tails were forked and they were magnificently able to helicopter in the air like hummingbirds.

He had taken Tammy Savannah and her mother, the woman

with whom he had the indiscretion, Mary Raye Hobart. Mary Raye was an office worker who over the years had flirted and made her interest discretely known to Joe-Bob. She was a clerk who had worked for him at his television studio offices long before he and Colleen had been sleeping in separate beds, in the opposite ends of their house.

Joe-Bob Jones was tempted, and after years of suppressing his carnal desires, he succumbed. He and Mary Raye had a tryst in a rundown motel room in Marietta, Georgia, outside Atlanta. Afterward, he could never forgive himself.

Mary Raye, however, had other plans. She was going to have his baby, then blackmail him for the rest of his life. Joe-Bob had no choice but to acquiesce. All his teachings to his dutiful disciples; all his unrebukable wisdom, would be for nothing if his congregation discovered his sin.

Over the years, as Tammy Savannah grew, Mary Raye refused to let Joe-Bob see his daughter. The demands for money mushroomed. Eventually, Mary Raye told Joe-Bob's wife Colleen Winslow Jones, who had grown to despise Joe-Bob. Colleen, however, reacted paradoxically. She relished the idea of Mary Raye's blackmail. Together, these women who hated men, would relentlessly milk the Reverend Jones' ministry dry.

That day, Joe-Bob had met Mary Raye in Capistrano to tell her that he was going to come clean to his church and to the world. That he would no longer be blackmailed, that he owed it to his assemblage to tell them the truth—to confess his sins.

"She's going to kill you." Katrina stood up. She had tears in her eyes. "I've got to go."

"Where are you going, my child?"

"I don't know, but away."

"Please."

"No, I have to go."

"Are..."

"Are you going to be all right?" She contradictorily asked.

"Don't worry about me my child, no one is going to kill me. If she is there, Mahalia Hunt, or whoever she is...or my daughter; then I will embrace her with my unconditional love. No one will kill me."

"I'm sorry Reverend, I have to leave." Katrina could feel, palpate—that he was telling the truth. She also knew that Mahalia had gone totally crazy—that she was going to *shoot him dead.*

Robert Charles Davis

CHAPTER 46

The space shuttle *Orion*, or Orbiter Vehicle Number OV-108 was the eighth in a series of shuttles. The original design had remained fairly true to the progenitor *Enterprise* that was built and tested for landing in 1977 and then later transferred to the Smithsonian Institution in 1985.

The *Orion*, similar to *Columbia*, the ill-fated *Challenger*, and the *Atlantis*—devised as a launch vehicle, platform for scientific laboratories, orbiting service center for other satellites, or return carrier for previously orbited spacecraft—was modified to operate as an orbiting construction resupply ferry, with the broadening of its cargo bay from fifteen-by-sixty feet to eighteen-by-seventy feet.

In addition, *Orion's* three engines (SSMEs–Space Shuttle Main Engines) were modified to increase their liquid-fuel (hydrogen-liquid oxygen) thrust from 375,000 pounds (1.6 million newtons at sea level) to 525,000 pounds.

With these modifications, in addition to the much expanded internal nitrogen, oxygen, water and fuel re-supply tanks, the shuttle was capable of extended range, maneuverability and speed.

However, for every concession made to increase the load volume and weight capability of the shuttle, in turn, other operational equipment was limited. The onboard computers made to handle all data processing—HAL/S (high-order assembly language/shuttle) IBM mass memory 48 million byte data processing systems—were diminished from five to four. The basic crew of commander, pilot and mission specialist, with room for an additional four payload specialists, was reduced to five.

The three previous decks of the shuttle: flight deck, with flight controls and crew stations for launch, orbit and landing; mid-deck for eating, sleeping, hygiene and waste disposal; and lower deck, or equipment bay and life support systems, were modified. The lower deck was removed.

What before was a comfortable ride into space for seven astronauts, was a cram for five.

"*We need to get our asses out of here before this place blows!*" Maya yelled through her channel one intercom VOX mike as she pushed Jackson towards the Metallurgics Crystallization Lab door, and herself bounced pell-mell in all directions. "Hurry!"

"What the..."

"*LAV-10*, among its many other dangers, is highly unstable! I've seen these spectrograph readings before. With the pure oxygen atmosphere it'll explode!"

"What the Christ is this stuff?"

"It's hell!" she yelled.

Most of the crew of *Mir-Kennedy I* were already on board *Orion*. They had, despite Houston Control's orders, essentially abandoned the space station and were making last minute frantic preparations to depart their orbiting sarcophagus.

"Let's get the hell out of here!" Jackson ordered the stragglers. Only Commander Vrubel and Communications Officer Hobbs were still on board. The rest of the astronauts had been preparing *Orion* for its treacherous orbital burn.

"Should I radio Houston of our intent to land?" Hobbs asked as he propelled his way out of *Mir-Kennedy I*.

"No...not now," Jackson said, "Let's wait 'til we're on board the shuttle, and ready to roll."

"Roger," Hobbs replied.

"Go," Vrubel said, pushing Hobbs to the door. "Go!"

Vrubel and Hobbs were the first to hit the makeshift, already-detached alpha X-hoop docking module, held into place by one last stainless bolt.

Hobbs, then Vrubel, propelled themselves into the precarious, 4.5-ton docking module. Hobbs banged his head on the ingress steel-ribbed opening and ricocheted inside the polyurethane-coated foam interior. Vrubel next slipped into the docking module dead center, then ping-ponged into its umbilical chamber. The first explosion rocked the shuttle as the Biologics Lab disintegrated, separating the shuttle from the X-hoop and the rest of *Mir-Kennedy I*.

The docking module shook but did not disembowel from the alpha X-hoop docking module. Then a second explosion jolted the space station. This one engulfing the 123-ton core Russian *Mir* sub-unit in a ball of flames. Then a third, then a fourth cannonading eruption.

"Get your ass gone!" Jackson yelled as Maya pulled, ran and bounced her way to the docking module.

Orion was primed to go. Spacewalker/Pilot Randall Smith, who was also a Johnson Space Flight Center trained pilot had made his way into the commander's launch position from the pilot's seat.

"Let's go!" Solovyev implored on board *Orion*, "before it's too late!"

"No, we wait for Jackson and Mukhina!"

It was then that Hobbs scraped his way into the trembling shuttle's cockpit. Vrubel, however, had stayed behind to help Jackson and Maya. A shuddering fifth blast pounded the *Orion* and ripped it loose from the 9.53 degree attitude adjusted *Mir-Kennedy I*.

It was at that moment that Vrubel watched as Maya and Jackson were hurled out of *Mir-Kennedy I*.

Johnson Space Center, Houston

"We've had an explosion on board *Mir-Kennedy I*!" Flight Control Officer Bernie Johnson yelled to the manpower-thick ground control.

"Christ o'mighty!" Flight Director General Oliver Peterson

snapped. "Have you been able to re-establish radio contact?"

"Negative," Johnson brusquely replied.

"What about telemetry?"

"Still on line…" Johnson checked his thirteen soul read-out, two of which were already flatline (Pokrovsky and Shoyo). He also double-checked the computerized video panel along with Officer Randal Matlock. "Get me coordinates on those readings," Johnson ordered.

"Report?" General Peterson demanded.

"I'm not sure. There may have been separation from *Mir-Kennedy I.*"

"Shit," Peterson said.

"Are they coming home?" Matlock asked.

"Christ if I know," Johnson said.

"They have their orders!"

"What do you expect those poor bastards to do—die up there?"

It was then that crucial data relayed in from Anderson Air Force Base in Guam. Tracking Officer "Bo" Walter Huff read the hardcopy. "That's affirmative. We cross vectored them. I've got nine life signs in a cluster approximately 150 meters from *Mir-Kennedy I*, presumably in the *Orion*; and two seventy-five meters, but at different vectors. I'm having a difficult time getting an exact fix on the two. But they're definitely not together."

"Get me *NORAD* on the line!" General Peterson ordered.

"You think they're coming back in the shuttle?" a different controller asked.

"I'm not sure," Huff replied, "but it sure looks like nine of them might. My guess is that they're coming down."

"Damn it!"

Space Shuttle Orion

"We've been blown off of *Mir-Kennedy*!" Smith exclaimed. "Everyone on board?"

"All except for Vrubel, Jackson and Mukhina," Hobbs replied.

"Commander Jackson," Smith tersely spoke. "Jackson, Jackson!" There was no reply. "Jackson!"

Hobbs bounced out of the pilot seat and pushed his way back to the aft crew station. He squeezed between the other tight-packed astronauts. In front of him were two overhead tungsten and gold coated windows, facing the aft bulkhead for observation into the cargo bay. Another explosion, this from *Mir Kennedy I's* X-loop, violently rocked the shuttle. It rattled *Orion*, the percussion wave causing a gradual but continual separation from *Mir-Kennedy I*.

"The docking module's on the tilt. Shit!" Hobbs yelled to Smith. "It's bent, but still attached to *Orion*."

"What about the men?"

"I can see Vrubel, he's barely hanging onto the docking module. He's...he's moving. He looks okay."

"What about Jackson and Mukhina?"

"Nothing." Then Hobbs turned on the two aft television monitors that were lateral of the right window. "I'm going to use the remote arm; manipulating the RMS, I can use it as a periscope to find Commander Jackson and Maya."

"Affirmative."

The RMS (Remote Manipulator System) was a mechanical arm which sat in a cradle on the left rear edge of the shuttle cargo bay doors. It has three joints: shoulder, elbow and wrist. The shoulder was where the 50 foot flexible arm attached to *Orion*. The television cameras were at the elbow and the wrist joints.

"Let me give you a hand," Spacewalker Rusty Holloway said, as he crammed next to Hobbs. Holloway had special training in the Canadian-built RMS and its difficult to operate hand controller.

"Thanks," Hobbs said as he slid to the left aft portion of the flight deck.

Deliberately and precisely, Holloway manipulated the RMS out of its stern cradle, then extended the rigid arm straight on the perpendicular to the convulsed shuttle which was drifting even farther from *Mir-Kennedy I*. Holloway then bent the precise shaft wrist joint to ninety degrees in an upside down "L" and began sweeping an azimuth from the point of previous attachment of the docking module to *Mir-Kennedy I*.

Holloway scanned from a ninety degree wedge in all directions from the left shuttle delta wing tip to a line vertical of the RMS, then to the docking module, then stern. There was shredded, fragmented space debris everywhere. Then Holloway panned beyond Vrubel. He was pointing. Holloway quickly adjusted the wrist arm television camera to a positive forty five degree X-angle, a negative twenty degree Y-angle and a positive twenty one degree Z-angle. "Got 'em."

"Activate the auto track and I'll lock their position into the computer."

"Are they alive?"

"Yes. Looks like it." Holloway could see both Jackson and Maya. They were animated.

"Are they a safe enough distance away to fire the vernier thrusters?"

"I think so."

"Done," Holloway replied. He flipped the TV AUTOCOM (auto computer switch) which coordinated position targeting of the upper video monitor.

The aft and forward RCS (reaction control system) was comprised of forty-four small rocket engines that maneuvered Orion. There were thirty-eight primary RCS thrusters, each with 870 pounds thrust and six twenty-five-pound thrust vernier engines. The RCS thrusters were grouped in three modules, one in Orion's nose and one in each OMS (oribital maneuvering system) pad, mounted on each side of the aft fuselage. The vernier engines were for pinpoint delicate maneuvering.

Smith linked on the IBM HAL/S mass memory computer with the remote manipulator arm video, and fired the vernier engines. Slowly and meticulously, the intrepid astronauts inched within reach of capture.

Vrubel, whose radio communication had been crippled with separation of the *Orion* from the space station, reached out to the stunned Maya, then to Jackson. The blast had disabled *Orion's* external relay communication antenna, and therefore eliminated any communication between the space shuttle and the astronauts until they physically entered *Orion*, and were within limited intercom radio range of the other astronauts.

"You okay?" Jackson asked as he helped Maya.

"Yes." She had concussive space shock from the blast. The sudden catapult caused her to momentarily blackout. She felt like she had been hit head-on by a forty ton Mack truck. He, in contrast, was unflappable.

"Comrade..." Commander Vrubel asked Maya as she slowly, awkwardly pushed her way down the mangled alpha X-hoop docking module, "...go inside."

Jackson affirmed. "We'll ride the trip back home from here."

Though she had double vision and disorientation, her judgment was not impaired. "No," she said as she gathered the rest of her wits. "You're the most experienced pilot. You'll have to fly us down."

"I insist," Jackson said.

"We're running out of oxygen and we have no time to argue. It's your job—you have the training, you're the most qualified to land us at White Sands Space Harbor."

"Maya."

She scrupulously looked at him. "Commander."

"You realize," he said, "once I go in, the two of you will be out of radio communication." Jackson was well aware of the damage to the external communications relay antenna—and the fact that they had been unable to communicate with the *Orion*.

"Yes," Vrubel replied. "Go."

It was then, at that instant, he wanted to tell her—to say it. She took the initiative. She gazed into his reticent visor. "I love you," she said.

Jackson stood there. He wanted to make his mouth work, he wanted to move his lips and say those difficult words—to evoke the sounds from his paralyzed vocal cords. But he couldn't force himself *to say those words.*

"Let's go," Vrubel said. "Let's go..."

Maya grabbed Jackson by his upper right arm. For one fleeting moment she held him tight next to her. They locked glances. Then he was gone.

Jackson clumsily worked his way through the confining airlock, through the tapering connecting tunnel, and into the *Orion* command module. Several times he hit his helmet on the corrugated polyurethane-coated padding, then rough metal-edged walls.

Vrubel and Maya prepared themselves for their hazardous landing. They closed the three-inch steel inner hatch. The outer hatch had been mangled at the extreme one o'clock edge and what was left of it was misaligned by the explosion on board *Mir-Kennedy I*. They were alone. They each had an extra lithium hydroxide rebreather, which removed carbon dioxide from their Orlan-III DMA space suits, and two high-altitude ejection canopy riggings that thcy sliped into, though the chances of surviving an ejection were infinitesimal.

From inside the command module, Smith mechanically lowered

the damaged docking module into the cargo bay using the payload retraction switch. Slowly, it moved into position. It did not rest properly, the fit was stilted. Then he painstakingly closed the cargo bay doors.

"It's loose," Smith said, as he moved to the right pilot's seat from the commander's launch position. He adjusted himself into his uncomfortable titanium seat, and made room for Commander Jackson to slide into the commander's chair on the left.

"Can you do any better?" Jackson asked.

"If we have time to go outside and strap it in with the twenty meter kevlar-reinforced cable that we have in the cargo bay...maybe, but we don't. We're running out of oxygen."

"Will it stay in place?"

"I don't know."

"What are the odds?"

"I've got Holloway manipulating the remote arm over the docking bay," Smith scanned into his shoulder-high cargo bay video monitor. "Problem is, we weren't geared up to take on the docking module."

"Well, we'll just have to do the best we can."

"That's it, but it might not be good enough."

CHAPTER 47

The multitude at Texas Stadium, many from Dallas/Fort Worth and its environs as well as others from across the United States, Canada, Mexico, Central America, Japan, South America and Europe, was swelling. Nearly every seat was taken, and even more of the faithful wanted access into the capacity-filled stadium.

They were there for their risen Christ. They were exploding in evangelistic epiphany. The faithful's spiritual mentor had come to release them for *their* past persecution. It was *their* judgment day. The dutiful had made *their* journey. They, too, were on a mission of truth, enlightenment and hope.

A gospel group, the Holy Rollers, was on stage lilting. The three bi-directional monitor screens beamed the three New Christ Divinity Foundation vocalists worldwide.

Talk about love, how it makes life complete
You can talk all you want, make it sound good and sweet.
But the words have an empty ring, and they
don't really mean a thing,

Without his love is not to be found.
For love is surrender to his will.

The swallows of Capistrano with their blue and green metallic feathers swiftly flew over the hummock where Mary Raye Hobart and the young Reverend Joe-Bob Jones were arguing.

Six year old Tammy Savannah had bits of bread in her small hand. She had come to feed the swallows. In the not-so-far distance, Reverend Joe-Bob could hear the crash of the menacing surf on time-worn boulders and scraps. Around them, the haunting sycamore and birches sang in the off-shore breeze.

"I want the money!" Mary Raye demanded.

"This has to stop."

"I'll expose you, I'll tell the world. Your television audience. Everyone who you really are...*an adulterer, a sinner!*"

"That's why I called this meeting, Mary Raye."

"No!"

"Yes, Mary Raye."

"No!" She wisened quickly. She figured out his pathetic game. He was playing hardball. She could get more money out of him if she pressed him, manipulated him, skewered him—then ripped him to shreds.

"Have a seat," Jones said. She would go along with him for the moment. They sat on a weather-worn bench. There were splinters in the wood, and a piece of the middle board had cracked off at his end. It was uncomfortable to sit on. "I love my daughter," the Reverend said.

Mary Raye knew he did. This was her trump card, the leverage she would wield. Personally, Mary Raye didn't give a damn about Tammy Savannah. She was a burden, a big pain-in-the-ass—but she was Mary Raye's meal ticket...and Mary Raye made sure Tammy Savanah knew it.

"I know you love her," she stoically told him.

"Mary Raye, I'm sorry about what happened between us. It was all my fault, my responsibility."

Mary Raye had carefully planned Joe-Bob's seduction. She had devised her scheme when she knew that he was at his weakest, when he was the most despondent, when the ministry and his marriage were on rocky grounds—when he was vulnerable.

Joe-Bob had been depressed. He had gone the rounds with his

wife Colleen and it was all he could do to hold the New Christ Divinity Church together. That was when she would strike.

She had him meet her at the Rodegate Inn in Marietta, Georgia, to just "talk" about the ministry and "his" problems in private. She had rented the room and dressed in a slinky garter belt and thigh-high, seamed nylons underneath her school-marm, flower-print church dress. She wore no bra or panties.

She had methodically flirted with the Reverend in a low-key manner. He needed someone to talk to, and she saw the financial potential of exploiting his foible. Jones was a good man, but he had been without intimate knowledge for longer than he could remember. Secretly, he was often tormented by it.

At the motel, she had Keebler chocolate chip cookies and milk waiting for him, and a stereo cassette radio with Pat Boone and Patsy Cline tapes. She had placed her tippet over the bed light in order to soften the room.

At first they spoke at the table next to the window which overlooked the empty parking lot. The drapes were closed. He told his melancholy story for three hours. He cried. Then she placed his right hand in her grasp. He could feel their softness, their warm inviting welcome. Then she slowly moved his hand to her breasts. She unbuttoned her blouse.

"I've come to talk to you," he said to Mary Raye Hobart as they faced each other in Capistrano. He watched a pair of swallows dance and hover in midair, then fly off as quickly as they arrived.

"Go on."

"I've made a decision."

"And that is?" She was going to demand more money...and she'd get it!

"I'm going to go public."

"What?" she yelled and sprung from the park bench. A long, sliver of wood caught in her dress. It cracked off as she bounced up. "You can't..."

"I can't be blackmailed any more."

"You can't do that!"

"On the contrary, I can and I will." He stood and walked toward the cliffs. The St. Augustine grass and peat moss hummock sloped ever so slightly as it approached the surf. The sycamore branches in part shaded him from the sun.

Behind the trees, past the talking sycamores and birches, under a sole fan palm tree in the swaying tall grass, *stood an ominous shadowy figure—watching, listening, plotting.*

"You...you..."

"It's over. Tomorrow, I'm going to come clean. I've prepared a press release. I'm going to tell the world on my Sunday TV sermon. I'm going to take the heat...and whatever happens, is what happens."

Mary Raye slapped him hard. Joe-Bob's cheek burned crimson-red. She slapped him again. "You don't want her! You never did, did you?"

"You had Tammy Savannah to get to me, to blackmail me, didn't you..."

"Fool!" she screamed with spittle drooling from her mouth.

"I love her and I want my daughter. I can raise her with the Lord's love."

"Never. You will never have her! Not until you pay—until you bleed!"

"Mary Raye, it's over. Let me take her. It's all over." Joe-Bob looked for his daughter. *Had she overheard their argument?* She was nowhere to be found.

Mary Raye roared, "Never." She then ran to the cliff's perilous edge, looking for Tammy Savanah. "Tammy, Tammy let's go," she growled. She had venom in her words.

Joe-Bob rushed to Mary Raye's side. "It's got to end Mary Raye. I love my daughter, please let me have her. Please!"

"Never. I'll make you pay until the day you die. I'll soak your pathetic bones dry. I'll drain the guts out of your ministry, you scum-pig!" She leaned against a swaying, knee-high, single-row chain fence, that was the only barrier that stood between them and the crashing combers below. The swallows were flying frantically in slashing zig-zag and whipping serpentine. They sensed the turmoil so close to their nests.

"Please don't fight, mommy. Please don't hit her daddy, please," the paralyzed Tammy Savannah said from the limestone cliff walls below. "Please." Joe-Bob heard the fear in her voice.

"Mary Raye."

"To hell with you," she screamed. She slapped him hard and pushed his chest as tears of insanity welled in her eyes. "To hell with you." She hit him as hard as she could. She pounded his ribwall. "You'll pay! You'll pay!"

"No, Mary Raye, no!" He grabbed her tight. She continued to pummel him. "No." They fell to the ground and rolled underneath the guard chain. "No." He stood up and she fiercely kneed him in the groin. "Ahhhhh!"

He fell backwards and slipped on mossy grass. "No!" *He tumbled over the limestone edge and grabbed a rock crevice with his left hand as he skidded down the cliff's face.* It was the only thing that saved him from certain death.

"Mary Raye, help me please. Mary Raye!" he yelled, gasping for his life.

Mary Ray Hobart slowly, circumspectfully righted herself. She was unphased. She brushed off the dirt and sward. She stepped to the dangerous escarpment's edge and looked down at the Reverend and cackled. *"Die,"* she said as she ground her right foot into his gashed knuckles. *"Die."*

"Mary Raye. Mary Raye, please," he implored.

"Die!"

One hundred eleven thousand people had sardine-packed Dallas Cowboy's Irving Texas Stadium. A world-wide viewing audience of ten to twelve million would watch the Reverend Joe-Bob Jones' resurrection from the dead with his New Christ Divinity Foundation. They would be enchanted. They would be glued to their seats.

From above, through the oval-rectangular opening in Texas Stadium, flew a Sky Rider Aerochute stunt flyer. He was in a blazing red, yellow and green parachute canopy harnessed to a three-wheeled powered seat. The tricycle contraption, with pilot, flew at twenty-six miles per hour, had a take-off distance of 50-100 feet and could land in 25-50 feet. The Aerochute, or "paramotor," was powered by a 46 horsepower Rotax engine with a three-blade prop.

Behind the Skye Rider Aerochute, the stuntman streamed billowing red smoke from a seat-mounted canister and carried a fifteen-foot by sixty-foot bright red and white banner. It proclaimed: *"Jesus Saves."*

The daredevil flew in over the upper deck at the westward Gate 1, through the roof opening and eighty yards down field to the New Christ Divinity Foundation Holy Roller gospel singers. He spiraled twice in a tight figure eight to ecstatic cheers, then landed on stage in front of the Lord's singing troubadours.

The multicolored canopy gradually settled behind the stunt flyer on the parquet floor. The aerobat got out of his tricycle seat as it rolled to a slow stop. His flight suit was bright silver-white. On the front, in chest-size sparkly red letters, he had printed: "Jesus." On the back: the pronouncement "Saves."

He unbuckled to the raves of the crowd. Biff stood and pirouetted while spotlights illuminated his reflective red lettering. The throng howled. He raised his fist to the deistic air. He ran to one of the microphones where the Holy Rollers had been singing and began to chant: "*Jesus Saves. Jesus Saves.*" The crowd erupted.

"Could we get in please," Alex pleaded as he pushed his way past a line of several hundred who waited patiently, hoping to gain entrance. Pepper was at his side.

"I'm sorry," one of three New Christ Divinity Foundation security guards said. "But we're already beyond our limit."

Alex looked at his watch. It was 10:30 a.m. The New Christ revival had begun at 8:30, and Joe-Bob was scheduled to make his long anticipated appearance at 11:00.

"Please."

"I'm sorry," the stern guard reiterated.

"But it's an emergency!"

"What kind?" a bigger, cowboy-type security supervisor in a more official blazer inquired as he pushed his way to the commotion.

Pepper had squeezed close to Alex. "A girl, she has a vial," Pepper said, "She has a deadly poison—she plans on using it here. You need to let us through."

"Have you called the police?"

"Well, no," she and Alex had good reason not to call them, especially after the Invenco plant debacle outside of Cuba, Missouri, not to mention the St. Louis Zoo and Oshkosh. "Please, it's important."

"I'm sorry, but you'll have to leave. If you *have* a legitimate emergency, then you need to call the police and they'll intervene with us." The head of security had been conned by just about every ploy in his years working at Texas Stadium. In fact, he had heard *this one*, or one very close to this several years ago from some fanatic Cowboys fan and his buddy, who tried to weasel their way into a Dallas/San Francisco football game.

"Leave? But this is an emergency!"

"Look," the supervisor said. He was losing his patience. "You can wait in line, and if we get space we'll let you in, but after everyone else." He pointed to the back of the line.

"Please."

"Sorry, everyone else wants to get in too. We have to treat everyone the same, that's the rule. Now, I suggest you call the police or wait in line."

"Die you pig, die!" Mary Raye screamed. She ground Joe-Bob's bleeding hand into the blade-sharp rock with her inch-and-a-half heel. Joe-Bob frantically kicked, trying to find support for his feet. There was none. Luckily he found a toehold in a swallow's mud nest. It supported him temporarily, but just as suddenly as he braced himself, it broke away. Underneath, he had crushed two hatchlings to death. The remnants of the baby sparrows with their identical blue-and-green-metallic bodies careened to the cliffs below. A single feather—however, floated down to Tammy Savannah.

"Don't die daddy. Please daddy, mommy. Don't fight," she vainly cried. Tammy Savannah was trembling.

The feather wafted in pendulum breeze strokes. It nudged Tammy on the forehead with its stabbing, prickly end. It bounced, then bumped past her. She caught it in her palm and clutched protectively.

"Die you pig!"

"Please Mary Raye, please help me." Joe-Bob struggled to pull himself up under the crush of her scraping feet. He flexed his muscles and desperately attempted to wrench himself up from death's grip.

"I'm going to kill you, then I'll get everything!"

Then from behind Mary Raye came another voice —the bray of the person who had been lurking in the shadows on the St. Augustine grass under the sole fan palm.

"Die yourself, bitch!" the dark figure shrieked.

CHAPTER 48
Johnson Space Center, Houston

Flight Director General Oliver Peterson was 61 years old, cantankerous, grizzled and a pro at *double-entendré* politics. Each side was conniving—double-dealing the other—no one was playing straight pool. He knew that his next contact would be NORAD and Lieutenant General John "Chaz" Simpson, then Langley and CIA Director Gates. But those were "his" men up there.

He had, denying his conscience, ordered the crew of *Mir-Kennedy I* to a death sentence. There had been a blackout of communications since the employment of dihydroxy-organopyrethrum-Zeta-4 in the one hundred percent oxygen atmosphere.

Despite his orders, Oliver was playing out *both scenarios* as time was running out. He had discussed the alternative possibility with Dr. Perry Johnson at the Mills Farm Biologics Warfare Lab—and in the event he'd get the green light, the operation could go full scope— *immediately*. Already, despite his directives to the contrary, he had clandestinely ordered the Southern Hemispheric Melbourne, Australia Recovery Team in an orchestration of incredible military manpower—and sheer force of will—to keep the astronauts alive. They had gone from a readiness status red to a *green go*—and were en route.

"Harlan, General Simpson," he knew Gates personally from the Counter Driggs BBS covert spy satellite project they had worked on during the inception of the space shuttle Atlantis program.

"Oliver," Harlan answered on the scrambled NSA Vista II satellite transmitted video monitor.

"Oliver," the pretentious General Simpson spoke at the same time.

"My guess is that they're going to come down despite orders," Peterson said.

"And if they do?" Simpson asked Gates for reconfirmation.

Peterson interrupted. "We still have the Mills Farm alternative."

"We can't risk it," Gates somberly said.

"Gentlemen, why the communications blackout?" Simpson curiously asked.

"The risk of an electrical fire on board in the one hundred percent oxygen environment combined with the dihydroxy-Zeta-4 experiment was too great. Their only communication channel is through the *Orion*. We're waiting to hear from them any minute."

"I say we activate the Betsy," trigger-happy Simpson recommended.

"Oliver," Gates asked, "what do you think the odds are that they're coming in?"

"Honestly?"

"Yes," Simpson interrupted. He as well as Gates knew what the *Mir-Kennedy I* crew would more than likely do.

"They were ordered not to come down. But...if there is a possibility for Biosafety Level 4 containment, which I believe they can safely enter, then I think that they'd make a go for a landing."

"Are there any facilities that have the capability of Level 4 containment?" Director Gates asked.

"If I was them, and I was sure that I could land without incident, not contaminate the environment with their *possibly LAV-10* tainted space suits—I'd wait till the absolute last possible moment, then I'd head for the second alternative landing site—White Sands Space Harbor. We have the capability for Biosafety Level 4 containment there, if need be. Also, I think that there's a more promising possibility..."

"How long until they come down?" Simpson brusquely asked.

"If I was them...now."

"Harlan?" Simpson asked.

"I'd need to get the green light from the President...but right now, I'd say that was a given."

"Harlan," Peterson said. "I've been on the horn with Dr. Johnson at Mills Farm. There is another possible scenario. Though I think that our risks would be minimal at White Sands, there is another alternate landing site that would provide one hundred percent environmental isolation..."

"Gentlemen," Gates interrupted, "we can't afford to wait any longer. Let's get the Betsy in play."

"Harlan," General Peterson protested.

"Sorry. It's from the top," Gates said.

"Best decision you could have made Harlan," General Simpson said. "I'm just as sick about this decision as you, but it's the only way that we can still ensure that we'll preserve the lives of the American people through noncontamination."

"Bullshit!" Peterson said.

Edwards Air Force Base, California

The U.S. Air Force/Lockheed SR-71A Blackbird remains unmatched in its sustained speed and altitude performance—despite its aging subsystems and heavy workload imposed on the crew who operate the Mach3-plus aircraft. Though in part outdated by the Lockheed F-117A Stealth Fighter, designed to be invisible on radar, the Stealth Fighter had only a top speed of 646 miles per hour.

The unique high-speed, high-altitude environment in which the SR-71A operated made it ideal for General Simpson's mission.

Able to fly at 2,189 miles per hour and 86,000 feet altitude, the hypersecret "Betsy" ASAT (antisatellite weapons), which the Blackbird can launch during a crisis—was ideal for shooting down the 18,000 miles per hour orbiting *Orion*.

The two crew members of the Blackbird were strapped into the cockpit, the pilot in front, the copilot/navigator in the rear. They were not told what their target was, nor would it make a difference since they followed their orders with blind obedience.

"Mission tape?" the pilot asked.

"Roger," the copilot replied. The mission tape had been cut and installed just minutes earlier into the aircraft's ANS (astro-inertial navigation system). The tape provided navigation commands to the autopilot during the flight and automatically engaged sensors and their recorders when the aircraft approached and passed the ground positions designated for reconnaissance.

The Blackbird would fly a straight-line heading toward the shuttle's ground-tracked orbiting position.

"What do we got?" the pilot asked his copilot/navigator who was also the weapons officer.

"Astronavigation function on astro-inertial navigation system a go." The SR-71A located a white star illuminated on the mode selector button of the rear cockpit indicating that the system had positioned and was tracking at least three stars in its preprogrammed catalog of fifty-two stars.

"Flight level 250 (25,000 feet)," the pilot said.

"Two five zero," the copilot confirmed.

"Throttles to Mach 3.0."

"Three point zero."

The pilot advanced the throttles into afterburner range, and there was a sudden slight yaw to the right as the afterburners ignited asymmetrically.

"This for real?" the copilot asked.

"It is."

"Test run?"

"It's the real deal partner."

"Russian satellite or what?"

"It's anyone's bet. Gig's classified."

"No shit."

"Yeah. I don't have that information. Like to, though"

"What's your guess?"

"Don't know."

"My computer tells me," the copilot punched up the target on his side-mounted HUD (Heads Up Device) video panel, "the bogey has an incoming speed of 18,341 knots."

"Iran or Iraq. More than likely North Korean or Chinese satellite."

"I agree."

"Think it's a tactical weapon?"

"Probably."

"Missile?"

"No, satellite."

"You think?"

"Yeah, probably satellite killer, laser death-beam doomsday machine or something."

"Something like that."

"Let's go nuke us a satellite."

"Ride 'em cowboy!"

CHAPTER 49

Tammy Savannah Jones had seen her mother pushed off the cliff and to her death. Screaming, she fell 150 feet to the rocks below. A jagged granite chard ripped through her heart. Blood passed from her mouth and bosom in a ghostly bellow. In the distance, just off the coast on rocks that jutted through the surf, two oblivious sea lions barked. A lone dirty-white albatross flew through the swarm of swallows. It screeched, then departed for the mystery of the capricious Pacific.

"The bitch had to die," she calmly said.

Reverend Joe-Bob Jones incredulously looked up at his impassive wife, Colleen Winslow Jones, as he pulled himself from the cliff's edge. "I..."

"I knew all about you," she said. "She tried to blackmail me also. I knew that she had been blackmailing you. I know about your sea urchin daughter." Colleen gazed at the unsettling Pacific swells. "I have it all on tape." She pulled out a pocket microcassette tape recorder. "I could go to the police and tell them that you did it...that you killed her, that I was a witness." Then Colleen stepped to the edge of the escarpment and looked down at the pathetic Tammy Savannah Jones. She was frozen, petrified in fear, on the ledge thirty feet below. "He killed your mother," she said. "He pushed her off the cliff."

Tammy could not have seen Colleen push her mother, Mary Raye from behind. For all she knew it was true, her father did kill her mother—the mother who wanted to murder him.

"He killed her dead, child, and if you tell anyone, even one soul, then the police will take him away and hang him by his puny neck like a stuck pig—until he's dead, and you'll never have a father again. Dead as a doornail, dead as a duck."

That was the last thing that Tammy Savannah remembered. *"Her father had killed her mother dead."* And if she told on him—then the police would take him away and he would be hung by the neck until he was gone. Tammy Savannah withdrew into a confusional state of post-traumatic catatonia. She was plunged into a stupor. Her destiny was set in concrete.

The Reverend Jones couldn't utter a word either. The blackmail did not go away, it was just handed off. The baton traded from one relay runner to her successor.

Colleen Nazi-ordered Joe-Bob Jones to institutionalize Tammy Savannah, and to never see or speak to her again. He had no choice, he was forced to abandon the child he loved so much. Colleen coveted the tape that would be his *death sentence*.

On the following Sunday's service there was no mention of any blackmail, there was no self-revelation, no sinner's confession of adulterous misdeeds. The Reverend Jones' two million worldwide viewers saw a glum and dejected patriarch.

On Tuesday he hospitalized Tammy Savannah at Sunnyview Sanitarium in Macon, Georgia. She was diagnosed as having acute onset childhood schizophrenia. Her prognosis was poor, and her treatment included a menagerie of psychotrophic drugs: mesoridazine, triflouparazive, fluphenazine and haloperidol, among others. When she didn't respond to any of those, and became agitated, she was given dangerous, experimental anti-Parkinson medication. However, they soon caused extrapyramidal symptoms and were discontinued.

ECT was the treatment of last resort, and in fact was not indicated because of Tammy's preadolescent age. Yet, because of her immutable catatonia with mixed cycles of agitation, the doctors thought it might help. She received twenty-six ECT treatments. This was much more than the advised, and generally accepted, four to ten. Nevertheless, she did not respond.

Once a year, on her birthday, Joe-Bob secretly went to see her. He wasn't allowed to, lest Colleen expose him to the authorities. He did anyway. Tammy Savannah did not talk nor respond to anything he said. She was a vegetable. He was strong when he saw her, but cried tears of grief for the next 365 days.

Once, when Tammy Savannah was nine, Joe-Bob brought her photographs of the Mission at Capistrano, and others of the swallows that she liked so much. Those pictures, especially of the swallows with their blue-and-green-metallic feathers, seemed to elicit a sign of life from deep within. But the spark faded as quickly as it came.

Colleen worried that, one day, the mettlesome Tammy Savannah might come out of her stupor so, when Tammy Savannah turned twelve, Colleen sent Tammy to a far away sanitarium where Joe-Bob would never find her. He secretly tried, but was unable.

Time passed, and Tammy Savannah remained cataplexic until her sixteenth birthday, when suddenly—and paradoxically, she regained consciousness.

Her psychiatrists called it a miracle. They didn't know how to explain it. Tammy Savannah quickly progressed through a period of violent behavior, delusions and perceptual disorders, to one of borderline normalcy. She continued on antipsychotic drugs for a time, then moved to mild tranquilizers within a year. She rapidly made significant advancements.

Tammy's education also progressed quickly. Though she was non-communicative during the last ten years, *she did see and absorb everything around her*. By the time she was twenty, she had amazingly amassed the equivalent of a high school education. What she had lost over the ten year hiatus in non-functionality, she made up for with her voracious hunger for knowledge.

Tammy Savannah was eventually told about her father, the renowned television evangelistic preacher; and her mother's death. She was allowed to contact the Reverend Jones, but she didn't want to. As far as she was concerned, he, too, was dead. When Tammy was twenty-two, in the middle of the night during a spring thunderstorm, she escaped. She disappeared without a trace. She had a plan, an intent. *She had vowed revenge on her father, whom she believed mercilessly murdered her mother. Soon!*

Through the concrete tunnel, down the echoing corridors and into his lonely dressing room, Reverend Jones could hear the exhalted chants of "Jesus Saves." Then those incantations transshaped into, "We love Joe-Bob. We love Joe-Bob." The Dallas Cowboy Texas Stadium was on zealot fire—and so was the entire evangelistic world. "We love Joe-Bob. We love Joe-Bob."

The Reverend Joe-Bob Jones was not, however, their long awaited messiah. He was a lowly sinner. He had an affair—and he was at least indirectly responsible for his paramour's death; he had wrongfully abandoned his mentally disturbed child.

"We love Joe-Bob. We love Joe-Bob."

He was really an unpardonable sinner. His life had fallen into the iron grip of fate—and he was unable to extricate himself from the quicksand.

Twelve million people worldwide were waiting to hear his message, to share his heavenly vision. One hundred eleven thousand faithful were waiting for him to preach.

"We love Joe-Bob! We love Joe-Bob!"

This was the culmination. He had been given what very few people ever receive in life: a rare second chance. And before him lay one monumental obstacle—*or was it a blessing*—his daughter, Mahalia Hunt, Tammy Savannah Hobart, *who had come to kill him.*

"We love Joe-Bob! We love Joe-Bob!"

He looked at the enigmatic gift that he had received from Mahalia. It was wrapped in a tube the shape of his 6-3/4" Hoya De Monterey Excalibur cigars that he smoked only one, once a month. He looked at the green-foil paper and the eight-petal bow. He re-read the card:

"I am Tao. I am the Power. I am the Swallow."

He knew what Tao meant. Tao was the power within each of us to do whatever it is that we truly believe. She—Mahalia—was her own Power. *Her power was that she was going to kill him.* He could only love her and beg for her forgiveness.

He slowly, carefully removed the wrapping. It was the Hoya De

Monterey tube. He cautiously opened the cylinder. *There was no cigar.* He inverted it and gently tapped its end. Out spilled a blue and green metallic feather. It was in perfect condition—each barb of plumage was flawlessly unspoiled.

"We love Joe-Bob! We love Joe-Bob!" the restless flock chanted. The crowd was stomping their feet on the concrete deck, and on the Astroturf stadium infield grounds.

He was ready. He rose and looked one last time in the mirror. It was time for him to go. But before he walked the corridors into the seething mass, he found a safety pin on the vanity-light makeup counter. He took the pin and clasped it onto his white shirt that was open at the top button. He had tight-pulling black suspenders that looped over his shoulders. He wore a conservative sports coat, but as always, he would remove it before speaking. He was a common man. He was one with his congregation. *He was a sinner.*

Joe-Bob pinned the blue and green feather to his cardboard shirt like he would have fastened a pearly carnation. Tears welled in his *mesto* eyes. "Forgive me God. Forgive me for my transgressions."

His aides were at the door. They had already knocked twice. They told him that they were ready. Joe-Bob swung his jacket over his left shoulder. He was going to walk out there—before the whole world and wear his guilt. He was going to bear his scarlet letter.

As the Reverend Jones emerged from the concrete tunnel, the throng railed in applause. Sic cameras zoomed down on him from different angles. Three of the best profiles projected on the massive monitors. A prophetic gospel song boomed over the speakers:

Face to face with Christ, my Savior, face to face what will it be?
When with rapture I behold Him, Jesus Christ who died for me.
Face to face I shall behold Him, Far beyond the starry sky;
Face to face in all His glory, I shall see Him by and by!

Joe-Bob had memorized the perfect sermon. It was short, only forty-five minutes. Though it could have been much longer, too much would have bored his faithful. Forty-five minutes was just right. He ascended the stage to the exhilarated chants of his 111,000 divine followers. His heart was pounding.

"We love Joe-Bob! We love Joe-Bob!"

He walked slowly, deliberately to the podium, to his prepared notes waiting for him on the oakwood lectern. In addition, his script was projected on two clear, shoulder-height, symphony conductor teleprompters that rose from both sides of the podium.

Joe-Bob stood there in an impeachable trance. He could not forget the moment that Mary Raye Hobart fell to her death on the Pacific rocks. Before him he saw her body with the granite shard piercing her heart. *He was responsible.* He gazed down at the innocent little girl, the naive six-year-old that he would be forced to inexcusably abandon. *What would she look like now? Why did he do it? He should have had the force of will to stand up to Colleen. Why did he let Colleen blackmail him?* he asked himself. His answer was: *My daughter's here to kill me—to make me pay for my sins.*

The Reverend stared into the multitudes. His eyes were truthful, honest and remorseful. His suspenders nipped into his doleful skin and told him that it was time to start. The six dissecting cameras caught Joe-Bob's face, his pensive look, his charismatic aura—from all angles. "*This feather...*" he said, pointing to the blue and green swallow's feather pinned to his white shirt, above his left bosom.

"This isn't on our script!" the director exclaimed inside the 48-foot SatCom 5 satellite communications truck/trailer outside the stadium "Where is..." he flipped through his copy of the Joe-Bob's speech. He was in a broadcast panic.

"*This feather,*" the Reverend Joe-Bob Jones continued, "*is why I am a sinner.*" He pointed with his now trembling right index finger to the blue and green hatchling feather as he unpinned it from his starched shirt. He held it gently in his palm. He then lifted it, presenting it to his flock. The cameras zoomed in. "*This feather is why I am going to die today. I am a sinner. I am not worthy of your trust and respect.*"

CHAPTER 50

Dr. Joanna Knight was still disoriented when the NSA agents arrived at the Missouri Apiary Suppliers at 253 Pier C Street. It wasn't until midnight that she was ultimately hustled to the Mills Farm, Virginia, Biologics Warfare Lab. She was dog tired and still felt the hangover effect from the thiopental or sodium pentothal which her abductors had given her in their attempts to make her talk. En route, on board the Gulfstream IV she was debriefed by two operatives: agents Martin Collins and Thomas Frazier. They wanted to know about the autopsy that she performed on Roscoe J. McMahon III, CEO of BetaTec. She explained in the best detail she could. She told them what she knew about her abduction, which was scant since she was drugged at her Las Vegas home on Plaza De Cielo. Jo suspected that she was injected in her neck, though she couldn't remember specifics.

The Biosafety Level 4 research lab at Mills Farm, Virginia, was a top secret installation. By the time Jo got to the debriefing room, the cogs in her razor-sharp mind had resumed proper working order.

"Dr. Knight." Dr. Perry Johnson was with seven bespectacled, lab-coated scientists. General Felix Orlov introduced them. Jo did not pay attention to the names listed rapid fire. She had other things on her mind that were much more important.

"Mind if I smoke?" Jo asked out of common courtesy. It steadied her nerves and allowed her to think more freely.

"Actually, there's no smoking," one of the General's attachés said.

"I'll have one anyway. Anyone got one?"

Three of the eggheads reached into their lab coats for packs. They were closet coffin-nail puffers who smoked under lab-counter evacuation vanes. One pulled a soft pack of Winstons out of his shirt pocket; the other two had hard packs in their hip pockets.

"I'll have the Winstons." She took a cigarette and also matches that the technician handed her, and lit up.

"Coffee?" one of the scientists asked.

"No, thank you."

"Let's get down to brass tacks," Dr. Johnson said.

"It's your show," she said raising her sardonic eyebrows.

"Jo, mind if I call you Jo?"

"Done your homework, huh?"

"Yes. Jo, tell me what you can about Roscoe McMahon's autopsy."

"You don't have the body, the tissue sections and my notes?"

"No."

"You gotta be kidding?"

"No," General Orlov replied.

"Ta...didn't think you did. But...you knew about McMahon being taken from my autopsy room, and me getting kicked out of my office, didn't you?"

They hesitated in answering. A circumspect General Orlov glanced at Dr. Johnson. Orlov replied first. "Yes."

"Good. Now let's do it this way," she said impatiently. "Let's cut all the goddamn crap, and cut to the chase 'cause otherwise everyone's ass is going to be dead. Don't you agree, Perry?" Jo asked as she inhaled her Winston, and then blew out three perfectly sculptured smoke rings. She admired her handiwork.

General Orlov and Dr. Johnson looked at one another. Jo stood up and walked to the walnut credenza at the side of the conference table. She had changed her mind and poured herself a cup of coffee.

"What about the disc? We found an imprint of a disc behind a picture in your study. Does it mean anything?"

"Oh...that." She smiled and filled a cup two-thirds full, then remained standing next to the credenza. She leaned back into the wood, trying to ease the pain in her back. "Coffee's a little strong. Been on the burner too long?"

"Cut the crap, Dr. Knight..." Orlov said.

"Listen, you son-of-a-bitch, if you don't remember—if your file is not replete enough on Joanna Knight M.D.—then let me refresh your myopic short-sighted memory. I, sir, had security clearance *zenith—get it? Zenith*! I know all about this goddamn project of yours. Kapeesh? Now if you want my help, because I sure the shit believe that you need it, then it's a two-way street." She irately paused, took another sip of tar-strong coffee. "Got it, pal?"

"Go ahead, Dr. Knight," Dr. Johnson conciliatorally said. "Please. I'm well aware of your previous security clearance and your unblemished reputation."

"Tit for tat."

"Tit for tat?" Johnson replied.

General Orlov expressed disapproval, "Yeah."

"You first," she said.

"Go on," Dr. Johnson replied, "ask away."

"Just how far has the *LAV-10* project progressed?" There was silence. Neither Dr. Johnson nor his associates spoke. "Look," she reminded them, "Dr. Guyader at the CDC had already contacted me about assisting him. It was me who called Guyader when I discovered the scope of this operation and was freed in Long Beach. If it wasn't for my goddamn call, your weasel-ass NSA agents wouldn't have joined the show, and I wouldn't be here right now—and you wouldn't know about the thousand or so drums of deadly TTLV-1 in the Long Beach warehouse, would you?"

"It's not quite what Guyader might have told you," General Orlov eased up. "*LAV-10* was a covert project that was being worked on by a traitor, a Russian cosmonaut, Biologics Engineer Gregov Pokrovsky on *Mir-Kennedy I*."

"He's dead," Johnson said.

General Orlov continued. "Apparently he got a dose of his own medicine."

"Seems that Pokrovsky was smuggling *LAV-10* down to earth

on *Mir-Kennedy I* resupply cargo tugs," Dr. Johnson said.

"You still have the problem with gravitational flip?" Jo asked.

"Yes, how'd you know about that?" Johnson asked.

"Remember, I was involved with the original project, back when *LAV-10* was TTLV-1."

"Yeah. Anyway, Pokrovsky had perfected two versions of *LAV-10*. One we believe was airborne. It's the 'A' derivative; and another is vector borne—only works via skin contact. It's the 'B' derivative. The deaths..."

"McMahon?"

"Yes. We believe he was exposed to the 'B' derivative," Dr. Johnson said.

"We've since recovered a 'B' vial, but not an 'A'," General Orlov said.

"Are you sure that there's an 'A' out there?"

"Yes," Johnson replied. "absolutely. Furthermore, we believe that it might have fallen into the wrong hands."

"Shhhit," she said.

"Yeah," General Orlov echoed.

"What was on the disc?" Johnson asked.

"Nothing. It was nothing at all." Jo school-girl smirked. " Just my will, a letter to my daughter, my apology to her for me being such a lousy mom."

"Do you think that your captors thought that there was more to it?" the general asked.

"Yeah, that's probably why they kept me alive. That and the fact that I, of all people, ended up doing McMahon's autopsy. What are the odds?"

"Amazed me," Dr. Johnson agreed.

Joanna paused again to reflect. She was particularly intuitive, "CIA?"

"No, not really," Johnson answered. "Some are, some aren't..."

"Go on."

"They're an organization within the CIA. They used to be called the 'Armory', or the 'Inner Circle'. We prefer to call them scum. They're an international group of criminals—some CIA, others KGB, MI-6, some industrialists—who banded together to steal arms, chemical weapons, biologic warfare and industrial secrets and sell them to the highest bidder, like the North Koreans, the Iraqis, the Iranians, etc."

"What about the *LAV-10A*?"

"We're tracking that down right now," Orlov said.

"The girl has it," Jo said. She was referring to the laser print that Alex enlarged from the video in the Missouri Apiary Suppliers warehouse. Then Jo told them the *entire* story, in detail, about her rescue in Long Beach, the photo with the girl, and the cut-off "*Te*" and "*St*", which Alex and Pepper deduced to mean "Texas Stadium."

"That's everything," she said. It took nearly two hours to tell her story.

"Christ," Dr. Johnson said as he wiped sweat from his brow. He withdrew a notebook and a four-color pen, that were packed into his lab coat. He was extremely anxious.

General Orlov immediately placed several calls on an encrypted 15-key, 164,000 bps telephone, and began barking orders.

Jo paid close attention. Orlov made no attempt to shroud his conversation in obscure references, or coded dialogue. Then Jo asked, "What about the astronauts on board the space station?"

"*Mir-Kennedy I*?"

"They're running out of oxygen and they...can't come down," Orlov replied with sincere dismay.

"What happened?" Jo asked.

"They had an accident on board and they've gone into their space suits. There might be contamination of their suits with *LAV-10A*. And, as you know, even the smallest molecule can be deadly. They don't have much time."

"I wasn't aware of this."

"It hasn't been made public," Orlov said.

"Look," Jo thought out loud as she sat back down in her chair with her cup of stale coffee. "You have two problems. First you need to get rid of those toxic barrels of TTLV-1 at the Missouri Apiary Suppliers warehouse in Long Beach. It's potentially just as deadly as *LAV-10*."

"We didn't even know that they were there until you debriefed the NSA team en route," Johnson said. "We thought that stuff had been deep-sixed long ago."

"Well it hadn't. The second problem: When I was doing the autopsy on McMahon, I noticed something funny. His body had that mothball smell, the same *stench* from years ago. God, I couldn't forget that smell. But, the cerebral spinal fluid was different."

"How so?" Johnson asked.

"The color. In the deaths that occurred in Invenco, in the post-mortems we noted that the cerebral spinal fluid was slightly congealed, but didn't give off an exothermic reaction. In the original research with TTLV-1 we thought that the flipping could be eliminated by binding TTLV-1 to manganese dicarbonate. The idea was that it would make the TTLV-1 stable and prevent mirroring."

"So?"

"So, I think that's what Pokrovsky was working on in the space station. And if it wasn't with manganese dicarbonate, then it had to be something similar to it. He had to use our original research, but with the technology of the space station and the employment of a weightless environment—new options in the development of TTLV-1 had to have opened up."

"So what you're saying is that..."

"*We can stop the LAV-10 from flipping.*"

"Are you sure?"

"That's right. We did it temporarily with TTLV-1, in our experiments twenty years ago. The problem was that the manganese dicarbonate bonds didn't stick. But if Pokrovsky developed a zero-G *LAV-10*, then all we need to do is *cool* the *LAV-10*, whether it be in the 'A' or 'B' version to less than ten degrees centigrade and theoretically it should be safe."

"That explains why Pokrovsky was infected. He was working at ambient space station temperature," Johnson deduced. "And the other astronaut..."

"Other?" Jo asked.

"Yes, we had a second death on board *Mir-Kennedy I*, Japanese Flight Engineer Futabatei Shoyo. But he, too, was exposed at room temperature."

"So, what would also work?"

"What?"

"Bromochlorodifluromethane. We tried that before. You should have that data on microfilm," she snipped.

"What's bromochlo-whatever?" General Orlov asked.

"Halon, as in *Halon fire extinguishers!*"

"Jesus," Dr. Johnson said in startled realization. "That's right! Get me NASA on the horn, now!" he ordered one of his egghead assistants. Then speaking to Dr. Knight, "You realize that there's *now* hope for the astronauts?"

"Yes."

"You know Washington will never approve of this in time," Orlov said. The encrypted telephone rang. The cacaphonous brapping noise sounded like a dying goat. General Orlov answered. He spoke briefly and said, "It's for you Dr. Knight, CIA Director Gates."

Dr. Joanna Knight took another measured drag on her Winston. She languidly exhaled. She watched the smoke crest out of her mouth in rings. Nonchalantly she raised the receiver to her ear.

"Long time no speak."

"Yes," Gates said in a reserved intonation.

"Can't stay away from old friends, huh?"

"No."

CHAPTER 51
Space Station Mir-Kennedy I

"Houston Control. This is Mission Commander Scoop Jackson. Houston Control this is Jackson over."

"Roger, Jackson this is Johnson Space Center, Houston, Flight Director General Peterson. What's your status?"

"There're eleven of us on board *Orion...*"

"Commander Jackson, telemetry's shown us separation from *Mir-Kennedy I*, is this affirmative?"

"Roger, Houston. *Mir-Kennedy* blew with dihydroxy-organo-Zeta-4 application—that and the one hundred percent oxygen environment. We lost the X- and Y-hoops along with the docking module."

"Any casualties?"

"None."

"Commander Jackson, we hadn't heard from you for awhile, what's your plan?"

"We've been off air. We were concerned about another electrical incident."

"You know...there's no roundtrip ticket on this mission? You've got your orders."

"Houston, we're going to need to change those. We're preparing for deorbital burn."

"*Orion*, you're not authorized for a return trip."

"Houston, we'll have to ignore your nonauthorization. I'm sorry to say, but we're coming in."

"Repeat *Orion*, you do not have clearance for landing."

"Houston Control, let me make this clear, we're coming in. We believe that we have devised a protocol for complete isolation and..."

"*Orion*, we cannot allow you to land," General Peterson said slowly, and with grave regret.

"Listen Houston, we've devised a scheme for complete isolation, one hundred percent money back guaranteed. No fuss, no muss. We're coming in to the second alternative landing site at White Sands Space Harbor. We've already got the data on our computer and can download it on command."

"*Orion*, that's a *negative*, repeat a *negative* for New Mexico. Do you read me, that's a *negative*."

"Houston there are eleven souls on board, and two that are already dead. It's my responsibility to ensure that we have no more fatalities. We're goddamn about out of oxygen, and you have the equipment to contain us and provide emergency life support in Biosafety Level 4 containment."

"That's a negative, *Orion*."

"That's a screw you! Repeat, that's a screw you! We're coming down!" Jackson toggled off the air-to-ground communications channel in disgust, and ordered Communications Officer Hobbs to begin the download to Johnson Space Center Houston. Hobbs did such, and in two minutes, thirty-two seconds, Houston Control had the information.

"You ready to rock-and-roll?" Spacewalker/Pilot Smith asked with trepidation as he began running down his reentry check list.

"Let's do it," Jackson replied.

SR-71A Blackbird

The Blackbird was rapidly bearing down on the space shuttle *Orion*. At Mach 2.99 and 70,000 feet, the SR-71A was fifteen minutes from target engagement. A low rumble buzzed throughout the supersonic jet, and could be heard and felt in the tempered-steel airframe. The curvature of the Earth was readily apparent, and the sky above was dark blue. Despite the thin air, there was enough friction on the aircraft to generate substantial heat.

"Getting a little hot in here," the copilot said. He could feel the calefaction through the narrow windows of the rear cockpit, even while wearing his thick U.S. Air Force high-altitude pressure suit gloves.

"Yeah, I'd say so. Give me a fix on the Betsy target."

"Betsy—bearing mark three-five-nine. We've deviated," the copilot said as he looked into one of the windows of the ANS control head in the rear cockpit. They were three-tenths of a mile right off course.

"Let's correct with manual override."

"Override to you."

The pilot carefully nudged his ANS astro-inertial navigation system course adjusting control, since at Mach 3.0, even with slight course deviation they would be far from their destination. Slowly, then quickly, they came back on beam.

"Course corrected. On the blackline."

"Blackline confirmed."

"Give me a countdown from sixty seconds."

"Roger, we'll take out the bogey. Target in three minutes."

"Let's nuke us an unfriendly."

"Yee-ha!"

Space Shuttle Orion

Tension on board the space shuttle *Orion* couldn't be cut with a Ginsu knife. Jackson knew that they probably would be shot down. He just hoped and prayed that Johnson Space Center, Houston and White Sands Space Harbor would have compassion, that they would implement their downloaded reentry and Biosafety Level 4 isolation plan.

"Check OMS engine status," Jackson ordered Smith as he began working down his own checklist.

"Pressure, vapor isolation switches all closed," Smith replied tersely.

"TANK ISOL switches open."

"Open."

"CROSSFEED switches closed."

"Closed."

"Check aft LEFT RCS (Reaction Control System)."

Smith pressed switches OP, then TANK ISOL all four—GPC (General Purpose Computer). "RCS CROSS FEED—GPC MATER RCS CROSSFEED—OFF."

"RIGHT RCS."

Smith completed the same operation. "Off," he said.

"BOILER N2 SPLY (boiler nitrogen supply) switches—on. BLR CNTRL switches—on. BLR CONTRL PWR/HTR (power/heater) switches A. APU FUEL TK VLV (auxiliary power unit fuel tank valve) switches—CL."

"Roger."

"On computer keyboard enter: OPS 3 0 2 PRO."

"Enter OPS 3 0 2 PRO."

"FLT CNTRL POWER switch ON."

"On."

"ADI (attitude direction indicator—attitude) switches INRL (inertial), ADI ERROR—MED, ADI RATE—MED."

"Med, med."

"Let's kick this puppy over and pray they cut us a break and believe in our numbers." With rotation hand controller, Jackson fired the OMS engines and maneuvered to deorbit attitude. He compared attitude shown on the screen with that on the ADI. They were where they were supposed to be.

"Everyone ready for a ride?" Smith asked. There was affirmation from the nine astronauts on board the *Orion*. Vrubel and Maya were incommunicado in the mid-fuselage cargo bay, precariously tucked away—cocooned into their polyurethane-coated foam, jerry-rigged docking module.

"We're with you," Computer and Metologics Officer Zvezda, as well as Holloway, replied.

"Let's do it." Corddian Spacewalker Solovyev said in blithe Baltic monotone.

"Comrade Mukhina," Vrubel asked across the darkness, "You know that this is probably an exercise in futility."

"I do."

"You know that even with the data we provided Houston, and even though it makes sense—that *we can be placed in Biosafety Level 4 isolation* and *LAV-10*, if there is any on our space suits, will not come in contact with Earth atmosphere; that the embarrassment potential of *LAV-10* is too great for either government to allow us to land."

"I understand that."

"Then why did you come on board? Tell me the truth. You knew that your mission to stop Pokrovsky was potentially a suicide mission."

"I did."

"Then why?"

"Because the risk of an unperfected *LAV-10* being released to the public overrode any risk of my own death. Which is why Houston will have to shoot us down."

"I agree. I probably would have done the same."

"Yes."

Vrubel slipped slightly toward Maya as he adjusted his ejection chute gear. He was already strapped into the docking module with *Orion* flight suit zippers, snug-tight straps and taut bungee cord belt and shoulder harnesses. He needed, however, to loosen one of his tiedowns. The weak G-forces from the space station explosion tugged against him at a peculiar angle through his torso.

"Maya, I heard you and Commander Jackson."

"I..."

"Love is a funny thing, isn't it? It doesn't control its place of affinity or its time, does it?"

"No."

"It's somewhat like a virus. One day you're fine...and the next you're afflicted."

"Yes"

SR-71A Blackbird

The slick-flying Blackbird burst through the thin atmosphere at three times the speed of sound. It growled, rocked and shook as it arrowed toward its destiny.

"Target sixty seconds," the copilot said.

"Shock wave spike aft of Betsy," the pilot said.

"Roger."

"Center of gravity at twenty-five percent mean aerodynamic cord."

"Prepare for the kick and flutter with release."

"Roger, ready for kick and flutter."

The pilot was particularly excited to nail this bogey, which he was by now sure was a North Korean spy satellite with air-to-ground laser capability. What else could it be? "Let's knock that slant-eye scumball out of the sky."

"Target fifty seconds," the copilot said.

"Active laser guidance system."

"ASAT laser guidance a...lock."

"Armed Betsy for kill."

"Armed and...initiated."

"Target forty seconds."

"Flying the blackline."

"Target thirty seconds."

"Let's kill us a bogey."

Space Shuttle Orion

"Number One APU FUEL TK VLV switch—OPEN?" Jackson asked apprehensively.

"Open," Smith replied.

"Number One APU CONTROL switch—START/RUN."

"Start/run."

"HYD PRESS (hydraulic pressure) indicator—LO green."

"Low green."

"HYD CIRC PUMP switches—OFF."

"Off."

"DAP (digital auto pilot)—AUTO MODE."

"Auto-mode set."

Commander Jackson then pressed the left and right OMS (orbital maneuvering system)/VAPOR ISOL A and GPS. Then OMS ENG switches to—ARM/PRESS.

"On board computer programmed to White Sands Space Harbor."

"God be willing—White Sands."

Jackson pressed the EXEC computer keyboard to begin countdown. "OMS burn ignition: five...four...three...two... one...ignition."

The orbiting maneuvering system engine burn was thunderous. The riveting six thousand pound monomethyl hydrazine and nitrogen tetroxide rocket burn lasted two minutes, forty seconds. The *Orion* shook and thumped the astronauts into their body-contoured seats. "Burn complete," Smith said with cut-off and relaxation of the gravitational forces.

The Orion descended from 17,000 miles per hour, 245.49 mile mean altitude orbit. Jackson and Smith went through a meticulous check list verifying aft left and right reaction control systems, tank isolation switches, crossfeed and helium pressure/vapor isolation. Then, upon Jackson's direction, Smith entered into the computer keyboard: OPS 3 0 3 PRO, followed by ITEM 2 4 (for roll), ITEM 2 5 (for pitch), and ITEM 2 6 (for yaw).

Jackson maneuvered the *Orion* into a nose-up attitude of thirty-two degrees. He was apprehensive—not about their landing at White Sands Space Harbor—he could do that with his eyes closed, but *when they'd be shot down.*

"CABIN RELIEF A and B—ENA ANTISKI - ON."

"On."

"NOSE WHEEL STEERING—OFF."

"Off."

"ENTRY ROLL MODE—OFF."

"Off."

Then Jackson pushed both speed brake/throttle controls full forward. He carefully maneuvered the *Orion's* control surfaces to ready the hydraulic system for entry and landing. He prepared to dump propellants in the forward reaction control system overboard and shift the *Orion's* balance point for entry. Then, there was a sudden unexpected violent jolt!

"What the?" Hobbs shouted as the jolt jerked him in his seat.

Jackson switched his left upper video screen to aft cargo bay monitor. "It's the docking module," he said. "Christ, it's coming loose!" Jackson could see that the docking module had, as a result of the two-minute forty-second OMS burn, smashed against the left upper cargo bay door.

"Is there anything we can do?"

"No, that's it. We'll have to ride it down best we can."

"Shit, are you sure we can't..."

"No dice, this is now or never. We're committed to land."

"Shit!"

"It's going to screw up our balance," Jackson quickly scanned his instrument panel and ADI. He couldn't get Maya and her safety off his mind.

"Keep a sharp eye on item thirty-seven EXEC. Watch the roll, pitch and yaw!"

"Roll at zero. Pitch twenty-nine, yaw zero."

"Keep it on there goddamit! Keep it up!"

SR-71A Blackbird

The three-times Mach flying Blackbird was rapidly closing in. Its razor-sharp wings sliced the paper-thin air at two and one-half times the speed of a bullet.

"Target twenty seconds," the copilot said, now fully focused.

"Unlock coupler, let's get us a bogey!"

"Betsy free to fire."

"Target ten seconds and counting."

"Let's nuke us a slant-eye satellite!"

"*Target five...four...three...two...one...Fire!*"

CHAPTER 52

"*This feather*," the Reverend Joe-Bob Jones said, holding the blue and green metallic feather before the worldwide audience via satellite, "*is why I'm going to die today. I am a sinner.* I have committed adultery. I am not worthy of your adulation. I'm sorry."

The crowd noise lowered to a dull rumble.

"Twenty-eight years ago, I committed a transgression. I violated the Lord's commandment: *Thou shall not commit adultery*. Though I went to jail innocently, for crimes that I did not commit, for embezzling money I did not take, I have really paid for my trespasses. I beg for your absolution."

"You're a murderer." A woman in all black, wearing a macabre veiled hat stood up. She held a 9mm Beretta in her hand. As she pointed it at the Reverend Joe-Bob Jones, security guards rushed her. Twelve burly men surrounded her and the stage in a shielding flood. Joe-Bob waived them off.

He continued. It was time for his long overdue recompense. "Twenty-eight years ago I had an indiscretion with my secretary. Her

328

name was Mary Raye Hobart." The stillness thickened.

Mahalia steadied her jittery arm as determinedly she worked her way up to the stage. She pushed past the burly security guards. She was careful, however, to keep Joe-Bob dead in her sights.

"As a result of that *one-time* mistake, an inadvertent seed was sown. From that accidental seed came an innocent child. Her name was Tammy Savannah Hobart. She is my daughter. I did not have the courage to give her my name. For six years I was blackmailed by her mother. I paid her, in part with contributions from you." He spread his arms broadly.

"On March 28, twenty-three years ago, I decided to put a stop to the blackmail, to come clean to you, my beloved congregation."

"That's not true!" Mahalia screamed. The Beretta shook in her crazed palm. "You didn't care about me." She walked up to the podium and eased the Beretta snuggly to his temple. "You wanted me to die!"

Alex and Pepper tried everything to get in, but security at Texas Stadium was still tight. They agreed, back in Long Beach, that despite Jo's "contacts," that they didn't want to risk calling the authorities. Jo would do what she could at her end. She would disclose all to Dr. Guyader at the CDC, then the other *"powers that be"* that she still had a connection with. They'd handle Dallas from their end.

"Remember," Pepper said, "it was the Cuba City Police who showed up outside the Invenco plant and later the farmhouse where that farming couple was murdered." It wasn't worth the roll of the loaded dice.

They jogged around Texas Stadium. There was no way that they were getting in, no matter what. Pepper eventually agreed to stand in line while Alex made one more loop—but nothing. Then, just past eleven, when Joe-Bob Jones had begun his show business sermon— after Pepper had moved only a few feet closer to the entrance—there was a burst of activity with the security guards at the front gate. They were barking into their two-way headsets. Four of the burly guards that had been blocking the entrance disappeared into the mammoth stadium, leaving only one troll in their way.

"Let's go," Alex yelled, yanking Pepper by the hand. They made a break for the opening. "Front row seats everyone, front row seats," he shouted. "Let's go, they're letting us all in!"

There was a stampede. The charge of 250 faithful created enough diversion for Alex to sneak past the overwhelmed security guard.

In another corner of Texas Stadium, but inside and flanking the stage, was the Ray-Banned man from the Long Beach Missouri Apiary Suppliers. His backup included two of his California cronies and twelve other undercover operatives.

"You spot her?" the double-agent asked.

"It's her," Frank replied from the other side of the stage.

Inside and overlooking the parquet-floored platform, in a box at the twenty yard line between the lower and upper deck, a sharpshooter anxiously asked, "Do you want me to take her now?" He eased his finger on the trigger of his Israeli Galil 7.62 Sniping Rifle as he positioned Mahalia's face in his cross hairs, square between the eyes.

"Not yet, not 'til I'm sure she has the vial."

"I didn't want you to die my child. I love you," Joe-Bob Jones said as he turned to his daughter. Sweat beaded on his brow. She continued to press the Beretta deep into his temple.

"Your mother was blackmailing me. We went to Capistrano to talk. I wanted to tell her, to profess my love for you..."

"That's not true!"

"To tell her that the lies had to end"

"You hate me. That's a lie!"

"I wanted you to come live with me, no matter what the consequences. I had to come clean to you, to my congregation, to the world."

"You lie!"

"I told your mother, child, that I was going to confess my sins to my ministry. That you would be with me."

"That's not so!"

"Tammy..."

"You..."

"I love you Tammy Savannah."

"You do not!!!!" she screamed.

"I love you."

"You killed...you killed..." she shook violently, as if the electroshock therapy treatments again had her in their vicegrip.

"It was an accident. She hit me, we struggled...then she fell."

But Mahalia knew different. Her mother was pushed.

"We were fighting on the cliff. I slipped over the edge. I was hanging by one hand, by my fingertips, by the last breath of my life— and she tried to help me, pull me to safety..."

"That's not true either!" Mahalia knew what the truth was. She was Tao, she was the Power.

"Your mother fell to her death child."

Then Mahalia could see it as clear as day. She was there. She was on the craggy ledge. The ubiquitous blue-and-green-swallows of Capistrano swarmed in zigzags and spiraling serpentine, all around her. Below the surf and swirling tide pools raged on jagged boulders. Above, the sycamore and birches snapped in the crisp air. Unbeknownst to her father, *she did see Colleen Winslow Jones, his wife, push her mother to her death.* "You killed her!" Mahalia said. "You killed my mother. You were responsible for her death!"

"No child, it was an accident."

Alex Seacourt and Pepper Knight entered through Gate 8 near the Will Call Window. Alex pushed, then shoved his way through the crushing throng, out of Tunnel 27 to just behind the Dallas Cowboy's bench and the forty yard line.

"Alex, what do we do?" Pepper asked as she ran behind him, grasping his hand, so they wouldn't get separated.

"We stop her!"

"How?"

"I don't know. Follow me."

They pushed their way through the incredulous faithful. The crowd was in shock, as they watched Reverend Joe-Bob Jones' revelations on the three giant monitors. "I've got an idea."

"Close in on her now!" The Ray-Banned agent ordered. "We need that vial intact if she's got it on her. Don't shoot until I give the order!"

"Got it."

"I want two of you in from the right, two from the left, and two from the front and behind. Mingle with the security guards. Make it quick, and if you have any problem, show 'em your ID."

"You want her dead?" one agent asked.

"No, asshole! We need the vial first, then kill her!"

"No problem boss."

"You put me in an institution. You had me hospitalized," Mahalia Hunt quivered.

"I did," he said through tears. "After your mother fell...you became catatonic. You couldn't talk or walk or eat. You were frozen in time. You were in a mental hospital from age six until..."

"*I escaped*. Is that what you're going to say...*that I'm crazy*!"

"No, my darling..."

"Don't call me that," she pressed the gun tighter to his temple.

"They said child, at sixteen you woke up, that you came out of your coma."

"I...did."

"They said you were getting better, but that I shouldn't come to see you. That you weren't ready for me yet."

"That's not true!" she raged.

He knew it was. Colleen, his wife, had moved Mahalia to another institution when Colleen discovered that he was visiting Mahalia on her birthday. Colleen threatened to release the incriminating tape recording of Mary Raye Hobart's death to the authorities if he saw her again. His hands, or so he thought, were tied.

"You killed my mother...*father*."

"I love you, child." He reached to his side to hug her.

"No!" she pushed him off. Her finger wanted to explode on to the gun trigger.

"Should I take her out?" the sharpshooter asked from his platform booth, a second time.

"Not yet!" screamed the leader. "Not until I give the order!"

"I...saw her."

"Saw?" Joe-Bob Jones asked sympathetically.

"I saw her," Mahalia repeated, but this time with an emerging tic in her left cheek. "She pushed mother...to her death. Your wife...she pushed her. I saw..."

"I'm sorry child."

"But...you were responsible!" she railed.

"Tammy, that's when I put you in the hospital."

"You?"

"You weren't well after your mother's...death."

"I saw her." She bitterly remembered all. "I...I had sixteen years to plan my revenge, to plan my escape. I saw your wife push my mother."

"Child, you were catatonic."

"I was...pretending."

"Until you escaped?"

"No!" she pressed her body next to his. The security guards enveloped her. The Ray-Banned agent and his men moved closer. They surrounded Mahalia, just behind Texas Stadium security guards.

"I planned," she continued, "your arrest, your wife's embezzlement."

"What are you saying daughter."

"Don't call me that!...*father*!"

"Tammy," he again reached out to lovingly embrace her.

"No!" she drill-pressd the cold steel all the way into his brain. She looked vaguely familiar to him now.

"I worked for you when I *left the institution*."

"You..."

"I had the *same job my mother did*. I was a board operator at your television complex. I knew Colleen was blackmailing you. So...when you had your financial crisis with Inspiration Village and raised $25 million...*I talked her into embezzling half the money*.

"Then...*I* went to Switzerland. *I* dressed up like you and *I* forged your name and opened the bank account with the stolen millions. Then *I* called the police!"

"No...."

"I set you up to go to jail! To go to hell, father!!!"

"No child. Tell me it's not so."

"It is!"

"God forgives you daughter. I...forgive you. I love you."

"No, you don't love me! You can't!"

"I do. I love you Tammy."

"Fa...fa...it was I who sent you to hell for five years...to prison to rot...you...can't love me."

"I love you child, and always will. I forgive you. Please... forgive me."

"No, it's too late," Mahalia's facial tic worsened, "...now...I'm going to kill you."

"Child I surrender to your love." He waved off the security guards. "Do what you will with me. The Lord's salvation is my penitence."

"Father...It's more than just about you now." She again began to have those uncontrollable psychotic thoughts. The ones that the "*zines*" didn't help. She reached into the left pocket of her jacket, and *pulled out the double-sealed, yellow-red vial with LAV-10A. On it, smack in the center, was the cherry-red lipstick impression of Mahalia's lips. "I have a bigger surprise for you and all men everywhere!—the Doomsday Kiss!"*

CHAPTER 53

CIA Director Harlan Gates and Dr. Joanna Knight had been comrades in arms twenty-three years ago at Invenco. It was long before the Distinguished Intelligence Cross, the Distinguished Intelligence Medal, the Intelligence Star, and the Career Intelligence Medal. It was a time when Gates was bucking to make a name for himself and he was assigned to the Biologics Warfare unit. Dr. Knight didn't know what his real interest was in the project, except that he was one of the many nameless and faceless consultant-observers working for the CIA. That was long before the NSA's covert involvement.

Gates, as Jo remembered correctly, was a cool cucumber. But Jo knew how to work him. She gleaned that he was at Invenco as more than an "observer." She understood the real underpinnings of his clandestine assignment—that he wasn't there to assure Congress that their cutting-edge research funds weren't being squandered—and she called him on it.

"Jo, it's been a long time." He spoke with amity.

"Harlan, I see that you've made it into the sleazy big time, huh?"

"You still have your wits about you, don't you?"

"What do you expect after I've been *pentatholed-up*. I got to tell the truth, or don't I always."

"That never stopped you before."

"No, it didn't," she sarcastically said.

"Jo, tell me, what's the story on Halon?"

"You've been listening?"

"Of course."

"Where are you?"

"Now I can't tell you that, it would take all the fun out of the cat-and-mouse game."

"Screw you."

"Jo."

"Where?"

"D.C.," he said.

"Figured as much."

"So why don't you bring your ass over here. Let's have some coffee and solve this shit—instead of your bullshit subterfuge."

"So?" Harlan reasoned that Jo knew that the whole "legitimate" United States Intelligence world would be listening into General Orlov, Dr. Johnson and the rest of the white lab-coated stooges' conversation.

"So?" She took another sharp puff on her Winston.

"Jo, are you sure about Halon?"

"That," she blew out a culled smoke ring, "and ten degrees below Centigrade. Check the data, it's all there in black and white from twenty-three years ago. The shit doesn't change."

"You're positive?"

"Sure as rain. I'd bank my life on it."

"No, you're banking the lives of eleven astronauts on it."

"Them and millions of others, Harlan."

CIA Director Gates, a man of action, took the horse by the reins. Within ten seconds, he was on the horn with NORAD and General "Chaz" Simpson. The ASAT laser-guided Betsy had already been let loose from the SR-71A Blackbird.

General Simpson was praying for a miracle. *He got it!* Instantaneously, he relayed the command to the intrepid crew of the Blackbird. With lightening quick reflexes—with only microseconds and fifteen nautical miles prior to target actualization, and annihilation of the space shuttle *Orion*, the copilot/weapon's officer of the SR-71A veered the anti-satellite Betsy off course and self-destructed it seventy miles past the incoming target.

Gates next contacted Houston Flight Director General Peterson and gave him a new directive for *Orion*—one of the alternatives they had discussed covertly.

Finally, Harlan contacted a distressed President Climan, whom he had been working with hand-in-hand—playing crafty point guard. He informed the President of the turn of events.

"Bill, I've got the skinny for you..."

"Give me good news, Harlan. I'm sick of hearing all this discouraging bullshit."

"Well, this is how it goes down. First with regards to the shuttle, we've got a go on Earth landing..."

"Thank God...I didn't need to be known as the President who shot down the *Orion*."

"And it's just as we've discussed—it's the alternative scenario."

"Good, you can fill me in on the details later, but more importantly, any more about *LAV-10A* and the immediate threat? What's our status?"

"Yes, Mr. President, here it is: first about Khalifa Ali Al-Megrahi and the Hamas."

"Go on," President Climan spoke with measured apprehension.

"Seems that the Hamas had run some *side deals* for Rinerson..."

"Peter? Your Associate Director of Chemical and Biologic Weapons?"

"Yes...had to do with oil money and funneling some of the Armory's profits through an Oman sheik, Ajila Madadhi...for a cut of course. In any event, Rinerson had double-crossed his own partners. It was Rinerson who arranged Ambassador Perov's death. Blaming it on the Arabs was the easy way. Fact of the matter is that the Hamas wanted to take responsibility."

"So it was Rinerson who had Perov killed?"

"Yes, my guess is that he deliberately exposed the others—Perov, Mun and Nyerere to the *LAV-10B*..."

"The surface contact *LAV*?"

"Yes, not the airborne stuff."

"So your guess is that Rinerson got too greedy for his own good and wanted to eliminate his partners, and in the process he accidentally exposed himself."

"Yes, either that or one of his right-hand men, possibly ex-CIA or FSB, decided that he could take the game farther and double-cross Rinerson himself."

"So Rinerson kills off his partners, and then Rinerson gets it from one of his own confidants?"

"More than likely. And I think that we've found the *LAV-10A.*"

"Are you going to be able to secure it in time?"

"I sure hope so."

"I do too...for all of our sakes."

They were fifty-six miles above the surface of the earth. Space shuttle *Orion* was thirty-six minutes away from touchdown. They were streaking into the atmosphere at 17,100 miles per hour. Suddenly, the ECC Emergency Control Panel channel light flashed on.

Jackson knew that this was Houston Control's last attempt to contact them, to tell them that if they attempted to land at White Sands Space Harbor, they'd be shot down.

"Dump the propellant?" Spacewalker/Pilot Smith asked. Once they'd discharged their fuel and oxider, they were a dead stone coming in rock fast for a landing without thruster power.

Jackson did not answer. He looked at the left flight deck console ECC. The emergency system transmitted on a different channel than the rest of the shuttle's radios and wasn't tied into the two orbiting TDRS (Tracking and Data Relay Satellite) East and West Systems.

"Dump the propellant?"

Jackson hesitated, then reluctantly toggled on the ECC channel and placed the communication on his line two, HOT mic for the entire crew to hear.

"Jackson, this is Flight Director General Peterson," he was screaming at the top of his lungs, "We have new coordinates for you. Have you dumped your fuel?"

Jackson glanced at Smith, whose finger was itching to flip the ITEM 3 7 EXEC switch. "No," he replied.

"Then link us back onto normal air-to-ground communications and we'll up-load new coordinates into your system one computer. But you've only got seconds before blackout and we miss the window," General Peterson implored.

The work inside the *Orion's* cabin was furious. They had almost no time before blackout which they would enter into at fifty miles above the earth's surface, and traveling at 16,700 miles per hour. It was then that the shuttle would dramatically slow to 8,275 miles per hour. They would not break out of radio isolation until thirty-four miles above the earth's surface. Any new ground coordinates that were fed into the *Orion's* HAL/S mass memory computer had to be done immediately, since during reentry the tremendous energy of the shuttle was dissipated by atmospheric drag. This generated a great deal of heat, which in turn would ionize air molecules near the spacecraft and form a sheath of electrically charged particles that blocked radio signals between the spacecraft and ground. They would be out of radio communication during one of the most critical portions of the flight. The computer was still inputting information as they entered electron blackout.

"Did we get it all?" Jackson asked.

"It's hard to tell," Smith replied as he double-checked the computers. "We could have been loading Houston's back-up on number two. I hope for our sakes it was."

It was then that the *Orion's* RCS (Reaction Control System) primary and vernier thrusters unexpectingly fired on the left nose, then the RCS primary and vernier thrusters ignited simultaneously on the right aft. The *Orion* spun to a southeasterly direction. Next, the two pod mounted space shuttle OMS (Orbital Maneuvering System) rear engines fired, followed by ignition of the three space shuttle main engines. The space shuttle slammed into a vectored bullseye shoot.

"Where the hell are they taking us?" Hobbs asked.

"They're bringing us home," Jackson replied, "and we won't know where that is until we're out of communications blackout."

"You want to bet," Hobbs said. He had already gotten busy on his C-band navigation computer which was tied into the geostationary orbiting TDRS (Tracking and Relay Delay Satellite). In less than two minutes he had the unbelievable answer. "*Antarctica!*"

CHAPTER 54

"*I have the cure for AIDS!*" Mahalia Hunt thrust the lipstick kissed vial to the heavens for all to see. She looked back at herself on the three monitor screens. Mahalia lowered the vial and pushed the eerie black veil from her face. Her bizarre make-up, her black-brown lips and the macabre tear she painted under her right eye were ghostly. She ran her tongue around the vial. "*This is the Kiss of Death! This tube of antidote is the only one in the entire world—it's a cure for AIDS—and I'm going to destroy it so no man, no man anywhere can have it! And then...I'm going to kill you father! For men, all men, are evil—and all men need to die!*"

"I don't understand. Please Tammy Savannah."

"Move in—carefully," the Ray-Banned double-agent ordered. "No matter what, don't let anything happen to that vial!"

"It's a done deal."

"Got ya!"

The CIA double-agent drew closer. They wove their way

beyond the rattled security guards.

"Stay back or I'll shoot!" Mahalia ordered as one of the double-agents approached her.

"Please daughter, please, I implore you, don't hurt anyone. Give me the vial."

"Stay back, I warn you!" she spoke to all who began to close in around her.

"Tammy..."

"It's not Tammy," she howled. A noticeable stutter became apparent in her voice, "it's Mahalia!"

"Mahalia, please, stop this madness, put down the gun," the Reverend Joe-Bob begged.

"Hurry." Alex tugged at Pepper as she followed behind him. They worked their way through the throng, around the stage, and approached from the rear. Alex shoved past two wired security guards and wedged himself abreast of two of the Ray-Ban man's agents.

"It's time to die father," Mahalia said impassively.

"Stop Mahalia!" Alex cried. He rammed past the approaching shootists. "Please Mahalia, don't do it."

"Who...who...are you?" she asked. The sudden intrusion momentarily caused her to regain her teetering sanity.

"Mahalia...please put down the vial and give me the gun." Alex reached out to her.

"Never!"

"Mahalia, that vial's *not* a cure for AIDS. If you drop it, you'll kill everyone. *It hasn't been perfected. It has the opposite effect. Please.*"

"What?"

It was then that there was a hailstorm of bullets. The projectiles raked in from all angles, and riddled Mahalia Hunt's psychotic body. The sharpshooter in the platform seating popped off two rounds into her crazed head. They exploded her brain like a papier-maché piñata.

Mahalia danced with each incoming slug as her body sank to its knees—while reflexively in her left hand she held tight the *LAV-10A* vial, and with the right the Beretta.

The Doomsday Kiss

Then, in agonal involuntary skeletal muscle contraction, her left hand opened and the *doomsday vial* slipped through her fingers.

CIA Headquarters
Langley, Virginia

Associate CIA Director Henry Dulles slammed into Gate's office. The double doors cracked on their copper hinges as they ground shut. "Harlan, we've got action at Texas Stadium!"

"Jesus! Does she have the vial?" Gates asked.

"I don't know. We have our men on the way. They should be there in ten minutes."

"What about the local authorities?"

"They notified us."

"Christ! Are they there?" Gates asked.

"Some are working off-duty security for the rally."

"And?"

"The girl has Reverend Joe-Bob Jones held hostage at gun point. It's being broadcast everywhere!"

"What about the vial, what about the goddamn vial?"

"I don't know."

"No matter what, don't let that vial get into the wrong hands! We gotta stop her, otherwise..."

"We're all dead!"

"You got it pal, now get your ass on it, now!"

Texas Stadium

As Tammy Savannah, a.k.a. Mahalia Hunt slumped to the parquet stage floor—and as the blood splayed in all directions, the vial of *LAV-10A* plunged to its disintegration on the buffed, shiny deck.

"No!" Alex screamed as he dove for the vial. "No!" In the blink of an eye, and a diving leap—he caught the doomsday vial in the palm of his hand—*only inches from shattering... the beginning of the demise of the entire human race.*

Only instinct and the deeply suppressed love that s*he had for her father* prevented her from firing. Her attention refocused, Mahalia *reflexively squeezed* the hair trigger of the 9mm Beretta. The bullet lodged in the Reverend Joe-Bob Jones' heart in front of millions of viewers worldwide. Ironically the bullet came to rest between the right and left ventricle in the intraventricular septum, the same spot that the rocky scrag eviscerated Mary Raye Hobart, Mahalia's mother, twenty-three years earlier.

In his agonal breath, now exonerated before the entire world of a crime that he did not commit, and possibly one he did, the Reverend Joe-Bob Jones said, "I love you Tammy Savannah. I forgive..." he coughed, then sputtered traces of bloody sputum, "...you. Please forgive my transgressions. I..." Rivulets of crimson oozed from his mouth, "love y..." Then he died.

"Get the vial!" the Ray-Banned man ordered, "then shoot him!" However, Pepper, who stood next to one of the assassins, overheard the CIA traitor bark his orders into the thug's headset. As the killer reached up to lay waste to Alex, she grabbed his semiautomatic .32 Ruger Mark II handgun and shot him in the gut. "Fuck you!"

Three assassins dove onto Alex, then a somersaulting fourth and a fifth. By now, the police had arrived and the security guards had joined the fray.

They were too much for Alex, subduing him with their force. Shots spit out. Two, three and a fourth. But Alex was able to dodge the bullets by twisting, wiggling, kicking and biting.

"Everyone stay where you are, now!" an Irving City Police officer yelled as he entered the skirmish with his Colt 45 drawn.

"I've got to stop them!" Alex implored as he shoved his way to his feet, and the double-agent assassins retreated into the anonymous chaos as more and more legitimate cops arrived.

"You're under arrest!" a second police officer said to Alex. "Hands behind your head, now!" He, too, pointed the muzzle of his 45 into Alex's face.

"Fuck you," Pepper yelled from behind them as she buried her newfound Ruger into the unsuspecting officer's rib cage. "Let him go now!"

The CIA and other intelligence double-agents had more than ample time to escape. Mahalia's shooting and the subsequent murder of her father, the Reverend Joe-Bob Jones, was enough of a diversion to allow them to disappear with ease.

"Now that I have LAV-10 I will control the fate of the world!" the Ray-Banned man snarled. *"I have the cure for AIDS that can be sold at any price!"* he barked as he sped out past the parking stadium bus lot, and the stream of incoming cop cars—Irving, Dallas, Fort Worth, Grande Prairie and the Dallas County Sheriff that arrived.

"Is it safe?" Frank asked. "What about what that guy said?"

"What about it?" Ray-Banned man snapped.

"What if *LAV-10's* not a cure, that it's the opposite..."

"Shut-up!"

"But...shouldn't we..."

"Shut up! That pest, for your information, that you were referring to, is Dr. Alex Seacourt, and by now he is as dead as a fucking doornail. He doesn't know shit about anything. What we've got is the cure to end all cures. The cure to AIDS, and possibly just about any other virus known to man. Screw him!"

"I was just asking."

"We'll be worth billions. Our entire organization will have more money than we'll even know what to do with. It's worth more money than God!"

"All of you back off, now!" Pepper ordered. "Alex are you all right?" she asked as she carefully bent down, still watching the cops, and assisted him the rest of the way to his feet with her free hand. She continued to press the .32 Ruger into the Irving police officer's rib cage.

"Where's the vial. Who has the vial?" Alex asked as he quickly scanned everyone.

"Any of you?" Pepper demanded of the cops.

"Miss, please put the gun down. Please," the police officer requested.

"Miss," another approaching cop said, "do you know how much trouble you're in right now? Put the gun down."

She pressed the automatic deeper into the cop's scrawny ribs. He grimaced. "Who has the fucking vial?"

"Not us," one high-strung cop said.

"I don't know," another replied.

"Shit," Alex said as he finished his scan of their milieu, "they must have the vial."

"I know where it is," a timid, very religious camerawoman from SatCom 5 said. She had melded into the mix without notice, but was very much on top of everything. "A man with dark sunglasses ran out of here. He had it in his hand."

"Which way did he go?" Alex asked.

"Gate 5."

"Give me your gun!" Alex ordered of another cop without hesitation. "Give me your goddamn gun, or she'll shoot!" The Irving police officer who had the .32 Ruger drilling into his ribs nodded a desperate "yes."

The officer in front of Alex handed him his standard issue Smith and Wesson. "Now, which way, show me," he implored the camerawoman.

"You come with us," Pepper ordered the Irving cop. All the other police officers apprehensively made way for them. She was becoming comfortable in her role of terrorist.

Alex, Pepper, the SatCom 5 camerawoman, and their hostage Irving police officer made their way through the mass of hysteric bodies, and disappeared into Aisle 17 behind the monstrous stage and then out Gate 5. Not far behind was the posse.

"Where?" Alex asked. They stood in front of the bus parking lot. DART, Gray Line, Overland Stage Lines, Central Texas Trailways, Big Star Custom Coaches, and Vaught Charters waited for the holy.

"Here. They were parked in a limousine. I followed them out. Then I came back in for all the action."

"Did you get their license plate?"

"No."

"Did you notice what kind of limo?"

"No."

"Was there a name on the limo, like Billy-Smith's Limo Rental or something?" Pepper intuitively asked. She sensed the Irving police officer hostage moving away from her gun. "Don't get any wise ideas. You understand?" she said in a gangster voice as she repositioned her Ruger, and jammed it deeper into the cop's ribwall. He nodded in affirmation.

"No idea," the camerawoman replied.

It was then that Alex saw him: the stuntflyer who had landed inside Texas Stadium with his single-seat Rotax engine, and thirty-six by twelve-foot parachute laid out behind him, between the buses, the Gray Line and Central Texas Trailways. The bright red, yellow and green airfoil was spread flat on the asphalt. The rip-stop nylon had not been folded, and the harness lines and rigging were pulled straight in anticipation.

"Pepper can you fly anything?" Alex asked as an idea blossomed.

"Anything!" she answered without hesitation.

He nudged her without saying a word. He let his eyes do the talking. He didn't want to give his plan away to the cop. The SatCom 5 camerawoman saw the Skye Ryder Aerochute and knew exactly what he was going to do.

"Mind if I," she raised her Sony Beta video camera to film the odd-ball flying machine, "for posterity?"

"Shhhh!" Alex whispered.

"Anything!" Pepper said in reaffirmation.

CHAPTER 55

"Get him now!" Dallas Police Sergeant Wilcox screamed at the top of his lungs into his radio.

"Sergeant," Yancy Hawkins, a gung-ho rookie posted outside of Gate 6, yelled, "he came out this way! He's between Handicapped Parking and the north Bus Lot."

"Watch it, they're armed."

"Got ya, Sarge."

"Hawkins, are there any more than the two of them?"

"No."

"Dispatch, this is Wilcox, we've got a hostage situation. Get SWAT down here *now*!" he bellowed.

"Any men down?"

"Yes, two."

It was then that Wilcox was corralled by macho Steve Green, who aside from being head of security for the Reverend Joe-Bob Jones' revival, was an off-duty SWAT officer. "We'll have security corner these pricks in five minutes. There's no way out!"

"He killed the girl!"

"What?"

"Didn't you see him shoot her? I want them both taken out!"

"Wilcox, I'm not sure that's what I saw," Green said.

"That's what I saw and that's that. This is my goddamn show." Wilcox got on the horn. "Which way to Gate 6?" he quickly asked Green.

"Follow me." They ran toward Section 22 at the corner of the Cowboy sideline and just past the end zone goal line.

"Get me all available manpower," Wilcox spat into his mic. "We've got to stop this maniac before he kills anyone else."

"So you can fly anything?" Alex asked as he swiftly scanned his treacherous surroundings. Panicked people were screaming and running in all directions. Cars were in a crunch to go nowhere, and hysterical drivers were pounding on their horns. And then there were the police who were rapidly converging on them.

"Listen pal," the hostage cop said, "no one wants any trouble, put the gun down."

"Shut up!" Pepper said. Then looking at Alex, "I can fly fucking anything!"

"Hey you," Alex worked his way over to the ostentatious Aerochute pilot. The gutless man raised his arms. Though he was a stunt flyer with balls of steel, he wasn't prepared for a cocked-and-loaded 9mm Smith and Wesson in his face.

"Da, da, don't shoot," he stuttered.

"I'm not going to shoot you, I just need to borrow your chute."

"Hey...listen..."

"Cover me," Pepper shouted wildly to Alex. She was getting comfortable in her new-fangled role as Bonnie to Alex's Clyde. Alex took aim at the cop, and then motioned the born-again Joe-Bob Jones flyer to work his way next to the police officer.

"Down on your knees," Alex ordered both of them. The camerawoman who had given Alex and Pepper directions had made her way to the scene. Wild screaming in the background became more apparent, and cop cars converged on them from all directions. Officers barreled out of their cars with weapons drawn.

"Don't shoot 'em," the camerawoman said, as she began filming

Alex live. She wore a wry smile.

"Don't worry," Alex winked into the shoulder-resting video camera, "I don't know how to use the gun."

Pepper made her way to the high-profile Aerochute. The bizarre-looking contraption was basically easy to operate: It was a nylon parachute hooked to a three-wheeled chair that had a fan behind it. She pulled the rigging lines out, then swiftly scanned the powerplant: "No big deal." Ram-air canopy—simple airfoil with front airfoil that inflates the double surface and forms an open front end wing. Small control stick for steering control during ground operation, two large sway bars on either side of the seat which act as 'rudder pedals' and are pushed separately or simultaneously to provide turning power and/or lift augmentation similar to flaps (by depressing both)... "Piece-of-cake. Always wanted to fly one of these toys."

"Hurry!" Alex exclaimed as he flashed the Smith and Wesson at the defiant cop, who might have been getting some wise ideas.

"Look son..."

"Son?"

"Look..."

"Do you realize that I'm old enough to be your father?" Alex asked impertinently as he quickly glanced at Pepper who was double-time setting up the Aerochute.

"Well, I mean if it wasn't for the hair. Just, you should give it up..."

"My hair? What about my hair?"

"It's not that you're losing it or anything." The cop knew exactly what he was doing—he was distracting Alex while three other police officers clandestinely moved in to overpower him. "See," the cop motioned to remove his stiff cop-hat.

"Funny stuff," Alex snapped. He scrutinized the cop with a keen eye.

"See," he pushed off his hat to show Alex the front of his own thinning hair. "I've got the same problem..."

"I don't have any problem." Alex irritatedly said.

"I started Rogaine. You know, it..." the cop said.

"Shut up you asshole!" the Aerochute stunt flyer exclaimed.

"It's over-the-counter."

"Yeah," Alex said, thinking maybe. "My..." then Alex saw the two police officers that were coming in from an angle from between the buses—a Greyhound and a Chartered DART. He quickly made his way back to his cop hostage, who was on his knees. Alex pressed his gun to the cop's forehead. In a low voice he said, "Sorry." Then to the other officers. "Get the hell out of here! Or else!" Busted, the espied cops backed off.

The Black Limousine

The Ray-Banned leader flipped the cover on his Algorithm Secure-cell mobile phone. He took care of his business using his corrupt friends on the "force" and *other* avenues to frame Alex Seacourt for the Mahalia Hunt and Reverend Joe-Bob Jones shootings. Videotape imaging can be altered through high-resolution matrix morphing. *No problem.*

"We're going to be richer than God," he snarled as they cruised down 183 heading west. "I've got it handled so that that jackass Seacourt will be framed for the whole deal."

"Rock and roll," his lame compadre added.

"We've got the *cure* for AIDS and I've already got it sold for three billion big ones! Fuck—why even take bids?"

"Yeah, fuck!"

"In one hour we'll deliver the goods, and then be off to Rio, the Copacabana, the Jockey Club and hot Latin pussy."

"Party-fucking-time. Three billion. Three, cool billion."

It was then that the Ray-Banned man withdrew his silenced Ruger Mark II and twice drilled his "compadre" between the eyes.

"Too much to share and too many idiot mouths to tell stories," he smirked to the limo driver. The steely-eyed driver looked into the rearview mirror and smiled back.

Texas Stadium

"I need more room," Pepper screamed at Alex. Cop cars had surrounded them, and heavily armed personnel had swiftly penned them in.

"Give it up," Wilcox boomed over the bullhorn. "Give it up or we'll shoot."

Alex could see two black SWAT vans roll into the parking lot toward Gate 6, between them and handicapped parking. "They mean business?" Alex nervously asked the hostage cop.

"Give it up," the police officer said.

"The Rogaine?" Alex asked trying to be a smart-ass.

"No..."

"Let's go," Alex pointed the gun at the stunt flyer. "Give her a hand."

"She's right," the Skye Ryder Aerochute aerialist said. "She'll need more room to take off."

"Well," Alex scanned the packed parking lot. There was a grizzled chartered Greyhound bus that was parked in front of them. Its side panels were dingy dirty, and it, like the Jesus Skye Ryder Aerochute stunt pilot, had a banner on each side: "Joe-Bob Jones Saves." Its engine was running. The driver had cowered inside, and ducked under his pancake steering wheel. "If I move this," Alex said, pointing to the bus, "would that give her enough room?"

"Maybe. She'll need to gun the throttle to produce enough airflow to inflate the canopy, and she'll need to run out for about fifty to seventy-five yards."

"Well?"

"Maybe."

"Make it happen!" Alex pointed his gun at the stunt flyer, then to the troublesome cop and brave camerawoman. In the background, all around, Alex could hear the automatic and semiautomatic weapons. Any minute he would be hamburger meat. "Come with me." Alex gestured the cop up, and sandwiched himself between the police officer and the camerawoman, with the cop in front of him and the gun to the back of the officer's big-target head.

"I know that you didn't kill her," the camerawoman said.

"No kidding."

"I've got the whole thing on film."

"That's good. Then show it to them," he referred to the whole world of righteous cops, SWAT guys, and the Texas Stadium security guards.

"That's not a bad idea."

"What do you mean?" Alex surprisedly asked as they squeezed their way between two jammed buses, and then to the chartered Greyhound. Alex saw two other surreptitious cops waiting for him. The camerawoman took the initiative.

"Don't do a thing or he'll shoot!" she yelled. She feigned the "shakey terrors." The police officers backed off.

"Thanks."

"No problem," she replied.

"Let's go," Alex pushed the gun deep into the hostage cop's nape. They made their way to the bus.

SWAT Headquarters van within the parking lot

"I want you to take those fuckers out!" Wilcox ordered as he made his way into the armour-plated SWAT van.

Lieutenant Joseph Simonetti was the sagacious SWAT Commander. And though he knew that his men could probably do that in a no-brainer second, he was not willing to risk losing an Irving City police officer, nor a pesky journalist. Plus, he wanted to be one hundred percent sure of his mission—and that meant to be certain that it was Dr. Alex Seacourt who killed Mahalia Hunt and the Reverend Joe-Bob Jones—not someone else.

"Not yet."

"Look," Wilcox raged. He had a hidden agenda. "Take those fuckers out, or I'll do 'em myself!"

"Not till I see the tapes!" Simonetti barked. He was not one to be bullied, nor take his responsibilities lightly.

Wilcox stormed out of the SWAT van, slamming the door behind him, with a "fuck you" under his breath.

"Open up!" Alex kicked on the Greyhound door. The frightened bus driver crept further down in his seat. "Open up or I'll shoot the cop." What was Alex saying? He too was immersed in the role of *nouveau terrorist*—just like they taught him in Moscow at the antiterrorist germ warfare seminar.

"Do you have to be so dramatic?" the camerawoman asked.

"No. Should I say it in a deeper voice?"

The bus driver reluctantly responded by pulling back the doorhandle. They quickly climbed in. "Pull up there," Alex pointed. Two silver and blue Texas Stadium security patrol cars, that as a matter of usual business had parked in front of them. The nose of one car and the rear of the other blocked their exit. "Move it!" Alex commanded.

"Through...them?"

"Now!" Then Alex ordered the difficult cop into the first seat. "Get his handcuffs," he told the camerawoman.

"You shouldn't do that," the cop said to her.

She did anyway. "Now cuff both his arms around that bar." Alex pointed to the security bar that separated the passenger in the first seat from the driver. "Listen," Alex barked at the cop, as the driver increased speed. Alex turned and pointed the gun at the driver. "Drive!"

The Greyhound rammed through the two Dodge Challenger security patrol cars with a *crackling smash*. "I don't want any trouble. I'm a good guy and I'm here to help."

"Then give it up," the cop said, "if you're a good guy."

"Look, would you just shut up." Alex demanded. "The bad guys, and they're not me, have a vial that can kill the whole world, get it? And we need to stop 'em..."

"I can get the film, everything on TV," the camerawoman said again, as the bus lumbered to a screeching stop—the Greyhound driver had done his damage and was afraid to venture farther. Police cars converged on them from everywhere.

With attention diverted elsewhere, Pepper gripped the .32 Ruger in hand and prepared the Aerochute. The tricycle wheels of the Rube-Goldberg contraption creaked, then the ram-air canopy, as if hit by a hurricane gust, burst open. At a less-than-brisk twenty-six miles per hour, the gravity-defying parachute spiraled straight up.

Pepper's bold flight, once noticed and out of range, was followed by a hailstorm of bullets. That was Alex's cue to plow forward through the multiple police-car barricade. Alex jumped deckward, slamming into the door handle and change bin, then jammed next to the driver. He thumped down his foot hard onto the gas pedal. The Greyhound careened through five unsuspecting cop cars, and the closest of the two SWAT vans. The volley of bullets that was at first directed at Pepper, was redirected to the charging bus.

Shot after shot penetrated the body of the Greyhound, all clearly aimed to miss the driver. The road-worn tires were shredded, along with the luggage compartments, undercarriage and every exposed side and back window. Glass flew indiscriminately everywhere.

Nevertheless, the bus plowed ahead, the wheels spinning as burnt-rubber smoke filled the air.

"Duck!" Alex yelled.

Suddenly the dirty cop Wilcox jumped out the shattered rear window, after the last of the projectiles rained out.

"And don't stop no matter what!" Alex ordered the frightened driver who "*ca-jink, junk, a-junked*" the wheel-rim riding Greyhound.

CHAPTER 56

"Goddamnit," Lieutenant Simonetti yelled as Alex's Greyhound careened past their barricade. Then he grabbed a pair of binoculars and saw the insane Wilcox pulling himself up on the back of the bus. "Stop them!" he railed.

The Dallas SWAT sortie team and cop cars from Dallas, Ft. Worth, Irving, Grand Praire and the Dallas County Sheriff accelerated toward the bus. The Greyhound rattled full-speed ahead to downtown Dallas, onto the John W. Carpenter Freeway, over the Diversion Channel and the Trinity River Greenbelt Park, toward the heart of the city—to the pulse of over a million people.

"Let's go!" Alex yelled. Traffic in front and behind them quickly separated like Moses parting the Red Sea.

"Don't kill me, please," the terrified driver begged as they clamored the pummeled Greyhound in spark-flying fourth gear.

"I'm not going to kill anyone."

"Don't believe him," the cop said, "he shot the Reverend Jones."

"What are you talking about, he didn't shoot anyone," the camerawoman chimed in.

"All of you shut up. And you." Alex barked to the driver, "floor it!" Alex looked out the shattered front window.

In the rear, Wilcox flailed. He kicked his legs from side to side groping for a foothold. Alex looked to the sides and to the back of the bus. He saw the multitude of cop cars closing in from all directions.

"I can get it on TV."

"How?" Alex asked. He was desperate for a solution.

"Drop me off anywhere. I'm press. I'll flag down the police and they'll take me to the nearest mobile news van—guaranteed."

"Give it up," the persistent cop said.

"Would you just shut up!" Alex turned around and looked at the police officer. He stared at him. Then he realized it was his job—the cop was just trying to do his job.

"I've got it all on tape," she said. "It's all on tape!"

Alex then looked hard into the camerawoman's devout eyes. "Okay. Let's do it!"

It was at that moment Wilcox crawled over the alumium ribbing lining the rear of the bus and in through the shattered window. He dropped onto the rear floor and drew his revolver. "Hands up, you fuck!"

Alex turned from the camerawoman and toward the back of the Greyhound.

"Drop it!"

Alex let the Smith and Wesson slip through his fingers.

"Unhandcuff him," Wilcox ordered as he swiftly scrambled forward and pointed to the handrail, and the police officer who was handcuffed at chest level. Alex reached into his pocket for the keys. "Easy," Wilcox warned.

"Look, this isn't what it appears to be," Alex said, "I've got to get that vial. The bad guys got..."

"*I know.*"

"I didn't kill anyone."

Wilcox moved closer. "It's time to die pal." Alex slowly rolled the keys in his hands to the handcuffs. His eyes never left Wilcox's revolver.

"Look, that vial *isn't* a cure to AIDS—its a super "on-off" switch. It can kill everyone if it gets out. We gotta stop 'em…"

"Shut up and uncuff him." Wilcox loomed over Alex. "Then I'm going to kill your fucking ass. Nothing personal, just business."

At that moment, right in front of the chartered Greyhound, Pepper flew past the front of the bus, her Skye Rider Aerochute, with its bright red, yellow and green ram canopy billowing out around her. With only inches to spare, the bus driver slammed on his air-brakes.

Wilcox flew into the dashboard head first onto the door opener. His gun fell from his hand. Alex was thrown on top of him. The corrupt cop violently pushed Alex off and sprung to his feet. Alex fell back onto the cop handcuffed in the first seat. Then Wilcox threw a punishing sidekick into Alex's gut. "Uhhh."

"You fuck," Wilcox raged as he plowed a powerful right cross into Alex's chin. Wilcox was an ugly, brawny man. He could hold his own against anyone. "My employer has had enough of your shit Seacourt." He then lifted Alex up, and drilled another punch into his face. Alex flew back onto the center aisle rail of the fifth left seat. His lip bled, his jaw throbbed, and his ears rang.

"What are you?" Alex spluttered blood from his mouth.

"You stuck your nose where it wasn't wanted. Now it's time to die."

"Put your hands up!" the camerawoman yelled. She had set the camera down and grabbed a gun, holding it on Wilcox.

"What are you doing?" a startled Wilcox asked. The Greyhound driver nervously looked in the rearview mirror.

"Get 'em up," she ordered. She turned to Alex, "It's all on film. Live." She had shot everything, including Wilcox's incriminating admission.

Alex looked outside. From all directions the authorities were converging on them. The remaining, unscathed SWAT van was behind them. Men with "double-ought" Street Sweeper scatter guns and M40 Remingtons piled out of the van. "Get your ass out of here," she said to Alex, "I'll get it on the tube. Go!"

Alex looked out the remnants of the bus' shattered windows. He couldn't see her. He knew that Pepper had come for him, and though he couldn't find her, he had to trust his instincts. She had to be out there, at the least somewhere above the Greyhound.

A gust of crosswind had propelled the ram canopy and dragged her to a less than controllable height in a whipping tooly. She gunned the Rotax 503 engine, and straightened her wobbly course. Then she ascended to 150 feet above the bus and spun down in tight circles.

Pepper saw Alex pop out of the bus, and divebombed towards him. As she did, the cops converged on them.

"Stop," one cop yelled.

Another got on his bullhorn and ordered, "Halt or we'll shoot."

With abandonment Alex climbed to the hood of the bus, then hopped onto its roof.

"Freeze," another cop screamed as four other cops with their semi-automatic guns charged the bus.

"Don't shoot!" the camerawoman screamed as she jumped out of the chartered Greyhound with her video camera slungover her shoulder. "They're on board!" She pointed to the bus and ran to safety with tears streaking her cheeks. "That's not them!"

The camerawoman's outburst bought time for Alex and Pepper to escape, as Alex leaped to the Aerochute's right rear tricycle wheel and grabbed on tight. Pepper gunned the engine. By the time the cops and SWAT team realized that they were bamboozled, Alex and Pepper were long gone.

"Jesus," Alex said as he pulled himself over the skeletal lateral rail, up onto the seat and on top of Pepper.

"Not bad flying, huh!"

"Yeah." His gut was sore from Wilcox's sidekick—and his inept gymnastic wrangle. He was bleeding slightly from his lip.

At twenty-six miles per hour, the ostentatious Skye Ryder rose to one thousand feet above ground level. It was a height that Pepper belived would keep them safe enough from bullet fire. Below, they edged towards Regal Row, then U-turned, heading north of Texas Stadium past the University of Dallas at E. Northgate.

"Where'd they go?"

"I think to the airport," Pepper replied. She pointed to the Dallas/Fort Worth International Airport. It was left, over their shoulder just a few miles away.

"Let's do it!"

CIA Headquarters
Langley, Virginia

"Harlan, they're gone!"

"Where?" Gates implored. He needed answers and a location, now!

"Outside of Texas Stadium," Director Dulles replied.

"Do they have the vial?"

"I don't know."

"Dr. Johnson," Gates flicked on the scrambled NSA Vista II satellite videoconference telephone. Dr. Johnson was waiting at the Biologics Warfare Research Facility at Mills Farm, Virginia. "You buy into the Halon theory?"

"I don't know, it's risky."

"Perry, it can't be 'I don't know.' It has to be one way or another. We have no time!"

"Dr. Joanna Knight's as good as they come. If she thinks so then...I don't know. We still should do some controlled testing..."

"Damn it man. What do you say the odds are?"

Dr. Johnson scratched his head in perplexion. "Fifty-fifty," he said.

"Fifty-fifty?" Gates asked,

"Without first running the usual double-blind studies in a controlled Biosafety Level 4 airlock environment free from all exogenous contamination, at calibrated standard temperature and pressure, I'd say that..."

"Cut the techno jagron!"

"That would be my best guess."

"Shit!" Gates said. "Make it happen, now!" he ordered Dulles.

"Done boss."

Dallas

From the east, closing in rapidly on Alex and Pepper at 120 miles per hour were two Bell Jet Ranger police helicopters.

"Now what?" Pepper asked.

"God I don't know." He looked down at the Dallas/Fort Worth Airport which they were swiftly approaching from the southeast. The terminal was divided into four half-circles along the north-south International Parkway: 2E, 3E, 4E and the East Hyatt Hotel were on the east of the International Parkway; 2W and the West Hyatt on the west side of the parkway. Two sets of runways ran north and south on the east of the airport: the 13,400 foot 35L and 11,388 foot 35R; and two sets of runways ran north and south on the west of the airport: 36L and 36R, both 11,388 feet. Two additional runways, 31R and 31L ran on the diagonal from the 10 o'clock position to the 4 o'clock position. At the northern most tip of 31R, and the northeastern tip of 13R, were the East and West Air Freight Buildings.

"What do you think?" she asked as she quickly studied the field and the terminal's layout.

"I think that we should try Air Freight first," Alex said as he pointed to the two obvious locations where he anticipated that the bad guys would have gone.

"As good a place as any."

"I'd figure that if they're going to go, they're leaving by private jet."

"I agree," she said.

From behind them, and to the right, the first of the Bell Jet police helicopters blew past the Skye Ryder Aerochute, turned on a pinpoint, and then blocked their forward progress. The second contained them from the rear.

"Give it up!" the Dallas Skypatrol cop shouted from the Bell Jet Ranger. "Land or we'll shoot you down!"

A Delta 747 nonstop to San Francisco was holding on runway 35L, ready for final clearance and take-off instructions from the tower.

"Tower, this is Delta 1857 ready for take-off on 35 left."

"This is Dallas/Fort Worth Tower, over."

"Tower, to repeat IFR clearance—you have us vectored to heading two-four-zero degrees immediately after takeoff. Maintain two thousand feet and expect filed altitude in ten minutes...What the fuck..." the dumbfounded Delta pilot exclaimed as the ram-canopy Aerochute surrounded by the two police helicopters buzzed overhead.

"This is tower. Can you repeat?" It was then that the controller saw the furious action on the field. He threw off his head set.

"What the hell?"

"Fly low," Alex ordered frantically, "Screw the cops. Go for the

East Air Freight terminal. Do it!"

"Got it!" Pepper zipped a 360 degree looping right turn, then repeated the maneuver to the left in a twisting dip.

The first police helicopter pulled up, afraid that he'd hit the Skye Ryder and down their chopper in the Aerochute's rigging. The second hung right in there with Pepper.

Alex and Pepper buzzed the East Air Freight building. There was no limo. The second chopper stayed close on their heels. "Head for the West," Alex ordered.

"You're sure bossy," Pepper said as they buffeted in the Jet Ranger's blade wash.

A third, then a fourth copper-chopper entered the fray.

"Hold on," Pepper howled as she skud-ran the field, only feet over three American Airlines 747's and popped aloft Terminal 3E. She zipped barely inches from the side of the East Hyatt Hotel, then snaked around the FAA tower, and yards past the south face of the West Hyatt. She cut a beeline for the West Control Tower, and the West Air Freight. Beneath them traffic: American, Delta, Lone Star, and Sun Country Airlines ground to a halt.

"This is Amanda Carlyle, live with *Texas News 5* with a late breaking story…" With that introduction, the station rolled the infamous video footage shot the by the spunky camerawoman. Scenes of the Reverand, and Mahalia's grisly ends, the bus chase and Wilcox's confession were beamed first in Dallas, then throughout the world.

"Unbelievable," she said, after the camera stopped rolling.

"Not there," Alex yelled as they spun again in a reversed 360 degree spin. From the ground what seemed like hundreds of cops were swarming in. Again, a chopper cornered them, and this time stood its ground. The remaining three choppers closed in from the sides and rear.

"Give it up! This is your last warning."

From every direction, uniformed police officers disbursed with amazing agility onto the tarmac. They jumped out of their tire-squealing cars.

"Fire at will!" the airport police sergeant ordered.

CHAPTER 57

"Brace yourself!" Pepper yelled as they headed straight for the parking deck. With automatic and rifle shots zinging through their nylon canopy, and with virtually no protection—they dive-bombed over the International Parkway, straight for the third floor parking lot opening.

At 26 miles per hour, they flew in a ground-pouncing swoop. At the exact instant they slid through the perilous five-foot concrete opening, Pepper pulled down tight on both right and left sway bars on the sides of her seat. Her chute stalled. Then instantaneously she cut the 46 hp Rotax engine. They went rolling into the garage, past parking spot Section B number 27 and 28 into an empty stall between a beat-up station wagon and a '95 500 Mercedes SL.

"Christ!" Alex yelled.

Pepper wasn't even phased. She quickly reeled in the deflated ram-air canopy as a car searching for a spot squealed to a halt. One behind it, and then one behind that, smashed into each other in a chain-reaction fender bender. "Pretty good, huh?"

"You're nuts!" Alex exclaimed as he steadied himself, then tried to stand. He had borderline vertigo airsickness. Alex, however, remembered his urgent mission. "You do this for a living, I presume?"

"All day long. Now find the limo, I'll take care of them," she said referring to the cops.

"You're not done?"

"Far from it," she said as she pushed the tricycle Aerochute frame, and headed toward the other end of the garage. She swiftly laid out the ram-air chute on the concrete, and again started up the engine.

"What the..."

"Go," she ordered Alex. He figured she knew what she was doing.

Alex ran through the parking structure, down an east stairwell, and headed north to the airline-ticketing street level for the 2W and 2E terminals. This is where he thought that it would be most likely that he would find the limo, if it was even here.

As he dodged incoming traffic, out the opposite end of the parking structure, Alex saw Pepper take off. Just as she reached the end of the parking-structure drive, she gained altitude and swooped out toward the east terminal. This was enough, at least temporarily, to take the heat off of Alex.

Two additional helicopters arrived. These, however, were not the police choppers, but military Bell AH-IW SuperCobra T700s. The cops made way for the big boys.

"This is incredible," *Texas News 5* reporter Amanda Carlyle said as she viewed satellite-relay video from another *Texas News* remote at the Dallas/Fort Worth Airport shoot-out. She pushed the mic into SWAT Commander Simonetti's face, "Clearly the man you're after didn't have anything to do with the Reverend Joe-Bob Jones' death."

"I... " the usually articulate Simonetti was at a loss for words.

"Lieutenant Simonetti, what are your men doing to apprehend the *real murderers*, and what about the *LAV*?"

"I..."

It was then, alongside the curb, that Alex saw a 24-foot, black Lincoln Towncar limousine. The limo was idling as a man inside finished his cellular telephone call, while the driver and two assistants discretely bagged the slumped compadre. They dragged the "black-vinyled" stiff out of the car and stuffed him into the trunk. The Ray-Banned double-agent pushed open his curbside door and got out.

"Meet me at the satellite terminal," he told one of his assistants. Alex recognized him from the Missouri Apiary Suppliers, Long Beach warehouse. Just then, the double-agent turned his head and saw that Dr. Alex Seacourt was *still alive*. "Get him!" he yelled as his cronies slammed closed the limo's trunk. "*Kill him!*"

The first assassin reached into his jacket and withdrew a silenced .32 Ruger Mark II. The second one whipped out a silenced blue metal .38 Beretta. "Zap, zap, zap," shots came flying at Alex in a flurry. Alex tore into the packed airport lobby, pounded past the airport security, through the passenger-crowded metal detector, and raced toward Delta Airlines and Gate 16 and 17.

"Stop him," a uniformed Dallas/Fort Worth airport cop yelled as he got on his radio to call in the reinforcements. However, most of the airport police had already dispersed into the 4E Terminal Parking Lot, and then out onto the tarmac in pursuit of Pepper. "Stop him!"

The two assassins sprinted through the metal detector and a third flew over two security ropes, all with their guns drawn.

Shots railed out at Alex with total disregard for the safety of innocent bystanders. An Arkansas-bred actuary was struck in the shoulder, and shards of formica and fiberboard splintered as a counter was nailed with aberrant rounds.

Zip, Zip, Zip another clumping of death-dealing bullets were blasted by the lead man as the travelers screamed and ducked away.

Alex ran left, past the Delta Crown Room, the foreign currency exchange, the shoe shine, snack bars, phones, gates for Aeromexico, Atlantic Southeast Airlines, and the chapel—slamming into an agoraphobic man trying to purchase flight indemnity coverage. He was inserting his Visa into the airport insurance machine, when two shots plowed into the Teleticket machine, one whizzing through the man's duffer's hat, flinging it to the ground.

"Get her!" the Chief of the the airport police screamed over his radio. Police cars, copper-choppers and military helicopters went after Pepper with a vengeance.

She, however, was too smart for them. Despite the slow maximum speed of the Skye Ryder, she had a clear maneuverability advantage over the ground forces.

"I want her shot out of the sky!" the enraged Dallas Police Air Patrol cop yelled. "Get that bitch!"

The fourth nimble, blue-trimmed helicopter had attempted to box her in, when she made a reverse tight loop around the East Hyatt Regency, then deftly swung next to the FAA Tower, bumping her ram-air canopy on the concrete side of the structure.

"If we shoot we might hit someone in a room," the police sniper said in helicopter number one.

"I don't give a damn..."

Then the pilot in the first police chopper said, "I don't give a shit what you do or don't want to do with that woman, I'm not going to fly in any closer to the FAA Tower. We knock that sucker out—and it's my ass, not to mention we lose control of the airport and Love Field. You want to risk that?"

"I don't give a f..."

It was then, that a Bell AH-IW SuperCobra twin turbo—with under-the-nose M 197 three-barrel 20 mm gun, ATGMs (air-to-ground missiles) and AAMs (air-to-air missiles)—plunged in front of the puny Bell Jet Ranger copper-chopper.

Alex ran to the last exit in the people-packed semicircular terminal, then headed back outside through the baggage claim, towards ticketing and street level. "Stop!" a Dallas/Fort Worth airport police officer yelled as Alex vaulted the wrong way through the metal detector entrance. Behind him, more rounds exploded. Splinters of wood and faux granite wall sprayed in all directions. Screaming and hysteria were everywhere as the assassins trampled over the terrified travelers.

Alex ran straight to the parking structure. As he hit the doors flying, two Dallas Airport cops were waiting for him. Alex skidded to a stop on the high-polished floor, made a wide, sweeping loop—and doubled back downstairs to the 24-hour airport train.

Zing, another bullet, then two, then three more whistled past him.

The north-south train was an automated transit system that pro-

365

vided transportation to and from the terminals and the nearby Hyatt. The red train covered terminals 2E, 2W and the North Reduced Rate Parking. Black: the Hyatt and terminals 2W, 2E and 3E. Yellow: the Hyatt, 2W, 2E, 3E and 4E. Blue: 3E, 4E, the Hyatt and the South Reduced Rate Parking.

The yellow airport train was pulling out, heading north for terminal 3E. The doors were already closed. The single cabined, floating-wheel transport was en route. Alex dove for the automated train. He barely, only by his fingertips, grasped the roof of the transit and flailed over the rear window. *Zing! Zing!* two bullets cracked into the car's rear wall and to the left of him, inches from where he held on.

Zing! A bullet cracked through the train's rear Plexiglass window. Inside passengers ducked for dear life. *Zing!* Alex was struck in the left forearm. The force of impact ripped him to the concrete.

The second heavily armed Bell SuperCobra charged from the northeast and plowed past the second and fourth Bell Jet Ranger copper-choppers that were closing in on Pepper.

"This is U.S. Marine Corps AH-1W Bravo one," the pilot squawked from his death machine, as the Bell police chopper lined Pepper up in its sights for a clean kill.

"We copy, Bravo one."

"We'll handle it from here."

"It's covered Bravo one. We've got the situation under control!" The chopper one officer yelled. He was ready to shoot down Pepper.

The U.S. Marine Corps AH-1W immediately spun from its strategic position ready for Pepper's annihilation to dead square with the outgunned, undersized, Bell Jet Ranger police chopper. "I said," the SuperCobra pilot forcefully repeated, "we'll handle it!"

Another shot bit into the concrete ground behind Alex. Dazed and confused, but knowing that he had no other choice but to run for his life, Alex got up.

Two shots sailed past his left ear, barely missing his head.

He heard one of the double agents in pursuit fall to the concrete tunnel floor. Then shots rang out in a confusing barrage from in front and behind him. Alex did the only thing he could do—he dove for the deck.

Two assassins, and a third were taken out in the savage firestorm by unidentified men in front of him. One of the men beyond Alex fell as a .38 hollow point exploded in his chest. Then, as suddenly as it commenced, the firefight abated.

With their guns drawn, a team of undercover NSA agents approached Alex. Alex knew for sure that he was through.

"You okay?" a tall man asked Alex. Then he and a bigger man helped him to his feet.

"Yeah." Alex shook himself off, brushed his shirt and forced himself the rest of the way to a standing position. His left arm throbbed. He pulled back his ripped shirt to see a superficial entrance and exit wound on his deltoid muscle. He'd live. He ripped off the rest of his sleeve and put pressure on the wound with the frayed cloth. It stopped the bleeding, but not the pounding.

"Do you have the vial?" the first man asked.

"No. Who ...are you?"

"Who has it?"

"Who are you?"

Another of the men whipped out a wallet from inside his sports jacket and flipped open his badge. "NSA," he said.

"National Security Agency?"

"Yes," the lankier one replied. "Where's the vial?"

"He's got it, he was going to the satellite terminal."

"Man with the sunglasses?"

"Yes."

The NSA agent immediately got on his radio. "Satellite terminal now! Send in the cavalry!"

"Where's Pepper?"

"She's safe."

"What do you mean?"

Then, as suddenly and breathlessly as the men arrived, they ran off, except for the second, who was clearly eager to leave, but remained at Alex's side.

"Let me help," Alex said to him as he put pressure on his aching shoulder.

"No," the NSA agent said, "you've already done enough." Then he got an emergency call on his hand-held radio. Alex could hear gunshots in the distance.

Though Alex's ass had just been saved by the NSA agent, *he still didn't trust anyone*. Despite everything, Alex needed to be sure that

Pepper was all right. "I need to find her," he said.

"Follow me," the irritated agent ordered.

Then on the scamper he commanded, "You know how to use this?" He tossed Alex a 9 mm, chrome-plated Beretta.

"Yep," Alex replied. His left forearm pounded. Alex slowed. The agent continued with his undaunted gallop. "Come on," he commanded.

"Just a second. I'll catch up," Alex shook his left arm, that again was bleeding. The agent couldn't wait.

Slowly Alex unfurled his makeshift pressure dressing, and refolded it into a twisted tourniquet. With his right hand and the gun shoved into his pants, he tied a taut square knot. The NSA agent had vanished.

Sluggishly, deliberately, Alex made his way up to Terminal 3E, the American Airlines terminal. Brandishing his sidearm, and with the continuous screams of the panicked travelers, he shoved his way past the crowd. Alex jog-trotted to Gate 33. He looked like guerilla-warfare death in his crimson splattered undershirt—with a trail of blood dripping onto the terminal carpet. "Is there a way out onto the tarmac?" he asked a frightened American Airlines counter employee.

"Yes," she squeamishly replied, staring at his gun.

"Take me there, now."

The check-in clerk led him to an "Employees Only" exit door that led to a flight of stainless steel stairs, and out onto the tarmac.

"Thanks," he said.

"You're bleeding."

As Alex ran out onto the tarmac, the first of the Bell Super Cobras took a direct hit by a Soviet RPG-7 rocket shoulder-launched from CIA double-agents positioned outside the Satellite Terminal. The traitor crouched one hundred feet from a swept-wing Learjet 45 that was fueled and ready to go.

Overhead, the second Bell AH-1W, Bravo two, stormed in and laid waste to the rocket launching man with its three-barreled 20mm gun. Despite this, the Learjet 45 began to creep out of Gate 30, where it looked like any other departing plane. The Lear appeared to be avoiding the lethal fray.

A fierce firefight broke out on the tarmac. There were more CIA double-agents than Alex had even anticipated—and except for the Bell AH-1W SuperCobra—they seriously outnumbered the NSA men.

CHAPTER 58

Antarctica—the opposite of the Arctic—is the southernmost continent covering five million square miles. It is essentially circular, except for the Antarctic Peninsula which reaches toward the southern tip of South America some 600 miles away, and toward two principal embayments, the Ross and Weddel Seas.

The continent is almost wholly overlaid by a continental ice sheet representing about 90 percent of the world's ice. The average thickness is about 6,500 feet.

Mean temperatures are generally 20 degrees F (11 degrees C) colder than those in an equivalent latitude of the Arctic, thus making the Antarctic the coldest region in the world. Wind conditions vary throughout Antarctica. South of Australia, it's often called the "Home of the Blizzard" due to the almost continual gales pouring down the passes from the interior; gales from the ice plateau sometimes hitting 200 miles per hour.

The Wilkes Subglacial Basin is a vast glacier in a 35-mile stretch from the Australian Antarctic Territory into Adelie Land.

This is where the space shuttle *Orion* was going to have a million-to-one shot landing gear-up.

"Frigging Antarctica!" Hobbs exclaimed. "They gotta be goddamn kidding!"

"Where?" Jackson asked incredulously, as he quickly scanned his left aft cabin bay video monitor. The alpha X-hoop docking module that Maya and Vrubel were in was shaking violently. "Give me that again?"

"Antarctica?"

"Are you serious?"

"I don't even have this information in my TDRS NAV computer. Hold on. I've got an idea." Hobbs plugged into a second program, this one with the updated Jeppesen navigational-plate aids—not relevant for *Orion*, but relevent to commercial pilots—and one that Hobbs downloaded on his computer. "Got it!"

"Where to?"

"They're going to crash land us on...best as I can make out...at approximately 140 degrees 12 minutes west and 71 degrees 22 minutes south."

"In English?" Smith asked.

"Somewhere west of the Prince Albert Mountains."

"Where the F's that?"

"He means on flat land or a glacier, or what?" Jackson asked, speaking for the entire crew, all of whom were listening anxiously on the open channel intercom mode.

"On a glacier."

"Smith, you have anything on the NAV computer yet?" Jackson asked.

"Got it now," Smith replied as the data from the Johnson Space Center, Houston came on screen. It flickered, then intermittently buzzed. "Seems that we've up-loaded everything but the landing co-ordinates."

"Once we leave blackout, hopefully we'll be able to pick up the East or West TDRS and Houston computer, unless..."

"We're too far south, as in past their 130 degrees geostationary orbital positions," Smith said.

"Exactly."

"How long until we're out of blackout?" Jackson asked Hobbs.

"Three minutes."

"Do your best to regain contact." Then speaking to Smith, "Can you guesstimate our exact landing coordinates from the trajectory that was programmed in, less what data we're missing?"

"Possibly."

"I need better than that."

"What about the landing gear?"

"It'll be a belly-down landing."

"Yeah, but if we do that, then we lose gear-down drag...which significantly slows us."

"I know."

Hesitantly, Smith asked, "Will the *Orion* survive the stress of the belly-down landing?"

"Do we have a choice?"

"No."

Enterprise-type Nuclear Carrier
USS George W. Bush

A nipping wind blew across the sea-water kissed steel deck of the George W. Bush—sending a chill down the spines of those swabbing topside, as the vessel steamed southwest of the south island of New Zealand, forty-nine miles west of Fiarland in the Jasman Sea.

"Got'em," Commander Richard Monastersky, the carrier's intelligence officer, shouted.

The Combat Direction Center of the USS George W. Bush was bathed in a shadowy turquoise-colored light. The room was relatively small with a low ceiling and a grooved metal floor. Six men monitored the equipment in the computerized combat nerve center of the ship. The men, schooled in the art of threat analysis and operation, identified threats in the air and on the surface with the *George W. Bush's* own radar and the increased coverage from the airborne AWACS Southern Hemisphere Command Center.

"This is AWACS Southern Hemisphere, Big Mama. Copy?"

"Got 'em comin'—hot and slippery."

"Roger, Bush. Vector us in on their immediate heading. Relay to Trident C-141D STOL force. Copy?"

"Done deal, Big Mama, relay to Trident C-141D STOL force in progress."

Thirty-four stormy miles above the surface of the Earth, and twelve tedious minutes prior to touchdown at 8,275 miles per hour— the *Orion* broke out of communications blackout.

"Space shuttle *Orion*, space shuttle *Orion*, copy. Space shuttle *Orion*, copy?"

"Roger, Houston, this is *Orion*," Jackson answered as they descended rapidly over the southern Pacific towards New Zealand.

"*Orion*, this is your babysitter, Big Mama AWACS Southern Hemisphere Command Center south of Brisbane, Australia. How ya holding up?"

"Just cool, Big Mama. What else?"

"*Orion*, talk to us."

"What'cha got for us?"

"*Orion*, were you able to download the entire reentry data from Houston? Our scuttlebutt suggests negative."

"Roger, Big Mama, that's a negative."

"Copy a negative."

"Big Mama, can we up-load the remaining Houston data?"

"That's impossible *Orion*, repeat cannot do."

"Roger, Big Mama. You make us all enthused up here."

"*Orion*, how much did you get?"

"I believe," Communications Officer Hobbs said apprehensively, "everything but the complete landing coordinates, glide slope and autoland. We're basically missing the most crucial information."

"We can up-load you from here with everything but autoland. Will that do?"

"Gotta Big Mama, we're at your mercy."

"Roger, *Orion*. *Orion*, give us what you got on the landing coordinates."

Hobbs scrupulously reported. "140 degrees 12 minutes west, 71 degrees 22 minutes south. I don't have seconds."

"Right on target, except 13 minutes west, 15 seconds and 12 seconds."

"13 minutes, 15 seconds west, and 22 minutes 12 seconds south."

"Roger."

"Big Mama are we going to have support on touchdown? We're running a little short on oxygen." Jackson asked.

"That's an affirmative, *Orion*. Your alternative *approximate* ice cube landing site was anticipated eighteen hours earlier..."

"*Approximate?*"

"That's correct. General area. Anyway, *Orion,* we needed presidential authorization..."

"Otherwise you were going to shoot us down?" Hobbs said.

"That's...a roger, *Orion.* Sorry, but it was business."

"Big Mama, how long you going to stay with us?"

"As long as we can. In the interim, we'll up-load specific area landing site coordinates and glide slope."

"Roger, Big Mama."

"Uh...," Hobbs interrupted again, "What do you mean by approximate."

"We mean, *Orion,* the best possible guesstimate landing site.

"We're dropping you in on a glacier. Also..."

"Also?"

"You're...going to have some rough going on your landing. We've got thirty to fifty knot gale-force cornering crosswinds."

"That's beautiful."

"It's the best we can do."

"No shit."

"And it's a wheels up landing."

"Yeah," Commander Jackson said, "we figured that out already."

"Awesome," Hobbs said sarcastically.

"That's it gentlemen. Let's stop the chatter and get your TDRS NAV computer up-loaded."

"Roger, Big Mama."

"One thing," Jackson asked. "You're landing us on a glacier...and you're going to have oxygen for us when we hit the streets, right?"

"Gentlemen, we'll do the best we can."

"In blizzard conditions?"

"That's it."

"Well," Jackson said feigning approval, "let's make it a pretty one."

"Standby for up-load, *Orion.*"

Hobbs was already on the up-load program. In anticipation, Spacewalker/Pilot Smith programmed in the new verbal coordinates and came up with one more fire of the OMS (Orbital Maneuvering Program), then Smith began plotting their four roll reversal, speed-breaking S-turns before landing. "Do we have enough fuel?" Smith asked Jackson.

"Do we have a choice?"

Orion continued its critical descent. At 5.5 minutes to touchdown and 83,130 feet they fired their OMS and then the RCS (Reaction Control System) roll thrusters one last time with elevators now ready to control the Orion's rolls. Smith then cut the thrusters and began dumping propellants in the forward reaction control system, and second the fuel and oxidizer tanks which held propellant for the SSME (Space Shuttle Main Engines), the OMS and Reaction Control System. They would be going in dead stick.

Suddenly, a thundering crash riveted the crew, and an overpowering vibration shook the *Orion*.

"What the?"

"It's the docking module!" Smith exclaimed as he looked into the aft left cargo bay video monitor screen. The alpha X-hoop docking module had shaken loose, and was whipping in erratic 8 to 10 foot, three-per second shudders.

"Is there anything that we can do?" Jackson quickly asked. It was everything that he could do to help Smith maintain control of the *Orion* with the RHC (Rotational Hand Controller). "Hit the speed brakes, now!"

"That'll bring us in short!" Smith yelled over the deaf-defying rumble.

"Hit the goddamn speed brakes, or all of us will crack up!"

Smith pulled back the finger-grooved, speed brake handle to one hundred percent. Then suddenly...*Bang!*

C-141D STOL Transports

"AWACS Big Mama, this is Trident leader. Copy? AWACS Big Mama copy?"

"Trident leader, this is Big Mama, over."

"Big Mama, we're closing in on target *Orion*, touchdown Nexus," the pilot, Lieutenant Colonel Dawson said as he and his crew were violently thrown about their transport cabin. "Jesus!"

"How's the weather up there Trident leader."

"Bad!"

"Keep us briefed, Trident. Our window of opportunity is about to close. We need to make this one count."

"Doing the best we can, Big Mama." The first of the three C-141D STOL Transports was rocked by a powerful updraft, then a barrage of wind-twisting turbulence.

"Copy. Big Mama out."

Space Shuttle Orion

As quickly as the vibration had begun, it abruptly abated to an unexpected minimum.

"*We've lost 'em!*" Smith screamed. "*We've lost 'em!*" Smith flipped his video screen to the portside cargo bay camera, which gave them a better view of the storage bay and vent windows. The docking module had ripped free. The right cargo bay door was all but gone, and the left was shredded back and bent open.

"God!" Thoughts of everything he wanted to say to Maya raced through Jackson's mind. "What about the doors—can you close them?" he asked Smith, since one hundred percent of his attention was on landing the shuttle.

"Release the speed brake, we're losing too much speed!"

"I don't know. One's gone. We gotta pitch the nose up otherwise we'll develop drag in the bay."

"Shit!" Jackson was beside himself. He wished he had told Maya how he really felt. He thought in an instant that she was going to die. Without the extra weight of the docking module, the *Orion* was dangerously off balance—the already precarious center of gravity had shifted—and there was nothing that they could do. A second shimmer began to develop. "Dump the rest of the propellant, *now!*"

"Been dumping," Smith howled, while at the same time he continued to attempt to manipulate closed what remained of the destroyed left cargo bay door.

"CSS (Control Stick Steering) to PITCH and ROLL/YAW—ON."

"To pitch and roll/yaw on."

"Adjusting glide slope to 1.5 degrees."

"It's not responding!"

"Pull back the nose!"

"Glide slope to…" Another loud bang sounded as a portion of the right cargo bay door violently ripped off. The shuttle buffeted and shook in the thirty to fifty knot gale-force winds. "…1.5 degrees"

"Picking up speed brake to seventy-five percent."

"First roll reversal S-turn."

"S-turn."

Commander Jackson frantically began his series of several drastic banking maneuvers, "roll reversals," or S-turns, to control the *Orion's* descent.

"Second S-turn."

"Number two."

"Speed brake at sixty-five."

"Sixty-five percent."

"AIR DATA PROBE switches to DEPLOY."

"Deploy."

"Third S-turn."

"Number three."

"Begin terminal area energy management."

"Begin."

"Head for NAV Computer generated way point."

"Way point to alignment."

"Read," the *Orion* again shook, this time in a waffling stagger as a portion of the left bay door slammed against the reinforced HRSI (High-Temperature Reusable Surface Insulation) tiles at vent door number three, "altitude and air speed out loud."

"Altitude and air speed. 350 mph, 2,000 AGL (Above Ground Level)...310 mph, 1,500 AGL...300 mph 1,200 AGL..."

"Shit we're not slowing down enough! I'm increasing pitch to 5 degrees—we don't have the goddamn drag of the landing gear!"

"Pitch to 5 degrees."

"Read the speed and altitude in hundred feet!"

"270 mph, 900 AGL...250 mph, 800 AGL..."

"Still too fast! I'm increasing pitch to 8 degrees..."

"235 mph, 500 AGL...220, 300 AGL..."

"Too fast. Deploy the draft chutes now!"

"Nose down!"

"BOOM!" at 190 miles per hour, the space shuttle *Orion* slammed belly down into the 6,921 foot deep glacier on top of the Wilkes Subglacial Basin. They ragtag ground and shimmied into the relentless wind.

"Hold on!"

The tempered aluminum-honeycombed forward, the mid and aft fuselage body of the space shuttle *Orion* quaked, and two of the three primary thrusters, along with the boron-epoxy rear assembly and the left delta wing, crushed in an accordian sandwich. While pounded in the gale-force winds, the ship slid for two miles until it came to an abrupt stop on the gnarled stubby end of the torn left delta wing.

The aft fuselage, body flap, OMS (Orbital Maneuvering System), RCS (Reaction Control System) pod, forward fuselage, lower forward fuselage and RCC (reinforced carbon-carbon) nose were demolished. The aluminum, 122-foot structure of the *Orion* absorbed the impact and concussion of the crash landing, which allowed the upper forward fuselage and crew compartment to remain relatively intact.

The punishing winds that shrouded the *Orion* blew relentlessly.

Ten minutes after the crash landing, two all-terrain C-141D "short" STOL (Short Takeoff and Landing) transport planes with their advanced laser and IR (infrared) optics and designator rangefinders landed in the driving storm. The recovery team, with their ANIPUS-7A night-vision goggles and thermal viewers and in their Biosafety Level 4 space suits, found the space shuttle *Orion* without delay. The suffocating astronauts received their life-giving oxygen supply in the nick of time.

Eight minutes after the arrival of the C-141D "shorts," the astronauts were breathing uncontaminated clean air. Within twelve hours, the storm subsided to less than 17 knots, a portable kevlar/boron epoxy Biosafety Level 4 decontamination facility was airlifted in. The temperature on the Wilkes subglacial basin never rose above -23.3 degrees farenheit.

CHAPTER 59

Like Gabriel the avenging angel, Pepper incredulously touched down from out of nowhere in her flambouyant Skye Ryder Aerochute—right next to Alex.

The white and silver Learjet 45 snuck out of the Satellite Terminal in the middle of the hailstorm of bullets. It agilely spun south in a 170 degree turn—and headed to the southeast hold taxiway.

Fourteen jets, mostly American Airlines, two Delta 757's and an Aerojecutivo Airlines L-1011, were already impatiently parked on pods K and KK waiting for tower takeoff clearance. Dallas/Forth Worth Tower had closed down all incoming and outgoing flights during the skirmish.

"I spotted them from above."

"Are you okay?" Alex asked as he hopped on board the Skye Ryder, and they rapidly gained altitude. Alex could feel the blood begin to pulsate out of his aching shoulder. Below and to the east, blue smoke bellowed from the downed SuperCobra. The crackling of fierce gunfire prattled in his ears. "I thought they might've gotten you."

"Me?"

"Just worrying," Alex smiled as they headed in a beeline toward the taxiing Learjet 45.

"It's them," she said. "I saw the man with the Ray-Bans get into the jet and others with weapons came in and out. I'm one hundred percent sure."

"We need to stop 'em!"

"What with this?" Pepper asked as their seconds ticked away, and the CIA double agents' escape was imminent.

Learjet 2227N cut east on taxiway B tarmac and headed to a cut-off point a third of the way down the 13,350 foot runway 35L. They would be airborne in less than a minute.

With the diversion of the firefight, the "Armory" operatives, would escape to parts unknown, and with their air-defensive RWR and IR jammer avionics, and laser warning receiver, they wouldn't get caught. Not a chance in hell.

"I've got it!" Alex yelled. *"How close can you get to their engine?"*

"Of the Lear?"

"Yes."

"Front or rear?"

"Front."

"Which side?"

"Doesn't matter."

"Within a foot, maybe two, but our canopy might be sucked in by the engines' backwash, and we'd crash."

"Just get us there!"

The pilot hit his brakes and gunned the pair of Garrett TFE 731-20 engines. At the exact moment that the pilot released his brakes and jammed on full throttle, Alex —hanging upside down by his knees— flung the unfurled "Jesus Saves" banner into the right jet engine. The turbine sucked up the banner causing a freak static high-voltage discharge—disabling the Learjet's avionics system.

Only by inches did the Learjet, in its launch, miss the Skye Ryder

Aerochute. The turbulent exhaust propulsion was enough to suck in and invert the center of the parachute canopy, causing their Mad Max contraption to rip from its tethers and plunge to the tarmac. Alex and Pepper were violently thrown to the runway's surface.

In the rush to escape, Learjet 45 2227N rotated with full flaps down, at fifteen knots less than its 105 knot minimum take-off speed. With the right engine turbines jammed by the Jesus banner, it faltered—momentarily. The Learjet lifted off to 1,000 feet above ground level—then sputtered, nose-dived, and crashed four miles to the northwest, onto the lakefront edge of North Lake. The jet burst into flames.

Simultaneously, in a triumph of military panache, and last minute teamwork between the real CIA, NSA and Sheppard Air Force Base/Wichita Falls—four 1,000-gallon, Halon-equipped McDonnell Douglas AH-64A Apache helicopters converged onto the downed Learjet and inundated the fireball of twisted metal and graphite-epoxy composites, with enough Halon to suffocate any flames and contain the remaining *doomsday vial* of X23 LAV-10A.

Pepper had experienced rougher landings—like the time she broke her ankle at the Reno Air Races in '93 when she wingwalked a homebuilt Pitts 2,000 feet above ground level on a Cuban Eight that went awry, and she crash landed. Any landing she could walk away from was a good one.

"How's that for flying?" she asked as she tried to pop to her feet from her planted position, then yelped from the burning pain of her contorted left ankle, the same one she broke before.

"Groovy," Alex said sarcastically. His chest, abdomen, pelvis, neck and both arms throbbed. Slowly, he stood, and rewrapped his left forearm. It was killing him. "No more fun rides."

"Groovy?" she asked as she heard the trembling, limitless explosion toward the north, past the end of runway 35L. She saw the fireball flash of the Lear 45, and then felt the tremendous air-shock concussion wave. "What kind of word is that?"

"A good one," he winced. "I hope it's destroyed." Dallas/Fort Worth Airport cop cars blared toward them from all directions.

"A good one? That's older than my mother."

Alex looked north and east. He prayed. Then overhead, he saw the four AH-64A Apache helicopters chase to the billowing smoke cloud "It's...my word," he said with finality. "I like it."

"So what do you know?'

He hesitated. "So what do I know? Are you kidding?"

"No."

"We're almost dead and you ask me, 'so what do I know'?"

"So? What do you know?"

"Give me a break."

"No problem."

All around them, with guns drawn, cops barreled out of their cars. "Hands up!"

"Okay by me," Alex sighed with relief.

Chapter 60

Ninety miles north of *Orion's* crash site near the Cook Ice Shelf, the emergency high-altitude escape parachuted Vrubel and Maya— using their Orlan-III DMA space suits' life-support backpacks and portable oxygen system. They were recovered by the third C-141D "short" STOL transport. Their emergency locating transmitter was position-vectored by Big Mama AWACS Southern Hemisphere. They were immediately given life-needed oxygen refill cartridges, having lasted longer on their oxygen supply than the *Orion* astronauts.

Both Vrubel and Maya suffered from cerebral hypoxia. Maya was delirious and rambling when she was rescued. Nevertheless, both she and Vrubel would eventually recuperate. In the interim, they were transported to the *Orion* landing nexus and the temporary Biosafety Level 4 decontamination bivouac.

"Maya," Mission Commander Jackson spoke into his VOX mode mic from within his NASA extravehicular mobility unit. She was lying on a rigid army cot in her Orlan-III DMA space suit. She opened her hazel eyes to see the glare of his polycarbonate visor. "You gave us

"I did?" she asked as she shook the cobwebs out of her pounding head. She felt dizzy and heard a faintly audible buzz in both ears.

"You did. We thought we lost you up there."

Maya looked into Scoop's no longer unflappable eyes. He was showing his human side to her—that he, too, was vulnerable—that he could be touched.

"You know what?" she coughed. The clean, uncontaminated air felt good. It gave her vigor.

"No."

"You gave me...one hell of a scare, too."

"I did?"

"Yes, you did."

"Well, that's good."

"I know."

"Maya?"

"Yes...Scoop."

"Maya, you know...I've been a real jerk."

"I know," she said.

"Maya?"

"Yes."

"Will you forgive me?"

"For what?"

"For not being sensitive, for not being able to show you my feelings. I'm sorry."

"Well...that depends," she coughed.

"Depends on what?"

"If you're good."

He laughed. Jackson didn't expect her repartee this soon in her recovery. "I'll be good."

"We'll see."

"Maya."

"Yes."

"...I love you."

"I know," she said.

"Maya?" Jackson smiled. He knew that this was the beginning of another journey—one that involved more risks and greater heroism than that on *Mir-Kennedy I* and the *Orion*. This was a journey that scared him. And for that matter, scared Maya, too.

Chapter 61
Three Months Later

The drama was over. Worldwide, with the cooperation of the FSB, MI-6 in the United Kingdom, France's Direction Générale de la Sécurité Exterieure, the Foreign Intelligence Department in the Ministry of Foreign Korean government, and other public and private entities, seventy-one identified members of the Armory were either arrested or had mysteriously disappeared.

Disturbingly, however, there remained at least an estimated twenty-five to thirty-five unidentified, and possibly still Armory affiliates.

The only known vial of X23 *LAV-10A* was destroyed in the spectacular Learjet 45 explosion in North Lake. There was, fortuitously, no evidence of any contamination. Whether the *LAV-10* "l" flipping chemical was vaporized as a result of the fiery crash, or inactivated due to the Halon consumption, was moot.

For precautionary reasons, the eight-hundred acre lake, which was used for industrial and not recreational purposes, was cordoned off, along with a containment "hot zone" of all properties within a one mile radius.

As for the Reverend Joe-Bob Jones, in death he was triumphantly vindicated. He had risen to the level of deified martyr. The print media, especially the trash monger rags—*The National Enquirer, The Star, The Globe*, and the sleazy TV pseudonews programs: *Hardcopy, American Journal, Inside Edition, EXTRA,* and *Geraldo*—had a field day.

Mahalia Hunt's consort, Katrina Lee, was found four weeks later, in an alley between Bleecker and Hudson streets in Greenwich Village, dead of a heroin overdose. Foul play was suspected by the authorities, but was never thoroughly investigated. She was thought to be just another two-bit whore who met her demise.

CIA Headquarters
Langley, Virginia

CIA Director Harlan Gates tried to wear his usual "no-tell" poker face when FSB Chief Directorate Laventy P. Yezhov beamed on the Russian Sojuzkarkta satellite video teleconference line. Though he didn't want to smile, the corners of his mouth betrayed him. He and his organization had wrapped up this *LAV-10A* mess much to his liking. And though he wasn't one to gloat, he did pat himself once on the back. It was good to rout out the traitors.

"I appreciate your assistance, Harlan," Yezhov said, while sitting behind his opulent mahogany desk.

"Always a pleasure, Laventy."

"I just wanted to tell you again, Harlan, that without your cooperation I wouldn't have been able to plant Biologics Engineer Maya Mukhina on board *Orion*."

"That's what we're here for nowadays—to work together in a spirit of cooperation. Don't you agree?"

"Yes. If not, who knows what could have become of this world with *LAV-10* on the loose."

"That's true."

"Harlan?"

"Yes."

"One more thing—what about the business of dihydroxy-organopyrethrum–Zeta–4"

"Oh…"

"Well…"

"Before I answer, let me ask you—a tête-á-tête about Dr. Alex Seacourt. Why did you throw him into this?"

"Good question, Harlan. I suppose it calls for a tit-for-tat."

"Yes."

"When the 150 U.S. doctors participated in the Washington, then Rio and Moscow, anti-terrorist germ warfare training, we thought Dr. Seacourt would be perfect to get close to Roscoe McMahon, CEO of BetaTec in Las Vegas. Someone who we could innocently route to the Consumer Electronics Show…"

"And?"

"We sent him to BetaTec with some bait. We wanted to see if we could flush out McMahon. See if McMahan had any reaction to Seacourt asking about an *LAV-10* software. We needed a patsy. We had men watching both of them. We thought that by Seacourt asking McMahon about the *LAV* software, which of course didn't exist, we might be able to pick up a trail on *LAV-10*. We had no idea that McMahon would end up dying from the X23 *LAV-10B* in a double cross."

"What about Dr. Knight?"

"Purely coincidental. We had no idea that she was involved in the original project. And then for her to end up in Las Vegas as a pathologist at University Medical Center—and then she do the autopsy? What are the odds?"

"Yeah, and to have Seacourt arrive at the autopsy…"

"You've got it. When the 'Armory' operatives saw him at the hospital, they thought for sure that he had to be involved in some way with McMahon's death, or at least maybe a rogue agent trying to cut himself in on the *LAV-10* pie"

"So if it wasn't for Seacourt's blunder, we would have still been behind the *LAV-10* eightball—and that shit might have been released…"

"Must be American ingenuity, Harlan."

"I'd say so. You picked him."

"Yes we did, didn't we?"

"You did."

"Now, Harlan…there is still the matter of dihydroxy-organopyrethrum-Zeta-4."

"Oh, that.

"That."

"Well...let me explain..."

Boulder, Colorado

Alex Seacourt and Pepper Knight were flying west into the Rockies over Nederland and the Rainbow Lakes into the Roosevelt National Forest south of the Rocky Mountain National Forest. The aspens, ponderosa pine, white and douglas firs, Engelmann, blue spruce and piñon pines were resplendent; and lay beneath them like a burgeoning patchwork quilt.

Pepper was piloting the two-seater, star-spangled Pratt and Whitney 300 hp-powered Steen Skybolt biplane, which swung an enormous prop, and shrieked as it snapped through the air. After they reached a ceiling of 14,500 feet, Pepper looped the plane in a one-eighty and headed back toward Boulder at 13,500 feet.

Pepper was teaching Alex the aerobatic basics: steep power turns, the Chandelle, Wingover, Lazy Eight, aileron roll, snap roll, Cuban Eight, and Reverse Cloverleaf. By the time they were done his brain was addled.

Despite his impending vertigo, Alex was deliberately pensive. He had brought with him the Kershner Basic Aerobatic Manual. He studied it on the ground before they took off, and he was scanning the book's techniques while they flew. It made him queasy, but he wanted to get the moves down.

"Your mother?" he asked from the front seat with the wind blowing through his goggled hair.

"You know, it's not that bad from back here."

"What?" he turned partially to face her.

"You're not that bald."

"I wasn't talking about my hair. I was going to ask you a question about your mother."

"I was."

"Knock it off."

Pepper, the sprite, giggled, then whipped the Skybolt in a sharp dive and leveled off just above a stand of quaking aspen and cottonwoods. Then, she slowly climbed and did a quick snap roll when she regained altitude.

"You're good. Now, what about your mother?"

"Back at work in Las Vegas, at the hospital."

"No, I don't mean that, I mean you and she. Are you talking?"

Pepper popped a quick aileron roll to show her mild irritation at Alex's intrusiveness.

"Does that mean yes?"

She repeated the hellbent maneuver.

"Sensitive subject?"

"Yes," she replied above the Pratt and Whitney's drone. "I'm doing the best I can."

"What about your stepfather's death, Dr. Warner? Do you want to talk about that?"

"Not really. Maybe later."

"Well, just so you know, I'm here if you want to talk."

"Thanks."

"Yeah, anytime."

"Now it's my turn for questions," she said.

"Go ahead." Alex said expecting her smart aleck worst.

"What about all the drums in Long Beach."

"Of TTLV-1"

"Yes." At least she was asking a serious question.

"The government's going to bury them in a salt mine somewhere, three miles below the earth's surface. Pack it in a coat of Halon, move 'em in with spent plutonium nuclear reactor rods. At least that's what they told me when I was debriefed."

"Who're they?"

"Some CIA and NSA guys. I don't remember their names...except for the Associate CIA Director Dulles, and Dr. Johnson. There were a bunch of them."

"That's nice."

"Yeah, isn't it."

"I guess."

"Yeah."

"No Alex...I mean your balding hair."

"Screw you!"

Pepper pulled the Steen Skybolt's stick back and powered the nimble biplane straight up, then eased the stick forward. Momentarily the red and white acrobatic plane stalled, then rolled over and dive-bombed for the treacherous mountain top. "Yee-ha!"

The Last Chapter

Bolivar, Missouri
Outside of S.W. Baptist College
Denny's Restaurant

On either side of the road on his drive to Bolivar, were massive red barns, silos like silver bullets, tranquil white farmhouses nestled in thick groves of trees. The rich, rolling pastures were dotted with ponds, cattle grazed lazily on the slopes, and the soil was dark and loamy. An air of prosperity pervaded the landscape, as palpable as the aroma of freshly mown hay. It was Kodak country. Brightly painted billboards invited dallying travelers to family restaurants, farmers' markets and campgrounds.

"Black coffee, please."

"The same," the other man told the college-freshman waitress. Her hair was Goldilocks blond and her smile was infectious.

"So what about Cuba?" the first man asked in disdain. He was weatherworn but determined.

"Sheriff Brewer and two of his men on our payroll have been detained by NSA."

"Will they talk?"

"No."

"Are your sure?"

"Dead men tell no tales."

"You're positive?"

"They're in federal custody in St. Louis. Consider it done."

"Excellent," the first man said. He thought about his back-road drive to the sunrise meeting—through a one-street village lined with a general store, a gas station and a handful of white clapboard houses. "What about our operation on board *Mir-Kennedy I?*"

"Through."

"Alternatives?"

"Yes," the other man replied. "I've made sure that *one* of the TTLV-1 drums from Long Beach was misdirected."

"Misdirected?" the first man asked in sinister approval as he sipped his coffee, then blew on it to cool it down, before taking another taste. He decided he'd drive a different route back to St. Louis, but this time stop and do some sightseeing—smell the fresh clover, wheat and cornfields. "Where to?"

"It took some string pulling but I had it 'misdirected'..." There was a loud crash as another waitress, this one in her early forties with dyed rat-brown hair, and new on the job since yesterday, bumped into a businessman and his wife. She spilled an order of two eggs over easy with bacon, French toast, and two large orange juices.

"I'm so sorry," the waitress apologized to the first man as she quickly bent down and pulled a towel from her uniform bib pocket. "Sorry."

"Nevermind," the other man gruffly said as she briskly mopped up the orange juice. "Accidents happen."

In a tan 1994 Ford Bronco, a block and a half away, two undercover NSA operatives were listening to the conversation with their single earpiece wireless receivers. Everything was taped.

"Did you get that, Fred?"

"Dammit...no."

The waitress had spilled her service tray right next to the directional bug that five minutes earlier, Fred had placed behind the sec-

ond man's seat. Fred had followed him from Springfield.
"Damn!"

"Three weeks," the first man confidently told the second.
"It'll be done...and we'll be back on line."
"The new technology?"
"Should be good to go by then."
"Excellent. I'll see you in Memphis on the thirteenth."
"Count on it."
"I will," he said with certainty.
The cocksure first man slid out of the booth and stood up. He flipped two singles and a fifty-cent tip down on the table.
"Cuba?"
"It'll be taken care of."
"*Not a trace?*"
"My word on it."